EVENING SHADOWS

An Agents of HIS Novel

Sheila Kell

To Debbie Attenborough
You stood by me before I published my first novel,
giving me the nudges I needed
and telling the world about me.
It's been a spirited journey,
and I'm glad you've been part of it.

Titles by Sheila Kell

HIS SERIES
His Desire
His Choice
His Return
His Chance
His Destiny
His Family
His Heart
His Fantasy
A Hamilton Christmas

AGENTS OF HIS SERIES
Evening Shadows
Midnight Escape
Afternoon Delight
Bayou Sunset
Chasing Shadows at Dusk
Moonlight Exception
When Daylight Breaks

COASTAL INVESTIGATION SERIES
Deadly Betrayal
Read Between the Lines
Fractured Trust
The Final Hurdle

Chapter One

His life would, in all effect, end today. Everything he'd ever been would be no more. He'd quickly learned that the twists and turns life threw could impact life irrevocably and in only a moment. And all those little moments led him to this point. The point of no return.

In Baltimore's dreary weather and its on-again and off-again drizzle, Ken Patrick leaned on a cane, his hip aching from the healing bullet wound and the dampness in the air. The deep ache merely emphasized the need to do what he must.

He paused outside the steel door that led to the amazing life and people he'd known the last few years and didn't truly want to lose either. He and his conscience had struggled over this decision since his most recent injury, and as always, his conscience won the argument. No matter the pit of anxiety in his gut, his decision was made, and he'd put off following through long enough.

As team leader of the best men and women he knew—bar the men he'd served with as an Army Ranger—of Hamilton Investigation & Security, he'd failed once too often. Resigning from the team and HIS would restore the strength of the agency. Truthfully, Ken had been surprised they'd held on to him for so long, especially after the last FUBAR op. Okay, it hadn't truly been fucked up beyond all recognition, but it'd shown him he'd lost his edge. In his line of work, that could be deadly. Glancing down at the black cane he leaned upon, he sighed heavily at the reminder of why he'd shown up at HQ.

It'd been nearly a month since he'd taken a bullet in the hip—the same hip he'd been wounded protecting Madison Maxwell, now Madison Hamilton. At the time, he'd been focusing too much on Samantha Milton's safety—one of his sharpshooters—instead of concentrating on the protection detail as a whole. While things rarely went as planned, his distraction had put people in danger, including himself, and subsequently, he'd had to turn over the lead to his second-in-command, Rob Grimes, aka "Grits."

Thinking back to the day of his injury, he wanted to kick his own ass for being so stupid. His loss of focus had been the problem that could've ended more than one life, and even though everyone survived and the op had been successful, the entire incident was unacceptable.

Unable to keep the pain and weakness from his mind, Ken continued to deal with the repercussions of his stupidity. Taking the bullet wasn't what frustrated him most since it was always a possibility when on an op. Instead, the recovery rankled him. He required the use of a damn cane for support and had lingering pain while attempting to regain the flexibility and strength he would need to outrun or outfight any trouble in the field.

Trying to think on the positive side, Samantha had remained at his bedside while he'd recovered after surgery. Even though she'd assured him most of the team also waited, his heart absorbed the impact of her fussing over him. Since she'd come aboard HIS, they'd rekindled the closeness they'd shared what seemed like a lifetime ago. The heat that sizzled between them neared explosive. But, no matter what was building between them, they kept it strictly professional at work. With his injury, she seemed to be straddling the personal/professional line perfectly.

"Maybe while you're high on the drugs, I can finally beat you at darts," she'd teased after adding another pillow behind his head on the hospital bed.

Like that would happen, the woman may be able to hit a small target at record ranges, but she couldn't hit the bull's eye of a dartboard if she stood right in front of it. His mouth curved into the grin he reserved for her. "I prefer it when we're partners." He meant more than at darts but wouldn't push her, even though he felt they were on that precipice of falling into bed and burning up the sheets.

"I do too." Her soft voice almost escaped him. When he stared at her, he didn't know if the narcotics played tricks on his mind and showed him what he longed to see in her vivid blue eyes. Love.

He had to strengthen his body before he set them on the path from friends to lovers. First, though, he had to straighten out what lay ahead of him.

Even though he'd been assured that with physical therapy, he'd regain full strength without a limp, not being fully capable of doing his job chafed him.

Sick of having his own pity party, Ken slowly input his six-digit pass code into the keypad beside the door to HIS headquarters. Once the heavy door was released, Ken entered and ensured it closed with its automatic lock before he moved away from the entrance. His palms grew sweaty as nerves assailed him. He couldn't remember the last time he'd had that unsettling feeling. Even fighting his way through country after country, he'd never experienced the like of today. As his heart raced and with the combined awareness of his unease, he decided he could do without a case of nerves.

Ken limped down the carpeted hallway into the depths of

the structure Jesse Hamilton had constructed for a more secure building to conduct business in than the back rooms of his home. Frowning, Ken contemplated how his resignation would be received. Undoubtedly, they'd take it as a blessing so they didn't have to fire him. What was the point of having someone on staff who couldn't do their job? Cut and run…it was the best possible option for all of them.

With a heavy heart, he stepped into the spacious war room where their ops were planned, briefed, and debriefed. Ken stopped and took in the sight for the last time, branding the memory on his brain. Inhaling, he wondered what they did to keep the windowless room from smelling of the sweaty, dirty agents post-op before they'd have an opportunity to shower.

He sought out Jesse, the oldest Hamilton brother and head of HIS. With a glance around the room, he noticed the Hamilton brothers and their sister, Emily, crowded around her desk, looking at her computer monitor. On the other side of the large room, half the team huddled around each other, laughing. He expected they were playing at who could one-up the other. Although he never added one of his horrific stories, he enjoyed listening to others' acts of valor.

Hearing a round of "Congratulations," he swung his head back to the family. The men were each hugging their little sister and kissing her on the top of the head. Observing what appeared to be a personal moment between siblings twisted his heart. He missed the twin sister he'd lost when they were ten years old. His throat tightened at the memories. As if he didn't have enough grief to deal with today, he didn't need the losses that had impacted his family at the forefront of his mind.

When Jesse spotted him, he broke away from the family and strode toward him. Knowing Jesse would slap him on the shoulder, Ken planted his strong leg so he wouldn't stagger under the man's strength. Not that Jesse was generally stronger than him, but right now, most people were.

As expected, he received that powerful slap on the shoulder. "How are you? How's the physical therapy?"

Ken wanted to scream about how painful the damn PT was. Between the stretching and twisting he'd endured with this injury, he'd convinced himself that it was torture in repayment for his failure. The only benefit he'd seen to date had been the reduction in pain, but the doctor said that occurred naturally with his recovery, so he wasn't ready to credit physical therapy as anything other than a dreaded requirement.

Attempting to exude an air of nonchalance, Ken shrugged and acted as if all was well. "It's fine. I'm fine." Oh, how he hated that word, especially when a woman used it, but it slipped from his lips before he could recall it.

Jesse raised a dark eyebrow. "Okay," he dragged the word out. "Then how long before we can make you active again? We miss you out there."

Garnering his resolve, Ken looked around, then back at Jesse. "That's what I came here to speak with you about. May we talk in private?"

"Sure." Without further question, Jesse led the way to his office in the back corner.

Ken's mind raced to outrun the indecisive thought, trying to rear its ugly head. After this, what would he do about Sam? Just the thought of her in danger made his gut clench. He'd promised to protect her, and he'd orchestrated her being a member of HIS so he could watch over her, but his resignation would make it difficult to have her back. Then again, on ops, he focused so much on her that he jeopardized himself and his team. He'd puzzle out how to keep that promise later, but it wasn't like he'd done a bang-up job so far at keeping his word.

They entered one of a few offices that had been set aside for admin work, initial op planning, and private meetings. Ken settled into a burgundy leather chair and glanced at Jesse's large mahogany desk. Somehow, he kept it immaculate, and Ken wondered if Jesse just slid everything in a drawer at the end of the day so it looked like he'd been productive. Then again, Jesse didn't do anything half-assed, so Ken figured his boss took care of business as needed on the admin side.

With an assessing gaze, Jesse leaned back in his chair and crossed his fingers behind his head. "How's it really going?"

Ken thought for a moment about how to answer. He didn't typically share his private life, but he'd always given Jesse what he asked. "It's taking too damn long to heal, but the doc says it's coming along fine."

Jesse appeared to contemplate his answer, making Ken even more nervous. He wanted to wipe his sweaty palms on his black cargo pants, but didn't want to show Jesse that he was anything other than the strong agent he'd hired.

"Okay, trust the doctor. Don't rush it, or it might not heal correctly." Before Ken could say what he needed to say, Jesse continued. "The rest of the team will be back in a few days. Rob's doing fine, but I'm looking forward to you taking back over. If you approve of his ability to lead a team, we're planning to split the team since it's so large, and that'll give each group a team leader and a smaller team to bond together since many ops only take a select number of operatives." He paused. "You'd still lead as a whole."

Jesse took a breath and seemed to wait for Ken's

thoughts on his suggestion, but they were jumbled. His boss's plans included him, but Ken's participation would be a liability to HIS. It didn't matter which way he looked at it, his injury was debilitating. No amount of his boss's desire to welcome him back or create the whole family vibe they had going in HIS would change that fact.

Since Ken remained quiet, Jesse plowed forward. "You'll see less and less of me, my brothers, and our wives in the field." He smiled. "Kids grow up too damn fast, you know? We'll still be involved, but we want to stay close to home and take over our investigations. Which reminds me." Jesse snapped his fingers, turned, and opened a desk drawer, then pulled out a small stack of yellow file folders. "I'd like to go over a few candidates with you and get your thoughts." Jesse must've thought Ken had a question about the folder color because he shrugged and explained, "Em decided we needed to color-code things for easier filing for her. Yellow for candidates, then red and blue for the two teams we'll have. I have no idea what color she's reserved for the family." Jesse grinned and shook his head. "Anyhow, I want you to be a part of the interview process. I don't want to drop someone on you that might not mesh well with how you lead. We'll also involve Rob if you think he's ready to select the right candidates for his team. No matter what, you're still the ultimate team leader."

Ken's gut clenched. Why did this man have to be such a great leader and friend? When Jesse had contacted him before his enlistment in the army ended and offered him this position, he hadn't hesitated to accept because someone needed to be at Jesse's back. In the army, Ken had saved his team leader's life twice. Jesse always argued three, but Ken didn't count the third as he hadn't meant to step in front of the bullet meant for Jesse. Thank God for Kevlar. But, the main reason Ken had leaped at the opportunity was that Jesse had offered a perk that allowed him to comfortably leave Georgia, knowing HIS could help him keep track of Sam.

Until now, he'd never thought his decision to join the agency questionable.

With his stomach churning up a thunderstorm, Ken cleared his throat and looked his boss in the eye. "Sir, I've got something to say." "Sir" slipped from his lips as it always did. In part because Jesse had been an officer and because his mother instilled manners in him, that stuck.

Jesse's shoulders visibly tensed, and he placed the folders on his desk. His eyes narrowed, searching as if he could extract the truth without words. "Go on."

This time, Ken did wipe his hands on his thighs, although it did nothing for the clamminess. Pushing past the lump lodged in his throat, Ken bit the bullet. "I've come to resign." His heart hurt over those words. When he'd said goodbye to the army, he'd been sad, but nothing like the sudden emptiness he felt. HIS had been his new family. The place he felt needed, wanted, and, yes, loved. Emotions roiled up inside him. Loss… sadness… grief. Good God, if he cried, he'd whoop his own ass. This was nothing but smart business.

The silence in the office resonated through to his tortured soul.

"No." Sitting up straight, Jesse let the simple word stand as if law.

"No?"

"I don't accept your resignation."

Flabbergasted at the firm response, Ken tried to figure out what to say. "Sir, I don't think you understand. I'm leaving."

"Where are you going?"

Son of a— Jesse was deliberately making this difficult for him, and he didn't appreciate it one bit. "You know what I mean."

Leaning forward, his forearms on the desk, hands clasped, Jesse looked intent and authoritative and every inch the intimidating officer Ken had known. "Tell me why. I think after all we've been through, you owe me that."

A sudden flash of the losses they'd sustained over time settled deep in his bones, adding to the ache from his hip. Too many men. He still had a lot to reconcile in his life. A whisper of Sam's name played havoc with his ability to remain focused, and a hint of weariness flitted through him, making him doubt his choice.

His prepared speech vanished, so Ken just shared what his heart held. "We've been through a great deal, and in each instance, I'm glad you were there. But, sir—" Now came the hard part. With a dry mouth, he continued. "I'm stepping aside so you can find someone more competent than me. I've failed you too many times. This bullet and the time I've been laid up on my ass have helped me realize I've lost my edge, and I don't feel you can depend on me any longer." Damn, but that had been hard to say. At least he'd told the truth, believed Jesse would understand, and let him be on his way. Alone and jobless. But the men and women with the agency would be led safely on their ops.

"Huh" was Jesse's only response.

Seeing no need to explain further, Ken grasped the armrests and prepared to stand so he could clean out his locker and return his issued gear.

Jesse surprised him with, "When have you failed me and HIS?"

He should've resigned with AJ—the baby brother—

instead of Jesse. It might've been easier.

Ken dropped his hands back to his lap. "Well, there's this." He gestured to his hip.

"While I'd rather you hadn't been shot, you prevented our client from being killed. I don't see the failure."

Frustration slipped into his bloodstream at Jesse's pushing back. "It was my fault she was in that situation."

"No, it wasn't. She ignored your directions. That would've happened to any of us." Jesse drew his brows into a V-shape. "What else? It can't be only this instance. I know you better than that. You're not a quitter."

The words slammed into his chest, and he wanted to puff up and argue, but he had been a quitter this time. The team deserved better. He'd make Jesse understand. "Let's start with Madison. I made a stupid move, and she almost got shot."

Jesse steepled his fingers and tapped his two forefingers together. "You did right by attempting to clear the place. Besides, my new sister-in-law appreciates you taking a bullet for her. Excuse me, a bullet graze." Jesse waved his hand in a gesture that said his statement had been no big deal, and he needed to continue bringing it on.

"Well, there's Caitlyn. I didn't leave the house protected."

"Okay, I'll give you that one, but only because I think you should've hit my brother over the head to knock some sense into him. Because he was crazy in love with Caitlyn, Matt had taken the lead from you, and he shouldn't have. We promised in the field that you'd lead. I'm sorry to say that with those women who have since become our wives, we haven't lived up to that bargain. We all got a bit emotional."

Ken raised his eyebrows and almost tossed his head back

in an unexpected full-belly laugh. The men had gone over the top with their women. He'd never seen the like before. Thank goodness they were all married. "A bit?"

With that, Jesse smirked and squirmed. "This isn't about my brothers or me. This is about you. What else do you have, because I'm not seeing why you should resign unless you have a better job?" He cocked his head and quirked that damn brow again.

Something told him he already knew Ken's answer. "No, sir."

"You don't like us anymore?"

If he didn't know better, he'd think Jesse was enjoying this. "I like the team, but that's not what this is about."

"Hmm."

Damn him. Maybe if he thumped Jesse over the head with his computer monitor, he'd fire him, and this would be done. Ken cleared his throat and wished he'd grabbed a bottle of water for his dry mouth and parched throat. "Look, you know what happened in Kate's case."

"I don't blame you for that, Ken, and neither does my wife. You shouldn't blame yourself for what happened."

With deep sorrow, Ken closed his eyes a moment before speaking and looked at Jesse's blue shirt since he couldn't look him in the eye. "Les."

Jesse stiffened. "You weren't even there. You went to take care of your mother after your father passed away."

"But I should've been there."

Heaving a heavy sigh, Jesse stared at Ken as if assessing him with a new eye. "This is stupid. You know things can and will go wrong, no matter how much planning and preparation go into it. Our clients' actions sometimes create unexpected problems. You're doing an exceptional job with us. We've had hundreds of ops go well, and I attribute that to you. Don't let the few that didn't stay with you. You know to learn from them and move on. In fact, you're the one who told me that when I kept trying to dwell on the team failures our ops suffered in the Middle East. Listen to your own advice."

He had said that and was surprised Jesse still remembered it—and had listened to it. In no way did he want to leave HIS. It just seemed the right thing to do. It left him conflicted about Sam, but he'd led her on that assignment that could've gotten her killed. That wasn't the right way to protect her.

Of course, with Jesse not accepting his resignation, he could do one of two things—walk out without a backward glance or stay. With everything in him, he wanted to stay, but the fear of failure rested there heavier than it ever had. And one of those times, Sam could pay the price, and he couldn't live with that.

He wasn't due back from his medical leave for a while, so he could work on controlling that emotion. His concern for Sam had gnawed at him for years, and when he'd finally been able to do something about it, he'd screwed up. She'd come to trust him, and he couldn't lose that. They couldn't lose it. It'd become the foundation of their personal and professional relationships.

Inside, a switch flipped as if new life had been breathed back into him. It shouldn't be so easy to change his mind, but, dammit, he didn't want to leave these courageous men and women. He wanted to stand by them. To fight the battles that matter.

"Okay, I'll stay." With those words, his heart lightened, and something inside told him he'd made the right choice. He shouldn't have allowed his despair to overwhelm him into making the wrong decision.

"Good," Jesse agreed. "Now, tell me what's going on between you and Sam."

Shit. *She's had my heart since the day we met,* didn't seem the appropriate answer, even though it held the truth. *If I have anything to say about it, we're about to become more than friends,* probably wasn't the right thing to say either. No matter if he stayed or left, he'd have requested this one thing. Staying as the team leader gave him a stronger voice for it. He only hoped she'd forgive him.

Ken cleared his throat so he'd have the firmness in his voice to match the resolution he held in his statement. With a desire to see her safe, he didn't even blink when he stated, "About that…."

Chapter Two

Moving away from the toxic environment in Columbus, Georgia, had been good for Samantha. Although not free of her internal demons, she enjoyed her new life. Being happy and positive had become more manageable, except when someone tried to be overprotective or treat her as if she couldn't hold her own. Thankfully—and unfortunately— only one person did that at HIS. Ken Patrick. The tall, brown-eyed hunk who rode a Harley and wore his long blond hair in a low ponytail appealed to her more than he should.

With a heavy heart and her cell on speakerphone, Samantha Milton sliced a tomato to make a BLT sandwich. The tantalizing aroma of bacon floated through the house, making her mouth water and her stomach rumble. While she fixed her lunch, her best friend Beverly Shodun, in her heavy southern accent—Georgian, to be specific— continued her rant. This time, it referred to her perceived injustice of the men who'd deployed with her husband being alive while he was dead and buried. Since she'd heard it so often, Sam realized she could repeat the outburst word for word at some point during the tirade.

Since Bev's husband's funeral, her bitterness only deepened. Her friend still blamed Jesse and Ken for their husbands' deaths on that ill-fated op. Worse, she wanted the army to charge and hang them. Yes, she wanted hanging as their punishment.

Over the last ten years, Sam had overcome the shock of

seeing the army chaplain and her husband's battalion commander walk up her drive and knock on the front door to share the news of Lance's death while on a "training op." *Training op, my ass.* Lance hadn't broken OPSEC and told her about the op. He'd promised to come home to her. She hadn't expected it to be in a U.S. flag-draped coffin.

She and Bev grieved together after seeing the two men bearing life-changing information. Initially, they laid the blame on anyone and everyone they could. After her mind cleared, Sam came to terms with her husband's death as no one's fault but the foreign renegades who'd killed him. Ken had risked his career by explaining to her what had actually happened. He'd called them "tangos," but she used "renegades." Ken tried to be a rock and help her through her grief—whenever she allowed it.

Memories rushed forward, and Sam closed her eyes to absorb the force of all that had been powerful in her married life. Lance Milton had been a good husband who'd always been there for her with the right words, the perfect touch, and more love than she thought anyone could share.

Sam sniffed and closed her eyes again, but this time to ward off the tears trying to break free. Before his final op, Lance had told her that if he died, he didn't want her to continue to grieve, that she had to live…and love again. Neither of them had any idea how difficult—if not impossible—that task would be. In jest, he'd suggested she marry his best friend, Ken Patrick.

"I still can't believe you work for them," Bev spat.

Heck, Sam had been so lost in thought she'd missed all Bev was saying until now. She knew by "them," her friend meant Jesse Hamilton and Ken Patrick, the leadership on the fatal op that cost her and Bev everything. Well, not everything for Bev. She had a son with her husband.

Unfortunately, Adam Shodun never had the opportunity to see his only son. Bev had been pregnant when he'd left for the final time, and she'd delivered not long after becoming a widow.

Before Sam could form an appropriate response, Bev continued. "I still can't believe the army didn't discipline them." Her venomous reaction shouldn't have startled Sam, but she hadn't been ready for it.

She sighed when she realized her friend paused as if waiting for Sam to speak. Dropping her head, Sam squeezed the bridge of her nose with her thumb and forefinger and said, "Bev, I've told you this before; it's a primo job. It's elite and difficult to get hired into, even with all my years on the police force. I love it and am glad I'm here."

Seeing Ken again after so long and feeling their heated connection sent her spiraling. While the memorable kisses they'd shared long ago had touched her heart and imprinted themselves on her soul, and if truth be told, still haunted her, she'd been slow to open her lonely heart to a possible future for them.

"But they just left you home while they went out to save the world."

Sam shook her head at the uninformed statement. "No, they didn't. I mean," she corrected, "I didn't go, but a few members, including Jesse and Ken, didn't either." She halted and almost clamped her hand over her mouth. Knowing how much her friend hated the two men, she'd just given her the opening for another tirade.

Ignoring her response, Bev plowed forward. "You were doing fine on SWAT. I don't see why you had to leave and move so far away. I miss having you here. Brunch on Sunday isn't the same. All the other wives talk about are their new husbands and kids. You were the only other single woman."

Her appetite was gone. Sam left her sandwich on the counter and strode into the living room, then dropped onto the red leather couch that came with the apartment. Sam would've chosen differently, maybe a lovely vintage piece like she'd had when she lived near Bev. Instead of moving everything, she'd sold anything and everything and chosen a furnished apartment. Thank goodness Bev wasn't here. She would have gone nuts over the owner's poor taste and pushed to have him refurnish it. When Sam purchased her own place, it would be away from it all, and she'd decorate it to her taste. She just wasn't sure where that place would be. Sometimes she saw herself and Ken furnishing a home together. Then a slight uncertainty about remarrying crept into the dream. Not uncertainty about Ken, but her feeling she'd be cheating on Lance. It made no sense since her husband died, but when did love make sense?

But Bev only cared about having her best friend close, and Sam couldn't fault her for that. What bothered Sam was that her friend knew how painful talking about the issue she'd faced on the force was for her, yet Bev regularly brought up the subject. "You know the men on SWAT were harassing me. I'm strong, but didn't want to take it anymore." She'd worked hard for her spot with the team, but the men didn't want a woman working with them.

Needing to change the subject before Bev went on a rant, Sam tried again, hoping for a different answer. "Bev, why don't you move up here? Since you don't have to work, you can live where you want."

"I'm not leaving Adam's home."

Sam sighed in disappointment. Her friend wouldn't let Adam's death go enough to move her life forward. No one expected her to forget Adam and the life they'd shared. Bev needed to rebuild her life; no one could get her to do that.

She worried about how Bev's behavior affected Cody, Bev's son. Being an honorary aunt, when Sam hadn't been working, she'd taken Cody away for some special time. Unfortunately, by the time he'd reached the age of six, he'd figured out his mom wasn't typical. Typically, anything that reminded her of her husband's death sent her rage at the U.S. Army, the Ranger team, and anyone else she felt responsible, including the chaplain who came to break the horrible news. But mainly at Jesse and Ken.

As a friend, Sam had tried many things to help Bev move on from the past and that moment of initial sorrow, but she'd failed. Miserably. Reminding Bev, she could have two things—like Sam—where she didn't forget but moved on in the world.

Sam had almost declined the job with HIS since she'd wanted Cody to have someone, for lack of a better term, sane in his life. Bev wasn't insane like someone who needed to be committed or who would do harm to herself or her child. She didn't give Cody the love Sam would've.

"What happened to you? You used to feel the same way that I did."

"I did in the beginning, Bev, but I opened my eyes and realized I have a life to live. And, after all, I've been through with my career, I've learned that sometimes the best-laid plans are useless when all hell breaks loose." As she looked back, it'd taken too long for her to come to this conclusion, but come to it, she had. A rightness of that realization—and the bitterness she'd released against Lance's team leaders— rested in her soul.

Bev huffed in indignation. "You did nothing wrong on that op."

Realizing her friend had switched back to her SWAT

days, Sam took a deep breath to remain calm. "A hostage died," she seethed, knowing what Op Bev meant, but at least she was off her revenge kick. The image of the woman in the jewelry store would never leave her. The woman was kneeling, with her long, dark hair wrapped in the gunman's hand. Her head had been pulled back a moment before Sam's eyes had connected with hers. Though she doubted the hostage saw her since the woman's eyes were wide and full of fear. Per procedure, once Sam had found the optimal location, she'd radioed in the situation from her perch on the rooftop across the street. It would have been an easy shot for her to take out the lone gunman with his weapon pointed at the hostage's head. She'd tried to impress upon the negotiator the urgency, but he'd shut her up. Some negotiators thought themselves God. Unfortunately, this negotiator failed, and the next moment had instilled itself in her mind as the gunman fired his weapon, and the hostage fell with a bullet in her head. The approval to fire came too late to save the woman. Sam's light touch on her trigger brought down the murderer, but there had been nothing she could do to bring back the woman's life.

"Didn't you say you weren't given the order to fire or free clearance if you felt it necessary?"

At times, Bev surprised the hell out of her and talked reasonably about the situation.

Frustrated, Sam jumped up and all but stomped to the kitchen to pick up the sandwich she no longer wanted and dump it into the garbage. "The fact that I was cleared didn't change that the woman died, and I could've prevented it."

"Adam always told me that no matter how good the team was, sometimes people die because they couldn't be everything to everyone."

If only Bev would listen to her own words.

"I know. Lance used to say something similar. Jesse also explained that to me, although he prefers that everyone remain alive."

Her gut twisted at how damn confused she was. As an agent of any law enforcement or military team, saying "shit happens," which was what it boiled down to, was easy. For the survivors, not so much. Sam, being on both sides, made every day a struggle, not knowing which emotion would rule the day.

"Dammit, Sam, quit that job and move back here. You know the department will take you back."

And they were on that road again. She didn't believe her friend would ever stop trying to get her to move back to Georgia. "Bev," she said patiently, "I'm here now." *Near Ken once again.* "Like I've said, I love working with this team. The types of ops make a difference. Thankfully, there's little to no red tape. Plus, there are women on the team, and the men seem to trust them and treat them as equals." With how the male-heavy team had treated her so far, she wasn't plagued with the fear or insecurity that had haunted her once the men of SWAT began their campaign of sexual harassment. "Can't you understand how this perfectly fits me?"

"You won't think it's perfect after hearing what I say."

Sam quietly groaned. She refused to ask or reopen this topic. If it weren't for her love for Cody, she'd have reevaluated her friendship with Bev. She'd expect a friend to support her in her decisions, not try to bring everything down, so Sam moved back to Georgia and was as miserable as her friend.

"I've been investigating. Having someone inside investigate what I can't get my hands on as a civilian."

"What are you talking about?"

"I'm talking about what really happened the day our husbands died."

Frustrated, Sam silently counted to ten before she responded. "We know what happened. You have to let it go, Bev."

"No, Sam. We know what they wanted us to believe, but there's more to it, and I have proof that'll make you rethink who you work for."

Chapter Three

Finally cane-free but still limping, Ken was again about to approach Jesse with the same request. He had to think of something to sway his boss's mind about letting Sam go. Although he'd been shut down on his first request, he wouldn't give up. It would be best for her as they took on more dangerous ops daily.

He didn't know why he'd thought she'd be safer with HIS than SWAT. The thought of her nearby had seemed perfect at the time.

The problem was he couldn't tell Jesse it was for his peace of mind and to calm the frantic beating of his heart for her safety. She'd solidified her spot on the team as a much-needed asset with her quick eye and dead-on shooting. She put the other two snipers on the team to shame. And Jesse happened to be one of those. Her ability to hold her own made it more difficult to achieve his goal.

He'd gritted his teeth long enough, worried about her each time the team went out to a precarious situation. He'd promised her late husband to protect her however he could, but that had already been a commitment in his heart. Before he'd left Fort Benning to join HIS, he'd tried diligently to get her to quit the police force. Stubborn didn't begin to describe the woman. When she'd made SWAT, he'd about lost his shit. A man on a mission, he'd shown up on her doorstep and insisted she give up the team. His disapproval had made her more determined to stay on the job.

Reagan's laughter floated into the hallway at the open

doorway to Jesse's office. "Please, Daddy." That pleading voice always did him and the other agents in for whatever she wanted.

"You can, but you can't force anyone, pumpkin."

"But, it's for a good cause."

Jesse chuckled. "It is, but still—"

Cutting her father off, Reagan turned to him. "Don't you think so, Uncle Ken?" Ever since she'd been little, she'd begun calling every agent "Uncle," and they all loved her as if they were. Boy, did she have them wrapped around her cute little finger. Him included.

Noting Jesse's reluctance, he hedged, "What're you asking?"

She heaved a heavy sigh, as if he should know what she'd been discussing. "The jar?"

"Jar?"

Nearly bouncing with excitement, she said, "Swear jar."

Oh, hell. Most of HIS may as well hand over their paychecks. They came from military or law enforcement backgrounds, which occasionally led to foul language. "Why a swear jar?"

The nine-year-old smile made him feel like he should've, once again, known the answer. "College money."

Ken looked at Jesse, who only shrugged. "I see." He didn't because, with a millionaire mother and wealthy father, college would be a drop in the bucket. Yet, he knew they didn't spoil her—the agents were good for that—but still….

After a kiss on her father's cheek, Reagan skipped out the door with a girlishly decorated jar in her hand. Ken stared at it and swallowed. They'd always tried to curb their language around the children and did a pretty good job. On an op though….

Jesse shook his head and turned his attention to Ken.

Jesse waved him into the office in a blue polo shirt with the HIS logo over his left breast. "Come in. We need to chat."

Hell. He didn't like the sound of that. Still, he entered and sat in the familiar chair facing the desk with a stern-looking Jesse behind it. "Yes, we do." Although he couldn't imagine they had the same topic in mind.

As he sat, he figured if he couldn't get Jesse to dismiss Sam, he'd have to convince her to resign. Somehow. His gut clenched, and he felt like a heel for what this might do to her and their relationship. Selfishly, he wanted her near him and happy. As a civilian, her life wouldn't constantly be in jeopardy, and he wouldn't be a bundle of nerves. He and Jesse had thought getting her out of SWAT had been the wise thing to do since they'd found out about the sexual harassment, even though she hadn't filed a complaint. Some men liked to brag way too often. And while he'd wanted her out of SWAT, maybe they should've hired her to do the computer work with two of the Hamilton siblings, Devon and Emily. Then he'd have fulfilled Lance's request to keep her safe. Finally.

He'd love to marry her, not only because he loved her, but if he did, he might persuade her to avoid a profession where she risked her life, whether it be police, SWAT, or HIS. Something inside his heart flipped at the two being together as husband and wife. Then it sank in, knowing she'd never agree to such a thing if he pushed her to give up what she loved.

In truth, he'd hoped she'd be safe by his side and not as an agent, yet he knew he'd have to go slow with her. A lifetime ago, he'd had two chances with her. Their kiss had been hot and searing the first time they'd met. Not ready to commit to a relationship, he'd pushed her away and into Lance's arms. When he'd felt ready to build something between them, he'd touched his lips to hers again, only more gently. It'd been a year after her husband's death, and she'd put a screeching halt to the intimacy. He'd been right to fear it too soon after Lance's death, but now was the time for them.

While she'd followed his direction as a senior agent and her team leader, he'd focused more on being her shield than allowing her to spread her wings, so to speak. Hell, after each op, he wanted to pull her into his arms and kiss her until they couldn't stand. It would happen soon, but he wouldn't wait until an op occurred.

If things didn't go his way with Jesse, she'd see him later today as they had a serious topic to discuss. Deep down, he knew he had no chance of winning, but he wouldn't go down without a fight. The only upside—and he meant only —was she'd been added to his team in the split. That allowed him to watch out for her as best he could.

Funny how with Jesse refusing his resignation, his strength and confidence in commanding the overall team had returned. They'd find another sharpshooter to replace her. Heck, they had piles of unsolicited resumes from people with impressive experience. A woman he'd worked with on a government-sanctioned mission would be an excellent choice. Finding her was another matter, as who she worked for hadn't been solved.

With all the danger that came their way, he wanted to admit that he liked Sam working with him, knowing that her skill enhanced every mission. But that contradicted his desire to protect and focus on her when she was there. Without her realizing it, the woman scrambled his brain. He had to break through this clutter to return to normal. Although something tickled his mind that since he trusted her, he shouldn't worry and let her do her thing, and he would do his. Then, a response that she might get hurt slapped it away.

He knew his views were archaic, but dammit, he wanted her safe—always.

"We've got an abduction."

Straightening himself in the seat, Ken's mind focused, and his heart pounded, adrenaline readying to spill into his veins. The switch flipped, and his mind tuned into the problem. "Child or adult?"

"Both. Listen, I don't have all the particulars yet." His jaw clenched. "Or the go-ahead."

Ken knew Jesse would get them airborne as quickly as possible, even if that meant getting the go-ahead in the air or on the ground. Whether family or police, or government had agreed they'd want HIS to handle the situation, they generally took too long to pull the trigger.

"The team is coming in now. I need you and Rob to agree on that split and not let anyone on Bravo team disappear. When I'm ready to brief them, I'll come to the two of you."

Waiting sucked. Once Ken knew someone needed their help, he wanted to be there pronto. "You're going to send out Bravo team?"

"Have to."

A stab in his chest would've been easier to take than his boss's remark on his injury and the impact. Taking a deep breath, he remembered Jesse didn't have a problem with his injury, and the decision made sense.

"Because I think they'll need the extra manpower, I'm also going to send a couple of my brothers." He held up a hand to stop Ken's rebuttal. "I know I said we'd leave these missions to the agents, but they want to help, and, if at all possible, I'd like to keep a full team intact in case something else comes up on the fly." He sighed. "Look, this looks like it could get messy. The asshole"—Jesse regarded the paperwork on his desk before looking back at Ken—"one Ronald Wheeler, owns an arsenal and has beaten his estranged wife more than once. She filed for divorce and sole custody, and Ronald doesn't appear to be taking it well."

An angry fire blazed in Ken's gut, ready to erupt. There should be a special place in hell for men like this. Ken stood. "I'll take care of Rob. If you need my team, they're yours."

Jesse's lip quirked up at the end. "Have them on standby. If this becomes a multi-state chase, Rob may need the backup."

Exiting Jesse's office with the yellow folders from before, Ken hoped Jesse received the particulars and go-ahead quickly, as they all knew, every moment counted in an abduction case.

In the war room, Ken found Rob still in his all-black attire, striding out of the locker room. When they approached, Ken grasped Rob's hand at chest level and smiled at his friend. "Welcome back." He nodded as agents walked by them, ready to debrief.

"Glad to be back."

"How'd it go?"

Rob grinned. "Piece of cake."

Ken almost snorted out loud. "Only a few bullets flying?" While true, it had been said in a lighthearted, jesting manner.

"I'm thinking we need to train the team in evasive driving. I imagine Brad could help, but it wouldn't hurt to get them onto a professional course."

Brad Hamilton had once been a U.S. Secret Service agent. Although he hadn't been an official driver, he'd somehow managed a few driving classes that had helped

HIS when trouble had arisen. Now that Brad would stay back more often, Rob's idea had merit.

"I'm sure Old Man won't fight it." He rubbed his chin in thought. "Maybe two per team." Old Man was Jesse's designation, similar to a commander. Ken couldn't call him that outside of an op or in discussion with the team. They'd been too close. The same held for Sam.

Rob showed surprise for only a millisecond before he returned his features to his blank expression. "Teams?"

Nodding, Ken led him to one of the empty offices. "Teams as in two. One for me and one for you."

Ken sat behind the desk, and Rob took a chair in front of it. "That's not a bad idea."

A sly grin spread across his face before he told Rob, "It'd include a raise for you, of course."

Rob shrugged as if it didn't matter, but Ken knew the man saved nearly every penny he made. "I wish I could take credit for the idea, but it was Old Man's. The family is stepping back. They're available for special ops or when our numbers aren't enough. But they'll take over the investigative side, freeing us up for the field."

Rob nodded. "I figured they'd step back at some point." Almost as an afterthought, he asked, "How's the hip?"

At the question, Ken automatically rubbed a hand over the wounded area. The skin was still tender to the touch, but he'd never admit such. "I'll be fine. Back to ops in a couple of weeks."

"It'll suck not working side by side with you."

"I'm sure we'll have some ops that require both teams." Ken knew one was in the offer stage. Once Jesse accepted it, most of the team would be gone for as long as it took. Due to the need to expedite everything since it included a child abduction, Ken expected to hear about it shortly.

"I imagine that'd be the case." Rob half stood. "I've gotta debrief."

Per Jesse's orders, Ken was to delay Rob while he pulled the specifics for that op and ensured Rob accepted the new team leader role. "Since everyone was here, we thought we could present the team concept to them."

"Christ, Boss, the team is exhausted." He didn't care for "Boss," but he'd been dubbed that, and that's what the team called him. Except for Sam, in private. And the Hamiltons. Maybe because they'd grown up together, the brothers had never stuck with any nicknames they'd been given in their careers.

"I know, but this is important and shouldn't take long."

Spotting the paperwork Ken had dropped on the desk, Rob scooted forward. "Okay. Let's do this."

"Including us, there are twelve agents. We'll each have a sharpshooter and a field medic."

Rob looked up from his perusal of the list Ken had handed him. "But we only have one medic—Rodney."

Reaching across the desk, he tapped his finger on a name listed on the paper. "We've hired Ash McNabb. Casper was a D-boy and a paramedic before he became a Green Beret, then Delta."

Rob whistled, as he should for someone with such elite experience: respect and all.

"As for team designations, I'll lead Alpha team, and you'll lead Bravo team."

A grin split Rob's face. "Still making me second, aren't you?"

"Filling these big shoes is hard," Ken jested.

"Big shoes, my ass."

Ken chuckled. "You're just jealous."

Rob snorted. "You just keep thinking that."

"All right, let's get back to this so we can get you out there and announce it to the group." Motioning his head toward a single sheet of paper, he explained, "That's the suggested breakout. But this will be your team, too, so it's not set in stone until we both agree."

"So your sniper is Sugar, while I have Nemo."

Ken nodded in agreement. "We'll beef up that position to two on each team as soon as we can find sharpshooters that fit."

Looking up from the list, Rob smiled slyly. "How about we switch?"

Without warning, Ken bristled at the remark. Although it felt like jealousy, he refused to admit it. "What's wrong with Nemo?" Neftali, aka Nef, aka Nemo, had also been a SEAL, so he and Rob should get along excellently.

"Nothing. Sugar's just better to look at."

Anger raged through him, and he could've sprung over the table and strangled the man if his hip and professional restraint hadn't held him back. Sam was a million times better to look at, but he didn't want anyone else to believe that. He'd attempted Jesse's approach when he'd attempted to resign. "No."

His second-in-command laughed. At him. What the hell? He hadn't done anything that warranted the humorous response. He decided moving on would be the best option. "I'll keep Rodney for a medic, and you can use Casper. He shouldn't need any training."

Sober again, Rob nodded. "That works."

Glad to be back on track, Ken split the once larger team. "I'll keep Franks, Cowboy, and Stone. That'll leave you, Romeo, Celeb, and Speedy." He looked up from the list. "Any issues?"

"You have more former spec ops than I do."

"Remember, you're gaining a Delta for your team." To move him off that topic, he added, "Also, we each have someone formerly from the FBI—Stone for me and Romeo for you—which can help in investigations when the Hamilton clan isn't available. The rest are a mix of backgrounds."

Rob leaned back and nodded. "That works for me."

Jesse walked by the office and nodded at Ken as he continued toward the war room.

With a grimace, Ken spoke, "Your team is up now. Old Man is waiting to brief the team. You can debrief the op you just completed while in the air. There's no time to waste on this one."

Rob surged to his feet, and all appearances of exhaustion evaporated. "Then why the hell have you kept me here?"

Not wanting the vulnerable position of being seated while Rob stood over him, he unfolded himself from the chair and held out a hand, staying Rob. "Calm down. Old Man had to get the information. We haven't wasted any time except right now. Get out there, and I'll get the team." With that, they both strode out, Ken falling behind because of his limp.

Jesse quickly introduced the team breakout when the team assembled in the war room. As expected, no questions were asked. The men and women trusted their leadership's judgment, which helped tremendously in HIS op success. "Bravo team, you're up for this one. Let's go. Alpha team, you're on standby."

With the room half empty, Ken called his team together near the end of the conference table. As they huddled around, he asked, "Anyone have questions or concerns about our splitting up the teams?"

"I'm glad you did it. It's better than arbitrarily being put on standby or never knowing if you'll be chosen for an op,"

Danny Franks, former DEA, offered.

"I agree," Mike—Cowboy—a former Air Force Pararescueman or PJ, added.

"What about the brothers and Kate and Rylee?" Franks asked.

"They'll be more administrative. That's not to say they won't augment an op like this one, but the teams are it for the most part." He didn't add because they'd all seen the change. Kate and Rylee—former FBI agents and Hamilton brother wives—had already slowly been pulling back on ops.

"Who decides who goes?" Sugar asked with that light Southern accent that sounded like music to his soul. The team had quickly dubbed her with a call sign of Sugar because her accent was "sweet as sugar."

Ken smiled. "That's one of those administrative things. Old Man will ultimately decide, but the plan is for rotation."

"Hell, I'm gonna miss Rylee out there. She's damn good." Joe Stone, a former FBI agent and called by his last name, must've realized how that sounded when Sugar gave him the evil eye. "Now, wait a minute," he begged off. "I'm not saying just because she's a woman. I'm saying it because she was FBI, and we stick together."

While they knew he was joking, a small argument broke out where Franks stood his ground for the DEA. When he disparaged the SEALs, Ken stepped in to keep a full-out war from happening.

"All right. We all know the Army Rangers are the best, and anyone who argues can sit out the next op."

Completely ignoring him, they all talked at once. He fought not to smile. This group was predictable.

"So what do we do when Bravo team is on an op?" Rodney, a former Navy SEAL and medic they referred to as Doc, asked quietly.

"We'll be on downtime, out on an op of our own, or on standby to support them however we can. We'll also train. Lots of training." Ken's experience was that when the topic of training was spoken about, several groans sounded. Not from this group. They wanted to stay on top of their game.

"All right, I need to debrief with those who just returned and do the quick turnaround. I've read the police reports, but I need to hear why bullets were flying." Some police departments either lacked the resources to handle certain situations or needed the help that the government wouldn't provide, or they welcomed their assistance, especially with a successful resolution. But they always hated it when bullets flew, even if HIS didn't fire first.

"Hell, Boss, you know they don't fly unless we have to," Stone said belligerently, taking up for his old teammates.

Ken sighed heavily. "Yes, but when they do, they don't usually hit an off-duty police officer."

"Whoa, wait a minute," Franks said. "I understood our attorney already said it was a clear case of self-defense. We couldn't help it that the cop tried to kill Romeo."

It didn't surprise him that Grits had called their attorney while returning. None of them wanted jail time for doing their job. "I'm not saying the team did anything wrong. Everyone needs to be informed of what happened before, during, and after, so we can learn from it. We know that different states react to us differently, so understanding each state can only help us. Knowing how the police react to every incident can help us improve our responses. Revisiting what occurred before the incident can only strengthen us in lessons learned."

Franks, Stone, and Doc nodded. Sugar and Cowboy watched him, not in disagreement, but more as if they wanted him to continue or add more.

"After we debrief, you're released for the day. We'll meet back here tomorrow for training. Remember, you're on standby to back up the team. If we need you, Devon will send out the alert." Every agent, by requirement, carried a cell phone, and if the emergency text pushed through, it required only one thing—get your ass to HQ on the double.

"When are you back on ops?" Doc asked.

"Not soon enough." And no way in hell would he allow Sam to go on one without him.

Chapter Four

In her Baltimore apartment, Sam woke from a catnap to a pounding on the door and automatically reached for her weapon. Not finding it, she bolted upright, and in a split second, she had her bearings. Tossing her legs over the side of the sofa, she wiped a hand down her face to remove the remains of another dream featuring Lance. This time, however, it morphed into Lance's final moments, where he told her all she'd learned from the information Bev had overnighted. In her dream, she'd vowed to avenge him. Then, when Jesse and Ken visited her after Lance's death, she reacted differently than the first time they'd arrived. Later, her and Ken's kiss had them on the edge of a cliff, ready to fall. That was the point she woke.

With a quick glance at her watch, she swiveled her head to peer outside the window, where dusk had fallen. Bright streetlights broke through the darkness, brightening the small part of the sidewalk. Her thirty-minute nap had turned into a couple of hours.

Three knocks came again. Not knocks. Someone pounded a fist on her door, aggravating her. She had a feeling she knew who that might be, and although her pulse leaped at the possibility, she planned to be cautious since she didn't expect company. A quick thought jolted her heart. Had they been called for backup, and she'd missed the call? She snagged her cell phone from the side table and noted no alerts or phone calls. A relieved sigh slipped through her. Thank goodness.

Looking down at her clothing, she shrugged, deciding her cut-off jean shorts and navy crop top, with the words *Don't Even Think It* stretched across her breasts, would have to do because she planned for this to be a short visit. The top fell a few inches above the waistband of her shorts. Heck, if she reached her hands above her head, she'd probably provide a nice bra shot of her ample chest.

With a chuckle at her doing that for company, she checked the peephole and guessed right. Ken Patrick. Unexpected heat crept through her body.

Before joining HIS, one of her more imprinted memories of Ken—and Jesse—had been when they'd arrived after the Ranger team returned stateside and completed their lengthy op debrief, including the interviews, the statements, and all that went with the success of their op, but also the loss of two special operators. Sam had listened to the two men offer support from the team, actually, all Ranger teams, but her grief had been too strong to grasp what they'd selfishly offered. Ken hadn't given up.

Ken and Lance had been best friends before she lost her husband, and she and Ken had a close relationship. Although she'd never forgotten, to be fair to her husband and marriage, she'd put their first kiss to the back of her mind. They'd remained friends after her husband's death, but she'd drifted in mourning. About a year after Lance's death, Ken kissed her, asking to become a more significant part of her life. When she'd been too numb to give him more, he'd finally given up and moved to Baltimore. After that, she'd felt abandoned, which she knew was ridiculous as she'd had no hold on him.

When Jesse had sought her out for an opening at HIS, she'd accepted, knowing Ken was an agent. She'd missed their friendship and maybe him even more. Even with Bev as her best friend, she'd felt lonely.

Knowing what she'd just learned about Lance's death, the job offering had been fortuitous.

When she'd walked into her interview with the five Hamilton brothers, their sister, and their foster brother, she'd almost freaked out at the intimidating interview panel. The atmosphere in the room had changed when Ken—dressed in all black, including a tight T-shirt with his hair pulled back at the base of his neck—slid quietly into the room. Leaning against the back wall with his arms crossed over his massive chest. A calm had settled inside her at Ken's reassuring presence.

Once she'd joined HIS, Ken's agenda confused her, keeping her a little off-balance. Their friendship had started afresh outside HQ, but had a different feel. With Lance no longer a barrier, the possibility of what could be excited her. The attraction had zinged between them whether they were on or off duty. The only thing holding her back was whether to go down that road from friends to lovers.

On the flip side, he'd done everything HQ could to hold her back from doing what she loved. He'd even hovered and informed Jesse she wasn't ready for an assignment for what seemed the longest time when she'd been more than ready. When she'd finally deployed, he'd again hovered.

Warring over her growing feelings for Ken and the new intel she'd received, her stomach revolted, knowing she had a difficult decision to make. She wished she'd never heard or seen the official information Bev had acquired. Her life had been moving forward on a positive note. She didn't know how to reconcile everything she'd been told with everything she'd read.

Damn that report. She'd felt alive again, and now this…. Betrayal buried its way into her heart. Had Ken lied to her about what happened when Lance died?

While regaining calm, she peeked in the small mirror on the wall by the door to check herself. Boy, how she wished she'd had time to down a few chocolate-covered mini-donuts. She'd never admit to the unhealthy indulgence she usually fell to in times of stress or deep thought. After this visit, she'd probably need an entire bag because she couldn't bring herself to share what she'd learned. What he already knew and kept secret.

Even as a flash of Bev reminding her of her loss and convincing her the men should pay, her commitment wavered. Not only did she think she couldn't kill anyone except those on a mission who deserved it, but Ken…? Her heart lurched in her stomach. She couldn't believe she had promised Bev she'd consider the idea.

After a quick tug to tighten her blonde ponytail, she swung open the door to a frowning man.

She couldn't handle being close to him, especially now. It was too difficult to be around him. Once again, she felt in mourning. This time, it was the loss of what could've been. With the hope she'd piss him off enough that he'd leave before entering her apartment, she pasted on her best fake smile and, in a syrupy voice, stated, "I don't recall inviting you."

It didn't work. He narrowed his eyes, and if she hadn't

been trying to repel him, she might've laughed at a glare she didn't find intimidating. That was until he briskly pushed past her into the living room, motorcycle helmet in hand.

As he passed, he left behind the scent of a rugged man who wore a woodsy cologne she didn't recognize—not that she was an expert there. The familiar scents reminded her of their time together and their passionate kisses. Time had changed for them. Seething at his brisk manner and all she'd learned, she closed the door and followed him into her living room.

When she confronted him, his eyes bulged out, and his jaw clenched.

"Wha—What the hell are you wearing?"

His harsh tone surprised her. While they'd been professional at work—keeping an apparent distance she always respected—at home, they let their guard down as friends. She had reason enough to be angry, but he shouldn't. He'd never spoken to her thus.

Knowing what he meant by his question but not allowing him to goad her, she looked down at her clothing, then back at him. "Clothes?" Typically, at work, and most of the time she'd seen him off-duty, he dressed in a black T-shirt, cargo pants, or camo if the op deemed it appropriate. But today, he'd tossed that for those damn snug jeans again that made her body crave him. It didn't help that his gray T-shirt with the HIS logo was probably too small. Or so it appeared.

She wanted to return before speaking with Bev, and her world had changed. Only she and Bev knew it had, but that didn't change how her moving forward could weigh heavily on her conscience.

"Dammit, Sam, that shirt is too short. You shouldn't be wearing that in public."

His absurd commanding arrogance may work when battling an enemy, but she refused to take it from him.

"First"—she pointed her finger at him to emphasize her point—"I'm not in public, and second, I didn't make you my fashion police."

He blustered, and that brought a pleasing sensation in her chest. How he got tongue-tied around her made what she had to do all the more challenging.

"What do you want?" Realizing she'd balled her hands into fists, knowing what he'd done, she slowly relaxed them at her side so he wouldn't notice.

"We need to talk." Gruff. That personified the man.

"Well then, let's have a seat." She gestured to the sofa.

Ken waited for her to sit.

She wanted to yell what she'd learned and toss the reports at him and demand that he tell her the truth, but the impact of the intel was still too raw, and Bev promised more information soon. Instead, she focused on his curious visit. "Can I get you something to drink?" she asked like a prim and proper Southern hostess.

"I'm sure you can, but will you?"

To keep from lunging at him, she bit her tongue—hard enough she probably had blood flowing. He constantly corrected her on the proper usage of "can" and "may" along with "could" and "would." While aggravating, she understood that things like that—wordplay—on an op could make a big difference in the execution of their mission. But she wasn't on an op. She was in her friggin' apartment.

Instead of responding, she headed into the kitchen and

yanked two bottles of water from the refrigerator. Hands full, she strode back into the living room and handed him a bottle on her way to sink into the sofa. After she settled, he dropped into the armchair.

She waited for Ken to open his bottle and drink. Her emotions were in turmoil almost every time she was alone with him. How could he have done such things as the army said? Could he have been so incompetent? It kept her head, heart, and body constantly at odds and always battling out her next move.

Waiting for the reason for his visit, she remained silent until he decided to speak. When he did, his words left her speechless.

"Would you like to grab a bite with me?"

Not only did she stare, but her mouth also dropped open at the question. Usually, she'd immediately grab her purse and have dinner with him. Now? Could she?

"Whatever night is good for you," he added.

Sam noticed a slight shaking of his hand as he tilted the bottle to his lips.

How could this tough man be nervous? That's what it had to be unless he had a medical condition she didn't know about, where trembling or shaking was a side effect. She couldn't imagine that. He had to be genuinely nervous. Intriguing.

A vision of the two of them at a table covered with a white tablecloth and a rose in a vase in the middle sprang to mind. The romantic atmosphere seeped through her imagination. Then it came to a screeching halt. In no way could that happen. She reminded herself she had to reconsider where she went from here, no matter how much her body craved his touch.

She cleared her throat to keep away her true thoughts. "I don't think that's wise. You're my…my team leader." *My friend* had been her first thought, but it made her feel ill that she could've trusted him with her life and Lance's.

He didn't appear to realize her change in acceptance of his previous dinner invitation from "Sure" to "No" this time. "I wouldn't be if you'd do some sort of desk work or quit."

He did not just say that. Anger flared up, rousing an inferno burning through every cell in her body. After all she'd done to get here and prove herself. She could choke him for being such an obstinate man. "Why are you so set on my no longer being a part of the team?"

"Because—"

Something inside her knew he'd made a promise to her husband, and that must be his goal. However, being a sniper was more challenging than being a police officer on the streets or in SWAT. She grumbled, "Sexist bullshit," under her breath. When he chuckled, she pointed a finger at him and narrowed her eyes. "Lance would've supported me no matter what."

Ken sobered and shook his head. "No, Sam. Lance didn't like you being a police officer."

With that blow to the stomach, she wanted to curl up into a ball. She could've gone to her grave without knowing the truth of it. If Ken, her husband's best friend, knew that, why hadn't her husband told her the truth?

That same hurt, plus a bucket load of humiliation, kept her from conceding the point. She jumped up from her seat to emphasize the strength of her response. "Bullshit. He never would've married me."

Ken rose as she did but remained silent and still.

She raised her brows in victory. "What? Nothing to say?"

Ken closed his eyes for a moment. When he opened them, he rushed ahead with words he would have known would tear at her very being. "I'm telling the truth. It isn't sexist like you think. Lance never approved of your profession because he feared you'd never come home one day, but he loved you too much to let you go." He stopped for a moment as if in conflict. Eventually, he sighed and continued. "He planned to get you pregnant as soon as possible so you'd give it up. He wanted you safe."

All her bluster rushed from her, and she dropped back on the sofa, fighting the anger welling inside her. "You say it's not sexist, but it sounds like a moronic and sexist idea." The next moment, before he could respond, her mood flashed, and she turned on him, pissed off. She couldn't believe he'd make this story up to bolster his standing with her. This change in his behavior reiterated what she'd read. "You're lying." Lance had wanted to get her pregnant to keep her from her job instead of for typical reasons—family, etc. He wasn't that type of man.

Ken dropped to one knee before her and took her hands in his. "I'm sorry, Sam. I really am. I didn't need to be so blunt. Who knows? Maybe Lance would've changed his tune and been your biggest supporter on this job. I promise I'm not sexist. I know you can do the job, but I also know you can die on the job."

She looked at him with wet eyes and tears sliding down her face. Die on the job. Could it be that easy?

After dropping one of her hands, he clung to the other as

he stood and pulled her up with him. Standing so close, her breasts touched his chest. Neither said a word. Her breathing quickened, and their gazes locked with a fire lighting and flaring between them. The one thing they'd been dancing around since she'd joined HIS.

Slowly, he leaned his head down, his lips covering hers. But it wasn't the chaste kiss she expected. It was full of red-hot passion that tried to make up for the last ten years of separation.

He teased her lips, and with no resistance, she parted them, then welcomed his tongue into her mouth. She mimicked his tongue's movement, putting every positive emotion she had for him into this foreplay before he deepened the kiss.

Her response came swiftly. Needing to get closer, she slid her hand up his rock-hard chest and wrapped her arms around his neck. When her breasts fit snuggly against him, Ken pulled her closer until sparks of pleasure drove through her.

She drank in all that he gave her at that moment when reality crashed in, and her blood turned cold.

Jerking back out of his arms, she covered her mouth in self-reproach. This was one of the men responsible for her husband's death. The intel reports told all. Bev had told her Ken hadn't saved Lance because he wanted Sam for herself. She hadn't believed her friend, but....

Sick to her stomach, she did the only thing she could. "Leave," she demanded.

He turned away from her. "As your team leader and a man who's always held our friendship dear, I support you. As your husband's best friend and someone I care about more than friendship, I don't want you anywhere near the danger that comes with this job." He turned back to her. "I'm having trouble reconciling the two."

Her heart wondered if there was more to his statement. Even if not, reconciling those two things had to happen. She had to allow things with her and Ken to progress and forget about what she'd learned. Or, she had to find a way to make Ken and Jesse pay for her husband's death.

She slammed the door behind Ken as she strode away. Could she really allow herself to fall in love with one of the men responsible for her loss? Not wanting to think it through, she dropped onto the couch. Lowering her head in her hands, she cried for all she'd lost and all she might lose.

Chapter Five

Where the hell had that come from? Ken had been a fool to kiss her while acting like an ass. He could understand—in a small way—if his action had been too much, as she hadn't verbalized her agreement to move to the next step. He couldn't understand why she turned him down for dinner and then used the "boss" bullshit.

To be complete, he needed her in his life. His heart had always been devoted to her, even from afar. He had to pull it all together.

He had to remember the most important part—she asked him to leave after he kissed her—no other words. Just asked him to leave. He'd overstepped his bounds, but she'd looked so defeated and vulnerable that he'd wanted to enfold her in his arms.

When the first agent on his team burst from the building, Ken refocused on his task. With the team split, he could devote more time to the cohesiveness of his smaller group. They'd all worked together, but now they had a chance to strengthen their bonds and become a smaller family. One who anticipated every move and countermoves their teammate would make. Plus, they had to get used to Franks —his team's new second-in-command—leading them when he couldn't. *Like right now.* The agents had become comfortable with Grits, but times had changed.

"Dammit!" Ken looked at the stopwatch in his hand. "It took you four seconds longer than our target time."

Not long ago, a training house had been constructed so

that they could practice rescues, which, unfortunately, outnumbered their protection details but were equal to their government-sanctioned ops, which kept climbing.

"Four seconds," he stressed, "longer to clear the house," he reiterated to a tired and sweaty team.

Dressed in full tactical gear, the team had run different scenarios inside the hull of a house with no air conditioning, without giving them time to rest between scenarios. They had to be ready to tackle a rescue even while exhausted. The rescue came first and foremost of any such op.

He had to get his point across even though he knew they understood. "Your delay could've notified the captors, and our op would've ended in recovery instead of rescue. Our goal for the victims is rescue."

No one spoke. Solemn, tired faces looked back at him, offering no excuses—which he wouldn't tolerate. He hadn't needed to tell them what taking too long could mean. They were hardened warriors. And warriorettes, if there was such a thing.

"Let's rerun it." He knew he'd probably pushed them far enough for the day. He worried that he couldn't go in and lead them if they were called up for an op right now. They had to learn to beat the clock without him.

"Come on, Boss. Give us five to catch our breath." Franks leaned over with his hands on his knees. Ken trusted him, but he wished the agent had more leadership experience. His DEA experience was good—but not enough. When he was back on his feet, Ken would work with him because his second had what it took.

Seeing how tired they were, he looked at his watch and grimaced. It was later than he'd expected. It wasn't like him to lose track of time. In truth, he knew he'd pushed so hard because Sam hadn't been acting as a sniper. She'd been right in the thick of it. They had to get it right to protect her, while he couldn't. "We'll call it a day and tackle this tomorrow. Make sure to clean your weapons before you leave."

Cowboy snorted and rolled his eyes. "Like you have to tell us that."

"Since Bravo team is out, you're on call," Ken reminded them.

Stone laughed. "You don't have to tell us that either."

"Wait," Franks said. "Don't tell me—make sure your gear is in good working order."

"Don't forget—make sure your go-bag is ready." Sugar chuckled.

"And the med kit," Doc added.

By this time, the entire team was either grinning or laughing. He'd give them this bit of fun because it told him they listened. Not that he'd had to tell them to do all those things. More honestly, they knew how to prepare. "Are you done?"

"There's plenty more." Franks flashed a wry smile. "Should we continue?"

Usually, he'd tell them to go fuck themselves, but he'd been trying to clean up his language so he wouldn't owe Reagan so much. That child's jar had already begun to fill. Plus, he did want to behave better around the Hamilton children. The Hamiltons had become his family. They'd taken him in and treated him as if he belonged. However, that pack of brothers could get overwhelming and opinionated when he didn't want the hassle. "No. Just get it all done."

After punching his code into the keypad beside the door, the team trudged through the war room to the weapons room. Once finished, Ken expected them to go to the locker rooms and get showers. He could use one also, but he'd survive until he arrived home. Not wearing full gear or running the drills, he'd survived the worst of the oppressive heat. Plus, even with the wind in his face on his motorcycle, he'd still sweat on the ride home.

The in-residence Hamilton brothers strolled into the war room, most carrying their gear, bag, and weapons. It was odd since a typical investigation didn't require tactical gear. "What's going on?"

"Trent needs some help," Jesse stated. Ken missed running the team with Trent McKenzie, a Hamilton half-brother. Although he'd taken to ranching in Montana instead of his spot at HIS, the brothers remained close. Well, as close as they had before. The brothers always respected Trent on the team, and since they'd grown up together, they knew each other better than most.

"What kind of help?" Ken nodded toward the bags AJ and Matt—Brad's twin—carried with Jake and Brad augmenting Bravo team, leaving Jesse and Devon—their former CIA computer guru—as the only Hamiltons at HQ —minus Rylee and Kate. He couldn't forget that Emily would also be there.

"Someone's slaughtering his cattle. He also found a stallion dead in his stall. His throat had been slashed. Plus other cruel actions," AJ said with a heavy dose of anger and disgust.

Hell. Anyone who harmed animals—and children and older adults, heck, anyone—deserved punishment. "Why aren't you sending my team?" He felt slighted, no, more like thoroughly insulted at being overlooked.

Jesse hesitated. "We're not sure your team is ready without you."

Ken couldn't help but bristle, even though Jesse was, in all probability, correct. Individually, they were strong, but with a new second-in-command, they needed time.

"Besides," Jesse continued, "we're making it a family reunion of sorts. The wives and kids are going." Jesse lifted two tactical bags that Ken imagined were for Kate and Rylee.

Unbelievable. Hadn't they just spoken of danger? "Are you sure that's wise?"

With a cheeky grin, Devon said proudly, "Have you forgotten two of those wives were FBI before they joined this elite group?"

Of course, he remembered. Kate and Rylee were incredible assets on the team. Together, they could clear an area faster than any of their spec ops brethren. "No, I remember. Does this mean Devon's going too?" If Rylee were going, her husband would probably travel with her. They'd need Devon's skills if another op came up.

Devon shook his head. "No. Jesse and I are staying back since we have Bravo team in the field."

He nodded, thankful they would have support if needed. He'd let them figure out the family thing and danger. However, none of it was new to them.

When the brothers went back to planning, Ken sought out his team.

"No, on the second run, I got the drop on the tango in the back room," Cowboy insisted.

"Bullshit," Stone said. "Sugar clearly had the bead on him first."

A frisson of pride filled him that Sam held her own, not that he doubted her for a second.

While he quietly held fast at the door, no one said a word to him, even though he knew everyone was aware that he stood there. They'd have acknowledged him had he strode into the room bearing news, but for him to stand there meant nothing more than he'd been observing.

Sam smiled without lifting her head from her task. "I do believe I did, Michael."

Looking up, Cowboy narrowed his eyes at her and muttered, "Don't call me that. The name is Vaughn or Cowboy."

"Whatever you say, Michael." Her grin broadened.

Cowboy's face turned red, and Ken held his breath. Cowboy could be lethal, and he appeared to be headed toward anger. Then he surprised Ken by relaxing and shrugging. "Okay, *Samantha*."

Her playful interaction with the team fit in well with the dynamics. It sucked keeping that professional distance from her when he wanted to pull her into his arms. First, he'd ask her why she broke their kiss, told him to leave, and avoided being alone with him.

Sam regarded Cowboy for a moment and laughed. "Touché."

With that, Ken walked into the room to the tables where the team was working.

"Hey, Boss," Doc said without breaking from his work.

Taking an empty seat, he nodded in response—even though Doc couldn't see it. "The remaining brothers are taking off."

Everyone stopped what they'd been doing and snapped their attention to Ken. "What's going on?" Franks asked.

"Some trouble at Trent's place."

Cowboy whistled. "That's a big place with a shitload of land to cover."

"They're taking Kate and Rylee also. Along with the rest of the brood."

"Well, hell," Franks said. "Who does that leave us as a backup if we get called out?"

He knew they'd balk at this—whether being passed over for the op or because they'd be left with Franks for the first time if called out—but they'd find out the truth when they walked into the war room. "Jesse and Devon."

Cowboy snorted. "So you mean Old Man."

"Hold on," Franks said. "Devon can hold his own out there. You've seen him."

"Yeah, I've seen him kick some ass. He surprised the hell out of me, but he doesn't go out," Cowboy argued.

Needing to put a stop to it, Ken jumped in. "Look, we need Devon back here on his magic computer. Besides, since I'm down, Old Man will automatically go with you to support you."

Tension filled the air. He should've told them when they split the team instead of waiting until after they'd had a tough training session. Even though they'd love to work with Jesse, they probably felt like they were being punished. It resembled having the principal take over the class instead of the teacher. No one liked that. They feared they wouldn't meet the standards.

"You didn't tell us that," Sugar said in a strange voice. Ken couldn't tell if she was happy or angry about it. "I thought Franks would lead us."

Ken shrugged. "It's the only way you can go. Since we brought the group down to smaller-sized teams, we can't afford any shortages. It'll take us some time to add more agents."

The team worked in silence. Then Cowboy piped up. "I still say on the second run, I got the drop on the tango in the back room."

Laughter filled the room, and the tension disappeared.

Sam slapped the table beside her weapons. "Done." She beamed with pride. "And it's not even my piece. It's just that crap you guys carry.”

A bit of grumbling went through the men since they knew the M4 she’d used today was nothing to laugh about, even compared to her top-notch sniper rifle. As for the handguns they carried, HIS allowed the men—he had to remember women also—to carry what they felt most comfortable using—mostly Glocks, but plenty of SIGs.

For rifles, they’d all argued over their favorite—M16, AR15, AK47, and M4. After weighing everything, Devon purchased them M4s, which they all enjoyed, even if they grumbled about how their service weapon had been superior. The grumbling ceased when he provided them with M203 grenade launchers to attach to the rifle. Devon promised to look for anything better. Ken figured that meant before it was sold to the military or civilians.

Bragging rights for the first to complete their weapons cleaning were held in the balance. Some non-tangible reward seemed to go with it, but Ken hadn’t extracted that information from them. Smartly, they kept it to themselves because he’d have to lecture them on doing it right instead of doing it fast for a reward. Although he remembered those days as a Ranger when the teams had done the same thing.

Picking up her weapons, Sam stood. “I’m off to shower. See you guys in the rec room.”

Ken hadn’t realized he’d been blatantly watching Sam’s backside as she exited the room until the snickers reached his hearing. Turning his head back to the men, they abruptly quieted but kept smirks on their faces. Had he been that obvious? Apparently so.

Tipping his chair back on two legs, he thought of something to say to take their mind off his wandering eye. “Did I tell you that Em’s pregnant again?”

Cowboy shook his head. “That family is a regular baby

factory."

"Only if you put them all together. Separate, they're not too bad," Doc said.

A stabbing pain gutted him. He hadn't thought much of children before, but having a family….

Without looking up, Cowboy stated, "I'm not having kids."

"That's because you haven't learned how to make babies," Stone said.

"Fuck you."

Franks made a tsking sound. "It's a good thing you're not having kids with language like that."

"Are you kidding me?" Cowboy asked. "What about all your language?" He looked around the table.

"We're trying to clean it up—at least when we're home. Reagan gave us a tongue-lashing the last time we were with the family. Then she introduced us to her swear jar." Franks shook his head. "That girl is way too grown up."

"What type of military team doesn't use foul language?" Cowboy persisted.

"One that isn't only military," Franks responded. "Some of us were taught manners."

Before a military versus law enforcement argument broke out, Ken stood. "Look, your language is your own, and so is whether you contribute to her. Just be respectful around the kids. That's all the brothers, and I ask."

As he exited the room, he smiled when he heard Cowboy say, "Well, hell."

While Ken finished a little paperwork, the team played darts in the rec room. He was unsure whether they waited for him so they could depart together or if they really wanted to play the game before they left for the day.

After finishing, he joined them and played a round—

getting his ass handed to him by Stone—before they all called it a day. Jesse and Devon were huddled around Devon's computer when they left and gave a nod goodbye.

As the team fanned out to go to their vehicles, Ken closed in on Sam. He had to try again, apologize, or smooth her ruffled feathers. "May we speak for a minute?"

Probably still bristling from their last meeting, she stated matter-of-factually, "No."

Nearly struck dumb at her easy dismissal, Ken stood momentarily, then strode toward his Harley. He needed the wind in his face to clear his head. Somehow, he'd been going about this all wrong. He had to get his head straight for what he wanted with her. And what he could reasonably ask of her.

He saw Sam digging a ringing phone from her black purse out of his peripheral vision. As she answered the phone with a "Hi, Bev," his curious ears perked up. Could it be Beverly Shodun? He'd never forgotten the woman threatening to have him arrested if he approached her again. Since her husband died on one of their ops, Ken and Jesse had offered condolences and assistance. Since she wouldn't allow them near her, they checked on her from afar to ensure one of their teammates' widows was adequately taken care of, even if it couldn't be by them.

Of course, Sam, as someone on the police force, had known the reality of ops was different and not once blamed him or Jesse.

He glanced at Sam over his shoulder. The two women had been two peas in a pod. He'd never understood it because, in his mind, Sam's friendship had been too good for the woman he'd deemed selfish.

Maybe it was time to check in on Adam's widow and her son again to ensure they were still doing well. Cody had to be about nine or ten by now.

Knowing he shouldn't intrude, he turned back to his bike. Ken's blood ran cold at Sam's following urgently spoken statement, and he whirled around to face her.

"When did he go missing? What do you mean kidnapped?"

Every team member froze as they tried to get to their vehicles and turned to Sam. Ken's blood ran cold at the questions she'd asked.

She turned, and their eyes connected. Instead of the woman who was pissed off at him from their passionate kiss, she turned back into the focused woman who happened to be the best damn sniper he'd known. Her expression wrenched his gut. Even through her strength, fear clouded her eyes, and he'd never seen that in her before.

Without thought for themselves and the rest due to them, after a long, hard day of training, the men moved in and surrounded Sam. They knew they'd just drawn an op and were already focused on learning what details they could from her side of the conversation.

Even though they were only steps away from the building, Ken pulled his cell from his pocket and speed-dialed the HIS emergency line. When Jesse answered, he quickly stated, "We have a kidnapping. We're returning now. Sam's on the phone with a Beverly, maybe Beverly Shodun. Her boy should be about nine or ten."

They began to shuffle her toward the door they'd all departed through a few moments ago as individuals going their separate ways. They returned as a cohesive team.

"Oh, hell," Jesse responded. "His name is Cody, and he's nine, almost ten. Devon and I are ready for you."

"We're walking in now." Until they reached the war room, Ken would keep his phone line open to relay anything

Sam said, so even the few seconds it saved could mean time rescuing the boy.

As the men led the way down the hallway, Ken followed Sam, listening to every word in case she forgot to relay something. As she slowed her pace, she turned away and lowered her voice. Curious, he leaned in from behind her and barely overheard her words. When he did, he stepped back because her statement startled him.

"Don't you remember who I work for? I thought you wanted me to kill two of them, not bring them to help you."

Chapter Six

*C*ody abducted! Sam's heart had skipped a beat, and fear lanced its way through her system at record speed, leaving her determined yet with weak knees. Even though she knew this disturbing act occurred, she couldn't comprehend why someone would do such a thing—especially to the Shoduns. Bev had no money, and Cody was a good kid.

Knowing how much Bev despised Jesse and Ken, Sam had been surprised that her friend would call for help. Of course, Sam would help no matter the backup, and the team's experience would be extremely beneficial.

"I don't want them. I want you."

Feeling Ken move closer, she began walking again. When she entered the war room, Jesse and Devon's stern, expectant gazes almost threw her off balance. Even though she didn't discount her skills, she knew success would need more than Sam alone. She had to convince Bev to allow them to rescue Cody.

"Is she home?" Devon's quiet words told her HIS would be involved, and she'd bet even if it were against Bev's wishes. They didn't mess around when a kid was involved. They'd pull in any resource they could find, which included, as she noted on one op, some black ops friends of theirs. That had been a surprise when they'd just appeared out of nowhere.

She nodded, refusing to speak so Bev wouldn't realize she'd shared information with the people Bev hated most. They'd start their search at Bev's, hoping there were clues or

Bev could offer up something they could use to locate Cody.

She closed her eyes in the hope that the plane hadn't departed. She'd never been more grateful that HIS had leased a private jet to ensure they had a rapid response.

Turning her back to the men, she kept her voice low, hoping they wouldn't push her until she could talk Bev into their coming or at least calm Bev down enough to get the information they'd need. "Bev," she said soothingly, hoping to quiet the hysterical woman, "you know I'm there for you and will do everything I can to rescue Cody, but I can't do this alone. I need HIS. You need HIS."

The crying from her friend nearly broke her heart. No parent would want this to happen to them.

"I don't want them anywhere near my son," Bev said vehemently.

With a frustrated sigh and knowing time was of the essence, she gave up trying and turned back to the men. She shifted into her warrior mode because friend mode had failed. This was no time to hold a grudge or let hatred take over. She wouldn't tolerate it on Bev's part…or her own. Nothing mattered except finding Cody. "Give me the particulars." She'd rather have had the call on speakerphone to keep them moving forward quickly, but she feared Bev would hang up, and that couldn't happen. If not that, she would say something that she really shouldn't about what they'd discovered about Ken and Jesse. The thought made her blanch, the information still not settling well in her gut.

Bev needed to get off the phone to await a call from the kidnapper. Suppose it went down like that. Besides, she didn't need to know that Sam planned to bring the team with her. Bev needed them more than she cared to believe.

Sniffing and sounding like she was trying to stop her crying, Bev asked, "What do you want to know?"

The men reappeared, and Franks tossed Jesse his tactical vest. Cowboy handed Ken his vest as if he planned to go. She eyed him while Bev composed herself. Why his vest? With his injury, he couldn't be much help.

As Bev answered Sam's questions, she watched the byplay in the room as the team saddled up. Jesse was surprised by Ken suiting up because he cocked one eyebrow at him in question.

"It's Adam's son. I'm going." There had been no question in Ken's words, only a matter of fact. She'd heard that tone before, but as far as she knew, it was reserved for an op.

Sam's gaze bounced back and forth between the two agents, curious about Jesse's response. Despite Ken's injury, while he couldn't help them in the field, he could lead the investigative side of the crime while the team traveled to wherever the hell they needed to go. And she would go to hell if she had to rescue her pseudo-nephew.

She tossed another question at Bev, who seemed more focused, despite the tremor in her voice, as she told Sam what she knew.

Jesse nodded at Ken. "All right." He glanced around the room, and Sam followed his gaze. Devon had a phone nestled between his shoulder and ear. He gave a thumbs-up before returning to typing furiously on his computer.

She nearly sagged with relief, knowing that meant the plane hadn't departed and become theirs. Knowing Trent would agree with priorities. She didn't feel guilty.

The men stood over the table, looking at what Sam thought might be a map of Columbus, yet appeared to be waiting for a command to move out.

Knowing she had enough information for them to start and the need for Bev to keep her phone line open since she didn't have a ransom demand, only a note that said *No police,* she ended the call. "Okay, I'll be there as soon as I can." She estimated it would be a few hours, but she'd have to double-check before she promised that. Bev's wails began again, and Sam took a deep breath, wishing she could calm her friend through the phone. But it was useless. She just needed to get to her.

"Bev. Bev. Listen, I'm coming to you. We'll figure this out. You stay where you are in case Cody comes home or someone calls. Remember to keep your phone line open and don't do anything rash. Your and Cody's lives are too valuable. Don't fret. I'll help you through this." She and six well-trained men on location, and one left behind to do that magic he did on the computer, were also needed. They were the best. She was confident with that knowledge.

"Hurry," Bev said through wails.

Sam's heart broke for her troubled friend. She'd do whatever it took to find Cody, even bringing the men Bev never wanted to see. Sam would beg for forgiveness after they rescued the boy.

Instead of immediately briefing in the war room, Jesse caught everyone's attention. "All right," he said, without looking at Ken, "I'm going to tag along as an extra gun. Now, grab your gear and get your asses to the airfield pronto. We'll meet in the usual spot and brief in the air."

Without another word, her four teammates departed, leaving her, her team leader, and their big boss. She appreciated the team, knowing she needed to ride with them to the airport. Ken and Jesse would make all the decisions, although curiosity over who'd lead this time, since Ken was injured, wandered through her mind.

Jesse looked pointedly at Sam and then at Devon. "We'll conference you in while Sam briefs us on the road. Is the plane ready and staying with us in Georgia?"

She thought it was a little late to find out that information. Then a bit of fear grabbed her. The jet had to remain available after their boots hit the ground. They fought the clock.

"The pilot had already pre-flighted for the fam's trip, so the plane will be ready before you get there," Devon responded. "Everyone will agree you have priority. I'll get the closest airfield information to the pilot so she can change the flight plan before you arrive. The plane and pilot will be at your disposal during the search. I'll also get a weapons clearance for both airports."

Jesse nodded, then turned back to her and Ken. "Let's go."

The three walked at a fast clip to the back of the building, where they kept their vehicles. They climbed into a waiting, black SUV. The other team's vehicle had departed.

Before their SUV had even been moved out of Park, Jesse connected his phone to its Bluetooth. Once completed, he phoned Devon hands-free so they could all hear.

"Go," Devon said in answer.

At this point, the necessity of brevity to get the ball rolling had her spurting out single words and short phrases of what she'd learned from Bev as she answered his questions. "Nine years old, male, six hours." Since Bev had been gone most of the day, six hours was the best guess.

"Ransom demand?" Devon shot questions at her rapid-fire, barely giving her a chance to breathe.

"No."

"Police?"

She knew that meant the police weren't contacted and involved. Although she wished they had been, she also knew HIS would be limited if they were, since it wasn't their neck of the woods. Then she thought about Fort Bragg and Jesse and Ken's past Ranger experience. Her heart leaped. If needed, help would be available.

"Note stating not to contact them."

Devon didn't miss a beat. "Witnesses?"

"Unsure. I couldn't get anything else from her. She did well answering questions for a while, but then…. She's just so overwrought." Hell, she realized she'd gone into a narrative instead of keeping to the short response. Although this wasn't her first kidnapping rescue with HIS, it was the first time she'd been the resource and had a personal investment in the case.

The clicking sounds from Devon's hands flying over his keyboard were her response. She'd always wondered how he found the information he did—some of the legality of it made her wonder—but when it came to rescuing children, she never questioned his ability. He'd always said the information was out there. You just needed to know where to look. Then, he'd give that adorable grin and wink, adding, "And not get caught."

"For hire or pro bono?"

She knew it meant how deep they could pull from their pockets, although she had an inkling that, depending on the situation, if a client's budget was exhausted, they dug into HIS funds for rescues. Since she'd never been in this situation—where she knew the client—she hadn't considered a thing like a bill for services rendered. "I don't know if she can pay or—"

Jesse interrupted her. "Pro bono."

Relief whooshed through her. The last thing Bev needed was to deal with a ransom demand and a bill for their expensive services from the men she despised, no matter if they rescued her son.

Ken jumped in. "Beverly Shodun. Her husband, Adam, was killed on an op Jesse and I led."

A knife to the gut ripped up her insides as she thought of that op. What she'd experienced with Ken and Jesse's leadership and actions warred with what she'd recently learned about their leadership efforts on Lance's final op. But people changed.

"Christ," Devon breathed. "I remember now. Okay, Sam, please tell me everything you can about Beverly and her friends. Is she seeing anyone?"

The time for brevity was over. He had the basics to start his computer magic, so now the investigation part began. "I don't think so." The questioning lilt of her voice must've alerted everyone to her newfound uncertainty. She hadn't asked Bev this question, yet she'd expected that if Bev had been dating, she'd tell Sam about it. Besides, Bev was too dedicated to Adam's memory.

"We'll find out," Ken stated from the driver's seat.

"As for friends, she had acquaintances, but I think I'm the only one she calls a close friend. Bev suffers from—" she hesitated "—depression." She gulped, hating to expose her friend's problems, but knew anything could be relevant. "Among other things. I've been trying to get her into counseling. She hasn't gotten over her husband's death." She didn't glance at Jesse or Ken but somehow knew they'd been thinking about that fatal op, and Sam's husband had also been killed. Absorbing the new information and how Bev wanted her to help enact vengeance tore at her.

She mentally shook herself back to the person who kept those types of emotions deep inside. Strength and focus were needed, especially since Bev would go into a fit when she arrived with the men.

Delving into more detail about what she knew about

Bev, she recalled her friend's habits, routines, and more. The longer she spoke, the more she realized Bev needed her help, whether she wished it or not. And not just in rescuing Cody.

She wouldn't just suggest after this. She'd make it happen, even if she had to drag Bev to a doctor and counseling herself.

Ken asked the million-dollar question. "Why do you think someone kidnapped her kid if she's not rich or socially prominent?"

That had been gnawing at Sam's belly. Bev hadn't told her of anything she'd gotten herself into or anyone she'd started seeing, so Sam couldn't figure out why. The only thing that came to mind made her sick to her stomach. "Maybe—" She couldn't spit it out. It tasted so terrible on her tongue.

"No. It doesn't feel like sex trafficking," Jesse said. "They wouldn't have left a note, even if it's not a typical kidnapping note."

The four quieted, and Sam prayed they'd get a good lead when they met with Bev.

Devon broke the heavy silence. "Let me see what I can do. I'll have a report for you before you land." He disconnected the call without waiting for a response.

Sam's gut churned at the realization she was about to learn more—personal and financial—about Bev than she'd ever known, and because of her friend's instability, she didn't think she'd like it all.

In the rearview mirror, she caught Ken's gaze. "What do you think really happened, Sam?"

She bristled at his question, which raised doubts they believed all she'd told them. In no way would she tolerate that misplaced sentiment. "What do you mean? Cody was kidnapped? What else is there?"

"Well," Jesse took over the sudden interrogation, pointing her way, "it did take her six hours to contact you."

"We can ask her about that when we get there," she responded sharply, wanting to kick herself for not asking that question. "Maybe she thought Cody was at a friend's house."

"Does she often leave him alone? I mean, he's only nine," Ken asked, though she caught the hint of disapproval in his voice.

"Almost ten," she said in retort. She hated to admit that Bev did, which was why Sam had tried to be around when she knew Bev planned to go about town doing who knew what. She frowned in disappointment. "I'm sad to say that she sometimes does." Trying to justify her friend's behavior, she added, "So do many people, whether right or wrong."

Sam hoped Bev would be cooperative—for Cody's sake. It'd be a toss-up for sure. No matter her friend's desire, HIS would take over to find and rescue Cody.

She hoped Devon found something quickly that pointed them in the right direction. They'd already lost time, and the longer Cody remained with his kidnappers, the chance of rescue diminished. With a sinking heart, she admitted that they might be too late.

Even working with a smaller team, Alpha team had more than enough men to follow any leads. And with the practice Ken had them doing to build a more cohesive team and mock rescues, she had no doubt they could handle this.

Ken cleared his throat and asked cautiously, "Did you tell Beverly that Jesse and I are coming?"

Sam fiddled with a strand of hair that escaped her ponytail to think of the situation that could explode. "Well," she breathed before finishing, "no."

Jesse chuckled. "This will be interesting since she

threatened to have Ken and me arrested the next time we came near her."

"Or," Ken added, "shoot us on sight if that didn't keep us away."

"Does she have any weapons in the house that you know of?" Jesse asked, and when she didn't hear a chuckle accompany the question, she knew he was serious and maybe even a bit worried.

Sam's breath caught at the impact of what he'd asked. "Yes." With a heavy sigh, she had to disarm her friend as soon as they arrived, or things could turn ugly.

Chapter Seven

Why had he pushed to come on this op? Being out of action, he didn't know what the hell he could do. Sure, the desire to rescue Adam's son took precedence, but the statement he'd overheard from Sam filled him with dread. Since she spoke with Beverly then, he could only imagine she was referring to him and Jesse. It didn't take a genius to figure that out. But shit, ten years was a long time to find them accountable for an ambush that no one could have predicted. Sure, he'd expected that from Beverly because she blamed them, but what of Sam? They'd started rebuilding their friendship, and they had an obvious connection, an attraction. His only hope was that she'd just repeated what Beverly said. Any other possibility didn't sit right.

By the time the plane landed in Georgia, darkness had set in, and the team had an information overflow from Devon about Beverly. Unfortunately, none of it looked promising to provide intel on Cody's location. However, they'd follow up on each lead and ask questions until they found something usable.

His men split into pairs, with Franks and Cowboy disappearing in one direction. At the same time, Stone and Doc went in another, dropping most of their gear in the waiting SUVs instead of entirely donning it, not to alarm whomever they questioned. However, he, Jesse, and Sam loaded up in full gear in case they encountered something at their destination and headed directly to Beverly's house to question her and search for clues.

Each time Sam put on her gear, his gut churned with worry. Not a typical worrier, he knew his feelings for her led to his need to protect her. While he'd tried to keep her from other ops or taken an overprotective stance while on them, this was different. Beverly was her friend, so he couldn't argue with her involvement in the attempt to bring the boy home. No. They would bring him home no matter what it took.

When they arrived at Beverly's single-story brick home, Sam asked them to wait near the SUV until she told Beverly they'd traveled with her. He'd loved Adam—Beverly's husband—like a brother, and his heart had suffered when he'd lost him and Lance on a covert op. They'd been true friends. He'd never warmed up to Beverly, probably because she'd been standoffish. After Adam died, she'd turned into a raving lunatic. He, Jesse, and the rest of the Ranger team held to taking care of their own, and Beverly was their own. She, however, hated the sight of them. He only hoped seeing them again wouldn't trigger something in her that delayed Cody's rescue.

While they waited, he and Jesse exited the SUV and leaned against it, surveying the area around them, keeping an eye out for anything suspicious. Although they didn't know the neighborhood, some things, like a vehicle watching the house, were everyday out-of-place things. Yet, they found nothing that caught their eye.

"What'd you think?" Jesse asked.

"You mean if she'll shoot us?"

"Among other things."

Now might be the right time to mention that possibility, but Ken needed to learn more to be extra alert. He couldn't wrap his head around the woman thinking such a thing.

"Yeah, something doesn't seem right."

"That's an understatement," Jesse agreed.

"I hope she'll work with us. For Cody's sake." He couldn't imagine any parent not, but if Beverly still held a grudge against the two of them and couldn't see beyond it, they'd have to allow the team to work. If that were what they had to do, he'd order it, and the two would work in the background at another location. Maybe another Ranger's nearby home.

"While Sam didn't say it, I'm worried Beverly could hide answers to the investigation with the two of us here."

With a sigh, Ken silently agreed. It was too late to change their decision for him and Jesse to be on the case. It seemed vital they were here, leading and setting up a command post. "I think we'll let Sam take the lead in questioning. We can jump in when needed once we figure out Beverly's mindset. Otherwise…." Ken shrugged.

Jesse nodded. "I was thinking the same thing."

Waiting for clearance to enter Beverly's home, his mind continued turning things over. It still baffled him why this particular kidnapping happened. He had an inkling that Beverly either wasn't telling them the truth or was holding back. There had to be something they were missing. Knowing Beverly didn't want them near her or her son—as she'd strongly stated years ago—he could understand her hesitancy to work with them, but not Sam. She'd called on Sam without the presumption that they'd come with her. No matter who she expected to ride to the rescue, her son's life hung in the balance. They had no idea what ordeal he might be facing, and they needed every bit of information to bring him home.

Ken turned to Jesse, his heartbeat quickening. He should tell Jesse what he'd overheard. But, only hearing one side of the conversation might have Sam's loyalty questioned without the true meaning of the words. Of course, "kill" was not something to be misunderstood. But there were too many unanswered questions.

Instead, he asked, "Are you taking the lead?" He had mixed feelings about which one of them should be in the role, but, dammit, he wanted to lead. He needed to do it. He'd had too many times sitting on the sidelines. Inactivity had nearly killed him. Not physically, but in spirit. Each time the team went out with Grits, he'd envisioned every possible scenario—good and bad. When they couldn't receive regular updates, he'd gone about nuts. Leading this team was who he was, and he kicked himself for almost walking away from it. Without it, he felt like his identity had been stripped and beaten with a baseball bat.

Jesse gave him an emotionless expression. Every team member had mastered displaying blankness since it was instrumental in interviews. It sucked when one member used it against the other, though. Jesse raised an eyebrow in question. "You're the field team leader. You make the call."

Damn, he appreciated that Jesse, being the head of HIS, didn't automatically take command from him or Grits. Their boss believed in the continuity of the team and now teams. He had to decide which held more importance—his pride or the op. It took a moment before he realized he could have both without compromising the op. Nodding, he voiced his decision. "I'll take the lead for the investigation, but once the team hits the field, it's you since I can't be there."

"I can evaluate Franks for you if you want."

Ken had wanted to do that. He'd had Franks do parts, but leading a full op from start to finish without him or Grits hadn't happened. He couldn't wait and knew Jesse would be a good resource. "Thanks."

"You know you can be there. You just have to decide."

"It could compromise the safety of the team." He knew what Jesse meant, but had mixed feelings about taking that position. In one instance, he could protect Sam. In the other, he could hold her back if trouble arose. He had too many hard decisions to make, all of which revolved around an op that tightened his gut into knots.

"Like always, as a sniper, Sugar would position herself far enough away from the hands-on action. Plus, you're almost back to your full potential. I'd even say you could go in the field if you could run for longer distances without weakening."

Ken didn't want to sit back on this rescue, so he agreed to the latter part, but with Sam pushing him away after the kiss, she might not appreciate him acting as her spotter. It meant the two of them—alone.

With a tight nod, he requested, "I'd like it if you evaluated Franks's leading on the ground."

"Done."

Movement at the house grabbed their attention, and Ken reached for each of his sidearms. Seeing Sam, he released them. He whistled while Jesse shook his head when Sam exited carrying a rifle—not her own—a handgun—not the one on her thigh—and a shotgun. "I'd rather not leave temptation for her."

Ken deciphered that Beverly hadn't released her grudge against them. He reached out and accepted the weapons. "I'll put them with ours." Sam, removing the guns, told him they'd decided correctly not to take their rifles inside. They wouldn't go unarmed as they each had one or more holstered handguns on their body. He opened the case that held their weapons and added theirs. Then, he closed the weapons locker and secured it in the SUV before turning back to Sam. "Do we have a green light?"

She nodded, but he noticed her clenched jaw.

Uh-oh. "Is she going to work with us?" Frustration at the time spent waiting gripped him, and Ken wanted to go inside and shake the woman until she realized how her action left her son in danger.

On an exhale, Sam responded, "Yeah. Although, don't expect her to be nice."

Ken figured that to be an understatement. "We don't need nice. We need cooperation."

"Listen, while she's agreed to allow you—HIS—to help, I think it'd be better for me to question her. I think she'd open up more."

He and Jesse turned to each other, and both had small quirks at the corners of their lips.

Sam caught this exchange. "What?"

Turning back to her, Ken nodded. "We already discussed that and think it's the right way to go. But I need you to consult with us throughout in case we have more questions."

Solemnly, Sam nodded. "I can do that. Let's get in there and see what we can do to find Cody."

Jesse took a step forward. "Let's go save this boy."

With a narrowing of her eyes, she responded, "Let me go in first." Then she whirled around and took the lead.

Stepping into the house behind Sam, Ken first noticed the photos of Adam alone or of him and his wife with and without her pregnant belly displayed prominently in the central area. It'd been close to ten years. He'd have hoped she'd moved on somewhat for the boy's sake. He wondered what impact this had on the kid. On the one hand, the boy knew what his father looked like, but what the hell was she telling her child about Adam?

After some finagling from Sam and a trip to the kitchen

cabinet for a bag of chocolate donuts—what the hell was that about?—Beverly sat at the small breakfast table in a nook that opened to the kitchen. While Sam sat down at the table and opened the bag of donuts, giving one to Beverly and taking one herself, he and Jesse looked at each other and raised a brow at the interrogation food.

Instead of questioning it, he and Jesse remained stoic and sipped on the bottled water Sam had offered. They ignored the freshly brewed coffee, not wanting a stimulant that crashed in their system, plus who knew if she'd poison it. Okay, he knew that wouldn't happen, especially if she drank from the same pot. All he knew was that if her look when they'd walked in the door could've killed, Sam would've been digging their graves.

While Sam worked to soothe Beverly, Jesse slipped off to investigate the home. Ken held the note left behind—an odd one since there had been no ransom request—at the corner with a tissue in the tips of his fingers, even though he was sure Beverly's prints compromised what might've been there. Still, they'd expedite it to the lab. Even though Sam wasn't asking kidnapping questions yet, he remained close, listening. It was amazing what crumbs could be found. That must've been Sam's intent.

Jesse hadn't returned when Sam began asking their standard questions. He had to hand it to her. She knew what to ask and how to handle Beverly, who kept giving sideways glances at him and searching glances, probably seeking Jesse's location.

Most of what she'd answered gave them nothing new to work with. While unspoken, the question of whether she could've harmed her son had been there. It was statistically the likely cause. Heck, several cases had made national news. He couldn't stomach the thought of her hurting the boy.

Ken didn't get that gnawing feeling that she had something to do with Cody's abduction. Right now, though, he didn't trust all Beverly told them.

Sam reached over and covered Beverly's perfectly manicured hand on the table. "You already told me some basics over the phone that will help us, but I need you to tell me about the note." Her soft voice held a soothing quality that had a no-nonsense effect.

With her free hand, Beverly wiped her nose with a much-used tissue. She sniffed before responding. "I found it on the table when I got home."

Some instinct wanted him to walk over and wring the woman's neck for leaving the child home alone to take care of himself. Hell, for ten minutes while she popped to the mailbox or something, but for six hours or so! She deserved to have her kid taken away, not by abductors but by a loving family. Every little boy and girl deserved that, but the world was wild. Not a day passed that he wasn't thankful his parents had provided a loving home.

He'd been blessed with two wonderful parents who loved him no matter the grief he gave them. Since his father passed, his mother's greatest wish was for him to marry and give her grandchildren. He choked up a bit, thinking about his father. How he wished he'd at least given him grandchildren.

A new resolution set inside him. He may not have been able to give those things to his father, but he could give them to his mother, who held the same hopes. An image of Sam flashed into his mind.

If only he'd asked her out before Lance had instead of pushing her away. He'd been a fool, but he'd realized it too late. The Ranger team had an unwritten rule that you didn't infringe on another man's woman. He'd heeded that rule, but the more he'd been around her, the more he'd fallen in love.

Refocusing, he paid close attention to Beverly's expression and eyes while she answered the following questions.

"Show me where on the table you found it?"

Beverly pointed to a spot closest to the open kitchen area.

"Were any chairs out of place?"

Stopping her sniffing, Beverly appeared to consider the question. If there had been, they might also get a usable print to send to the lab. Unfortunately, she shook her head. "No. I don't think so."

"That's okay, Bev. Let's focus on the note again. Tell me what you did when you found it."

"I—I—picked it up and read it. Then—" She moved her hand as if mimicking the motions she'd completed. "At first, I didn't understand. I mean, just those couple of words confused me. When it dawned on me what it might mean, I dropped it and ran through the house looking for Cody."

"What'd you do when you couldn't find him?"

She looked at Sam for the first time since they'd begun the note discussion, and Beverly had almost seemed in a trance. "I called his friends' parents. None of them had seen him."

The tears flowed once again. He couldn't blame her. He could not imagine what she must feel, but dammit, he needed to understand her answers.

"Okay, what next?"

Jesse sidled up to him and briskly shook his head before focusing on the two women. That meant nothing useful. He wanted to sigh, but didn't want to feel that resigned. He hoped the men positioned outside found something that might make a difference.

"Where have you been?" Beverly shot at Jesse, completely ignoring Sam, trying to turn her attention back.

"Investigating." Jesse sipped the water bottle he'd picked back up as if nothing seemed amiss.

"I didn't give you permission to walk about my house." Beverly half stood before Sam halted her with a hand on her arm and that soothing voice.

"Bev, he's just doing what I would've done."

She turned to Sam. "I don't want them walking around."

"Sit down. They have to do that in order to help us locate where Cody is being held. You want that, don't you?"

Looking as if she were in a daze, Beverly nodded and sat, although she turned her gaze to him and Jesse.

"Okay, Bev, tell me what you did after discovering Cody was really missing."

"I called you," Beverly stated as if it were a no-brainer.

He wondered how long Sam's patience would last. They'd found out absolutely nothing except that the woman was a negligent mother. She said she had no friends—although Sam needed to challenge that, asking about her lunch dates. As far as she'd admitted, she dated no one and had no ex. While she went out a great deal, she didn't frequent the same places regularly. She wasn't aware of any stalkers. As far as she knew, no one wanted to harm her or her son. While Adam had left a nice insurance policy, they had no real money. No neon signs on her or Adam's parents' sides. And the list of dead ends continued.

His nerves and muscles tightened. Every minute counted, and this crap of no clues took too much time away from searching for Cody. When Jesse opened the door to Franks and Cowboy, Ken silently hoped they'd found something. Even a nugget of gossip would be better than what they had to date.

Motioned over by a nod of Franks's head, Ken set down the water bottle and gave Sam a short nod. The newly arrived agents pulled Ken and Jesse as far from Sam and Beverly as possible to keep them in sight and from overhearing.

Without asking Ken, Cowboy slipped back outside to watch over the house. Franks talked low and concisely, and with the information they'd learned, rage surged through Ken like none he'd ever felt on an op. He tried to contain the emotion enough to take over the questioning, but as he worked to release the tension in his jaw and body, he still dealt with his blood boiling and sparks of anger shooting through his body.

That lying, conniving woman deserved to be horsewhipped, and he'd be the first in line to do it, no matter how much Sam protected the bitch.

Chapter Eight

Ken barged back into the breakfast nook. Looking up at him, Sam knew the agents had new information, something terrible based on Ken's angry face. Ken was almost red with what was controlled rage. He stopped and touched her lightly on the shoulder, which calmed and reassured her, much to her discomfort. Being angry at what he supposedly did and the man he'd shown himself to be was a constant battle in her confused brain and heart. Her problem with Ken aside, she had an inkling Bev held something back. Something critical, and even with Ken's calming touch, her body tensed at what he was about to say. Before he spoke, he removed his hand from her shoulder and put his hands on his hips. He made a formidable presence that even had her a bit unnerved. Yet, that could be from the loss of his touch.

"Who the hell is Alejandro Ramirez?" he barked.

While she knew that Ken—and indeed Devon—had to know who this man was since it appeared her teammates brought the information back, she focused back on Bev since she'd ignored Ken's question.

"Who is it, Bev?" Her soft, soothing tone had disappeared. Tired of running in circles while she treated Bev like a friend instead of a client, she gave up all pretense of patience. Becoming more and more disconcerted by her friend's actions and knowing because of them, she'd probably lost her team time they needed to find Cody. She no longer cared if Bev hated her or ended their friendship. The boy mattered more than any of that.

Bev fiddled with the same tissue she'd held since Sam began questioning her nearly an hour ago—straightening it, folding it, then crumpling it. "I don't know what you mean." Her shaky voice and unwillingness to meet either of their gazes belied that point.

"Bev, to get Cody back, we have to question everything. It's the only way. No one will think anything different of you or Cody. We need to know the truth." It angered her to no end that her friend, Cody's mother, would hold out on them. She couldn't make sense of it. Maybe the information on this individual was wrong, and he had nothing to do with the Shoduns.

"Sam, make them all go away. I don't want to talk about this with—" She waved her hand at the men with a disgusted look marring her features. "—them around."

That meant she knew Alejandro, whom Ken had asked about, and he might be important. Her instinct wanted her to tread easily again, but she persevered and distanced herself to do what they needed to bring Cody home safely. "No," Sam said forcefully. "Tell us about this man, or I swear to God, Bev, we'll knock on every damn door in your neighborhood and ask the question."

Bev's shocked, then wounded look didn't sway Sam to be easy again.

"He's, uh—" Her hands shook despite her death grip on the tissue.

Having enough, Ken answered his question. "She's been dating him."

Sam sat stunned for a moment. Her friend—her best friend—had not only kept that information from her as a friend but also in the investigation.

"Is it true, Bev?" She couldn't hold the disbelief laced with unleashed hostility out of her voice. And, honestly, she didn't care. Although she'd never used the term "bitch slap" before, now she understood its meaning and provoked need. Yet she held back. They were here for Cody. She'd deal with Bev after he'd returned home.

"Well," she hedged, "he and I…."

Good God, she might reconsider that slap. "I'm tired of playing, so don't push me. Now"—her assertive voice had Bev snapping her head up to look at Sam—"you two what, Bev?"

Shock didn't begin to describe the woman's expression. "Sam, why are you being like this?"

She didn't fall for the wounded routine. She'd seen it before when Bev didn't get her way. "So help me, God, I will come across this table and beat your ass until you give me the information. Now," she bit out and stressed each word, "tell me about this man."

"I didn't tell you, Sam, because I can't imagine he had anything to do with this. He wanted our relationship to be secret."

"Bev, I'm one step away from doing what I said. Now, tell us about him."

By this time, the entire team had returned, and most stood outside while Ken remained beside the table, refusing to sit.

Tearing a piece off that damn tissue that Sam wanted to yank from her hands, Bev began, "We used to date."

Sam ignored the pang in her heart when Bev confirmed Ken's statement. Had she been such a shitty friend to Bev that she hadn't felt compelled to share something as huge as this? This was the first time since Adam's death that Bev had dated anyone. Well, as far as she was aware. Who knew what else Bev had held back? "Used to?"

"We broke up last week. That's why I know he had

nothing to do with it," she rushed to assert again.

Gritting her teeth and almost hoping Ken would take over the questioning because there was no assurance she wouldn't explode, Sam took a breath and then asked, "Where does he live?"

Bev's hesitation before she spoke had Sam narrowing her eyes at her friend. "I don't know."

"Those are three words I don't fucking want to hear again."

Sam was startled at the force of Ken's words.

"Well, I don't." Bev shrugged. "He stayed at a hotel. I think he said he lived in Mexico. I never asked specifically."

With that information—as vague as it was—Jesse slipped from the room, pulling his phone from his pocket. God, she hoped Devon could make something of the crap information they had so far about Alejandro Ramirez. That'd be a challenge since she imagined there were tons of men with that name. She didn't care how Devon narrowed it down for them—and he would—they'd pay the man a visit. She reminded herself that everyone was a suspect until proven otherwise.

The desire to close her eyes to it all—Cody's abduction and the changes in Bev—held firm, but her need for them to succeed held stronger. "Why did you break up?" If Bev didn't answer because the men were in the room, friendship be damned, they'd have to pull her off the woman.

"I don't know," Bev whined, but with her fidgeting, there was no question that she knew the answer. Yet, her holding it back and Sam's pulling teeth to get all the information made Sam wonder what the hell kind of relationship she had with this man.

She took a deep breath to calm herself. Either Ken noticed, or he'd had enough because he forced the question.

"Why did you break up?"

The waterworks started again, and Sam wanted to roll her eyes at the melodrama she'd initially fallen for and couldn't believe Bev's apparent lack of urgency to find her son. Unsettled, Sam struggled to contain her growing anger or unease. There was something off with Bev…with Cody.

"Beverly," Ken barked, "answer the damn question. A little boy's life is at stake, and I'll do anything—anything," he stressed, "to find him. We don't deal with bullshit in a case like this. Instead, we carry shovels with us in case they're ever needed to bury the bodies of obstacles."

If that didn't break the tension amongst the team, nothing else would. While all held back their grins at Ken's bluff since the situation didn't warrant them, his statement had the desired effect on Bev.

Open-mouthed and bug-eyed, she looked at Ken with fear. He did appear ferocious. A sexy, ferocious, but one had to be on this side of the table to see that. "He said—" She wailed, and Sam became sick to her stomach for the first time at for the first time with growing doubt of Bev's care for her son and his safe return home. She'd called Sam for help, but she wasn't helping. Sam didn't think it had anything to do with HIS. Bev had to be hiding something.

While they had to consider everyone a suspect—especially the parents—Sam couldn't believe Bev had her hand in Cody's disappearance. She knew Bev loved her son, no matter how poorly she showed it, and it took more smarts than Bev demonstrated on any given day to pull this off. But something didn't sit right, and she couldn't put her finger on it. Maybe this person—this Alejandro—had been the secret and hopefully the key to unlocking Cody's location.

Ken took one step closer to the table and thumped his hands on it, leaning forward. Bev jumped, and Sam no longer cared if the team intimidated her friend. "He said—" Her following words were almost lost in her next fit of wailing. "—I was an unfit mother."

Holy shit. If they'd had this at the beginning, they'd probably have Cody home by now because this man could be Cody's kidnapper. Her head hurt, but she might've been mentally beating it against an imaginary wall. After all the runaround from Bev, they finally had a suspect. *Alejandro Ramirez.*

Ken straightened and stiffened as Stone carried a box into the home. Sam hadn't seen Stone and Doc when they'd returned, although she'd heard it in her earbud. They'd remained outside to keep from crowding Bev and to watch for anything suspicious.

As Ken took fast strides to the door, Sam stood. "I'll be right back. You stay here and think if there's anything else that'll help."

Bev nodded, playing with that nasty tissue. Thankfully, she didn't turn to see what drew Ken and Sam away.

"The postman showed me the routing information on his little handheld tracker. It went through the post from Mexico, mailed five days ago. The return address says it's from Alejandro Ramirez," Stone informed them.

Sam imagined there had been a collective holding of breath at that news without knowing if that was correct. Two things came to mind—Bev was lying about when she'd last seen Alejandro, and because of the time the package was shipped, Alejandro might not be their man.

With a sinking stomach, Sam hoped that somehow— even remotely—this provided a lead to Cody. Then again, the questions of what this could mean to their investigation flared to life. It'd mean most of what they'd learned so far had been a lie, but if it led them to the boy, they'd deal with that later.

Ken pulled a knife from a sheath on his belt. "Let's open it. It may be nothing." Sam could tell from his intense focus that he didn't believe that. "He could be sending something of hers back like some couples do when they split."

"You don't really believe that, do you?" Franks asked a question she knew Ken had already considered. They all contemplated that question before taking similar action. It'd been ingrained in them.

Shaking his head, Ken motioned for Stone to carefully place the box on the closest coffee table.

"I'm curious," Ken said, "why he'd send something to someone he split with—someone who never stayed at his home in Mexico. If he wanted to reunite, there are easier ways." He held back for a second and looked around the box. He started to speak into his comm system when he thought better of it, and she knew why. They had to make sure they weren't dealing with a bomb. "Go get Cowboy," he told Franks.

Stone and Jesse looked expectantly at the door while she observed Ken. He slowly circled the table with his eyes riveted on the package.

When Cowboy entered, with Franks on his heels, their munitions expert ignored everyone and went straight for the package. Due to the height of the table, he knelt and began to circle as Ken had. After much more observing and handling it at close range, Cowboy stood. "There's nothing tied to opening it, but cut easily and shallow. I'm not psychic enough to know what's inside without my equipment…." He shrugged.

Ken nodded. "I want all of you to get back."

No one moved.

He looked at Jesse. "See, I can't even get my team to

follow my instructions."

Jesse shook his head. "We're keeping you, so stop it."

Sam's head snapped to Ken. What the hell was that about? She wanted to ask, but other things took precedence at the moment. Later, she'd ask. All she felt right now was that she didn't want Ken to die. Irony described her life.

"Don't worry," Franks said with a quirk to his lips, "if we all get blown up, Doc's outside. Who better to have tended to you than a medic?"

While a bad joke, it helped ease the tension that flowed through the group.

Ken knelt and slowly sliced through the clear tape securing the box lid. The brown box had no markings except for the shipping information. They'd send it off for prints, but if Alejandro resided in Mexico, he might not have prints in any US system.

Realizing she'd been worried and thankful nothing had happened, she sighed with relief. Now to the second part that had her heart thumping in her chest. *Please lead us to Cody.*

Opening the box took an excruciating amount of time. Going slow for a potential bomb made sense, but something inside her gut told her they'd find something about Cody. Which would mean Bev had lied about more than just when she'd seen Alejandro.

Once the lid was fully opened, the note, on top of a navy backpack she'd purchased for Cody, told them they'd been played for fools.

"He's better off with me."

Sam didn't know this man, but she wholeheartedly agreed based on what she'd seen with Bev today.

Chapter Nine

Ken knew his men and knew they didn't care how intimidating the group came across as they surrounded Beverly. The scowls on their faces no doubt covered the rage that built within each of them.

Ignoring Sam beside him and any feelings she had for her friend, he went in like a rabid dog after a bone. He ground out, "How long did you say your son has been missing?"

Beverly looked around the group with wide eyes. When her gaze landed on Sam, as if calling her back to her side but not seeing what she perhaps expected, her head fell in defeat. "I-I," she stammered, "I don't know what you mean." With what appeared to be renewed courage, the crazy bitch lifted her head and stared straight ahead, away from them. "I told you. It'd been about six hours when I called Sam."

His control might snap, after all. Why? Why would she lie to them? Either she knew it'd been more than six hours or that Alejandro had taken Cody. Either way, she didn't want to own up to it, creating a new level of concern for the boy. With the information the men had gathered, the notes and the backpack told them it had all been a lie. The question for them to resolve—albeit later—was why Beverly had lied to them. Even to Sam, whom she'd claimed was her best friend.

He crossed his arms over his chest to avoid reaching out and doing something he might regret. Might. "You want to try that again."

"What?" She gave them the same bewildered look. He had to hand it to her. Her acting had them in the beginning. Knowing they'd been played for fools while a child had been abducted set the team on edge. They didn't know this man or how he'd treat Cody. "I told you the truth."

Ken nodded to Franks, motioning to the room where they'd left the package. Once Franks returned with the backpack, Ken unfolded his arms and accepted it before shoving it before Beverly. "Does this look familiar?"

She turned her face away.

Beyond pissed, he pushed the backpack in her face so she couldn't ignore it, no matter how much she tried. He roared when she closed her eyes, emphasizing each word, "Does. This. Look. Familiar?"

She nodded. "It's Cody's." Her voice broke as she admitted what they'd already learned from Sam. Finally, they got one snippet of truth from the woman.

"When did he really disappear?" With his head, he motioned the men to the door before returning the backpack to Franks. They didn't need anything more from Beverly right now, but he hoped to grab one more grain of truth while the men prepped them to get to the airport. Not like he thought he'd get anything useful.

"I don't know." The crying restarted, but he had no sympathy for her.

"Why don't you know?" Sam asked. When Beverly didn't answer her, she prodded, "How long did you leave him alone?"

She sniffed. "I don't know. Maybe a week."

Christ. A fierce resolve settled in him. They'd do something they'd never done before when rescuing a child. They would return Cody from his kidnapper, but they wouldn't return him to his mother. Finding him a better situation would be a new goal for Devon while his team located the boy.

Ken caught Sam's eye, and they turned their backs to Beverly and departed without another word to her. Sam's heart had to hurt, but he couldn't do anything about it now. Not like she'd allow him to do so.

Like always, he had to hold those thoughts and emotions for another time. One day, he'd buck up and tell her the depth of his feelings. Even though she pushed him away after their kiss, they'd shared something substantial. She'd kissed him back with something powerful that he thought might've scared her. He wanted her love more than anything and wouldn't let her push him away.

First, they'd save the boy.

Giving one last look at Beverly's home, Ken climbed into the SUV. Because of all their wasted time, they wouldn't arrive in Mexico until nearly four in the morning —if they could fly out immediately. They could grab combat naps on the plane. When they arrived, darkness would hamper their recon efforts.

To include Devon in the call, Ken dialed him, then connected someone from each vehicle and used the SUV's Bluetooth to coordinate their plan of attack.

Without prodding, Devon started sharing the information. "I spoke with the pilot, and the plane is refueled and waiting with the new flight plan. I can confirm the address in Mexico on the package as belonging to one Alejandro Ramirez. So far, I haven't been able to confirm he's the one we're looking for, but based on what I pulled from the hotel, he's our best option. I'm working on getting photos of the man's house, whether satellite or other."

Ken waited for more. Jesse had slipped away more than once to pass the information to Devon and receive what their computer guru had uncovered.

Jesse shook his head.

Devon continued. "The man seems to fly under the radar."

Collective groans over the speaker matched his own. Nothing at this point equaled something terrible. One of two things came to mind: either Alejandro was truly spotless and had, in many ways, rescued Beverly's neglected child, or he was into something they needed to uncover. For Cody's sake, he hoped the first one fit. While not religious, he sent up a silent prayer that they were successful before each Op. His one for Cody was the same.

Devon forwarded the photo of the kidnapper to the agents' handhelds. The man looked like a regular guy. Never before had he wished someone had a distinguishing scar or feature.

"Here's the best part," Devon said with what could be interpreted as accompanying a grimace, "or worst part, considering your preference, the Lacandón rain forest surrounds him."

Great. He'd prefer the blazing desert heat to the unwelcoming air in a rainforest. High temperatures, moisture clinging to your skin, and humidity that could choke a horse were what they'd be challenged with handling. "We've had worse." However, he couldn't think of a single op to support that statement. Getting shot at and being on the run held more appeal than traipsing through that mess.

"You're high if you believe that." No one disputed Stone's statement.

Franks snorted. "At least we won't have to lie down on the wet ground as long as Sugar."

"Huh. If your job were so all-fired important as mine,

you'd survive that little inconvenience," Sam joked along.

"Inconvenience? Is that what you call it?" Stone laughed.

"Whatever it takes," she shot back.

"How often do you roll around in the wet grass?" Stone asked.

"She probably does it for fun," Franks butted in.

"She probably calls it combat training," Cowboy added.

"Come now," Doc said soothingly, "we have to give the little lady her due."

Ken guessed it'd be five seconds or less before Sam blew her top over that jest.

Sam sputtered, and from the passenger seat, he looked over his shoulder at her, strapped in the back seat. "Little lady?" Her voice rose with an edge to it. "Little lady?"

Chuckles sounded over the speaker from the other two vehicles. Like Kate and Rylee, the team had opened their arms to Sam and treated her like one of the team instead of a woman they needed to protect. That self-imposed rule of protection fell to him alone.

"When I think of a good non-curse word, you're all in for it. And, Doc, know that I won't forget."

"Don't get your panties in a wad," Doc said with a chuckle. "I was just funning. You know I've got a lotta love for you, honey."

"Hmph." Out of his eye, he saw her cross her arms over her chest. He couldn't be sure, but he thought he saw a smile on her face. Something inside told him she enjoyed it when the men joked and even when Doc called her honey. Of course, he also called Kate and Rylee honey, so maybe that's why she didn't fight it.

Thinking of her response to their kiss, he wouldn't believe she had broken it off because he was her boss. Perhaps he shouldn't have imposed his professional standards at work. By doing what he'd thought had been the right thing in not giving her more attention, he'd separated their personal and professional lives too much when they were entwined.

"We've got two snipers this time. Who's going in with us?" Ribbing set aside, Franks's question brought them back to the op.

Without much thought, Ken responded without consulting the snipers on his team or his boss. "The Old Man goes in under Franks's command," he started, referring to Jesse. "Sugar's our team sharpshooter." Calling her that didn't flow well, but he needed to do the same if the team used it once they were in operations mode. Keeping her out of the thick of it would keep Sam safer, and he'd act as her spotter.

"I don't know," Stone hedged, "she's a fine shot in close also. She almost kicked our asses in the mock scenarios."

"She's even better at long range," Franks countered. "She did beat the Old Man after all."

Jesse didn't argue the point. Instead, he grinned.

"It may've been just luck," Stone countered.

"What is this? Pick on Sam day?" she asked.

Someone snorted. He couldn't be sure, but he thought it might be Cowboy.

"You're the newbie," Franks answered.

"I've been with you for months now. I'm not new."

"Sure, we popped your cherry months ago, but you're still our FNG."

Sam had gone ballistic the first time one of the guys had said that to her. Not used to their military jargon, she hadn't understood that it meant first time in combat or, for them, first time on an op. She'd quickly searched the acronym on her phone and smiled as she confirmed, "Fucking new guy."

Except she'd replaced it with a girl.

Even though she'd been with them for a while, her argument had no merit. She'd be the newbie until they hired someone else.

"Sorry, Sugar. It wasn't until you were hired that they stopped calling me FNG," Doc said.

"But they call you Doc," she argued.

"Of course they do. I'm your medic."

"Wait a second," she interjected, "We just hired Casper, so I'm not the new guy."

Sam had a good point, but Ken had an inkling of what the men would say, mainly because they enjoyed teasing her. She took it like a champ and gave it right back.

"But he's Bravo team's FNG. You're ours," Cowboy said, and Ken thought there had been pride in his voice, even if the stretching of her designation was thin.

Asking no one in particular, she tossed out, "You just make up your own rules as you go along, don't you?"

"That's S.O.P.," Franks said.

"Standard operating procedure, my ass." Sam huffed.

Ken closed his eyes. He didn't usually mind their bickering—knowing it was one of the ways they passed the time as they waited and grounded them—but this case had him tied up in knots. Beverly had left her son alone too long to fend for himself. A week. For Christ's sake, who did shit like that? While he didn't know this Alejandro, the man might be right about how the boy was better off with him. Yet, he could be into crimes against children.

However, Devon's inability to dig up much on the man worried him. As far as they could tell, the man had resided in Mexico his entire life. So, why couldn't Devon give them a profile of him? And how had he come to be in a relationship with Beverly in the first place?

"Are you going to join us, Boss?" Franks asked.

Ken looked at Jesse, remembering their conversation on this subject. Not wanting to hamper the team, but with a burning need to be involved in this rescue, he answered, "Yes." At least none of them called him a "broke dick." He'd always hated that lingo, especially when women were around. Yet, soldiers still used it. Old habits were hard to break.

"Damn, it'll be good to have you back." Franks's statement told him a great deal about the man.

As they neared the airport, Stone interrupted the silence with a curse. "Whiskey Tango Foxtrot." That got everyone's attention—what the fuck always did—and only silence breathed through the three vehicles. "Boss, she's Oscar Mike."

"Son of a bitch." Jesse said what Ken would've. Why was the woman on the move?

"Should we follow her?" Franks asked.

"Let me see what I can do on my end." He'd almost forgotten Devon remained conferenced in the call.

Damn, the woman. What the hell was she playing at?

Torn on whether to follow the crazy woman or act on a lead that seemed solid, Ken turned to Jesse. "I know Trent needs the help, but can we get the fam if needed?"

"I already sent them out on a charter, but each took their gear and will return for whatever you need. Bravo team ran into a snafu, so they won't be available immediately."

Sam leaned forward before he could ask what had happened to Grits's team. "How do you know she's moving?"

Stone answered. "We put a tracker on her car. S.O.P."

Not willing to trust anyone in these types of cases, they placed tracking devices on every vehicle involved.

"We continue to Mexico. Watch where she's going, and we'll figure things out from there," Ken directed.

"I'll lose her in the air," Stone informed him.

Ken knew that already, but he had an idea that he didn't like. If what he suspected was true, she was heading where they were to either get her son back or try to reconcile with the man who jilted her. Hell, she might even give them away if she got there first. He had no idea how deep her stupidity went. If this were the case, they'd have to intercept her. A thought occurred to him. "Did you drop a tracker in her purse?"

"Yeah," Stone said. "It's not moving, though."

"Bev does change purses to match her outfits," Sam informed them.

Great. He'd have loved to know that before. It wouldn't have mattered since they didn't have that many trackers with them.

"Is she heading in the direction of the airport?" Ken asked.

"Yep, it looks that way," Stone responded.

"Devon—" Ken started, but hadn't needed to finish.

"I'm on it," Devon said. A few moments later, his low voice requested that Emily set up an alert if Beverly booked a flight from any airport within sixty miles of her home. Emily may be the financial genius of the Hamilton family, but she'd quickly taken to Devon's tricks for supporting the team.

They arrived at the airport and left the SUVs where someone would collect them. After grabbing their gear, they took the short steps two at a time, the urgency of their boots hitting the metal.

In almost no time, the team strapped themselves in, and the plane took off. Once allowed, the team, who should've been sleeping, pulled out something to keep their minds occupied until op planning. Cowboy held out a small iPad and, Ken knew from experience, played one of any number of games he had loaded on the device. Stone put on headphones and reclined in his seat. Doc opened a book, although Ken couldn't see the title. And Sam, dear Sam, she brought out a Rubik's Cube.

Ken called Franks over before he could deal a game of Solitaire.

As Ken watched the team, Jesse set up the laptop and connected to the Wi-Fi offered in the air. While not as reliable as a home connection, it allowed them to speak with home base. He turned away from the team as Devon appeared on the screen. Ken didn't worry about his picture coming in and out. He already knew what the man looked like.

"First, Beverly did purchase a ticket to Mexico. Because she appeared to be in a hurry, it's not direct, so you'll have time to stop her from getting in the way."

Ken ground his teeth. He hated it when parents tried to get involved. She wasn't the first and surely wouldn't be the last. Generally, though, the parents were more stable. "We'll leave someone at the airport to grab her as soon as she gets off the plane. Shoot us the info."

"Done," Devon responded. Sure enough, he had the info. Thank God for Wi-Fi and whatever Devon had done to boost it.

"You said two things," Jesse hedged.

Ken had a bad feeling about what information Devon had for them. A really bad feeling.

"It wasn't easy, but I got satellite images of Alejandro's house. Plus, a guard who works there is big with Facebook, and he posted a pic and made a few comments that can help us."

Ken and Jesse looked at each other and surmised that their boss thought the same thing based on their working experience. Having guards said a lot.

Devon hesitated, verifying Ken's thoughts. "It's a veritable fortress with towers and armed guards."

"Fuck." All went quiet in the cabin. The realization that this rescue had become more dangerous than expected hushed the team.

Chapter Ten

With the team engaged, each had their eyes on their handhelds, reviewing the pictures and information Devon sent.

"Stone, how's your Spanish?"

As with each op where English wasn't the primary language, they'd spend part of the flight learning a few basic phrases to get them through. However, Ken needed someone more fluent in handling the airport employees.

Stone shrugged. "Passable."

"Good. I want you to get over to commercial flight arrivals and keep Beverly out of our hair. I don't care what you must do, but get her on a return flight and see her to the airplane door. If you have to go and cuff her to the seat, do it."

Like any other agent, Ken knew that Stone would rather be in the thick of things, but he didn't complain about this assignment. "Cowboy, how're you feeling about clearing a path for us?"

With a quick nod, Cowboy answered, "I'm always good for blowing shit up."

"Doc, while I hope we don't need it, is the field kit ready?"

Doc didn't remind Ken that he'd asked that same question before they'd boarded their original flight from Baltimore. "Ready, but I like it looking nice and new." He ran his glance over everyone aboard. "Got it?"

While that statement often wrangled boisterous

comments, the team nodded and returned their focus to him.

On the laptop screen, Ken and Jesse pointed out areas they would recon for the best visibility and cover. After verifying the battlefield, they'd map out the rescue and their egress route, then get down to business. While they'd have to go in by vehicle and walk about five klicks to avoid detection, they'd have helo support to get their asses out of there and back to the airport. While only a short jaunt for everyone but him and Sam, they needed that quick transport.

"Once we split, Franks will lead Old Man, Cowboy, and Doc while we separate. And Stone, if he's able to return in time." Looking around the group, he received nods from the men used to the Hamilton brothers taking a back seat, but Sam looked perplexed and bit her lower lip. He'd give her a moment before she figured it out.

A light bulb seemed to be slowly burning in her mind. Then her eyes snapped to his. "You said you're participating. If Franks is leading the team, what will you be doing?"

"I'll be your spotter."

She narrowed her eyes. "I've worked without a spotter before. I don't need one now."

No one completely denied his directives. They would discuss them and sometimes find a better solution, but Sam's argument nearly spoke of insubordination. He wouldn't lie to himself that while he had that burning need to be a part of the op for Cody's sake, being near Sam, being able to protect her, also drove him to participate, even though his injury might hamper his mobility if they needed to make a quick retreat.

"Doesn't matter. You're getting one." His voice brooked no argument. She sulked like a child who couldn't convince his parents to buy her candy, which he found pretty cute.

"Once Sugar and I are in place, we can fill in the gaps and guard posts."

"Bad news, boys." As an afterthought, Devon said, "Sorry, Sugar, boys and girl." He winked, which made Ken think she'd moved into Devon's view. "He's suspected of trading arms."

"That'd explain all the armed guards," Franks said, even though that hadn't been a question for anyone.

"Boys and girl," Ken smiled at Sam, who returned it with a scowl he doubted Devon had received for the same comment, "not like I have to tell you, but this isn't going to be pretty. I know we all want to rush in and grab Cody, but we can't unless we want to put Cody's life at more risk than it might already be. You're working with a smaller team than you're used to." He waved his hand to silence Franks before he spoke. "I know we've had smaller teams before, and like then, we can do this without injury."

"I've called a friend of ours to see if any government agency is after the man. I'll let you know as soon as I do, so step light." Devon's words rested heavily in the air. No one liked to wait. But getting it right meant everything.

"We'll recon the hell out of that bitch," Cowboy said. He tilted his head to the side for a moment. "Does the no-cursing thing apply to ops? I mean, Reagan won't know."

Jesse grinned. "I don't think my daughter meant to stifle you." Then he chuckled. "And you're right. She won't hear you on an op."

"Thank fuck," Cowboy said. "I didn't think I'd make it."

He did not ignore the situation, but the levity relaxed the team, and he wholeheartedly approved.

"Although she's not allowed in the war room," Jesse said, "one of her uncles sometimes breaks that rule, and she may hear you or find out."

Cowboy growled. "Damn, Devon."

Devon laughed, pulling his hands from his keyboard and holding them up in surrender. "I don't know what my big brother is talking about. But," he pointed out, "if she happens to be here, I'll let you know before she has the chance to get in and chastise." He dropped his hands and cleared his throat. "Ken, I see a spot for you and Sugar to set up about a half mile out. Most of the area has a line of sight and elevation problem, so give yourselves extra time to recon."

At times like these, when they crowded around a laptop, he wished for all the big-screen TVs Devon had installed in the war room.

"The aerial is a bit fuzzy, but the complex is set up for protection. There's only one way in or out, except through the jungle surrounding him. If he's a paranoid bastard, there could be traps or guards. It appears he had the jungle near his home cut back, which means you'll have more open ground to cover than we'd like."

"No problem. Sugar will clear us a line," Cowboy said.

"Michael, remember I'll have you in my sights too," Sam countered.

Her joke sent a cold shiver down Ken's spine, the thought of what he'd overheard popping into his head. Indeed, if Beverly had asked her to kill anyone, she'd refuse. His head couldn't get around anything other than that refusal.

For the remainder of the flight, they reviewed the photos and the map. They couldn't tell if the jungle would be a friend or foe for them without setting foot down. They couldn't tell how thick the foliage was, and not having machetes could help or hinder.

During weapons check and camouflage paint application, Stone taught a few basic phrases in Spanish to include—to Cowboy and Doc's benefit—one beer, please.

After that, they each caught a combat nap. He, Franks, and Old Man were the last to sleep and the first to rise. Everyone was awake before the pilot announced their descent and buckled into their seats.

With another smooth landing, Ken applauded the choice of the pilot that Jesse and Devon had selected. The woman was worth every penny. While they taxied, the team grabbed their gear, suited up, and conducted a weapons check.

"GPS check," Ken directed.

Ken opened the door and dropped the stairs when the pilot cleared them. After a quick sweep of the area, seeing as best as he could in the dark, he led the team onto the tarmac near a hangar.

At zero-dark-thirty, they spread out and searched the area with NVGs to see through the darkness, but returned with frowns.

"Where's our transport?" Stone asked.

Damn, good question. Ken didn't give Jesse time to make the call to Devon. Phone in hand, he hit speed dial. Before he could utter a word, Devon rushed, "Stand by. I'm working on it."

This had to be the first time Devon had not had something ready for them. Even though he heard Devon speaking with someone—in Spanish no less—he asked, "What the hell happened?" He should apologize for his angry tone, but he couldn't. They needed that transport to rescue Cody and get there in time to stop Beverly from getting in the way.

"Okay," Devon said. "I received the call when you landed, that your transport hadn't arrived. I hired a new group, but it could be close to an hour before they arrive since they'll wake drivers. The vehicles won't be armored like the ones I initially hired, but since they're dropping you off so far away from your destination, you shouldn't need that option."

"Sen—"

"I'm sending their names and photos to your handhelds." Ken smiled at Devon's ability to anticipate.

The team had to do something they hated unless it was when they were in position—wait. Starting an op with a glitch left him with a sour stomach. Now more than ever, he didn't question his decision to protect Sam. She wasn't invincible, no matter how strong he knew her to be.

Chapter Eleven

Confused that Ken planned to follow and remain with her, Sam climbed into the waiting SUV. When the driver leered at her with open lust, even while she carried her gear and wore face paint, her skin crawled with disgust. Something about him screamed sleazy drug dealer.

A small part of her wanted to be childish and stick her finger in her mouth, mocking a vomiting act. But as a professional, she pushed that aside and remembered she had a KA-BAR on her waist, a small knife in her boot, a SIG Sauer on her thigh, and her new sniper rifle. Any of them would be helpful if he decided to act with his groin calling the shots.

With Stone escorted to the commercial terminal to head off Bev, the team split into groups of three for transport, and somehow she ended up with Jesse and Ken again. Thinking a bit irrationally, something inside her told her this op provided her an excellent opportunity to decide whether to walk away from the evidence Bev's investigator had uncovered or find a way to make the two men pay.

When she'd first scanned the investigation report Bev had sent her, the need for vengeance bled through her veins, and she'd allowed her friend to feed that desire until Sam had seen nothing but red. Reading it in black and white and knowing these men, she couldn't reconcile the actions they'd taken that fateful day.

Maybe that's why she hadn't planned any retaliation against them. Perhaps it had more to do with her and Ken's growing relationship. Either way, she had to reconsider all she and Bev had discussed. While she'd never committed to anything, Bev had asked her to kill them.

While Sam may be struggling to believe the new information, Bev would accept anything that laid the blame for Adam's death at someone's doorstep. Even after, Sam wasn't sure she'd stop.

And, now, she'd brought the men straight into Bev's orbit. What would happen after they found Cody? Could Bev forgive them since they'd brought back Adam's son?

Closing her eyes and holding back tears of sorrow, despair, and confusion, she knew Bev had not only shared the intel with her because Lance died, too, but because she was in the best position to take out Jesse and Ken. Her friend actually thought she could be capable of murder. Vengeance, yes, but still murder.

Worse, on a personal level, she couldn't get Ken out of her mind. His presence tilted all her emotions and thoughts. That kiss…nine years after their last had been better than she'd remembered. With the heat…the passion…her senses went into a whirlwind.

She loved being an agent with HIS. The camaraderie of the team and how they'd enfolded her in their midst told her she'd found a home. And the rekindling of a relationship with Ken had helped her bring back the female part of her that had died with her husband. All in all, this was where she wanted to be.

The question became whether risking that for something that happened in the past was worth it. Or did the dead require justice?

If Ken hadn't pushed her away all those years ago, refusing to become involved even though they shared an attraction that had never diminished, she'd probably never have dated and married Lance. She closed her eyes, dropped her head, and sighed. It'd all changed ten years ago, yet she couldn't push it aside. Ken had always been there. The before and after Lance kisses—as she referred to them—the hanging out with him and Lance, and Ken being her support after her husband died.

With her small backpack on the floorboard between her legs, watching her side of the road as she knew Ken did on his side on their ride to Chiapas, Sam continued her attempt to rationalize things.

Since their recent kiss, everything had changed. He'd finally decided they should be together, and God, she wanted him so damn much. Well, her body…her mind… and soul did, but she refused to give him her heart as she'd been fool enough to do that in the past. Plus, there was the mind-blowing development of his involvement in Lance's death to contend with.

Doubt swirled in her gut, her heart squeezing.

"Do you think Stone can get Beverly back on a plane?" Ken asked softly from beside her on the back seat. Not trusting their driver, they'd only spoken in low tones and not about op specifics.

Sam looked at him, and his gaze almost floored her. She'd never seen worry in his eyes, but she caught a flash before he pulled on his mask. With a brief shake of her head, she gave him her honest opinion. "I don't know. I should've gone to talk her into it."

"Believe me, that had been my initial thought. But two things changed my mind. First, your Spanish is horrible, and not everyone speaks English enough to understand your requirements."

She couldn't argue there. Without the little refresher on the plane, she couldn't find a bathroom on her own.

"Second," he continued, "I need you."

Her breath caught in her chest. Yet, her next few breaths became heavy, and for someone who had to perfect her breathing behind the scope of her rifle, her reaction knocked around something in her heart. "You—" She gulped. "—you need me?"

"Sure." He shrugged as if it meant nothing to him. "You're one of our most valuable assets."

Those words were the sweet-talking she preferred. She had never heard something so heartfelt as that from the PD or SWAT. In reply to his statement, she snorted. "'Bout time you noticed."

"Oh, Sugar." His fake drawl needed work. "I've always noticed."

Okay, that got too personal right away. She had to remain focused, rid her brain of all that crap, and pay attention to the op. Nothing else mattered.

Turning the conversation back to a safer topic, she mock-shuddered. "I hope we don't run into any big f—" She caught herself, and her gaze snapped to Jesse in the passenger seat. "—snakes." He didn't turn, but she could've sworn Jesse's chest moved, hiding a chuckle. Their challenge in living up to his daughter's request had made some headway, but the men had been right that sometimes it slipped out on an op. They'd try and try again until they got it right because they loved the little girl and all the other Hamilton children.

Ken chucked, whether at her for almost saying the f-word or her aversion to snakes, she didn't know. "I'll protect you from them. Especially while you're lying there as a perfect target for them to wrap themselves around your prone body."

That thought made her want to toss her piece and go

home—even if she had to hitchhike back to Baltimore. She'd dealt with numerous critters, including small, non-venomous snakes, and remained still. But boa constrictors that could be up to fourteen feet long? "Hell no" didn't even come close. Instead of reaching out and choking Ken like she would have liked, she smiled sweetly. "Thank you, oh knight in Kevlar."

"Anything for you, milady," he shot back and leaned forward as if in a bow. When he rose, his smile settled her, and she relaxed, caught up in their usual easy banter.

Jesse had the driver stop out in the middle of nowhere in the near pitch-black. They hadn't seen a house or soul for miles, and the paved road ended a mile or so back. There had only been jungle on either side. Who lived out here? Immediately, the stupidity of that question sprang forth. Their kidnapper and possible arms dealer did. Snakes must not bother him.

Before the drivers turned their vehicles around, the team had slipped into the jungle on the right side of the dirt road with her, Ken, and Doc wearing backpacks and the remaining agents their war belts, with rifles in hand and night vision goggles ready. They wore determined looks on their painted faces. By some of their excitement, she figured they missed their war games and looked forward to this trek. While she'd hike in the jungle to rescue Cody, she would not even consider this trip at any other time. Something was wrong with those men.

Jesse remained close to the edge of the foliage, watching to ensure the drivers turned back instead of continuing to warn Alejandro, possibly. They'd already learned that besides the indigenous Lacandón people, a few others lived out this way since the government sold only a few plots of land. It seemed Alejandro had enough money to grease some palms for his large parcel.

Sam didn't care about all that crap. She cared about a snake dropping down on her. She shuddered at the thought.

Even though they were miles from their destination—to throw off their transports and avoid the direct entry into Alejandro's home, they moved swiftly through small, well-used trails, striving for the closest thing to silence. While not wholly possible when the brush couldn't be skirted, all the animal sounds nearly drowned out their movements.

Ken led the group with his rifle in one hand and a GPS in the other to ensure they didn't chase their tails in the brush. At one point, they split to approach from different angles. Franks, who'd also had his handheld in use, led the remainder of the team off to the north side, but not before Cowboy grabbed her free hand with a "Do us proud, Sugar" before he joined the other agents.

That left her with Ken. He looked back at her for a moment before leading them east. At one point, he did a comm check with five responses of "Lima Charlie." They would take longer to settle on a location than the team. The distance didn't bother her, and with no wind, her shot would be assured if she had a shot.

The darkness receded as the morning light arrived, but only a bit of light filtered through the tree and brush overgrowth in the jungle. She preferred it because the lack of light didn't stop her from doing her job since she had a night scope in her pack. She didn't worry about her location being spotted because sunlight didn't glint off their weapons like the rest of the team due to some special coating Devon had ordered or added.

The humidity stifled her breathing, and her hair, although slightly damp, wanted to spring from its holder in a frizz like nobody's business. Looking at Ken's back, his hair was pulled back at the base of his neck. She wondered if his would also frizz when released. Wow, that's what she chose to think about?

Seeing something in their path that stopped her, her heart skipped a beat, and she stood rooted to the spot. Was it a snake hanging down from the bushes? A shudder rippled through her, and her heart pounded in a fearful beat, making it difficult to breathe normally.

Realizing she hadn't followed, Ken stopped and turned around. Maybe seeing her distress had him closing in on her. In a low, worried voice, he asked, "Sam, what's wrong?"

Her voice quivered as her shaky hand pointed to the possible snake. "Snake."

Without a word, he moved to where she pointed, and Sam wanted to cry out for him to stay away. As he surveyed it, then used his rifle to prod it, her pulse zinged back and forth.

Ken turned back to her. "Branch."

She gulped, then, as if her legs were concrete, she struggled forward, skirting the limb as best she could. He said no word about it or her fear.

"We're closing in on the location Devon marked," Ken noted.

Giving herself a mental kick, she cleared the clutter and focused on the op. Once again.

Her mind had cataloged their escape route, or at least one of them. Part of it contained primitive trails where it'd been traversed before. Not very wide, but better than forcing through the overgrowth with only KA-BARs. As the small potential area for her to set up came into sight, she knew it wouldn't work. But they tested it anyway because of the slight elevation. Her fear had been right, and while she wanted bushes to conceal them, she had to be able to find a hole that allowed her to have a clean shot into the compound and all around it.

"I don't know about this," she let slip.

"Aren't you a member of the one-mile club?"

Like distance would ever be a challenge. With the foliage around them, she doubted she'd find a clear shot from this far away.

"We can eighty-six this spot," she decided without wasting any more time. She sighted something that had her moving forward. "Follow me," she quietly directed.

Knowing that if guards were patrolling the jungle, they could be overhead, they didn't rush, even though she wanted to do so. She had patience galore when in position, but making it there with that much patience was a lost art for her.

More than once, they stopped each other to listen. Although they heard nothing, they still waited before moving forward again.

Ken touched her arm to stop her once again, and as she searched the area, he whispered, "Where the hell are you going?"

With a nod in the forward direction, they moved again, and she noticed his limp become more prominent.

Sam grimaced when they stopped. The area she'd sighted, while only covered in vines and some small leaves growing up from the ground, happened to be larger than she'd expected. Still, out of view from the compound and the open area around it, the space left them more vulnerable than she liked. They sat about one-third of a mile away.

Knowing the risks, Ken nodded in approval at her relocation. "See if you have a hole while I check out our six." He turned away and crept behind them.

Even though she saw nothing but his back, she nodded, flipped her hat backward, and settled on the uncomfortable ground. Her joking team had been right about her lying on the wet ground. The vines she'd ensured weren't snakes gave her the willies. She shuddered again at the thought of giant snakes and tried to put the phobia from her mind. Lord knew it was full enough today with non-sniper stuff.

It took a bit of positioning to find a hole with enough concealment for her and Ken and clear to the compound. Ken would have a more challenging time finding an opening. She usually worked without a spotter, so he might join the fray and leave her be.

Admittedly, having a spotter would be better, especially with the short distance and cover, but something besides her confusion about her husband's death had her wanting to reject his help. Thoughts of Cody and what she might need to save him made her freeze any personal opinions in their tracks. She could use a spotter to give her as much support as possible.

Ken nodded to her piece as they set up and asked, "How do you like it?"

Smiling at her new top-of-the-line sniper rifle, she nodded. "He definitely came through on this one."

"Devon says it's the Ferrari of sniper rifles, and although Jesse and Nemo each argued for their rifle, he assured them it's the most accurate as far as he'd found."

"I don't know about it being the Ferrari, but I agree on the accuracy."

Ken softly snorted. "He might've been referring to cost."

Rubbing her hand up and down the smooth barrel, she smiled. "I wouldn't disagree there."

His gaze focused on her hand and the unintentional sensual movement. His jaw clenched, but he swallowed hard. She realized what he must be thinking. Many men would, but that hadn't been her intent. Heat rose in her face, hopefully, covered by her green and black face paint. She stopped her movement and turned back to her task.

Ken cleared his throat. "Why didn't you go with the Barrett M82? You could shoot through concrete and brick to hit your target."

"While that would be cool," she said with a sly smile, "I want range, and the M82 isn't as long-range as this one tested at. Anti-material is the primary use of the M82. You didn't hire me for that."

"Aren't there some long-range shots with the M82? I thought I heard about one in Desert Storm."

She snorted. "Lucky shot."

She didn't expound, so he dropped to the ground beside her since, as she'd anticipated, if he set up the tripod to spot, he couldn't see. After he did a hasty search, he identified reference points and sectors. As he finally directed her to each target, he listened as she described every man in detail except underwear and eye color.

Franks updated them on the team's location, which she'd searched, and applauded them for blending so well. Then she briefed the team on what threats existed.

"Here's the 411. Four towers, North, south, east, and west. West is sleeping, and North is bouncing his head to the music instead of paying attention."

"Dumb asses," Cowboy inserted.

Ignoring that, she continued, "Two roving guards outside the compound. Two entry gates—west and east—five-hundred meters from cover to entry. The walls are about two and a half meters and scalable. House is fifty meters from the entry. There appears to be a barracks fifty meters south of the house. Size could house ten. Twenty with twin bunks."

Stone interrupted. "Am I too late for the party? ETA twenty."

Ken stiffened next to her. "Sitrep."

"Ran into a snafu."

It didn't matter what Bev had done now. It couldn't have been in Cody's best interest. Sam would petition the court for custody as soon as she returned to the States. Being a single woman would hurt her, but staying with Bev would hurt Cody.

Ken turned to her and narrowed his eyes as if she'd been part of whatever Bev had done now. "Go on."

"Her seat on the flight went unclaimed. When Devon researched further, he found she boarded an earlier flight—right before it went airborne—under her maiden name and old passport. She landed in Mexico about the same time we did and wasn't waiting at the airport. She's Oscar Mike again, Boss, and I'm guessing here."

A car approached as if to validate the intel, and Beverly Shodun sat in the driver's seat.

Chapter Twelve

Damn Bev. Why did she have to interfere? She'd called on Sam, and she had this. Of course, Sam brought HIS, which Bev didn't like or trust, but no one was better at rescuing children and hostages. They hadn't failed a rescue op—ever. Between them, they'd taken a few bullets, whether grazes or surgery required. But they'd brought everyone home safe and sound.

Did the woman really think she could talk Alejandro out of keeping Cody? Or did she want to reunite with the man? She once thought she could answer what Bev would do, but now….

That niggling feeling about the validity of the evidence Bev had presented her of Lance's death hit her full force. Could her friend be that devious, or did Sam want to believe it wasn't true?

"Sam…" Ken said.

She shook her head. "I have no idea."

"Shit."

No one said a word while Ken evaluated this monkey wrench in their plan. They'd always been flexible, but Bev had them wanting to rescue Cody to get him away from the madness.

"Do you think she'll tell him about us?" Ken asked.

Thoroughly perplexed with Bev's behavior, she shook her head. However, the thought frightened her because she'd pulled them into this. "I honestly don't know what she'll do. If he wants Cody away from her, she won't succeed. I think then if she was losing and wanted some leverage—" She bit down on her lower lip. "—I think she might."

Only a moment after Ken scrunched his brows, he pulled out the sat phone and called Devon to reschedule their ride, then told Old Man and Franks to move up the timeline.

"Stone, double-time it and fall in with Franks," Ken ordered after disconnecting the call.

Stone chuckled. "This is where I'd say some hooah bullshit if I'd been military."

Ken grunted his agreement, and Jesse said, "You bet your sweet ass."

"If you want to do it right, it's hooyah, not that army bullshit," Doc added.

Chuckles sound but only briefly. A stoic silence met the air over their comms.

Ignoring the silence, knowing Franks needed the chance to organize the team, he set out the ground plan. Later, he'd find out why the team hadn't been in position when he and Sam had arrived from their long trek. "Franks, we'll take care of the towers. I want you over the north wall. The extraction point is to the west. You might get stuck with a rover inside the compound. We're not elevated enough to help you there." He took a breath into a slight pause. "Damn, I wish we had floor plans."

"I can blow the entry gate," Cowboy offered.

After thinking about it for a moment, Ken declined. "No, we need to go in quiet. Beverly may have already announced our presence, so I don't want that big entrance. Use it if you can't get in the house or have a problem with the gates."

Jesse suggested, "We've got our silencers on. If Sugar uses hers, we'll have a small advantage until someone notices dead bodies around."

She didn't tell them that Ken had already told her to use her silencer, not that he would've had to.

"What is that woman about?" Cowboy asked.

Her mouth dropped open. Bev hadn't been in the compound long before she sped away like she had the devil on her heels. "Does she have Cody?" she asked, putting the car in her cross-hairs for a better view. Alejandro must've refused to see her or allow her to see Cody. Good for the man, but they would have Cody before the day ended. They were no longer waiting until nightfall when they'd have a better chance to slip in undetected.

"Not that we can see. She should pass near you shortly," Franks said.

A visual on Bev should've been good with the road in and out on their side of the jungle. But she'd have had to adjust too much and, even then, had too much blockage. They could only go with what the team had seen.

"If possible, I'm having that woman thrown into a jail cell. She's a menace to society," Ken said.

"I don't know about society, but definitely to her son," Sam added.

Ken didn't look at her as he spoke, even with his mic on, "We're not taking him back to her."

As she'd expected, that had been aimed at her, and no one contradicted him. Maybe that's why he didn't turn off his mic. He wanted to show her they were united in this.

"I'd hoped you wouldn't."

While waiting for Stone to catch up, they took a side track that was important to the end of this mission that surprised her. "Today, Devon will talk with our lawyers. We'll find him a better situation." He paused and turned to her, waiting until she did the same before he asked his question. "Do you want it to be you?" This time, he did turn off his mic so only she heard and followed his example even though it wasn't allowed on an op. With Ken as the boss and the delicate topic, she hadn't hesitated to mute hers.

Her heart pounded so fast she worried her chest might explode with hope and happiness. With HIS behind her, she could make this happen. She couldn't hold back her smile and didn't think twice about how she'd just shifted her rifle. "Yes," she breathed.

Smiling, he nodded to her rifle for her to be ready to reset. After they lined her back up and she'd had enough of him telling her, "Come up two clicks," and more, she finally told him, "Thanks for coming along, but I know what the hell I'm doing."

He chuckled, then told the team, "While we'd have loved the time to learn the guards' habits and schedules, with Beverly inserting herself, we don't have the time. There's no telling what she's done or will do next." He paused, and no one disagreed. "Devon promised the bird will be at the extraction point in two hours, so we get the party started as soon as Stone arrives and hoof it double-time to get our asses closer to home. If we see a major change in security, we'll know she outed us and will adjust accordingly."

Her stomach knotted again at Bev's stupidity in coming here. What if she had Cody hidden in the car? Damn, she wished she could've seen more.

While Ken double-checked that Devon had also confirmed the airplane pilot would be ready for liftoff when the helo dropped them at the airfield, Sam checked areas with her rifle for any tangos while playing the team's game of "find me if you can." She had a general idea of where they'd hidden, but the exact location was her goal. Their goal was to keep themselves hidden enough so she couldn't get them in her sights. If she could, someone else could.

"I'll be glad when we get back to the plane. I hope he restocked the chow," Cowboy said.

"It's food, not chow," Franks informed him. "If we're going to learn some of your jargon, you could at least use some normal speak."

"We do use normal speak. Mostly it's vowels, but still," Doc said with a chuckle.

The joking continued until Cowboy taunted, "You're slipping, Sugar. You should've at least spotted Franks by now."

"Screw you, you PJ," Franks tossed back.

Cowboy laughed. "Like that's a bad thing. A DEA fellow like you requires help from someone like me to keep your ass alive."

Sam smiled. "Well, if that's the case, he's screwed."

"You don't see me," Cowboy said, appalled at the thought.

"Oh, yeah, I do. I'd know that hat anywhere. Just had to be different from the rest of us."

Even the Old Man chuckled at that. As expected, said head slipped down out of sight.

She enjoyed that any team leader allowed this while they waited. Someone always watched and didn't participate, but the rest could do a bit of both.

"Sugar," Doc said solemnly, breaking her smile, "about Cody. We've got a few minutes to talk."

Her breath caught. She couldn't stand it if one of them told her he couldn't go home with her.

Ken touched her to get her attention and pointed back at the compound so they could get lined up again.

"We were talking on the plane," Doc began, and she didn't have to ask who with. Even before the team split, her four teammates—not including her team boss—had been thick as thieves. "Since we've agreed he can't go back home, we think you should petition for guardianship of Cody."

Had they heard her and Ken? She'd thought both their mics had been off. Her heart swelled at their understanding and what would be best for the boy.

"It'd be better for your chances for guardianship if you were married," Doc said.

She choked on her breath.

"Well," Doc continued hesitantly, "since you don't have a beau, we thought you could marry one of us."

Her head spun, trying to get around this conversation and the one her teammates must've had. While sweet of them, she didn't plan to wed any of them, but she'd play this game. "Oh, really. Who did you have in mind?"

No one answered immediately, so she wondered if they were still fighting it out or hadn't expected her to take the bait.

Finally, Franks came on the air as their apparent spokesman. "Each of us wanted to marry you." He paused, as hesitant as Doc had become nearer to this point. "But instead, we think Boss should do it."

Shock wracked her system, and she barely noticed Ken had stiffened beside her. He probably hadn't known their answer either. Just the thought of it tickled her belly.

When she got her voice back, she chuckled—although she didn't find it funny—and answered, "Well, that is thoughtful of all of you, but I'll pass."

By this time, Stone had joined them, and the transport bird was on its way and would arrive per the new schedule.

Instead of responding to the quips, Ken grabbed their attention. "Ready, boys and girls?"

"I've been waiting so long my ass itches," Cowboy said.

"Eww, that's gross," Sam responded.

"You sound like a girl," Cowboy countered.

"That's because I am, numbnuts."

"Ouch, that hurts," Cowboy mocked. They never should've started teaching her military jargon. Like learning a foreign language, she'd first known most of the bad words.

"Cowboy," Franks said, "you might not want to piss her off before an op. Your six may go uncovered."

Cowboy chuckled. "She'd never do that. Would ya, Sugar?"

"Gentlemen," Ken cut in, "and lady," he added, "lock and load."

Sam rolled her eyes. Everyone had been ready since they'd deplaned. Yet Ken said the exact words on every op. *You can take the man out of the military, but you can't take the military out of the man.* She'd heard the statement in passing and believed it to be true. While the men fought about which branch ruled the roost, they came together for an op.

"Are you ready?" Ken whispered near her ear.

Hell, she hadn't felt him moving closer. That lapse in her instincts didn't bode well for protecting her from Ken. Not physically, but emotionally. She gulped and whispered back, a little breathless, "Yes." How could she be ready when, once again, she couldn't control her breathing around him? She leaned down and looked down her scope to insert space between them.

"We're going through this fast, so that I won't guide you in for each target. I'll give you the first instruction, and then you've got to run on your own. The order is north, east, south, and west. I'll watch for other threats we need to take out."

She memorized the order and associated the tangos with

them.

Ken put them back on point without giving her time to take a breath. "Go to the north tower," he instructed.

Relaxing enough to slow her pulse and control her breathing but not enough to leave herself vulnerable, she got to business. "Contact." She didn't describe the target again since they'd already done that, and nothing had changed.

She walked through the steps with him to ensure she was aligned and ready. When they finally got to the moment she'd been waiting for, she held her breath while Ken announced the winds. She adjusted as he cleared her to fire.

With a light touch on the trigger, she took the first shot— and possibly life for today.

Chapter Thirteen

Proud as a papa, Ken watched Sam take out the four men in less than ten seconds without needing his guidance, only his initial wind call. Granted, he'd run her through it already. Her skill constantly astounded him. Without a second thought, he radioed, "Four tangos down."

Franks didn't waste time. The team took that as the green light since all that had held them back had been the guards in the towers. "Go, go, go," he directed. Then, to Ken, he added, "Oscar Mike."

With weapons at the ready, the men crossed the expanse around the compound in what he considered record time. Because of their location, Ken lost sight of the team as they neared the wall. Now he wished he'd had Cowboy blow the gate so he could observe them, but he knew a silent infiltration worked better for this op. He trusted Franks to keep them safe.

His next sight of the men was their climbing over the eight-foot wall. His confidence in them didn't waver. After a minute with them inside, he wanted to scream, "Sitrep." Impatience could kill a man in situations such as this. Maybe he shouldn't have come since he couldn't be with the team below during the action.

"They're at the front door," Sam informed him.

He abandoned the spotting equipment, dropped beside her, and looked through his scope. While he couldn't hold a candle to Sam's accuracy at this distance, he'd be bound to hit something on semi-automatic.

The gate appeared more imposing as he sighted it. Only tiny slits through the metal bars allowed for a bit of sight. To get a shot through there would be a phenomenal feat. Disheartened, he admitted, "I can't get a shot through there."

"That's why you've got me," she said without boasting. "If you need to feel useful, you can do that spotting shit for me."

Had he heard her right? That she needed him? It was a first and work-related, but their entire relationship was entwined between work and personal. He craved to tell her he loved her, but regrettably, now wouldn't be the right time. After. That's what he'd do. After they returned home and debriefed, they'd figure this out. No more running on her part and no more holding back on his part.

Before he had time to respond, Franks cleared Cowboy, and Ken saw movement near the door and heard Cowboy's "Shit's about to get real" comment he always made before blowing something up.

"Shit," Ken said under his breath. When munitions were used, knots formed in his stomach. It brought back too many memories of loss that had to remain pushed back to the recesses of his mind, or he'd be lost in emotional grief and guilt.

The team's focus had to be on Cody. Without even knowing the boy, they would give their lives to save him. They did not desire that outcome, but they'd do it. The child was an innocent who belonged at home. In most cases, home. In this case, with his loving godmother.

Before they could breach the entry, men rushed out of the barracks armed, seeking out the team.

"I've got your six," Sam told the team.

Ken squinted at the narrow openings in the gate again and couldn't believe her confidence. He didn't doubt her marksmanship, but she'd never had this barrier. At least as far as he knew. Maybe she had with SWAT. No matter, with her calmness and focus, he didn't doubt she could do this.

He focused downfield as Sam took a shot. A man fell, but another came in from the opposite direction. "Cowboy's three o'clock." At times like this, he loved to watch her but couldn't tear his gaze away from what was happening with his team. He could only imagine how beautiful she looked.

Damn. There were ten targets, and his team didn't have anywhere to take cover, so they hustled to the side of the main house. Sam took down another target before Cowboy announced, "Fire in the hole."

As the agents moved from the side of the house toward the door, they encountered additional men from the barracks.

Without fail, Sam took down any she deemed necessary. He called out any tangos trying to sneak in for an attack.

"Old Man's six o'clock."

She didn't fire, and he didn't know if that meant she hadn't heard him or didn't have a shot.

He tried again, wishing he could make the shot. "Old Man's six o'clock," he said sterner.

The shot rang out, and Old Man turned to see the man who'd been sneaking up from behind him. He glanced toward the gate and gave a two-finger salute to them.

Once they breached the entry, Ken's pulse raced, and he nearly held his breath while he heard the men calling, "Clear," as they went from room to room.

The hair on his neck stood up before he heard the rustle of something—or someone—approaching. He sensed Sam tense beside him. They didn't speak. They both reacted instinctively.

His rifle bit the dirt, and with a roll to his left side, he grabbed his SIG Sauer from the right holster, and as soon as his right arm broke free, he snatched his other SIG from the left holster. He landed on his back and aimed at two of the three tangos before them. In his peripheral vision, Sam had her handgun pointed at the other tango.

His heartbeat quickened with worry that he couldn't protect Sam. At least they had three weapons on three tangos. Had he not spotted for her on this op, she'd have been in a losing battle of weapons. With the calmness he'd mastered in battle, he watched every movement, twitch, or change in expression of the men. He had no doubt that he and Sam were faster on the trigger if they gave any inkling of firing.

For some reason, the men had their rifles lowered. It didn't take a genius to know things weren't as they seemed, and they'd have to shoot their way out of this because they didn't desire to become captives. Or dead.

As one man said in broken English, "You die," the other men began lifting their rifles. A second after he and Sam simultaneously fired kill shots, an explosion inside the compound shook the ground beneath them.

With the men on the ground, he sprang to his feet, grabbing his M4 in one hand and the spotting tripod in the other as he did. "Move." He didn't need to say another word before she had her gear stowed and stood beside him. It stood to reason that if any other men patrolled this area, they'd have heard the gunshots.

"Get to the extraction point," he directed, since they couldn't help before the op ended.

She nodded and turned to the west.

"I'll cover your six." While adrenaline surged through him, he wouldn't allow his slower gait to hold her back if he led. He hoped she didn't get into trouble before getting to the bird.

Over the comm system, he broke in and said, "Sugar's Oscar Mike."

The radio went silent momentarily as it seemed everyone held their breath. They knew something had happened for the sniper to move this early, yet they couldn't help. They had to complete their op first.

"Sitrep," Franks requested, and Ken heard the tiny spark of fear in the agent.

"Three tangos bit the farm."

After trudging through that thicket of the jungle, they broke through to a small trail, and based on the overgrowth, it didn't look regularly used. It took them southwest versus west alone, but using it could allow fast movement to escape anyone on their tail. They could turn back west when the best time warranted. He hated that the team hadn't recon'd it.

Knowing what Ken meant by his statement, Franks spouted, "Foxtrot Uniform."

Ken wanted to laugh at how Franks had gotten around flat-out profanity. The younger, blond man might have it right. With the bursts of gunfire in the area, he felt that "fucked up" might be appropriate.

"We're moving to Point Alpha." If they couldn't make that extraction point, they'd have to go to Point Bravo and wait until someone came to extract them later.

"Copy," Franks responded.

As they raced along the trail, the expanse between him and Sam grew further with each moment. His limp slowed him down.

Voices tossing out words in Spanish that he didn't understand—and figured Sam didn't either—breathed out through the jungle to the east. More than likely, that meant they'd found their friends and knew at least one person was on the run.

He had to get Sam to keep going no matter what—damned if she didn't turn around and run behind him to check his six. He'd been wrong about getting her to quit HIS. She rocked in her warrior-woman mode. It made him love her all the more.

Realizing the men were closer than he first thought, he whispered, "Blend into the jungle. If I get caught, you run and save yourself."

"What? No."

How could she think he wanted her as a captive or dead? He ground his teeth. He hated pulling the boss card, but dammit, he'd do it without fail if it saved her life. "Follow my damn orders."

Without a retort, she blended into the foliage. He followed her before they fanned out to distance themselves in case they were discovered.

The men, or new ones, were too close. It became apparent they were on his tail, and no matter what happened, he thanked God they weren't on Sam's. He'd endure anything to keep her safe.

About the same time he heard the shot, a searing pain to the back of his leg wracked him, and he crumpled to the ground, doing the last thing a soldier should. He allowed his weapon to fall out of his grasp. Before he could move, Sam appeared and used her boot to slide his rifle toward him. Lightning fast, she ripped the scarf she wore around her neck to keep critters from crawling down her shirt and swiftly wrapped a makeshift tourniquet on his leg. Without a moment to chastise her for disobeying him, she rose to one knee and faced behind him, her rifle pointing toward their threat. "Use my shoulder to get up," she offered.

He didn't want to need the help, especially from the one

he promised to protect, but he had to use her, or he'd be found. Taking a deep breath against the pain, he moved to get to his knees and fell, cursing at his failure. No way would he give up. The second time he tried, he gritted his teeth against the blinding shot of agony, then reached to Sam's shoulder to help him stand.

Three shots erupted from Sam's rifle. With her precision, she had no need for automatic.

Not a newbie to the type of pain that burned in his thigh, he thought Jesse might've made the wrong choice keeping him on the payroll after all. He hadn't fully recovered from being shot in the hip. They should just shoot him in the calf and foot and call it done.

Somehow, leaning heavily on Sam, he got to his feet. She slung her piece over her shoulder and took his rifle since he couldn't hold it with one arm slung over the same shoulder. Not at all arguing, he pulled his SIG, and they took off toward the west as best as they could. While one person could slip through the jungle with little noise, the movement of the trees gave away their path.

In the same situation, he found himself in, any man would appreciate the help from a teammate, but would push the teammate to save themselves so they could help mount a rescue or recovery, although he tried not to think about the last option. "Sam, go. I'll be right behind you."

"We've got a situation here," she said, tugging him along.

"Go ahead," Franks responded, albeit a bit breathless. Ken hadn't even been listening to what happened in the compound.

Ken broke in, "Have you got the package?"

"Roger."

Sam piped back in before anyone else could speak,

"Boss is shot, and we have tangos on our six."

"Don't you dare turn back," Ken commanded like the team needed to hear it. "Your job is to get the package safe. If we're not at Point Alpha in time, we'll be at Point Bravo as scheduled."

Although he wanted to climb all over Sam for asking for help, he held back. One reason was that he wasn't sure she really asked, but with the open mics, some things didn't need to be aired.

After he stumbled for the second time, Sam said, almost like she finally accepted their dire straits, "We're not going to make it to Alpha in time."

Releasing a heavy sigh, he agreed, "No."

The airwaves held only silence for the second time during the op. All chatter had ceased. If he were Franks, he'd struggle with how to save the boy and rescue members of the team. This would be the first time Franks faced this situation, but thankfully, Jesse could mentor and take over if needed.

"Doc, you're Shaggy," Franks directed the man to observe and play decoy if needed.

"Roger," Doc responded.

He felt better that Cody would be safe and that he and Sam would have someone to help rescue them should they be captured. Should they be killed, well….

Without realizing what lay ahead, they burst through the bushes into an open area that left them vulnerable. Sam halted and looked around. "Shit. We've gotta move fast across this. Can you do it?"

"I want to survive, so I'll do anything needed." A fear he hadn't known in a long time gripped his gut. The first men had meant to kill them. Why would this group be any different? As much as he didn't want to be a captive, he'd prefer that to death.

A small smile played on her lips before she went all commando on him again.

"Let's move," she instructed.

"Wait."

She looked at him with an impatient expression.

"Earpiece," he breathed in pain. In cases where they were captured or killed, giving the enemy access to their communications was utterly unacceptable because it could impede operations and put lives at risk. While he hated allowing himself to go blind, it had to be done. They'd keep their mics for now to relay information. The team had only a single earpiece that worked to transmit and receive, but their complete shipment hadn't arrived in time to depart, so he and Sam, being further from the action, took the more cumbersome models. Now, he was glad they had, as it gave him more time to communicate, albeit one-way.

Sam leaned away, and they both removed their wireless earpieces. Gesturing to the spot before her, he dropped his, and she stomped on it with her booted foot. Devon would be disappointed to lose these pieces. They also removed the SIM cards from their phones. He hated to destroy them, but they might not have had another chance before they lost the equipment.

"We're going together," Sam stated matter-of-factly. "Toss your arm over my shoulder." He did so, and she wrapped her arm around his waist. He'd relish her arm around him if things weren't as dire as they were. Trying not to shift his weight too much on her, they moved to safety.

Twenty feet into the clearing, his fear came true. His body tensed, and his stomach dropped. Fear for Sam gripped him, holding tight enough to suffocate him. His heart hurt.

The threat moved in from two sides—twelve o'clock

and six o'clock. Sam shifted them sideways so they could see both groups, and he groaned with the pain it caused. He really could use Doc right now.

He didn't know much about Casper, Bravo Team's new medic, but Doc kicked butt as a medic and warrior, even though he'd been a SEAL instead of an elite Army Ranger. If things hadn't been as dire as they were, he'd have laughed at that and maybe even over the air.

Taking a deep breath to control the throbbing, achy fire that wanted to tear his leg apart, he made a decision that impacted his heart. As much as he didn't wish it so, this could be the end, and he refused to die without telling her the truth. "I love you, Sam. I always have."

With time of the essence, he didn't allow her to respond before he announced into his mic, "Sugar's team down. Switch to channel Charlie," since he didn't expect the response from her he desired. As for the team, they'd check in on the alternate channel and continue with their op, knowing comms had been compromised.

"Drop weapons. Where be boy?" a short, stout Hispanic man asked with a heavy accent. When they didn't answer, he asked something that froze the blood in his veins, "You Ken Patrick?"

His breath caught, and his racing pulse froze in his veins. How did they know him? Damn Beverly. She'd given them away. With his ponytail, it hadn't been hard to identify him. Yet telling them the truth gave him a fifty-fifty chance of survival. Telling them a lie did the same thing. With Sam's life to consider, his decisions became even more difficult.

Sam twisted them to get a better view of the man, and he struggled not to cry out.

No bones about it. They were truly outnumbered. Two to…he glanced and counted…eight.

When Sam spun again, his leg buckled, and he pulled them to the ground. Oh, he wished she weren't here. He touched her cheek ever so lightly, wondering if this would be the last time he saw her. From the fierce look in her eyes, she'd pull everything she had for them to escape this group.

When the stout man took a step toward them, Sam spun as fast as lightning and, on her back, aimed his M4 at the man.

"Drop your weapons," the man insisted.

Sam slid a slight glance at him in answer. With the realization they had no choice—if they wanted to live at least for the next five minutes—Ken gave her a brief nod. They each tried to hold onto any weapon they could, but the men who stepped forward and searched them even found the smaller knives they kept in their boots. As expected, they took the comm systems—or what they'd left of them. After a moment of confusion, since they didn't find a receiver with them, they checked their ears, telling him their boss held his secrets of protection.

He hoped Sam had a weapon tucked away where these assholes couldn't find it. If he could gain his feet, they could make some headway.

The stout man became impatient. "Now, where be the boy?"

"Safe" was all Ken said as he glared at the man. Cody had been their priority, and he wouldn't give him up, even for his own life.

The man narrowed his eyes. "You Ken Patrick?" he asked again.

Curious but not stupid about the fact that they knew his name, he chose not to hold back any longer. He nodded. "I am."

With a nod, the man waved him forward and pointed at

Sam. "You come too."

Trying not to show his weakness, Ken tried to gain his feet, but unmanageable searing pain ripped through his leg, and he collapsed on his face. When darkness began to creep in around his eyes, he fought it. He had to protect Sam. He couldn't leave her alone with these men. He had no idea what they planned for her.

His angel leaned over him. "Come on, Boss. I'll help you up."

"Sam, save yourself," he said, knowing her chance probably dwindled because he lapsed into the darkness with her sweet face on his mind instead of covering her.

Chapter Fourteen

Fear skittered up Sam's spine as she swiveled her head from side to side, assessing every threat while assuming a protective stance over Ken. Being unarmed, she had to remain calm yet vigilant.

Before Ken had passed out, she'd been focused on one thing—their survival. Fear hadn't motivated her. It'd been pure determination. Yes, her heart beat overtime, and her pulse raced fast enough to win the Kentucky Derby, but since she'd learned to control her fear, she'd not allowed it to rule her. Fear alone didn't help someone survive. Skill and a level head were her best bet.

An acute sense of purpose drove her, and she stood solidly, at the ready. There had to be a way out, and getting them there drove her. Her stomach revolted because escape presented a challenge she couldn't overcome without Ken's help. Not only could she not overpower this many men at once, but even if they offered her the ability to slip away, she wouldn't leave him to his fate.

She'd sprinted back to help cover his six since he'd not been moving at full speed. Although she'd been surprised at how fast he had moved with his injury. She knew the prospect of death made someone forget an impediment to their survival.

His whispered words had thrown her. "I love you, Sam. I always have." She had no idea how to respond to that admission. And right now, she couldn't let her mind drift away from their situation.

Trying to wrap her head around this change in the men's directives, she wanted to rub her temples to ease the confusion. The last group of men said that she and Ken would die, while this group said to come. But it was their knowing Ken's name that unsettled her.

Then it struck her and made her want to strike out. *Bev.* Her friend had ratted them out, probably describing each one to gain affection from Alejandro. Anger swamped her at the betrayal of someone dear to her. It hadn't worked because she'd hightailed it out in no time, alone—no Cody.

Two men stepped forward to pick Ken up under his arms, and Sam's protective instinct went into overdrive. She didn't know what they had planned, but she didn't believe it involved medical care. Remembering her training, she returned her focus to any means to escape. She wouldn't go alone because they worked as a team in HIS, and their HIS commitment meant everything. "We've got your six." They weren't completely alone. The code word "Shaggy" had been transmitted earlier, and Doc should've headed their way. He just hadn't made it in time. He'd observe and communicate the situation.

Having learned more about the men of HIS, she imagined that once they placed Cody on the bird, two would accompany the boy back to the States, while the others would return to support in whatever role needed. Whether it be interference, negotiation, or rescue, and, dare she admit, recovery. She fought to control the shivers attempting to take over her body at that thought.

With clenched fists, she knew their chance of survival improved if they could escape—her mind refused to allow that to leave her thoughts—before reaching the compound, even though they didn't have the team as a backup. But she needed Ken awake and at least able to lean on her to walk because she couldn't do anything but drag him, and considering his dead weight, her efforts wouldn't move them fast enough to safety. If they could get away, they'd find their way to Doc, and he could do some of his field medic magic so they could get the hell out of there and to the secondary extraction point before the scheduled time of the helo arrival. It wouldn't do any good if they missed the window and had to evade for longer.

Her captor's fingers bit her right bicep hard enough to leave five-digit bruises before tugging her forward. At first, she dug herself in and refused to allow him to put distance between her and Ken. She wouldn't leave the man who'd made her feel again. Even things she'd never admit because they conflicted with all she'd recently discovered from Bev. Though in her heart, she now wholly doubted the "new intel" Bev had given her. Ken's admission and deep-seated need to save and protect him destroyed the demons that haunted her, removing the weight of the decision to respond to the report and setting her heart free.

Her thoughts almost stopped in their tracks. She hated to admit that she'd nearly allowed Jesse to die without verifying anything. Ken had broken her out of those thoughts when she hadn't taken the first shot to cover Jesse. Now, she would rely on him to save her and an injured Ken.

When the two men stepped away, dragging Ken forward, her body tensed as her blood raged. The fear she'd been pushing at bay turned to anger at the situation and these assholes. If they escaped—no, *when* they escaped—she'd remember every one of these bastards once she had a weapon again. Any weapon would do. Going from police to SWAT to HIS, she'd learned quite a few things about survival. Taking out a threat could be accomplished in many different ways.

Captive. She couldn't let it happen. If she could get closer to the man who'd removed her small knife—a gift from Ken on her twenty-first birthday—she had no qualms about using her pickpocket skills to lift it. In no way would she allow them to take her sexually. Her stomach roiled with the idea, and nausea rose in her throat.

In silence, they continued through the jungle and over the rocky area, unlike where they'd had cover. Thinking of the small rocks in the terrain and Ken not grunting or moving, her respect for his strength built. As far as she could tell, the bleeding on his thigh had stopped for the most part, but she only saw the back of his leg where his pants appeared stuck to his leg. No trail of red followed him.

Knowing better than to look around for any friendlies, she watched their guards, and her lips quirked as she held back a smile. Most likely afraid of the rest of the team laying an ambush, the men looked a bit afraid. She'd pinpointed the stout guy who'd spoken initially as the leader. Knowing their chain of command could be helpful at some point.

The brute holding her in an iron grip thwarted her attempt to slip toward the thief with her knife. His lightning reaction caught her the moment she stumbled in the opposite direction. *Dammit.* That also nixed her idea to fall and grab a rock. She'd find something once the man released her.

Before they entered that metal gate, she'd sighted her targets, but new guards in the towers grabbed her attention. Son of a gun. Then she remembered that if Jesse didn't accompany Cody home, he'd target them first. Mentally crossing her fingers that Jesse returned, she scanned the rest of the area—left to right, near to far.

Ken must've tagged it right that they had bunk beds in the barracks. HIS had taken out quite a few men, but more strolled the compound, inside and outside the adobe walls. If only she could feed the information to Doc, the remaining agents could formulate a good rescue plan. Somehow, she didn't think it would be as easy as Cody's since they'd trespassed, blown up shit, killed some people, injured others, and more because they didn't do things halfway. They either got in and out with stealth or dealt with crap like this. If it hadn't been for Bev's interference, this would have been a clean rescue where they wouldn't have known Cody was gone until HIS had him on a flight home.

As they traversed the lawn area between the gate and the house, the extra men guarding her and Ken abandoned them and moved to what she suspected were their original posts. If she understood Spanish better, she'd know what they planned for the two of them. Damn, she should've paid more attention to their quick language training.

The coolness inside the house surprised her due to the warmth outside. The outside temp had been tolerable, but she freely admitted she preferred the temp inside and the lack of heavy humidity that swamped the rainforest. In no time, her sweat-soaked shirt felt cool against her skin, sending goose bumps skittering up her arms.

After a quick scan for threats and finding only the remaining men, with an alert gaze, she searched for a weapon. In what appeared to be a living room large enough for two sofas, one loveseat, one fainting couch, and four armchairs, she searched out every door, reevaluated every person—the asshole with her knife hadn't followed them inside—every piece of furniture and its location, and more —so they could escape. Knowing Ken had awakened renewed her strength in their ability to make it. They just needed to find a way out.

"Hello, my dear."

Sam bristled at the endearment as her head jerked to the

barrel-chested Hispanic man who walked through the doorway of a connected room. His deep voice, when speaking English, held little accent. Swallowing hard, she reminded herself she couldn't allow taunts to bother her. If she played this right, she could get them released or, at the least, medical care for Ken until he arrived.

She voiced her assumption, "Alejandro Ramirez."

With a smile, he bowed his head. "At your service."

"Why do you have us here?"

His gaze flicked from her to Ken. With a raised eyebrow, he asked, "Ken Patrick?"

Refusing to confirm that information, she narrowed her eyes. "Why do you have us here?" she asked again.

Alejandro took a few steps into the room and sat in a burgundy leather armchair. Steeping his fingers together and bouncing his thumbs off each other grated on her nerves. "You must be Bev's friend, Samantha Milton."

So he did know her name. *Stay on target, Sam. Don't let him affect you.* "Why do you have us here?" she asked again, ignoring his reference to Bev.

"I want the boy back."

Since they hadn't had much information on Alejandro, she hadn't known what to expect. What she hadn't expected was the calm, cool man. "That's not happening." No sense beating around the bush there.

"Is that your final answer?"

Panic seized her, choking her response. What type of final did he mean? She wouldn't give up Cody. All she could do if they chose to kill them was stand between Ken and a bullet. She didn't wish to die or want the man she cared about to die.

Taking a slow, deep breath, she calmed herself as much as possible. Her heart, attempting to escape from her chest, had no such qualms. She could face possible death. "Yes."

His dark eyes searched hers, and he must've seen her steely resolve in her protection of Cody. Looking at the man holding her arm, he nodded down the hallway. "Take them away."

That opened the door to a multitude of options she didn't like. Her escort pulled her down a light-colored hallway. She kept craning her neck to ensure Ken followed. He'd pretended for so long that she feared he'd passed out again.

Once she ensured Ken accompanied her, she focused on their path, counting doorways and looking for—and finding —surveillance cameras. He definitely couldn't be up to any good if he needed cameras in his home. What had Devon said? They suspected him of being an arms dealer or participating in illegal arms trading. On a positive note, she might find arms to help with any investigation. On a negative note, their captors might have plenty of arms in their hands.

Her escort gripped her arm and stopped her forward movement. "Here."

Here appeared to be a small room with an iron cell door. He swung it open and shoved her through the portal. Stumbling, she saw the cot on one side of the room and a large bucket on the other. Disgust roiled in her, turning her stomach over and over. Who the hell kept a dungeon in their home? One up to no good. Had they held Cody in here? She hoped not. That doubled her determination to keep the boy away from this monster.

She continued to survey the room and reminded herself that Alejandro may have treated Cody very well. The agents had reported pulling him from the breakfast table, so he, at least, didn't take meals in here. It'd been a shame they couldn't have taken the time to locate Alejandro. If they'd had a larger team and more time to prep…. With a professional effort, she swept Cody from her mind and focused on her and her boss and their survival.

More or less tossed into the room, Ken kept up his façade of unconsciousness. As they slammed and locked the door, she dropped to her knees beside him and said the first thing that popped into her head. "Did you really say you loved me?"

Chapter Fifteen

Ken groaned and rolled onto his back. "Yeah. Now take a look at my leg." He dropped his head back and closed his eyes. Although he tried to hide it, his pain radiated through her, and Sam wished she could take it away.

He wouldn't have been shot if she'd gotten to him sooner and protected his six sooner. She should've realized he hadn't been right with her after ordering her to run. Forgetting he'd been injured had been unacceptable of her as a teammate.

But what of any other relationship? He'd told her he loved her. If he genuinely did, why now? Because they'd possibly been about to die? She didn't know how to handle the emotions his words evoked. They'd been dancing around the growing changes in their relationship, where their feelings went beyond what they'd ever admitted. Was she ready to make that jump, though?

His groan refocused the emotions that had her thoughts in a jumble. Helping him had to be her priority, but she sighed in near defeat. She had nothing to treat his wound, and based on how their captors had treated them, she didn't believe a doctor would arrive anytime soon. No one appeared to be guarding the cell, so she could request supplies.

Did Alejandro want Cody back so badly that he'd allow Ken to suffer without treatment? Maybe they could fill in the holes about the man that Devon couldn't dig up. Then she'd have to find a way to use it for their release.

Determined, she turned her attention to Ken's injury. A frown wove its way on her face. She couldn't see his injury. Without her knife, the fabric wouldn't give enough for her to rip it and enlarge the hole. When they'd purchased the BDU pants, it had been for durability, which didn't involve being able to rip them so easily.

"The shot's too high on your thigh to pull up your pants leg to see it." She didn't say that because of the finely toned, muscular thighs that made her drool, the lower pants leg wouldn't have pulled up over them. She'd wanted to get in his pants, but not like this. *Enough. Now's not the time to think of those things. Fix him so you can escape*. Although she feared her womanly reaction to his following action, she directed him to do the only thing she could imagine would help. "You're going to have to drop 'em."

A pain-filled chuckle rumbled up from him. "If I had a dollar every time a woman said that to me…."

Damn if her emotions didn't resurface when she wanted to keep her mind on nothing but the business at hand. Yet she smiled at his humor, but secretly wanted to give the women their dollars back, so to speak. Jealousy sprang up inside her. She hadn't felt it since Lance, but if she had to admit the truth—and what better time than now—she'd been jealous of the women Ken had dated when they'd all hung out together. In fact—

Stop this! After scolding herself some more, she realized much had changed. She'd changed to include going into a dark place with what Bev had told her to have the man she'd dreamed about tell her he loved her. And he'd said something about having trouble reconciling his two challenges with her. Yet things about both situations scared her. Knowing the timing couldn't be worse, she shoved everything but their survival to the back of her mind, adding a slam of a door to emphasize her will so she could be the warrior she'd been trained to be and take charge until Ken's condition changed for the better.

Investigating the two items in the room and searching the floor, the walls, and the door, her heart sank as she found nothing that could be formed into something sharp to tear his pants or protect them.

She drew her brows in concentration and frowned, thinking she must be missing something. Anything could be adapted for use. Captors tended to overlook the most mundane things, but either these men hadn't been that stupid, or they had been that lucky.

Jolting her from her thoughts of trying to figure out how to help them, Ken requested something she should've already done for him.

"Help me get to the cot. I'm afraid the blood has started drying my pants to the wound. Maybe we should wait until we get some water to loosen it instead of ripping it back open. If it starts bleeding again, we may have to start removing clothes." He winked at her—winked!—and somehow, with his pain and discomfort, he smiled at her. Was he actually flirting with her? Now of all times?

Shaking her head and banishing those thoughts, she ignored his playfulness. If it got him through the pain, she wouldn't stop him. Heck, for all she knew, he might be delirious. Her medical training extended to not much more than putting on a bandage. Okay, a little more than that, like the improvised tourniquet she'd slapped on his leg, but her ability to help remained limited without the right items.

What she knew was that he made perfect sense. And not the loss of clothing, but that the wound would start bleeding again, and she couldn't chance it going beyond a trickle or two.

It took some heaving, grunting, gasping, groaning, half-dragging, and Sam almost landing on her ass, but they made it to the cot. His pallor didn't appear as gray as it had earlier. The warrior she knew had returned, albeit with a grimace of pain occasionally. He had to be in agony. "How serious do you think it is?"

Clenching his jaw, he sat on the cot and patted the space beside him. "Come sit with me. Let me rest my head on your lap."

She gulped. That close? That intimate? She'd just fully emerged from the cocoon of her body's awareness of him.

"No funny business to worry about, Sam."

Her heart lurched with a mix of disappointment and concern. His voice sounded weaker. Without another thought, she slid onto the head of the cot and allowed him to rest his head on her lap. At the contact, warmth infused her and settled the makings of desire.

Dammit, hadn't she twirled herself in circles enough about this today? But he'd dropped a real giant bomb that she kept trying to put away for a later day, but it wouldn't stop shoving itself forward. She wanted to think about it, analyze it, consider it, and decide what to do about it, but she had to focus on the op, not the man. Nor how her pulse raced for him. Or the butterflies that twittered in her stomach. Or the breathlessness that overcame her when they were close. Or all the rest of her erstwhile responses and emotions.

"In answer to your question—" His Adam's apple bobbed as if he had trouble swallowing. "—I've had a bullet hit bone and stay inside me. This isn't the same."

Her body shook with worry. "Do you think it's just a through-and-through wound, then?"

"I'd be damn lucky if it did that and didn't tear any tendons or muscle, but it's possible. I know my leg's pain and limitations are worse than just a notch from a bullet graze. After a short rest, I can use it more than I have."

Scrutinizing the front of his thigh, the obvious presence of blood there meant the bullet had to have exited. With the hole where the shot went through his body in the front being more prominent than the entry point in the rear, she could probably get some give with the material, but as Ken had said, it stuck to his skin, so separating it could cause problems they didn't need.

Surely their captors would bring them water at the very least. Without thought, her hand moved to his head, where she softly rubbed it. His dark-blond hair had fallen from the band at the base of his neck. It had been odd to see Ken's long hair after so long with military-short hair. She scrunched her brow.

"What'd you see?" he asked, soft enough she had to lean over him.

She described their trip from capture to cell. He asked a question or two to clarify, but asked if she saw cameras in their cell. In surveying the room, none appeared, but that didn't mean listening devices weren't somewhere she'd missed.

Listening! Hope surged through her. She reached back to her low ponytail and hoped the object hadn't fallen. When she'd tightened her hair in the holder before capture, she'd shoved the earpiece between the elastic band holding back her hair and secured it as best she could. She hadn't been jostled enough for it to have fallen loose.

Her spirit lifted, and she grasped and removed the tiny mechanism. In case she missed cameras or they were overhead, she reached out her hand to his and leaned down. "Here," she said in a low voice, hoping he'd understand why she spoke as she did and not blurt out a response.

He opened his eyes and felt for the object she held. Eyes brightening, he whispered, "I hadn't thought of hiding it like that." When he closed his eyes again and clenched his jaw, she knew he hid the actual level of his pain from her. She ached for him, wishing she could make everything right with a kiss. It worked in cartoons. She barely held back a strained laugh.

Acting like she hadn't noticed his battle, she tried not to make him feel foolish for not considering hiding his. "I don't think it would've worked for you." His hair didn't have her full length, but most importantly, he didn't have the volume she used to lose the tiny mechanism.

His ability to toss out a brief smile warmed her soul. Yet he handed back the earpiece. All of a sudden, she remembered two things. First, for her to listen, the other part of her comm system had to be near, in working order, and activated. Which could be possible, depending on where the men who'd captured them deposited the equipment they'd gathered. Second, the team had been sent to another channel. Thankfully, she hadn't changed her radio to the new station, assuming she'd been about to lose it to some hostiles. But that also left her unable to listen to the new comm.

Something akin to a nod from him played across her lap. "This is a good thing for us. Go ahead now, but be prepared to put it back quickly. After they take me, please bring it back out and listen, but always hide it again before they come. They won't see it unless they're looking, but we can't take the chance."

Her heart raced, and she hated to admit that a slice of fear ran through her. "What do you mean, take you?" Had her voice betrayed that he meant something to her? That wasn't her intent, but his raised eyebrow made her wonder how he took it.

Took. Take.

That sinking feeling rose in waves. If they took him, she couldn't protect him. And with his injury, he needed her protection. While she was sure he'd never admit that, especially on ops, she didn't think him so foolish as to deny support. He was a good leader, and part of leading meant knowing when to ask for help.

He reached up with an open hand. Without hesitation, she placed her palm on his. His warmth radiated through her, leaving her wanting to cuddle with him. Cuddle? Yes, so she could hold him through the pain. Everything before this moment slipped away. Her blinders were off. Ken was her future, and she wouldn't let what they had go.

He squeezed her hand and didn't let go. "I understood enough of the Spanish I overheard. They're going to question me."

Something tightened inside her. Question to what extent? And why not her? Maybe they planned to offer him medical attention if he talked. On the other hand, she had nothing for them to bargain with except for Ken's life. Christ, they couldn't do that to Ken. Offer her life for Cody's.

"Why do you think he wants Cody so badly?" she asked.

"I don't know, but I don't think this is about Cody. Yeah, he wants him, but why did he give him up so easily? He had all those men available, and most didn't engage. And Bev…." He trailed off before outright accusing her friend.

She absently nibbled on her lower lip. Ken had an excellent point. But if not for Cody, then what? Had HIS wronged this man in the past? They didn't seem to know who Alejandro was, so it had to have been an unintentional act if that were even the case.

She'd ponder that later. Right now, she had to stay the course. "I'll get us out of here." Her tone radiated assurance.

She would. Somehow. She'd have to figure out how. Maybe when they brought food, she could overpower whomever it happened to be. They might be several meals away before she handled that. Would they drug or poison the food, though?

"I don't doubt you will. Listen in, and remember, someone will always monitor the channel, but they'll only speak every half hour with our set code words."

"Right," she said with a nod, her mind flipping back through their hastily drafted op plan. "Scooby-Doo."

He chuckled. "Yeah, Rylee picked that as one of our sets, and we happened to draw it for this op. We'll create some of our own now that we're split. When we have more time to plan, we'll create different ones per op."

Common code words were utilized on every op. Things like capture required a change of code words, and they pulled from a few, or the team leader created new ones. Ken had already used a standard one to tell them they were in a serious pickle. Making them switch channels at such a crucial time in the op only emphasized the depth of that trouble to the team. A team she'd come to trust and depend upon as brothers in arms when needed. But Jesse and what she'd almost allowed….

Full of restless energy and wanting to reassess their cell, she lifted his head, gently placed Ken's head on a pillow, and stood. As she paced to the cell door, she put the earpiece in her ear and, as expected, heard silence. Trying to peek down the hallways through the bars, she jumped back in surprise when a Hispanic man who looked like a thug approached. Too late to remove her earpiece, she tilted her head to cover that side.

In the briefest of moments, she ascertained his friend or foe status and, without hesitation, deemed him a threat. Not just because he was in the house since someone could be there to free them, but with his size, a big knife on his side, and a pistol on the other, she couldn't overpower him in her present situation. Unless she fought dirty, a smile twitched at her lips at what Kate and Rylee had shown her—and she would do just that to get Ken and herself out of this prison. But then, she'd have to get Ken out quickly.

Not hearing him approach didn't bode well for the two of them sneaking out. Sure, their footfalls would be quiet, but so would any pursuers'. She had to get a peek outside the cell since she hadn't paid enough attention to their path on the way inside. While she remembered parts of it, her worry for Ken had overshadowed the cataloging she should've been doing.

With a grunt, the man issued clipped orders. "You"—he pointed at her—"back."

Keeping her eyes on him, she slowly stepped backward. After her butt hit the wall, the thug unlocked and opened the door. Had he really thought her a threat? That almost made her smile because she could be, but he didn't need to believe that—just yet.

Another man slipped into the room and went straight for Ken. An emotional pain attacking all her senses whirled through her. On impulse, she stepped over to Ken, attempting to position herself between him and the new man, sure something terrible would happen. Her heart and mind told her that.

As the man placed an arm under Ken's and helped him stand, Ken called back to her, "It's okay…Sugar."

As he half-walked while being half-dragged from the room, in her ear, she heard, "Daphne." Their code word for the team regrouping. A burdened sigh of relief escaped her.

"Thank the Lord," she whispered. If Ken came out of

this unscathed, she'd allow him the chance to finish unfastening the love in her heart. She'd been a fool to believe that he would've intentionally harmed her husband, even if only half-heartedly.

So, if Bev lied, why?

Chapter Sixteen

After Ken endured several excruciatingly painful hours of interrogation, Alejandro Ramirez flicked his wrist in dismissal. "Take him back."

Even though almost every inch of his body throbbed painfully, Ken would handle whatever they gave him, provided they didn't touch Sam. He'd endure any physical or emotional harm to protect her. But Cody and his teammates also needed protecting.

"Let him think about his answer. We'll continue later," Alejandro told the guard.

The implied threat did nothing to Ken. He curled into the shell needed to survive while ensuring he had enough will and ability to escape. And whether it be by escape or rescue, he and Sam would leave whole.

"Jose," his host said to his goon, "don't touch the girl."

Ken wanted to ask if he meant don't touch her now or at all, but he didn't want to draw attention to his feelings for her. All special operators were trained to protect the op, including watching a teammate die to protect what they must. Said operators would take their last breath at the hands of a captor if it came to that.

In all his years, he'd never imagined someone like Sam —who held his heart whether she wanted it or not—could be the teammate in front of him with a knife to her throat. After the questions he'd been asked, their op had to change. He didn't know how to share that information with the team. The team itself didn't understand that the risk to the team had turned a new corner.

Even though he knew he couldn't move tonight unless HIS came in and dragged him out, he wouldn't stop trying to figure out a way to gain their freedom. That didn't involve providing Alejandro with the information he desired because, first, he wouldn't do that ever, and second, and most importantly, he didn't believe the man would actually free them.

Dragged from the room where he'd been tied, questioned, and beaten, he acted more injured than his actual condition to appear less of a threat. In his current state, threatening didn't define him, so he did not need to pretend to be worse. However, something gnawing in his gut told him to play the game.

Knowing every nook and cranny of the hallway would benefit their escape. The team—should they be able to rescue them—would already know this, but he and Sam had to be prepared to escape and not wait for rescue. Since the team had to regroup and make a successful plan with the small number remaining, it could be tomorrow before rescue arrived. Nighttime would be to their benefit this time.

If he had more days like today, or if they took Sam back, one of them could be seriously injured, *like the searing, painful gunshot wound to my thigh.* His heart pounded, not at his injury, but at the possibility of what they could do to Sam. If they hurt her, he'd find a way to kill them all.

Who was he kidding? He couldn't even walk by himself. That wouldn't make for a strong exit, with or without support. The term "liability" fit him, and he hated it. He shouldn't have joined the op. Sam would've outrun them and been safe.

When two men tossed his battered body into the cell, he fell into a crumpled mess and—at Sam's gasp—changed from overly wounded to hiding what pained him beyond all reason. He'd wanted to protect her, the woman he loved, but he couldn't, and that tore at his heart more than anything.

"Ken," she gasped, dropping to the floor. "Oh, my God." Her quavering voice struck at his heart.

"I'm okay," he assured her with his bald-faced lie. He probably should've saved his breath because she wouldn't fall for that. His condition was apparent. "Just help me to the cot."

The swelling in his left eye grew, and he feared it might close his eye completely, hindering his vision. He'd do what it took without it, but with it would be better. If he'd been untied—bad leg or not—he'd have kicked the shit out of the guy who'd used him for a punching bag.

"Are you sure you should move?"

Not really, but he didn't want to remain on the floor that had housed who knew what. "Just help me."

When she complied, he looked at her, and the tear that slid down her face startled him. First, her toughness and ability to focus on an op wouldn't have allowed for tears. Second, she'd turned cold toward him after they'd last kissed. Not wanting to know the actual reason, he didn't ask why she cried.

"Why did they beat you?" She strained to help him as he used her body and strength to stand.

The leg hadn't felt so bad when he'd been questioned quietly. When his torturer arrived and kicked him in his wound right off the bat, he crumpled to the floor. After that, the man's fists found a place to pound for every question he'd refused to answer or not given the answer they desired. While he'd prefer not to endure the beating again, they'd have to bring a whole helluva lot more down on him. Even then, he wouldn't break. His teammates knew this, so they wouldn't have to rush in blind. A solid plan could be formulated. But Sam…what if their captors…?

His woman held him up strong. He nearly halted in his limping tracks. *His woman?* Thinking they might not see another day, he'd told her his deepest feelings for her. Although not expecting her to respond in kind, he'd wished for something. They'd had months to rebuild their friendship and grow close. He'd felt it, lived for it. Yet she'd turned him away when he'd finally built the courage and kissed her.

Barely free of her hold, he dropped onto the cot and rolled onto his back. He tossed his arm over his eyes to block out the single light bulb hanging from the ceiling. Pain radiated up and down his torso, and he worked to push away what discomfort he could. He wouldn't be more of a liability than he already was on this op. He'd become mobile come hell or high water. A Ranger didn't know when to quit, no matter the obstacles. That philosophy had carried over to the agents of HIS.

He ignored her question. "Anything?"

Since she didn't wear perfume out in the field, it took her warm breath on his cheek before he realized her closeness. An enticing womanly scent clung to her, though only apparent at close range. "Just Daphne." Her soft voice soothed him, and a sigh escaped his lips as he relaxed a fraction.

They were regrouping, which he'd have expected at this point. If they followed the plan, only three of them would be available to rescue or cover them. Not good odds since he and Sam wouldn't have weapons, and he'd handicap their escape.

He'd forgotten entirely. "What are they saying at the top of the hour?" They needed to know the next open extraction point to find their way out of this miserable place.

Before she leaned away from him, she whispered, "Bravo."

Remaining quiet while she jostled him enough for her to sit and place his head on her lap took a monumental effort. Once there, it was worth every ache and pain.

When her fingertips glided lightly over the swelling of his eye and where he expected a bruise, it drew out another of those relieved sighs as temporary shivers of pleasure overrode the pain. If only he'd get the same relief from his other wounds.

"Where else are you injured?"

From the hitch in her voice when he'd first been tossed back in their cell, he'd known she wanted to check him for every wound. It had to be killing her just to wait for him to expound.

"I think they missed my little toe."

"This little piggy went wee-wee-wee all the way home," she said with light humor to match his.

Laughter lifted inside him, but the pain kept him from releasing it.

"Is it bad? How're your ribs? Your wound?"

She must've realized that he'd purposefully kept an arm across his chest and belly. However, he'd only answer what she asked. No sense worrying her any further. "The ribs hurt, but I don't think they're broken. The wound opened up again, but didn't bleed much as far as I could tell."

"And your face?" Her fingers whispered, featherlike, across his cheek.

With some pain, he formed a smile. "Would it make you think me more of a man if I said it was twenty big-ass bikers plus a couple of grizzlies?" Drinking in her light chuckle, he didn't care whether she answered or stroked his face and hair.

"Hmm. Men and their exaggerations. I'd give you a grizzly who'd been madder than a hornet's nest, but not more than that."

That felt like what he'd run into already. He just needed a short rest and would be as good as new. Or about as new as he'd been when he'd arrived.

"Did you find out why he wanted Cody so badly?" She fingered a strand of his hair, and his mind began that drop into blissful sleep.

Turning over a couple of things that nagged at him that he couldn't let go of. He should've addressed both of them before and clarified what his mind had conjured before they departed. Now appeared the appropriate time to start. "Sam, why did you hold back that shot?"

Her breath caught, and he noticed a subtle change in her. She closed herself off. "I don't know what you're talking about." She substantiated this with a furrowed brow and a questioning look.

He hadn't been specific, so maybe she didn't understand. "You didn't shoot the man aiming his weapon at Jesse when I first told you. It's the only shot that you didn't make within the span of a heartbeat."

"Oh, that shot." She acted innocent, but he didn't believe her for a second. "I just didn't see who you meant right away."

He may love this woman, but that doesn't mean he'd mindlessly follow her words and deeds. Yet something about this entire scenario eluded him. Not sure he'd get a different answer, he tabled that topic until a better time.

"What did they ask you?" she said, deflecting the questioning off her.

He sighed and wished he'd remember not to do that because it pained his chest. "I only had one question about

Cody."

"One? You've been gone for about half the day. Were you really that obstinate?"

And he'd suffered all those hours as they passed with the same questions, with only Alejandro and Jose, his new least-favorite person. "He only wanted to know if Cody was safe."

"He? You mean Alejandro?"

"Yes."

"He didn't want him back? That's odd. He wanted him back earlier. Why kidnap him at all?"

That's where it had gotten strange. "He wanted confirmation that Cody wouldn't go back to Beverly and that he'd go to someone who loved him and could give him a good home. If HIS couldn't do that, he wanted the boy back."

Her face brightened. "Good. We can promise that, so there's no need to hold us any longer." Looking hard at him, she must've realized what he hadn't told her. "There's more, isn't there? They wouldn't have beaten you otherwise."

How much to tell? He loved her, but in this case, he didn't know if he could trust her. One coincidence shouldn't sway his mind, but he couldn't let it go. The first non-Cody question they'd asked had him reliving her actions.

His mind couldn't settle on what to believe. If she'd been in on this, she wouldn't be in the cell with him unless her goal was to get the information he hadn't shared. But that didn't make sense either because she'd have the information they asked him for.

Because of his heart, he kept making excuses for her and didn't want her to be involved. He had to stop that and treat her like any other teammate. After letting everything brew in his mind again, he came to the same conclusion—love and trust firmly in a battle.

If he wanted to escape, he had to because he couldn't do it alone. The question was if she'd rat him out or help him. But would she only be helping him to further Alejandro's cause?

He couldn't figure out how she knew the man. She'd acted as if she'd never heard of him at Beverly's, nor when they'd been introduced upon arrival.

"Ken, what did they want?"

"He knew that even though he'd said otherwise, Beverly would call you, and you'd bring HIS. I think he'd planted that seed at some point."

If he didn't know better, he'd say her hackles rose. Whether that happened to be about the situation, the boy, or her friend, he didn't know, but she had reacted.

"He wanted HIS here." He watched her closely for any telltale signs of duplicity.

"I thought HIS didn't know him."

"I thought you didn't either," he accused.

Her hand stilled in his hair, and she stiffened. "What do you mean? The first time I've seen the man was when you did."

Her phrasing hadn't escaped him. It could be nothing, and he hated how quickly he'd come to not giving her the benefit of the doubt. She didn't deserve this from him, but he had to get to the bottom of it before any more trouble surprised the team.

"Seen?"

"What'd you mean?" She narrowed her eyes. "What are you accusing me of?"

Glad she hadn't jumped up and allowed his head to drop, he softened his tone. "I'm trying to see if there's a connection between you and Alejandro."

"I assure you there's no connection. The first time I even heard of the man was at Bev's. She never even told me about him while they'd supposedly 'dated.'" She paused before asking, "Why would you think there was a connection?"

"He knew about you."

She jerked, and it jarred his neck. While wanting to cry out, he bit his tongue, watched, and listened with his heart tied in knots.

"Me? He asked if that was my name. Obviously, if he figured Bev would call me, he must've known something about me." She paused for a moment. "So he expected me to bring HIS here? What for?"

When he waited too long, her penetrating gaze knifed through him. He had no reason to lie. She either knew already or needed to know.

"Ken, what does he want?"

"He wants Jesse…and me."

Chapter Seventeen

Sam gaped at him. She opened her mouth to speak, but no words escaped. Abandoning that effort, she lifted her chin and looked at the opposite wall.

Wanting to trust her, Ken closed his eyes to block out the pain and his unwelcome thoughts. He'd gone from wanting to get into her pants that morning to wondering if she'd been a traitor to HIS by late afternoon.

He still had the second thing to ask her. He probably should've asked this one first, but the other had risked a life, so he deemed it essential to feel her out. On the phone conversation, he'd partially overheard. He could have misinterpreted it, taken it out of context, and been way off base with the subject matter.

Kicking himself for not calling her conversation into question before they'd departed on this op or when he'd been with Jesse, Ken could only move forward and hope he hadn't risked lives by keeping quiet about Sam. He'd just never believed what he thought he heard could be true.

"You and Jesse?" she asked in surprise.

Hmm. His heart pressured him to believe her…to put his faith in her. The hardened warrior in him kept shutting that desire down.

Opening his eyes, he began, "Sam—" Fear that he wouldn't like the answer to his question clogged his throat, making it almost impossible to speak. "When Beverly called

—When she called you, I overheard something that needs explaining."

She visibly swallowed hard, and rocks tumbled in his bruised stomach. "Go ahead."

As a guise to still her hand on his hair, he grasped her wrist and held it, monitoring her pulse rate. "I don't remember the exact wording"—a bald-faced lie if he'd ever told one—"but it had something to do with you working for us and two people Beverly wanted you to kill."

Based on the way her pulse raced, he had no doubt the words had meant what he'd thought. The reality of that had him jerking away from her wrist and sitting up—albeit biting back a groan amid the throbbing of wounds—to put some distance between them.

He definitely should've asked that question beforehand, but he hadn't wanted to believe it.

Shifting forward on the cot, she left the distance he'd put between them. "Ken...I—It was Bev's desire. I never agreed to such a thing."

Hearing her sniff, he turned in time to see her swipe at a tear gliding down her dirty cheek. The face paint had blended with sweat, and it clung to her sleeve and hand. Still, her beauty astounded him.

No matter his pull to her, he had to escape and warn Jesse, getting them out of the area. Once they rejoined the team, he'd have Sam held to ensure she couldn't harm anyone or run back and help their enemy.

In a gruff voice, he announced, "If we get a chance tonight, we'll escape." How the hell he planned to do that eluded him. To save his teammates, even Sam, he'd find a way.

Her shaky voice turned his insides upside down. "I've been thinking the same thing."

Of course, she had. The woman exuded strength and confidence. He shouldn't have expected less. After seeing her risk her life for him, he'd understood how competent she was and that he'd wasted so much time watching over her.

Jesse and Stone should've been on the transport with Cody. Due to the situation, Franks and Cowboy would've returned to rendezvous with Doc.

It occurred to him that she'd said she hadn't agreed to Bev's wishes. But that shot's time-lapse made him wonder if she'd devised another plan with her friend. Why? If that were the case, she wouldn't have saved Jesse and returned to save him. Maybe he was overthinking it.

The groan that escaped him included a mix of physical and emotional pain. No matter his concerns, he just had to trust her to get him out.

"When the meal arrives, we'll overpower the guard or guards," Ken said.

"We?" she taunted. "How about me? I'm already wondering how far I can carry you once we're out in the open."

He scoffed. "I just need to lean on you, not have you carry me."

"You've never had a woman ride to your rescue, have you?"

"No," he said shortly. He guessed he'd soon learn how it felt.

"Right," she said. "Evening meal."

No meal arrived that evening.

* * * *

"I hope we're home for a while after this op," Lance Milton told his teammates over their comms.

With Jesse—Captain Hamilton—in the lead Humvee, Ken listened to his team, but his attention, like he knew theirs was, was focused on the surrounding area. They'd left civilization behind and passed only small spaces with a few shacks left standing. That didn't ease their threat, but it made things more challenging for a terrorist to follow them without notice.

"Why's that?" Adam Shodun asked with a chuckle.

They knew the answer before Lance even spoke, as he'd mentioned it many times.

"This time, I'm going to get her pregnant," Lance stated matter-of-factly as if he'd already done the deal.

With Lance being the closest thing to a best bud that he had, Ken knew the reasons for his need to impregnate his wife. Lance figured it'd make Sam leave the police force, so he didn't have to worry about her so much.

When they'd met Sam, he, Lance, and Adam had been drinking beers and talking shit at a sports bar. When Adam's now wife and then sex interest, Beverly, walked in with her extraordinarily beautiful friend, Adam moved faster than a rattlesnake striking to get the two women to the table.

Immediately, Ken felt a burning attraction to Sam. Her long blonde hair flowed past her shoulders and gleamed in the overhead lights. When her shining blue eyes met his, an instantaneous lust hit his gut with a bare recognition of a more profound emotion.

No question about it. He wanted her. However, unlike

his teammates, having a wife didn't fit his plans. Their job could mean their death at any time, and he couldn't do that to someone who counted on and loved him. He didn't understand how some of his teammates could.

Yet something about Sam tugged at him. With Beverly and Adam's heads together, oblivious to everyone else at the table, he and Lance had given Sam their full attention, and she'd divided hers between them. He'd chalked that up to her being polite.

Meeting her in the hallway, and with him being on his way to intoxication, he took one look at her in that sexy, red dress and her wide, smiling eyes and couldn't control his subsequent actions. Whisking her into his arms, he'd pulled their bodies close and melded their lips together. The touch of their chests and lips sent a pulse through his torso that frightened him.

Moving his lips, his tongue searching her mouth and dueling with hers, and his hands roaming her body, all wound into a fire that pulled him back to reality.

The depth of reach to his soul would remain imprinted in his heart, as would the hurt in her eyes when he told her that it would never happen again. Nothing would happen again. He'd then left.

Eventually, Lance asked her out, and the two fell in love and married.

His heart had crashed into a million pieces. He'd been happy for his bud and knew, listening to his plans for Sam, his emotions jumbled, knowing he'd pushed her away before they'd even had a chance.

"You say that every time. Maybe you're shooting blanks. You might want to let Sergeant Patrick give it a shot," Adam *taunted.*

Oh, shit. Why would the man say something like that? Even if he'd known Ken was in love with her, he didn't want Lance to know that.

To end this conversation and with Adam and Lance together in the second vehicle of their convoy, he halted their fun. "Eyes out, boys."

Something about the cluster of homes they approached bothered Ken. He couldn't say what because nothing looked amiss.

"Ken, you might want to put the pedal to the metal. I don't like the look of this settlement," Captain Hamilton said, confirming his suspicion.

Not questioning either of their gut instincts, he increased the speed of the already flying convoy. No one spoke, and without the need for an order, all followed Ken and Jesse's actions.

Passing the settlement on their left, Jesse leaned toward that side and scrutinized the area. Ken's adrenaline pumped double-time through his veins when he nearly turned completely around in his seat. He pushed the accelerator down further, even though it had little to go before it hit the floorboard.

"Fuck!" Jesse shouted before an explosion rocked behind them, and in the rearview mirror, Ken saw the fire bomb the second vehicle. "Stop," he ordered. Whether right or wrong, Ken did.

No man left behind. *No matter the branch of service, special operators didn't leave their comrades.*

The first and third vehicles halted, maneuvering into a support position, and the Rangers hastened out the passenger sides of the vehicles, using them as cover. During the firefight, Ken disobeyed Jesse's order and ran into the open to the second vehicle, now aflame and nearly destroyed. He didn't care if he received a bullet or died. Not only his teammates, but Lance had been in that vehicle.

Unconcerned about the heat of the door handle, he flung it open as fiery pain sizzled on his palm, and then he pulled out Lance, who'd been in the passenger seat, dragging him to a safe distance but close enough to protect. He returned to the Humvee and, because of the flames, couldn't reach anyone else. Without any cries of pain, he could only surmise they'd been killed instantaneously.

Returning to Lance, he did a quick triage, and his heart sank to his gut like a lead weight. Not only did Lance have burns on most of his body, but his hands also lay on his stomach, blood flowing between his fingers. Removing his hands, Ken saw the blood pouring from a wound to Lance's stomach where shrapnel had embedded itself.

Even though he knew his attempts would be futile, he placed his hands on the wound and gave it light pressure. He used caution to not press the metal further into him, creating more problems.

"Medic," Ken screamed over the gunfire that sounded around him.

"Ken," Lance said weakly, and Ken turned his attention from the wound to his friend's face.

Ken shook at the grief that racked him. He never liked losing his brethren, but this hit like home.

"I need a promise from you."

"Anything," he responded, tears forming in his eyes, yet he refused to let them fall.

"Take care of Sam." Blood trickled from Lance's mouth. "Please."

Things spun in his head, and a different feel reached his dream. "Ken," Sam said as his dream morphed. "Help me, don't let them take me away." His head spinning, he sat on the cot in their cell and did nothing while the guards took Sam, and she accused, "I thought you loved me."

With his heart pounding in self-pity and defeat, he remained seated, unwilling to pull her away. "I'm sorry," he said. "I'm not capable of saving you, just like I couldn't save your husband."

"You bastard! I knew I should've killed you after all."

Ken jolted awake, heart pounding and sweat covering him. His body racked with aches and pain, his thigh burning, he quickly recon'd the room to gain his bearings. Closing his eyes briefly to ward off the spots flashing in his vision, he silently cursed. *In captivity.*

"What's the matter?" Sam asked from beside him.

It'd taken a long time for them to agree on the sleeping arrangements. He didn't know which of the two held the title of the most stubborn.

"No, Ken. You shouldn't be on the floor in your condition," she'd argued.

"You shouldn't be on the floor, period," he'd countered.

"You're being argumentative when you don't have to be." Her eyes widened. "Like you used to be when I first met you. If you sleep on the floor, I'm sleeping there too."

"You're impossible," he'd huffed.

"I've been told that a time or two. I'm afraid I have to disagree, but people can think what they want. Now, I have a suggestion. Hear me out before you have a fit."

His eyes narrowed in suspicion. He didn't have fits. "Go on."

"We both sleep on the cot." She seemed proud of herself, nodding with her statement as if a done deal. When he went to argue, she'd held up a hand. "It's wide enough if we both sleep on our sides." She added, "Away from each other."

He'd agreed, if for nothing else than to keep her off the floor.

The heat from her body as she leaned over him, her hand on his shoulder, slid through his veins like a feel-good drug. With it, his pulse raced in excitement, and his dick came to life. Hell, when his body had responded to her in the past, their distance had kept the noticeability from her.

"Are you okay?" The concern in her voice reached deep into his soul.

"Bad dream," he answered, wishing he hadn't been so honest because he just knew what would come out of her mouth. God, his body felt like he'd been run over by a Mack truck before it backed up and did it again.

"Tell me about it."

Did she know her voice glided over his soul and left him feeling held in her embrace?

"It's nothing." On his uninjured side, facing away from her, his arm folded beneath his head, he kept looking forward. She'd turned over to face him and leaned over his shoulder somewhat.

"Turn over and talk to me."

Face her? In these close quarters? He'd have preferred talking in an intimate setting—maybe the bed after sex—but this setting…. He didn't know how to describe the turmoil racking his system over Sam…his love for her…her possible betrayal. Making it worse, no matter what she'd done, his body still reacted to her.

Before he turned, they both seemed to remember that he couldn't lie on his other side due to his injury.

"Sorry," she said. "Hang on."

Without turning over, he knew by the cot moving and the noticeable shimmying of her body against his that she crawled from her sleeping spot between him and the wall.

"Scoot back," she directed in front of the cot.

Although not sure he wanted the nearness or the conversation, he scooted backward with significant pain radiating down his leg and side. Renewed sweat broke out on his brow, and exhaustion settled inside his body. He'd not have made it if he'd had to move further than the foot.

Gently, she lowered herself to the cot and lay down.

"How do you feel?" She settled with her arm under her head and a narrow space between them.

"I feel better," he lied.

"Do you want to talk about your dream?"

Hell no came to his lips, but he didn't want to argue with her. No matter their past, fears, or accusations, his feelings for her were real, and right now, he needed the connection with her to focus on anything but their situation for a short while. With that in mind, he held tight to the trust issue and let his heart lead the conversation. "Do you remember the first time we met?" He didn't wait for her answer. "You had your hair flowing over your shoulders to about mid-back, about the same as you wear it now. The red dress with its frilly sleeves, or something that probably has a fashion name, I don't know. I liked that you wore it like a supermodel but weren't overdressed. As for the snug fit…," he said the last with laughter.

"If you weren't hurt all over, I'd smack you for mocking me."

In mock horror, he said, "Make fun of you? Not me."

"You used to always make fun of me." She paused. "You stopped once Lance died."

He raised a brow in question. "Really?" He wondered if she'd put it together now that he'd told her he loved her. "Sam, I've loved you since you entered that sports bar. I've never stopped. I've become the crabby old man I am today because I longed for you to be by my side and safe. Always safe."

As best he could tell in the dim moonlight streaming into the room, her eyes darkened.

Knowing they could die at any moment, he wouldn't pass up more time with her, no matter her transgressions. This woman held his heart, and he might be unable to save her life. Maybe she'd been involved in this, but love didn't always listen to reason.

With a hand that shook a little from his body's weakness —from blood loss, the beating, and lack of food—he gently placed it on her soft cheek where she'd removed most of her face paint with her sleeve. The strength of his longing moved him forward, but the possibility she'd deny him rolled in his gut. He couldn't stand denial a second time. "Sam, I'd like to kiss you. May I?"

It took her a moment, and that indecision almost had him pulling back in resignation. Then, she slowly nodded.

Euphoria hit him before he'd even kissed her. Just the fact that she'd agreed went a long way to mend his heart.

Leaning forward as if he had all the time in the world, his

eyes moved between her lips and eyes. The beautiful blues sparkled in the near darkness. That might've been his imagination from years of thinking about them.

Without a care for the small cut and slight swelling, his lips lightly touched the edge of hers, and that romantic nonsense lightning struck. He'd heard women talk about it and thought it a fluke the first time they'd kissed, but he'd admit it occurred. Some electrical current could flow between them when they touched, but this….

Her breath caught, and it brought a smile to his face. It'd hit her too. Moving over her lips to the far side, he placed another featherlight touch on her forehead. His slow seduction held equal measures of pleasure and pain. And not from his injuries.

Leaving the far side of her lips and noticing her breath mimicking his, he touched his lips to hers full on, but in a quick kiss.

Pulling back, he looked at her eyes, unsure what he'd see, but he hoped it'd be desire. Something better flowed between them. Something hard to explain but essential. He no longer needed the conversation about trust. Seeing it… feeling it in their connection told him all he needed to know. How could he have ever doubted her? They'd always been connected, but this new level had deep and real feelings that surely couldn't be a lie or anything she could damage or toss away. He believed in her…in them.

A small smile appeared as if both had realized it at the exact moment.

He couldn't wait any longer to savor the kiss and passion she held away from him. He'd wrangle it at some point soon.

Against her slight smile, he whispered, "I love you."

His lips reclaimed hers with a long-held hunger, and he enjoyed the sweet taste of her. A taste that he could quickly drink every day to work himself into a drunken state.

Before he could nudge her in that direction, she opened her mouth and welcomed him in. Their tongues immediately touched, and that longing grew, and he couldn't fight the arousal that tightened his BDU pants.

While his need drove him, he fed off her strength, desire, and passion. The intensity of their want skyrocketed between them.

Shifting his head, he took more of her, and their lips meshed so tightly they could've been one, and he wouldn't change it for the world.

Their tongues tangling set him afire. One kiss might not be enough. One kiss wouldn't be enough. But it had to be for tonight.

His lips loved hers long, tenderly before. Regrettably, he lifted them and chuckled when she moaned.

Pulling her close, regardless of the pulsing shot of pain from his injuries, he wrapped his free arm around her. After placing a light peck on her forehead, he whispered, "Sleep."

As she snuggled against him, Ken tried to calm his out-of-control hormones. He didn't know what tomorrow brought, but they'd survive it together with Sam at his side.

Chapter Eighteen

"**R**oadrunner."

The male voice in her ear roused Sam from sleep ever so slowly. Nodding off for the night in Ken's arms had been the most beautiful feeling in the world. A miracle considering their situation. She'd always relied upon herself and trained enough to never fear anything. Lying as they were, though, warmth flowed through her at the safety and strength, which far exceeded any she held for herself.

Her life held serious regrets, the most important being that she'd considered facilitating this man's death. The fact that she hadn't acted didn't make it right.

She needed a round with a punching bag to clear her head. She did not need to discover Ken's version of the truth the day Lance died. He'd given it to her so long ago. She never should've doubted him. The strong connection between them, or from her heart—although it was involved —but from knowing Ken…watching him in action… witnessing his morals…being tugged toward him were there. She mentally shook her head. The last one wasn't mind, but body.

What turned her inside out was that Bev had lied to her. Her new question became: Did Bev know the information was false—Sam's belief—and feed it to Sam, or had someone assured Bev of its authenticity? Either way, she'd been betrayed and had considered making a mistake that would've burned in her soul for eternity.

It saddened her that it'd taken such dire circumstances for

her to realize the truth. And the emotions she'd been blocking. Her feelings for Ken. Pity settled in her stomach. She and Ken may not have a chance after all this. It didn't help that their captivity and questioning made no sense. She also worried he might be unable to take much more.

He didn't fool her that he felt okay enough to escape. They could if she had to drag him. The thought of him being tortured again strengthened her resolve to help figure this out. No, they wouldn't give up Jesse, but if they could buy time—

"Good morning, beautiful," he said in a raspy morning voice as if he'd greeted her each morning for a lifetime.

"Morning," she mumbled. He looked like a mess. With smudged face paint that had made it to his shirt sleeve, to the bruising and slight swelling on his face. At least his eye hadn't closed up. She called that a plus.

Before she could worry about how to overcome her morning breath, she stiffened. "Roadrunner."

Ken's muscles tensed. "Shit." He released a heavy breath. "As much as I'd like to remain lying here with you, go ahead and get up. We're due for company."

Before she left his arms, he quickly kissed her lips. Her heart sang with that contact. She'd experienced something similar with Lance, but that memory had mostly faded. With Ken, her body hummed with only a touch.

"I wish they could say who." She scrambled off the bed. "I mean, I know they can't say in case communications are compromised, but still, I wish." At least they knew a new visitor had arrived. That could mean something to them or not.

"You slept with your earpiece in?"

She shot him a skeptical look. "Of course."

"Sam," he said as he stiffly maneuvered to a sitting

position on the cot. "What if they'd grabbed you from sleep?"

"It could've just as easily dropped from the ponytail holder in my hair."

Sam worried for him as he ran a hand down his weary face. For them. What did this new visitor mean? Granted, it could just be a neighbor stopping in for a visit. The sinking feeling in her gut told her this person or persons were related to their imprisonment.

Turning away, she mulled things over in her mind. Alejandro wanted Jesse and Ken. If their assumptions were correct, Bev ratted them out, and the man knew to expect them. But why just the two? That answer came quickly to her. The two men Bev wanted to die. Bev. But why would Bev have her son kidnapped?

Either Alejandro—out of some misplaced loyalty—was taking on Bev's desperate revenge or…. She didn't want to think about it, but everything made sense.

She whirled around. "I think—" She gulped and hoped to get the message past the enormous lump in her throat. "I think Bev might be behind this, and maybe her return. She could've gone home, but something tells me that's not the case."

How could her best friend do this? While she had no room to talk since she'd once considered the same scenario, she hadn't gone through with it. She also hadn't had someone kidnapped and put the whole HIS team at risk. Nor had she imprisoned her best friend.

"Yeah, I've been thinking about it the whole time. She became my prime suspect once you confirmed what you and Beverly had talked about."

She opened her mouth to speak and didn't know what to say. Although she'd never verbally admitted it, he'd seen right through her. She closed her eyes to the pain of what could have been. He had to know the truth.

"But Alejandro seems like a sane man and successful. Why would he do this for her?"

He shrugged and grimaced. "The only thing I can think of is for a twisted love. I just don't see how Cody fits into the equation."

"That's turning over in my mind, too. Ken," she hesitated, "I need to tell you something."

The air crackled with tension at her statement. "Go ahead."

His voice had taken on his "boss" role, sending shivers of dread through her veins. She didn't know what to do if he blamed her or turned his back on her. They finally had a chance, and she'd almost tossed it away.

"You need to know why Bev wants you dead, and I—" She couldn't look at him or speak. How the hell would she get through this? In no way would she look good. Not that she deserved it, but she didn't want to lose what they'd become.

Her heartbeat raced and pumped warm blood through her at a rapid pace. Fear for what he'd think gripped her. When he didn't speak, she continued, pouring out the story, making herself hold his gaze. "You know she blamed everyone for her husband's death and hasn't let that go. She still believed you and Jesse, as the officer and NCO of the team, should've been brought to justice even though the incident review showed nothing of the sort. Not long ago, she told me she'd had someone investigate it in depth and had proof you and Jesse were responsible."

His jaw worked, but he continued his silence, and she backed herself to the wall, hoping it'd hold her steady.

Her heart pounded, and she nearly felt faint having to tell

him what she thought. "She showed me the information, and I—" She gulped and cast her gaze down, unable to admit the truth to his face. "—I believed it." She looked up and used her hands to emphasize her hurried admission. "I didn't want you dead, but I admit to considering that you needed to pay since the army didn't do anything."

She paused, hoping he'd say something. When he did, her heart plummeted to her toes since it was one of the few things she wished he hadn't asked. "Is that why you held back the shot on Jesse? Did you hope he was killed?"

Her gaze snapped up to his and met the steel wrapped around his presence. How could she overcome that when she wasn't sure of the truth? Something had flicked through her mind when that held-back shot happened, and a small—minuscule—part of her mind thought the opportunity for Jesse to pay had been at hand. Ultimately, she couldn't do it. No matter if they'd shot her husband outright, she couldn't kill them.

She slid down the wall, pulling her knees up and resting her arms on them. "I'm not sure. Something slowed my reaction, but actually killing him—or you—wasn't something I could even agree to. Bev wanted me to. While I considered all options, I couldn't do any. Not only am I not a killer—bar op necessity—but I believe in you. Lance believed in you. I never should've accepted a word of the report she'd sent me."

The quiet stifled the small room. Disgust with herself riddled her body. She had to have his forgiveness, not only so they could continue on together, but so she could let go of the guilt as much as she could.

Pulling all her courage, she looked back at him to catch his gaze on her with what she guessed as consideration or confusion. But not hate. Not yet, anyway. "I swear, Ken, I never agreed to kill you. I never agreed to any payback. Yes, I considered something needed to be done, and yes, I listened to what Bev wanted. Ultimately, I know the kind of man you are and that the intel had to be false. Although it was too late to realize that."

"What'd it say?" The words seemed to be painfully yanked from him.

A weary sigh slipped through her and left calm in its wake. "It said a lot that I should've realized what was bullshit earlier. The summary is that—" She raised her brows to emphasize her next point. "Know that while it held Jesse responsible since he was the team commander, it also included you as the senior enlisted. Bev couldn't see differently. It said that you and Jesse stayed behind the rest of a larger convoy, and because you waited too long to return to base, you took an alternate route that went against the battalion commander's orders. When you were attacked, it stated that you'd refused to call in medevac either because of safety or to cover your tracks. It took an extra hour to get out of there, and the men died en route, not on the scene as we'd been told. The report speculated that the men could've probably been saved in the lag time if you'd called in a medevac."

Too late, she realized how ridiculous it sounded. She'd allowed her emotions to rule instead of her mind. Thank God she'd wised up before she did take any revenge. "Ken, I'm—" She stopped. Ken appeared to age ten years, and it ate at her gut.

In a weak voice, he asked, "Do you still believe it?"

"I told you that I didn't. I was a fool even to think that of you. I can't say how sorry I am. Maybe if I'd been brave enough to ask you, we could've helped Bev see the truth."

He worked his jaw again, and she knew it meant he did it

to keep his temper in check. "I doubt it would've mattered." He patted the seat beside him. "Come here."

She rose to her feet, walked to the cot, and tentatively sat on his noninjured side as if a bomb might be present.

He took her hand, and she waited.

"It breaks my heart you'd think such a thing of me, but dammit, I still love you. No, don't say a word. Let me finish. If the report seemed legit, I can see how you'd question everything. But God, I wish you'd come to me about it."

Pulling her hand up, he lightly kissed it, and Sam stiffened, unsure of what to expect next.

"Since you started explaining, I've been changing how I feel about everything. You not believing in me, not trusting me, and even considering harming me are hard to swallow. Yet, two things jumped up and grabbed the hurt I felt. One, I know how deeply you loved Lance, and as a grieving widow, something like that would turn you inside out, and coming to me would've been the last thing you could do. Second, and most importantly, no matter what you'd thought, while you said you hadn't decided whether to exact some sort of vengeance, you did decide. You decided not to harm Jesse or me in any way."

Her voice cracked. "Will you ever forgive me?" Waiting to respond to her confession, her stomach lurched, and her body ached, fearing he'd turn her away. She only hoped her stupidity hadn't cost her something she'd waited years for.

A life with Ken.

With her breath held, Sam searched Ken's eyes. She needed those three words…craved them. Not the three words most women wanted to hear—what he'd already said —but the other three words.

"It'll take some time to get rid of the hurt, but I love you, and, corny as it is, love conquers all. We trust each other on the job. We may need to work on that trust on the home front. We won't let what happened stop us from a future together."

Her eyes misted, and her vision blurred. He still loved her. How had she ever gotten so lucky?

"All in all, I forgive you."

Those magical words lifted everything from her heart until her passion for life, and this man resided there.

He dropped her hand and opened his arms. "Now come here. I need you in my arms. We'll make it through this."

She snuggled in, careful of his injuries, committed to convincing him of her loyalty. She'd grab this forgiveness and absorb it into her soul. She'd do whatever it took to earn and keep it.

Relaxed from him running his hand through her hair, Sam leaned back and looked at him. No woman could ever be so lucky as she was.

"What do we do now?" Hoping not to push it, she mimicked his prior action by finger-combing his disheveled hair. Damn, he looked handsome, even with bruising and swelling on his face. She caressed her fingers over the roughness of his bruised, whiskered jaw and split lip where the thin line of blood had dried. It had to have bothered him when he'd kissed her. Yet it hadn't stopped him.

"We wait. We don't know for certain it's her, and you know we've been surprised as hell at times."

That was true. Crazy people didn't always show themselves from the beginning. They checked out well, then went off their rocker at the most inopportune time. Like, there actually was an opportune moment for that transformation.

"Whoever it is won't have Jesse. He'll come back, but he has to take care of getting Cody home."

Her heart lurched, and she dropped her hand. "What will he do with him?" Cody's not being with people who loved him worried her. They hadn't planned to take him back to Bev's, so she didn't have that worry.

Ken shrugged, then grimaced. "Since you're not there, he'll probably leave the boy with his housekeeper since the women are in Montana. I imagine Jesse's sent for them to return for Cody's sake and ours. I won't object to any of them at our six."

"Good." Jesse's housekeeper would take great care of Cody. Heck, he'd probably be too spoiled to come back with her. "If it's Bev, maybe I can talk some sense into her," she said with hope, but the reality of that probably not being the case sat heavily in her gut. "If they're going all the way home, our backup dwindled in numbers."

"I imagine Jesse will find a way to make both happen. He always does."

A sudden thought stalled her. If it were Bev and she'd finally arrived—or come back to confuse HIS—what would happen to Ken? Alejandro must've been playing with him until she arrived. Bev's goal was death. Would she kill Ken today?

Bile rose in her throat, and she swallowed it down. No. She would not lose Ken. She'd almost made the mistake of losing faith in him. Never again.

She had to stop Bev before that happened. She'd learned the folly of her ways. Maybe she could help Bev understand the same and release the hatred before she did something she'd regret.

She swallowed hard. Bev had been too far-gone when she'd spoken to her last. She should've realized something when her friend finally agreed to HIS—especially Jesse and Ken—taking over the search for Cody. With frustration, she jumped to her feet, walked to the door, and held onto the bars tight enough that her knuckles turned white. How hadn't she seen this?

She shook her head. It was pointless dwelling on the what-ifs. She had to keep her teammates safe.

Damn that woman!

"Sam, come here."

She released a burdened sigh and turned back to the man who'd changed her. The man who'd always stood by her, even when she hadn't deserved it. A man she didn't deserve but refused to turn away. She'd been rendered powerless to do just that.

After sitting by Ken again, he reached over and clasped their hands together, resting them on her thigh. Some of her worries ebbed, or maybe he just instilled enough confidence in them to overcome anything.

"Take your earpiece and hide it in a gap between the bed and the wall. If our assumption is correct, I think you'll be pulled to visit with her. If it's not her—"

When he didn't continue, she turned and saw him working his jaw. Knowing Ken as she did, he wondered whether to fight them or not if they took her. It had to be hard on him since he wasn't at full strength.

"I'll be fine. No matter what. If you fight with the guard, they could hurt you worse—maybe even shoot you again—and that won't help us escape."

His Adam's apple bobbed. "I can't trust it's her, Sam. I can't."

Her eyes misted. "Here," she said, changing the topic, "let me see your wound."

The chuckle that escaped him lifted the heaviness of their previous topic. "Which one?"

Shaking her head, she stood. "Lie down and let me see

what you've got going on."

As he maneuvered himself back on the cot, he waggled his eyebrows. "Do you want to see *everything* I've got going on?"

His good humor told her he'd moved forward, and while they weren't perfect, they were together. So, like a giddy schoolgirl, she tittered and blushed.

After she poked and prodded Ken, she tore strips from the bottom of her T-shirt to cover his bullet wound since it had seeped during the night. Once finished, he stood and stretched to loosen up the kinks and tight limbs to prepare for whatever came.

Even though their stomachs rumbled, they didn't discuss the lack of food.

Heavy footfalls approached—she preferred that better to the silent guard—and Ken stepped in front of her, blocking her view of the door and the guard's view of her.

The air around her rattled with some noise. Ken actually growled at the guard—just one more thing to like about the man.

A key rattled in a lock, and a heavily accented voice directed, "Girl."

It'd been a good thing she'd been hidden, as somehow she didn't think he'd have appreciated her rolling her eyes. *Girl, indeed.*

"No," Ken asserted, animosity dripping from him.

Needing to see what transpired in their cell, Sam lifted herself on her toes, stretching her neck to peek over Ken's shoulder. He must've sensed her movement because he shifted to block her view. What she'd seen made her blood run cold.

The guard filled the entrance. No wonder Ken didn't want her to go. She gulped, and her heart pounded loudly in her ears. Going with this man would be wrong if she'd misjudged the situation. Very wrong.

Ken stiffened, and a trill voice interrupted the showdown between the two men. "Jose, you did great work on him," Beverly Shodun said.

Sam closed her eyes against the pain of witnessing the evil of the woman she'd called her best friend.

"Sam, quit hiding behind the man responsible for our husbands' deaths."

Before stepping around Ken, she whispered near his ear, allowing her hand to press against the arch of his back a moment, "Trust me." She'd lost that with him once, so she could only hope he'd give her a chance.

Clearing Ken, she came face-to-face with a crazy woman. "Bev," she said with feigned relief. "Thank God you're here. They've kept me locked up. Had I known you'd be here, I'd have complained louder."

Bev studied her as if judging whether to trust Sam. Crazy people had some sane moments. Bev would, too, so she'd have to watch herself.

With a broad smile, Bev waved her out of the room, and she followed. "I'm sorry. I just arrived this morning, and they didn't know."

Widening her eyes, she asked, "I don't understand. What about Cody? HIS rescued him. They were bringing him to you. Jesse and one of the other men left with him."

Bev stopped about midway down the long hallway. "You mean Jesse isn't out there waiting to rescue you?"

Furrowing her brow as if in confusion, Sam asked, "Bev, what's going on? This doesn't make sense. You hired us to rescue Cody from here. We did, and he's not here, but now you are."

She waved her hand as if to flick off the topic and began

walking with Sam on her left side. "Oh, that."

Sam bit her lip, waiting for Bev to expound, but she didn't. The cell door slammed behind her, and she wanted to look back at Ken and assure him she was acting, but didn't risk anyone noticing. Instead, Bev led her into a large dining room with bold red colors.

"Sit, Sam." Bev kissed Alejandro on the cheek before taking a seat beside him. Sipping coffee, he appeared perfectly sane. Yet he seemed to have a relationship with a crazy woman still. And it looked as if he'd bought into her scheme. Finally, Bev had the means to make trouble for Jesse and Ken.

She wanted to press Bev for her plans and their release, but she knew better than to let her cards show. Besides, her stomach rumbled, and they knew she'd had nothing since she'd been brought into their custody. She needed fuel to keep her strength up.

As she eased into a high-back chair, she thought her words through before she said them and what her possible rebuttal would be. "Are you going to feed Ken?"

She held her breath for the answer. The depths of Bev's sanity remained unknown.

Looking at her as if she were crazy, Bev halted before drinking her coffee and calmly asked if starving a man was expected. "Why would I?"

Sadly, she'd expected that question. "What do you want with him?"

Bev set her rose-themed china coffee cup back on a matching saucer. "He'll pay. So will Jesse."

Sam's eyes flitted back and forth between the two. Disgust swamped her when Alejandro reached for Bev's hand, entwined them, and kissed the back of hers.

Good God. Since Bev apparently had Alejandro's full

support, she also had the men employed at the compound.

"Okay, you'll have to explain everything to me. But I think, if you want to have him beat up more later, you'd want him aware of it instead of out of his mind with hunger and thirst. Or if you're waiting for Jesse to join us, you'd want to keep him alive. So, unless you plan to kill him right now,"—*Please, God, don't let her say yes*—"then feeding him makes sense. It doesn't need to be extravagant. Some tortillas and some water would even do."

Again, she held her breath. Something told her she'd do that quite a bit more with Bev in her state.

"That makes sense." Bev turned to Alejandro. "Would you see to that, honey?"

Didn't they have a ton of servants and guards? *Oh*, Bev must want her alone. Perfect. Time to play her role, and thank goodness Ken wouldn't see it.

Watching Alejandro leave, Sam turned back to Bev and put on an excited look. "Bev, you've done it."

The woman lifted a shoulder as if it meant nothing. "When you didn't make it happen, I had to do something."

Stuffing a piece of tortilla in her mouth to keep from spouting something that would blow her true feelings, Sam waited. After swallowing and taking a drink of bottled water, she sighed dramatically. "I know. I just never got in a situation where I could make it happen without getting caught. I mean. I wanted them to pay, not me. I've paid long enough. Just like you." *Time to pick up your feet with how deep you're shoveling it there, Sam.*

Having Bev scrutinize her every word and facial expression made the ruse challenging since she didn't want her to know that Sam couldn't have gone through any plan.

"I want Ken and Jesse to die, side by side, like Lance and Adam," Bev stated calmly as if that were a typical statement that didn't involve murder.

She closed her eyes against losing her husband, but she'd moved forward, and Ken had her heart now. She'd protect him with every fiber of her being.

"Well, then," Sam said. "We'd best get Jesse back here. Had I known your plan, I'd have made sure he hadn't been the one who took responsibility for Cody."

Bev didn't even wince at the mention of her son, and pain for Cody trickled through Sam's heart.

"Okay, tell me how many men are out there and who they are."

Sam almost snorted aloud at Bev's request. Like she'd rat out men who had risked their lives for this woman's son.

"Well, one man stayed behind, but the others left with Cody to return him home to you."

The click of Bev's perfectly manicured nails on the table grated on her nerves. "Will they come back for you?"

Walking a tightrope, she nodded. "Someone will. It might not be them, but someone will."

Alejandro walked up behind Bev's chair. "Where do we find this Jesse?" Returning to his vacated seat, he offered, "We could send someone to his home and collect him."

Water almost snorted out of Sam's nose at that. They could barely get on the grounds of Jesse's homestead if they had a passcode. Devon's system would catch them in a heartbeat.

"That could work," Bev agreed. "We'll keep Ken alive until then." She turned back to Sam. "Where does he live?"

Continuing to dig deeper into her acting skills, she shrugged. "I don't know. I've never been to his home." *Lies, lies, lies.*

Several ideas spun through her mind. If she showed her agreement with Bev, she wouldn't be returned to the cell.

She had no idea what they would do to her if she didn't agree.

Acting like a light bulb had gone off in her brain, and her path became clear, she excitedly said, "Wait, I know how we can get it."

"How?"

She smiled brightly. "An idea is formulating in my head to get that information, but tell me everything that's going on and your full plans, and I'll make sure we can make it work. Together." She nodded as if agreeing with herself and pasted on what she hoped displayed as a sinister smile. "Oh yes, I think we can make this work for both of us."

Chapter Nineteen

With a great effort that occasionally wavered, Ken bit back the aches in his body. Weak from blood loss, dehydration, and hunger, he wouldn't allow it to topple him. Putting light weight on his leg and limping around the room had been successful. It hurt like hell, but he could manage. For how long at a time, he could only guess.

Full of fear for Sam, he stood at the door. Even with the warmth from inside the ten-by-twelve space of his prison, the steel bars felt like ice in his hands. His gut twisted with worry about how her meeting was progressing. She'd asked him to trust her, and, in their predicament, he had no choice but to do so, even when his heart lurched at the way she'd greeted Beverly.

He didn't trust Beverly. If she'd convinced Sam of the validity of that damn intel report, would the crazy woman believe Sam still believed it and stood with her?

Calling himself all kinds of stupid, he should've been more thoughtful and more stubborn about their sleeping arrangements. Anyone could've looked in on them and fed Beverly their cuddling position, which Sam would've had to talk fast to justify.

Concern about whether Beverly would go nuts—more than when they'd left her—and hurt Sam had him shaking with a terror that emanated from deep within his heart. Although not wanting to admit it, a pang of outright fright tried to bubble up within him that Beverly might bring Sam around to wanting him and Jesse dead. The passing of their husbands had undoubtedly strengthened the bond between them.

Closing his weary eyes, he leaned his forehead against the inescapable cell door and wanted to slap himself for thinking such thoughts about Sam. She admitted she'd fallen for Bev's faulty info and couldn't get aboard the crazy train. She may've had a moment or two of weakness, losing her focus, but it'd only been a few days since she'd been fooled. He believed her, heart and soul.

In the months since she'd moved to Baltimore and they'd worked together, they'd tightened up their friendship and become closer daily. That growing bond helped soothe his bruised heart, as he knew the woman she was. The Sam he'd fallen in love with. The woman who'd smiled, and a glow of happiness and contentment surrounded her. That is the woman he'd given his heart to, even though she hadn't been aware of his love until now.

As for her heart, she may not love him—and he'd been prepared for that—but she deeply cared for him. In fact, he'd seen a raw, genuine desire in her gorgeous blue eyes—as well as he could see in the near dark. The small window, sitting up high with square bars, allowed very little light to spill into the room. She wouldn't't've been able to kiss him with so much passion or relax in his arms if he hadn't stirred something deep within her. And he would continue to stir up her emotions until she either made him the happiest man on earth or finally crushed his heart.

No matter her ultimate decision, he'd never stop loving her.

When HIS hired her, his body had hummed at the thought of being close to her daily, and he enjoyed every minute. Granted, seeing her in danger still didn't sit well with him, but even though he worried, they worked well together, and it only strengthened what was between them. He just needed to get them out of there so they could go home and crawl into bed together.

Lifting his head from the bars, he stopped himself from turning and pacing. He'd already figured out the mistake in trying that. Walking was fine, twisting not so fine.

Although Sam had searched the barren room, he'd checked every nook and cranny and come to the same conclusion. The room and sparse contents offered nothing useful. Any metal springs on the uncomfortable cot would've been a bonus, but instead, it had been made of wood and bolted to the floor with concrete screws he expected to be embedded very deep.

Even at full strength, he wouldn't have been able to break the legs from the floor or the wooden base of the cot apart. Then the other object—a disgusting bucket with the aroma of past use-had been their bathroom. Lacking a secure grip or any weight to make a difference, only the smell or actual contents would aid them momentarily.

A small chuckle slipped out, and he cursed himself for not remembering the pain in his chest when he did that. At least he felt confident the ribs weren't broken. Maybe a couple might have minor fractures, but mainly bruising. Although not having heavy damage hadn't been for lack of trying.

Painful breathing would follow him on escape, but he'd suffer like a champion. The leg, though. ...

Where had his thoughts been? Oh yeah, the bathroom bucket. At first, Sam had refused to use it, but she'd caved after a full bladder. But not before making sure he not only turned his back but he'd covered his ears.

After she'd left with Beverly and Jose—he hated that man and hoped to get revenge—he removed the small earpiece from the hiding space. More than ever, he realized, that'd been the right idea to keep it out of both their ears. He didn't know what Beverly would've done if she'd found it. Alejandro and Beverly's goons hadn't used the microphones yet, and he hoped they didn't figure out the frustration they could cause the team's members monitoring the station in case Ken or Sam broadcast. Not that the team would be fooled by mindless chatter from their captors, but it'd clog up the airway.

"Velma." Ken closed his eyes in relief. Franks had come up with a plan. Based on the few code words used, three men—as he'd suspected—were watching. One at each gate and Doc in the middle to play his role of Shaggy. Instead of leading the tangos to a trap, Doc would protect his and Sam's six and lead the hired guns astray. That was assuming that he and Sam could escape. What he wanted to hear, although he doubted he would today, was "Freddie." That meant he could expect the cavalry.

His hackles rose, and his heart leaped into his throat when he heard Sam's distressed voice calling for help. What the hell had happened? He'd figured that Sam would stay with Beverly and hopefully get him released. Instead, one of his fears had come true. It appeared Beverly had gone off the deep end—deeper than before—and since she couldn't bring Sam around to her way of thinking, she'd kept her as a prisoner.

"No!" Sam shouted, "I won't go back in there." Then louder, she screamed, "Bev, you can't do this! I thought you were my friend."

Shaking the bars to push his way through and effectively throttle the man holding Sam against her will, a deep-down rage exploded within him. His entire body shook to keep himself from snapping and hurtling over the edge and attacking the guard, which could make matters worse for them. Being utterly helpless behind bars, he held it all back. And being damn vulnerable hurt not only his chance of survival but Sam's, too.

He'd promised Lance he'd take care of Sam. Yet he found himself in a situation where he could not meet that promise, which cut him deep.

He blocked the despair that tried to push its way forward in his mind and heart. "Never give up" was a well-known motto for military special operators, and he wouldn't. There had to be a way. Had to.

Since it appeared Beverly didn't plan to use Sam to follow through on whatever lunacy she'd planned. He hoped Sam had been able to extract something that would aid them. Sam would've uncovered something if Beverly hadn't told her specifically. He believed in her abilities.

With his limited vision since the bars held him back, he couldn't see Sam, but he could tell by the shuffling and grunting noises that she struggled with her captor. Her pleading calls to Beverly went unanswered.

As a gentleman and man of honor, he'd never struck a woman. He'd taken some down and had to use some strength. But if Beverly harmed Sam, he'd rethink the honor he held to not abusing women. She'd messed with Sam, who held his heart. That meant she'd messed with him.

Somehow, Beverly would pay. HIS would ensure it. He'd appreciate it if only they could take care of it now.

Coming into sight from his left, Jose propelled her forward with a tight hold on Sam's forearm. She fought every step of the way, digging in her heels, attempting to wrench her arm away, and stumbling into the man.…

A smile broke across Ken's face, and he ignored the pain of stretching his skin on the bruises, burns, swelling, and abrasions. *Good woman.* He hoped she could reach the cell with the blade she'd just lifted from Jose. With the handle in her free hand, she flipped it and hid the blade inside her shirt sleeve so it wouldn't be detected. In fact, she'd lifted *her* knife. She'd been upset at being parted from it, bringing a smile to his heart.

In one of his weaker moments, he'd gifted her that knife. The three of them—he, Lance, and Sam—had browsed a weapons store. He and Lance were always on the lookout for something new and lethal. Sam admired a knife. Not just any knife, but a smaller one that would've been perfect for her. The boot-size blade remained in the locked glass case when they'd departed the store. She hadn't said a thing, but he'd seen her longing look.

Since he had no say in her career choice, he could only think of how to help keep her safe—on and off duty. He'd presented her with the knife for her birthday that year as a gift. Lance hadn't been too happy, but in the end, he'd relented. The way Sam's face had lit up with joy, he'd have happily pissed off his friend worldwide.

"Back," Jose directed.

To remove Sam from Jose's touch—that undoubtedly bruised her—Ken didn't fight the request, even though he longed to give the asshole a taste of his medicine. Backing to the wall, which took only a few steps, he collapsed to the ground and bit back his curses and exaggerated groan of pain. Knowing the trouble he'd have rising from his current position, he remained on the floor, challenging his nemesis with a lethal glare.

He'd considered rushing the man and the two of them making a run for it. He used the common-sense God had gifted him with and acknowledged his physical limitations. He'd recognized that leaving in daylight would likely be their death sentence. He'd never put Sam in more danger than he already had because he hadn't been able to get away with that damn limp of his.

Sam must've realized the same because they had a great opportunity when Jose opened the door. She could've shoved her knife into Jose's heart, and the two escaped, but she passed up the opportunity. Although he wished she'd stab the motherfucker for what he'd done to him.

She hadn't even seen the worst of it on his upper torso. The heat still flowed under the skin on each mark, with his salty sweat gliding over the marks. Ten in all. He'd not relished it, but they'd have to devise worse torture than that. Even then, he wouldn't give them what they wanted. Not Jesse.

As Jose shoved her into the room, Sam winked at him, then turned back to her guard and continued making a ruckus.

Something lifted inside him. Her smile told him they had hope.

Chapter Twenty

With an indignant grunt, Jose slammed their cell door, then departed the area without a word. Sam might've figured out something to help them, but he definitely couldn't tell by her behavior. The woman cursed like a sailor and even kicked the bars with her boot. He held back the smile at her reaction.

Once quiet, she turned to him and mouthed, "Trust me."

He nodded, and immediately the woman started caterwauling again. He awkwardly and, with some severe discomfort, stood on his own. Sweat dotted his forehead from the effort, and he knew that doing it himself took too much out of him. He'd have to suck it up, having her assist him if he wanted to walk.

Her following words jolted him—in a good way. Her melodrama brought a chuckle from him, but he bit it back and played the game Sam had started.

"Oh, Ken, hold me." She launched herself into his arms, squeezing him around his waist. She loosened her hold at his sharply indrawn breath of pain but didn't pull away. This, he liked. Her body was snug against his. No matter the injuries pulsing in his body, the heat between them sprang up to a roaring blaze that would one day soon be extinguished with the two of them naked and well-loved. Even then, he imagined things would smolder between them until they made love again.

"I can't believe how she treated me."

Automatically, Ken stiffened at her words. What had Beverly done to make Sam go on this much? Sure, he'd figured she'd been playacting for Jose, but he didn't know if she did now. Sam didn't appear injured, but he could've missed something. Or, it could've all been mental.

Then, the best thing happened. She lightly kissed his neck between her pretending to whine and sobbing. Enough to tell him she still playacted. She must suspect someone down the hall was listening. He wanted it over because even knowing her emotions weren't real, it sliced into him that she could be that pained by a woman she'd called a friend.

Taking advantage of her sham outburst, he reached down, cupped each cheek of her butt, and pulled her close. He leaned toward her ear before she could extricate herself and whispered, "How much longer are you going to behave like a crazy woman and not the superior warrior you are?"

When she leaned back, leaving little space between them, and narrowed her eyes, he silently acknowledged that it had been an unfair question if she still played a part. She unwound the weaponless arm and lifted a finger to his lips for silence. He, of course, sucked the slender digit into his mouth. What else was a guy to do in that situation? Her need for him to be quiet had been evident, but she could've just as easily put her finger to her lips. He liked her choice better.

Her gaze softened, and, to his satisfaction, an eager hunger clouded them. He itched to kiss, taste, and show her his love and desire. Without anything tangible to validate it, he knew it'd be the next best thing to heaven to be inside her. That day couldn't get here fast enough. He'd endure any amount of pain to make her his.

Instead of acting on his desire, Ken kept eye contact with her and focused on listening to their surroundings. Sure enough, the echo of footfalls disappeared down the hallway. Before he could speak and ask anything, she snatched her finger back, cupped her hands behind his head, leaned up, and covered his mouth with hers. Not just a peck on the lips, a deep, hungry kiss that gave him more than he could imagine.

A low, guttural growl escaped him. That act, and not just the actual meshing of lips, had his body humming with a pent-up desire that he would unleash on her one day.

He brought his right hand up and cupped the left side of her face with his thumb under her chin. With a moan, he pushed his tongue between her soft lips and searched for hers. The warmth and sweet taste of her nearly undid him. Their lips tangled, and he took seconds between each stroke to taste her fully. *Pain be damned.*

He had no idea if she realized how she affected him. If she had any sense—and he knew she did—she'd feel his physical need for her growing. She wasn't a blushing virgin, so she'd understand unless she chose to remain oblivious. Well, hell, he'd already told her, so it shouldn't matter.

With his left hand still cupping a perfectly rounded butt cheek, he tugged her snuggly back into him, and her pleasure-filled moan sent his pulse skyrocketing.

She wasn't a complacent participant in the kiss. No, she brought heat and lifted onto the balls of her feet to meld them closer. When her tongue dominated his, the heat shooting to his groin raced.

Even though he tried to remain aware of his surroundings, this woman took everything from him without asking. Their bodies snug against the other, and their lips fused, drove his anticipation, dreaming of the time they could continue without an audience.

Audience. He jerked his senses back to their surroundings. His chest heaving and his heart racing faster than a race car in the Daytona 500, he pulled away from their kiss and dropped his forehead to hers. Seeing her delicious breasts heave, he pressed a light kiss to her temple, took a deep breath, looked up, and prayed for the strength needed to see them escape alive.

Falling into a loose embrace, they didn't speak right away. After waiting longer than he'd wanted, he asked, "Are you okay?" He'd wanted to run his hand through the strands of her hair, but she'd been provided a brush to restrain her hair in a ponytail holder again and, based on the minty taste of her mouth, a toothbrush to freshen up. Why, then, did Beverly send her back?

"I'm fine." Her eyes misted, and that had him stiffening. Was that a woman's "I'm fine" that men had to be concerned about?

"I'm so sorry."

Her statements didn't get better as she said them. Concern laced its way through his thoughts. Cautiously, he asked, "Sorry for what?"

"I'm sorry I didn't see this coming from Bev."

One notch of his stress level was reduced. "Let's sit down and talk."

She nodded, keeping her gaze averted. He'd rectify her guilty feelings. In no way would he hold her responsible for that maniac's behavior.

As they shuffled to the cot and sat facing each other, she nodded to his food tray on the ground near the door. "You didn't eat much or drink water?" she asked. "You know we need to stay hydrated. I drank as much as I could with Bev."

Suppose it'd only been that easy for him. He needed fluids badly. That bottle would not touch his lips. "Drugged."

As she indelicately dropped back on the cot they'd somehow managed to squeeze on together to sleep, she shoved the knife into a boot sheath and focused her gaze on him. "What?" Her disbelief once again validated that he could trust her.

Nodding, he managed to sit without collapsing in a heap beside her. "Pinprick hole near the top of the bottle."

"That bastard."

Bastard? Not bitch? He must have missed something because her vehement response left no doubt in her statement. "What?"

"Alejandro," she spat out. Reaching over, she took his left hand into her soft right one. Absently stroking the back of it with her other hand, she continued. "He oversaw your meal prep. I thought he'd been gone as long as he had to give Bev and me time. Now, I see that it hadn't been the case." She squinted at the tray, primarily full of food. "What did you eat?"

The only thing he thought was safe. "The tortillas. After the water, I wasn't too trusting."

"Hopefully tonight it'll be better."

He squeezed her hand. "How can you say that?"

Gazing at each other, warmth flooded him at the glow that overtook her face. Her excitement and triumph were there for the world to see. "Bev and I came to an understanding." She reached into her pants pocket and extracted a bronze key resembling the cell door key.

Quick as lightning, he swooped in and gave her a light kiss. It took all his will to pull back and keep the vital conversation on track. He wanted nothing more than to devour her lips and make her his. He needed to escape to do just that. "You're amazing."

He reached out for the key, but her words froze his movement and optimism. "She'll keep hurting you until you give up Jesse because she wants the two of you here simultaneously to torture and kill. I assured her that no matter what, you wouldn't bring Jesse into danger. So, I agreed to get that information from you."

His hand froze, his heart stuttering a beat.

She quickly added, "It's a ruse."

He searched her gaze, only finding warmth. "Okay. Tell me."

"We're escaping tonight."

Chapter Twenty-One

"Tonight?" Ken asked. Hope laced his voice, but leeriness reigned. Then he shook his head. "It'll be too dark in the jungle. With all the overgrowth, little to no moonlight shows through. Remember, we used NVGs and a GPS on the way in. Beverly's goons confiscated all of it. We'd be flying blind in the pitch-black."

Biting the corner of her lower lip, Sam silently agreed. She'd been so caught up in their chance to be free, she hadn't considered the risk of leaving at night. She'd only thought the darkness would allow them to slip by the tower guard unnoticed. But they might not make it home if they did and ran into a predator—two-or four-legged, or even slithering—while unarmed.

"Before we talk about escape," Ken said, "tell me how you managed to get a key. I saw you lift your boot knife from the guard, but he'd have noticed if the key had gone missing since he needed it to lock the door."

She smiled with pride since she'd caught something he'd missed. Not that he wouldn't have seen it eventually, but she did first. "Haven't you noticed that the door has an automatic lock? They only need the key to open it. It locks automatically when closed."

He furrowed his brow as if searching his memory to substantiate her claim. The look on his face tickled something in her stomach. He exuded strength and stern resolve. Yet she knew he also had a softer side that drew her. The man with the combined attributes and the warrior willing to extend mercy to those who deserved it made up one hell of a man.

How had she ever even considered that he could've acted so maliciously? Like when Lance had been his subordinate, the HIS agents were under his command. If one of them died in the line of duty, she wouldn't blame him. She'd blame those who killed the man or woman she'd come to respect.

Seeing what that hate and misplaced blame had done to her friend, Sam was glad she'd wised up before it'd been too late. Watching Bev and the ugliness that had resided inside her for so long made her heart ache for her friend.

Even after the words Ken had overheard from the get-go, he hadn't treated her differently. He'd not set her aside on the mission, and he could've. He'd worked with her, but he could've done that for one of many reasons. To watch her. To participate. To give her the needed support. It didn't matter. He stood by her even before he'd discovered her intentions.

"Before we go on, I need to apologize again."

His fingers covered her lips. "Shh, you don't need to keep apologizing."

She nodded, and he moved his hand away. "Tell me."

"As we guessed, the kidnapping was her ruse to get us here. To get you and Jesse here." Damn Bev for doing this. "As we guessed, Alejandro is doing this for her. He appears to be crazy in love and wants to banish her demons. I think he wanted Cody to have a good home."

Sighing, she continued. "I screwed up. On the phone, I let it slip to Bev that we weren't on an op. She knew you and Jesse would be available, but couldn't chance you two not responding, so she involved Cody. You wouldn't step aside for a Ranger's kid." She sighed. "I think I was a little upset we didn't go out, considering most of the new team had been off, and I didn't pay attention to my words."

"It's okay. Jesse had a reason for making that call. We didn't pick up the last op mostly because of you."

The words slammed into her with the impact of hitting a concrete wall. She hadn't expected that answer. "Me?"

Nodding, Ken rubbed the wound on his leg and closed his eyes momentarily. "Yes, you. Based on the information gathered, the op Bravo went on—the rescue didn't need a sharpshooter. That doesn't mean it wouldn't, but at the time, it didn't. Because you're the best, Jesse wanted you available should we snag something last minute,"—he cocked his head to the side in a cute gesture, although he'd probably not like that term for it—"like this, that required your expertise."

She looked at him with watery eyes. Maybe this could've been prevented if she'd only spoken up earlier. Heck, Ken had been shot, tortured, and held in captivity. She'd never forgive Bev for the destruction she was delivering.

His thumb tapping a rhythm on his good leg, he gazed over her head. "Did she create the false report?"

Nodding, Sam bit her lip. "She admitted to it." This time she shook her head. "I'm not sure why because she's held a grudge against you and Jesse all this time, placing the blame at your doorstep."

"I'm guessing her hatred turned into a need for vengeance somewhere along the line. Why wait so long?"

Sick to her stomach, she guessed the answer as he voiced it.

"You. You were now in a position to do something."

"And I had told her that—" Her eyes widened.

Embarrassment be damned. "I told her I had feelings for you."

His tight smile faltered a bit, and a small quirk appeared at the corner of his lips.

"Since," she continued, "she realized she truly had no way to get me to take action, she attempted to manipulate me."

Ken nodded his agreement.

"And I almost fell for it." She jerked away and up from the cot. "God, I could kick my own ass." She paced the small space. "I thought—" She swirled back in the other direction. "I thought—" Tears filled her eyes, and she hated it. Not only because it made her look like a girl who couldn't hold her own on a mission, but Ken had to witness it. She stopped and dropped her head in her hands. A comforting hand stilled her shaking shoulders.

"Sam, getting upset at yourself will help no one."

She turned into his arms, her head buried in his shoulder. "Bev and I went through so much. I can't believe she'd go this far. You know we were friends before we married, remained friends during, and grieved as friends after. Maybe I was lucky because I also had you while I grieved. Maybe that made it worse for her. I don't know." She squeezed tightly around his waist. "I'm so glad we found each other again."

At those words, she snuggled in closer but cautiously around his ribs to avoid hurting him any worse. When a hiss slipped through his teeth, she pulled back. Had they retaken him while she'd been with Bev? No. They couldn't have. So what sparked that level of sensitivity?

"Ken?" Concern and bewilderment mixed in her question.

"It's nothing."

Reading the lie in his dark eyes, she tugged his T-shirt up. Her breath caught in her throat. "Are those cigarette burns?" she choked out.

Chapter Twenty-Two

Based on the fresh tears streaking down Sam's face, keeping the extent of his injuries secret had been the right move. While awkwardly sitting on the cot, he'd pulled her into his shoulder, rubbing her back to soothe her.

"I'm so sorry," she managed through his hold and her tears.

"Shh, sweetheart. This isn't your fault."

"But, Bev—"

"Beverly had you kept in this cell until she returned, and if you hadn't agreed to help her, you'd have probably been back here but without a key." His gut revolted at what Beverly might've done to her—or could still do if she discovered the truth. They had to escape before that happened.

Trying to turn the conversation away from his injuries and gloomy thoughts, he said with a light-heartedness he didn't fully feel, "A key that I can't use."

The desired effect happened. She stopped crying, almost with a halting of breath. "What'd you mean?"

The level of perplexity in her voice brought a smile to his face. She knew the reason, but her mental focus had left her.

He looked down at her, hating the redness surrounding her slightly puffy eyes. "Think about it, sweetheart. My arm is too large to reach through the bars and turn the lock."

"Oh, right." He didn't take his eyes off her as she leaned

away to sit back, sniffling. "My call sign is Sugar. But, I like you calling me sweetheart."

It had been way too long since this woman had been romanced. Maybe she had not remembered that he'd always called her that endearment, even after she and Lance had connected. "Don't worry. I'll remember Sugar when the time is right. Otherwise, I like 'sweetheart.'"

With her nod and the slight smile on her lips, he pushed forward even though he'd prefer nothing better than to pull her back into his arms.

"Okay, let's get back to the important task in front of us. Finish telling me about Beverly's plans and anything you learned that could help or hinder us."

Back in her warrior mode, the renewed strength from her reinvigorated him also. "As we've said, her ultimate goal is to ensure you and Jesse pay." Sam furrowed her brow. "Although she and Alejandro—who she'd never stopped dating—managed this rather quickly. I wonder if she'd already had this as an idea to draw you two out. Alejandro had offered to have the two of you killed. He's quite obsessed with her."

"If she doesn't go out much, how'd they meet?"

She shrugged. "They said they met at a hotel bar."

"You don't sound convinced."

"Maybe they did, and maybe they didn't. Bev"—she hedged—"was into some kinky stuff."

"Oh God, please don't get specific. The last thing I want in my mind is that woman dressed in black leather and carrying a whip." He squeezed his eyes shut. He'd done it to himself. "Dammit, too late." He reached up a hand to squeeze his eyes closed, hoping to block out the revolting image.

While she didn't laugh outright, he heard the levity in her voice. "She and Adam did well together with that."

He opened his eyes and stared at her. "She told you about her and Adam having sex?" Good God, what did these women do when the men were deployed? He'd expect they traded recipes, but it sounded like they traded whips.

"No. Stop worrying. She let it slip once. Anyhow, what I was saying is that she used to be on websites for that stuff, and she met a lot of people that way."

"And Alejandro is—" He didn't know what to call him. Master?

"I don't know. I'm saying that was how she met out-of-town people who enjoyed her preferences in bed."

"I can't deal with that right now." Taking her hand, he squeezed lightly, offering her silent support. "What did you two agree on?"

"Oh, since I told her Jesse had left with Cody back to the States, she fumed, and I formulated a strategy. I let her know they'd be at Jesse's house, but I didn't know the location."

Pride splashed across him, and he didn't hide the smile for her. "Why, you cute, little double agent."

She elbowed him in jest. She slipped her hand from his and covered her mouth when he grunted. "I'm so sorry, Ken."

"Don't worry about it. It didn't hurt. It took me by surprise."

"Are you sure?" The uncertainty in her voice almost broke him.

She'd asked for forgiveness, but exonerating herself might be more of a problem. Somehow, he'd help her, even though it would take time.

"Yes, but we're getting nowhere. Tell me what's going on, and no sidetracking."

That did it. That brought out her grin. His also. It's always been the joke between them that she couldn't have a conversation without branching off two or three times while never getting to the end of any story.

"Okay, let's see. She wants you two at the same time. You won't give Jesse up. I pretended not to know where he lived, so Alejandro couldn't grab him. I'm on a mission to worm the address out of you so that when I'm done, I can let myself out and tell Bev." She crossed her arms over her chest and proudly harrumphed.

Oh, how he wanted to chuckle at her and her satisfaction for being concise. Instead, he stayed on target like he'd challenged her to do. "How long did she give you?"

"Originally, she wanted the information before dark."

"And now?" he asked cautiously. What would the woman do if Beverly expected her to return and she didn't? He didn't like the ideas turning in his head. With her being unpredictable—

"I convinced her"—Sam's smile brightened—"that the morning would be better. Just in case I need to use my womanly charms on you to get that pesky old address."

He raised an eyebrow. "Resourceful, aren't you?" His smile sounded in his words.

"Are you patting yourself on the back since you made sure I was before you allowed me on my first op with HIS?"

He ignored that, but a chuckle rumbled through him. "Anything else I need to know?"

"Since I assured Bev the rest of the team left with Cody,

Alejandro recalled the men on patrol. Most of them," she quickly corrected. "I only overheard part of his conversation with Jose and one of the men who'd captured us. I asked Bev about it. She said they kept a roving patrol around the outside perimeter and some in the jungle. At her frown on the conversation, she gave me the impression he'd cut the number. I can't be sure of that since she didn't translate it all. I do remember my numbers in Spanish, though. If it matched his conversation, he's barebonesing it."

He mentally counted men.

"That's assuming we can trust Bev."

"Hmm." He rubbed his hand across his hard-whiskered face, trying to puzzle out what he wouldn't give for accurate intel. "Why is he dropping his numbers so low? He should be expecting HIS to attempt to rescue us."

"Maybe to give them some rest since I assured them there weren't enough HIS agents to mount a rescue yet, and we could get to Jesse before then."

"And they bought it?" He shook his head. "Obviously, they did. Do you think this is a trick? Did Alejandro know you were listening and wanted you to pass on false information? Or that Bev lied to you?"

"At this point, either of them could've."

It worked well for him and Sam that Alejandro relaxed his security, but it also bothered him. Then it hit him. The man had the same setup when they'd rescued Cody. This meant the men in his barracks were ready, and bringing the fight inside the gates gave them the advantage.

They were taking the fight outside the gates. "Once we leave the house, we have a bit of ground to cover before we hit the wall."

"Do you think your leg can take it?"

Probably not, but his life depended on it, so he'd go to hell and back if that's what it took. "I'll make it happen. I'll limp more than before, and as long as I don't spin around suddenly on that leg, I'll be there with you."

She settled her head against his shoulder. "You can always lean on me if you need it."

There was no question he'd end up leaning on her at some point since they had a lot of uneven ground to cover. "I might have to. Listen, if I tell you to run this time, I need you to do it."

She shot up, leaping from the cot, almost clipping him under the chin before whirling on him with fire in her eyes. "No."

Sighing, he knew she'd fight. "Don't argue. Just listen. That's a lot of ground to cover, and we must move fast. If we're lucky, Doc will see us and provide cover."

"How will he know what direction to expect us?"

He smiled crookedly. "Opposite the barracks."

She nodded. "What about the other guys?"

Without being with the team when one of their own had been held captive, she had no idea what to expect when it hadn't been discussed. It'd been a no-brainer to them since they'd become such a cohesive team. It reminded him how they couldn't go lax in their preconceived notions. "They'll stay on each gate to catch anyone hampering our escape."

"I guess when we plan these things, I never expect to be the prisoner."

"Come sit back down," he coaxed. She did, and he continued, "From the little bit of recon we did before dawn yesterday, on the north side, there are blind spots where the spotlights don't cover." The large spotlights covered a large portion of the area. Only a paranoid bastard would go to that level.

"How're you going to get over that wall?"

He might not, but he'd not tell her that. He'd get her over first, and nothing that happened to him after mattered. "It'll be fine."

"Any—"

"Son of a bitch," he burst out, reaching into his ear and removing the listening device.

"What?"

Soothing Sam's alarmed voice, he smiled. "She figured out those were microphones. I just had a blast of heavy metal in my ear." Ken started to stick his finger in his ear and rotate it around, hoping to reverse the loud music's effect. Dropping their voices back down to a whisper, he leaned close. "Why would she do that if you told her no one was around here?"

Sam appeared to have the same question and no answer. "I don't know."

"I don't think she trusts you as much as you think she does."

"I think you're right. Do you think she's overheard us?"

Doubtful, since they'd done quite a bit of talking across the room, even if softly. Their plans and strategy had been whispered. "I don't think so, but we'll keep talking low."

"Are you sure we can't get out tonight?"

Wishing he could agree, Ken shook his head. "If there are patrols—inside or outside the jungle—they probably have NVGs. We don't, so we can't escape any pursuers."

"Maybe I should leave now and give Bev some bullshit

so I can find our equipment."

He shook his head. If only it'd be that easy. "No, I don't trust how she'll treat you now, and I don't want to be separated. We have to hope since she told you this morning we have that much time. We'll break out when the sky begins to lighten, when it's not so dark, so we can get over the wall and into the jungle before dawn breaks and Beverly comes looking for you."

Having to put faith into something that a maniac promised bothered the hell out of him. He didn't see any other choice. If they left in the black of night, they wouldn't get far enough away to make it worthwhile. And that was if they didn't run into any other trouble, which was a big possibility.

"Do you remember all the turns from the front door to here?"

He hadn't fooled her by pretending to be unconscious when they dragged his sorry ass in here. "Sure. I can get us out. I just wish we had more than your knife."

"I'm more worried about finding the rendezvous point without a GPS to get us through that foliage," she admitted.

A grin of satisfaction crawled across his face. "If I know Jesse as I do, he anticipated our losing everything. He probably tossed almost every piece of his equipment to Franks and Cowboy with directions to get it to Doc before he and Stone departed with Cody."

That still leaves them in captivity for a while—maybe days. With no lunch or water, his apprehension grew. Was Beverly playing out the ruse and treating Sam like a prisoner? Or had she realized Sam's deception? His gut clenched at either possibility. He only hoped they brought some drug-free dinner because he needed something to rebuild his energy. He also required fluids. Badly.

To pass the afternoon, they reminisced about their lives with Lance and even times with Adam and Beverly. With each story, Sam relaxed, and a lightness appeared to fill her. Her freshly cleaned face shone with a glow of happiness.

While some of the stories involved only the two of them, neither brought up the two times they'd kissed before the other night.

Hearing steps approaching, Sam moved away from him. He reached over and slid her knife from her boot. A small surge of fear zipped through him. If Beverly had come for Sam, he'd die before allowing it a second time.

Instead, a man accompanying Jose appeared, carrying a tray with their evening meal. Ken's stomach rumbled with hunger, but eating food from a crazy woman bent on vengeance meant hunger reigned supreme.

Jose allowed the man to scramble in and out, placing the tray on the floor. Seemingly satisfied, the man retreated. When the footfalls stopped, he and Sam looked at each other.

She broke first. "Are you hungry?" Moving to the tray, she continued. "This looks good."

"I am. I'm even thirstier."

After setting the tray on the cot, Sam picked up a water bottle and examined it while she prattled on to appease anyone listening. "There's this perfect red dress that I have my eye on back in Baltimore. Do you think Kate would like to shop with me?"

With great effort, he held back the laughter at the thought of either of the two women spending their time in a dress store except for a special occasion. Then he remembered the red dress she'd worn the night they met, not the specifics, but that it'd been red and fit her perfectly. "I don't know."

"I know you and Jesse are close, so you could help me find out. Maybe I could go over to visit."

He rolled his eyes at her poor acting skills. "Maybe. Let's eat."

At his cutting off the conversation, footfalls continued away from them. He hoped Sam's questioning of him would be satisfactory enough to keep Beverly from coming early.

Sam put down the water bottle and shook her head. Knowing if he didn't drink his water a second time, they'd know he'd caught on to them, he hobbled over to the bucket and poured out the contents. The two of them would be long gone before it'd be noticed.

When she brought him the second bottle with a shake of her head, his confidence cracked, and blood roared inside him, dropping heavily in his stomach.

Beverly planned to drug Sam, too.

Chapter Twenty-Three

Worried about what Beverly might do since she'd expected both of them to be drugged, Ken hoped it'd just been something to make them sleep. He shuddered at the thought that she might've tried something more harmful to himself and Sam.

It'd shaken Sam that her friend—no matter how crazy—had tried to drug her after the afternoon they'd had together and the pact they'd made. A fake alliance, but Beverly wasn't supposed to have realized that.

Ken rose from the cot—careful not to wake Sam—and checked the hallway as best he could. With the latest development, they'd kept a watch, taking turns so they wouldn't be caught off-guard. With only the tiny knife, they'd be limited but not unaware. Noting no one and with all quiet, he reached for the earpiece and checked to see if the comm was open.

Beverly had switched to salsa music. Being a country music fan, neither heavy metal nor this worked for him. It definitely wouldn't work for whoever on the team had monitoring duty.

With a shrug, he had to go with what they'd heard last. After dropping it into his pocket so Beverly wouldn't find it after they'd gone, he began to stretch his injured leg. He had serious concerns over how well he'd do on the run. Holding Sam back and putting her in danger once again weighed heavily on his mind.

If things went as planned—or ad hoc as they'd need to do with a limited team—he and Sam could make it to the rendezvous point in two days due to how much he'd slow them. He imagined he'd have to stop for the night and rest instead of pushing forward. As a decoy, Doc should pull the guards in the opposite direction and follow up to pick up his and Sam's trail. Covering their trail also relied on whether they could rendezvous with Doc and gain weapons.

Not being sure-footed, they'd undoubtedly leave a path where they would cut through the jungle when they diverted off the main paths that ran through it to the house and main road.

Ready, he turned around and saw the slivers of morning light attempting to break through the heavy darkness. The time had come for them to leave. They had to get over the wall and to the jungle's edge before dawn broke.

With renewed vigor and adrenaline pumping, he touched the shoulder of the woman he loved, rousing her from sleep. Like him, she'd slept lightly, and within thirty seconds, she stood, ready to tackle the day's challenges.

Unable to stop himself, he pulled her tightly against his chest and, with his heartbeat quickening, captured her lips in a soul-searing kiss. Knowing this could be the last kiss they shared, he didn't hold back, wanting this moment to put a smile on their lips.

Moving his lips over hers, he nibbled and memorized the soft feel, the perfect shape that accentuated a beautiful face. As if choreographed, they opened simultaneously, tongues tangled, then mapped out the other's mouths in familiarity.

They'd shared several kisses while in captivity and held

each other close. He wanted more. He didn't give a shit how much his face and lips pained him.

He craved a future with this amazing woman by his side.

Without breaking their connection, he mouthed, "I love you" over her lips. He still didn't expect to hear it from her, but with the way she gripped him and suffused passion into their kiss, she had feelings for him, even if only desire. He could work with that. Building up from there was more appealing than if that need didn't exist.

He lifted his lips from hers with an unwelcome force pulling at him. "It's time." Before he let her go, he placed a lengthy kiss on her mouth. "Stay safe for me."

Sam looked up at him with those blue eyes that made him want to dive in and take a drink. "You stay safe for me. Don't ruin something we should've made happen long before now."

"Marry me," he blurted. His control had momentarily escaped him. It had to be that uncertainty they faced. Hell, he'd rushed to tell her he loved her when he thought they might die. Now didn't appear much different.

Her mouth dropped open, and her eyes widened with shock. Opening and closing her mouth like a fish, she finally got out, "I—" Without trying to finish that word or sentence, she stepped out of his embrace. Pulling the key from her pocket, she avoided responding and asked, "Are you ready?"

A slice of disappointment lanced him even though he shouldn't allow it. She had to realize they were destined to be together soon enough. Straightening his spine and focusing his mind on their path and threats, he nodded.

Sam reached through the bars at the door and fumbled a

bit until the key fit into the lock. She turned back to him before she turned it because they knew it made a light click. It shouldn't attract anyone unless they were close. They'd already zeroed in on how far they could open the door before it squeaked.

She looked back at him. Their gazes connected, and before a fierceness took hold, they had a final soft moment. They nodded—time to go.

Turning back around, Sam worked at lightning speed to unlock and open the door.

Ken slipped out and took a right. His leg, while painful, didn't interfere with his fast stride. It reminded him of the pain in his chest from the injuries to his ribs.

No matter the issues, he'd lived through worse. Just because the Rangers were some of the best didn't mean they couldn't be ambushed. Not a day went by that he didn't silently thank Jesse for getting evac'd out.

It appeared he needed Jesse to do that same thing again.

Stopping right before a hallway intersection that he'd almost missed in the darkness, the two of them plastered themselves to the wall. He peeked around, and with the glow from another portion of the hall, he cleared them. Grabbing Sam's hand, they turned left and hustled toward freedom, at least from the house.

As they passed each room, they stopped and peered in, looking for any threats. The house was quiet—as would be typical this time of the day. He hoped that whoever monitored the indoor cameras wasn't paying attention. They reached the final spot before the front door.

Staying hidden, they observed the foyer for activity, alarm systems, and the locks on the front door before moving into an open space.

Adrenaline pumped through his body, forcing his heart to hammer in his chest and excitement to flood his nerves. He could barely even describe how his senses calmed, honed in on success, and every step, every thought, and every emotion required such discipline to see it through to the end.

Assured the coast was clear—although he didn't doubt that possible guards were hiding—and with a nod, they moved to the door.

He figured that since Alejandro had a compound and guards, he must've felt safe enough not to have security in his home. Fool.

With a tug on Sam's hand, they slipped outside.

Since the east gate lay before them, they followed the front of the home to the north side as planned. When they ran out of cover, they found the path that held the barest of light, something they slipped through as only a shadow.

Letting go of her hand, he used hand signals to count them down. At the ready, they darted toward the wall. As they progressed, Ken noticed his limp became more pronounced as the struggle to use injured muscles increased. His gut clenched with fear that they'd get recaptured or killed. Biting back that emotion, he returned to observing his surroundings and getting out of there.

Once they reached the wall, he stopped, cupped his hands together, and boosted Sam. Although she had the strength to pull herself over a wall, she couldn't reach the eight-foot height.

Damn, if even at six-one and with his long arms, he had to hop to reach the top, which meant an almost unbearable pressure on his leg when he pushed off. With one try, he almost crumpled to the ground before his feet left the perched position, before jumping. If he remained here long, one of the roving guards might spot him. He started to jump again, but the pain radiating through his leg hampered the effort.

Knowing Sam waited on the other side prompted him to make another attempt. He needed less than a foot of airtime to grab the top and pull himself over.

He silently cursed and prayed. He'd done a great deal of both on this op.

Knowing he couldn't allow the first challenge in their escape to be his last, he shifted his weight to jump. When a masculine arm reached out for him, he froze.

Chapter Twenty-Four

Shoving her knife back into the sheath, Sam grabbed the M4 Doc handed her. Alert, she stood guard while he leaped up and reached over the wall to assist Ken out of the compound. It hadn't taken him long to join her after her failed attempts to help Ken. The only thing she could think of was to get to the team and have one of the men help. But she hadn't wanted to leave Ken either.

Doc must've seen her fruitless efforts to scale the wall back into the compound as he appeared at her side in no time.

How the large man moved so silently left her mystified, but his sudden appearance scared the crap out of her. The two remained silent. He'd tossed her his rifle and bolted to the top of the wall as if he'd been born to climb. Facing forward, she hadn't seen him pulling Ken over, and the silence unnerved her.

She could only surmise that Doc had been patient and remembered Ken had been injured. Since he'd watched when she and Ken had been captured, he'd surely watched the men drag Ken inside the compound. Knowing how she'd feel, it must've wrenched at the big man's stomach for not being able to help one of his own in rescue and give medical attention.

Hearing a whisper of a sound, she guessed their feet had landed. And she'd been right, except Ken collapsed and grunted right after that.

Instead of turning to help him, which her heart screamed at her to do, she remained vigilant.

After Doc helped Ken up and held him tall, he whispered in her ear, "The boys have the guard towers and gates. You watch the jungle."

With a nod, they moved forward, and she focused on potential threats, fighting her instinct to check on Ken. With Doc holding him up, they walked at a fast clip.

Less than fifty yards from the jungle, the high-pitched cry of an alarm ripped through the air. Fear climbed up her throat and churned in her gut. While her teammates were exceptional agents, none of those remaining were snipers. Although glad Jesse had left, having him now would've assuaged her worry. But if their men could keep the threats busy, that's all they needed.

As dawn met the skies, they entered the jungle and were plunged again into near darkness.

Doc stopped the group and turned to Ken, "Tell me."

"Through-and-through on the thigh. Bruised ribs. Not broken."

Sam added, "Don't forget cigarette burns." She could single-handedly kill Bev. After all, she'd put Cody and Ken through.

Doc raised an eyebrow at that. "Can you make it, Boss?"

"Yeah, I'm a little slow going, but we'll make it. You'll need to house me at Point Charlie because I'll never make it to Bravo today."

Gunfire from the fortress broke their conversation, and Sam wondered if the men could prevent too many tangos from escaping through the gates.

Doc nodded. "I'll pass it along. Here." He thrust a GPS tracker toward Ken. "Don't get lost and end up in Guatemala," the big man joked.

Since the Lacandón rainforest spilled across the Usumacinta River into Guatemala from where they stood in Chiapas—Mexico's southernmost state—landing in Guatemala could be a possibility with poor navigation.

"You seem to be mixing me up with Franks."

With a smile at Ken's response, Doc presented the Glock from his waist and handed it to her. It became apparent he wouldn't be joining them. Something else they'd briefed before the op. They planned for so many what-ifs that it astounded her. Now she understood why.

"Point Delta has a bag for you. We'll rendezvous with you before nightfall at Point Charlie. If we don't make it, continue to the extraction point tomorrow. Old Man and Stone will be back by then with the bird. In the meantime, we'll keep an eye on these assholes and keep them busy until you get to safety."

Doc stiffened, and she figured he'd heard something from the other agents. "Go. A few are on the move and coming this way. I'll take them out or lead them away, so you have time. More weapons are in your pack."

Before either could say anything, he pointed. "Go." Doc took off back to where they'd entered the jungle.

Without her assistance, Ken limped at a fast clip in the direction Doc had pointed. She followed with the Glock in her hand. Routinely, she turned, and her alert gaze swept 180 degrees behind them in case someone slipped through or had already been in the jungle.

Where another small animal trail connected, they turned

onto it, following the GPS with its programmed path to Point Delta.

She started when the gunshots moved from the compound into the jungle. Doc putting himself out there as bait didn't sit well, but she'd have done the same for him. By leading the hostiles astray, she and Ken had an increased chance of getting away.

Ken stopped and turned right into the jungle without a trail to follow. It didn't appear thick, although they'd have to weave through low-hanging vines.

Maybe Ken sensed her presence. Perhaps he caught her in his peripheral. Maybe he knew she'd be there. Whatever the reason, he didn't look at her before he led them through a place where she knew snakes existed, and if one dropped on her shoulder, she'd unload the magazine she had on it. Protection be damned.

After turning to check their back trail, she almost bumped into Ken as he leaned into some big-leafed plant. Had they had more time to prep, they could've learned a bit about the flora and fauna of Mexico's Lacandón rainforest.

When he pulled out an olive-green backpack, she almost wept with relief. And when he reached behind it and pulled out a rifle—not just any rifle, but Jesse's sniper rifle, where he'd changed the barrel for their close-in situation—she almost gasped with relief. She hugged it to her chest, her confidence in their self-protection growing.

Instead of squatting down, Ken bent over to pick up and check things in their pack. Seeing his discomfort, she crouched before him and conducted an inventory of the bag. She spied an M4 for Ken, hidden against a tree. Jesse and Stone must've turned over their supplies. This group had the best support system she'd ever witnessed. Maybe if the men she'd worked with on SWAT had accepted her as these agents had, she might've enjoyed the job more than she had.

In her inventory, she first saw a full water bladder with, she suspected, electrolytes and thrust it at Ken, knowing he needed it first as he'd been the longest without something to hydrate. She wouldn't tolerate his gentlemanly manners when they needed each other to survive.

Finding a SIG in a rear holster, she checked the ammo and handed it to Ken, who passed her the water back. They placed the holsters and sheathed knives on their backs and sides, each with a full hand. The setup wasn't ideal, but with a rifle that, for her at least, took two hands to hold when firing, her choice would be to keep it in the bag or reach it in a flash.

Going back to the bag and seeing extra clips for their handguns and rifles, she distributed them, and they filled their pockets. Handing back a sheathed knife to Ken, another KA-BAR in a sheath near the bottom caught her eye.

Briefly picking through the items, the sight of food bars made her mouth water. She handed Ken one and took one for herself. They needed one on the go and couldn't wait for more. As she nearly guzzled the water, her gaze caught a blanket and two NVGs, which would be handy in the jungle. Excitement grabbed her when she came across a night vision scope for her rifle. Shuffling around the other items, she spied one for the rifle they'd left with Ken. There were more items they could use, but the small first-aid kit had her just as thankful as the weapons. No matter how much he fussed tonight, she'd clean him up if they didn't rendezvous with Doc. She wished they had time now, but getting them to safety took priority since he wasn't bleeding out or anything that severe.

As she was about to close the bag, her gaze landed on the golden egg of equipment—next to their weapons—an earpiece. *Heavens be praised,* she wanted to shout.

Jesse, I'm sorry I ever believed Bev. Giving us your gear may save our lives. Thanks, Stone, for also leaving your pack.

After handing Ken the components of their lifeline, she secured the bag, and without asking Ken his preference, she slung it over her shoulders. When he didn't protest, her concern for his health mounted.

He looked pale and had begun to sweat when this would've been a cakewalk any other time.

Time to move forward to get them closer to home. "Where is Point Charlie?"

"Las Golondrinas waterfall."

Quickly searching her memory of the map they'd studied, she grimaced. "That's a good clip."

"Not as far as the evac point. Don't worry, we'll make it," he assured her, although he'd done nothing of the sort.

"All right." She hadn't noticed him breathing so heavily, but realized she needed to pay better attention.

"Look," she said before he took off, "you need to get used to having a woman rescue you instead of the other way around. Sure, you can care for yourself, but you're injured and not at your normal capabilities. Lean on me, and we'll get through this."

He chuckled and folded his arm over his ribs. Her heart cried out in pain for him. "You just make me love you more each day."

Flustered, she just stared. He freely kept admitting his love for her. She needed to survive this to know what she truly felt. Too much was wrapped up in their situation, and it shouldn't be a consideration for something so life-changing. No, not changing. Life-defining.

Before she could go down that road, he said, "If I remember correctly, we'll follow hiker and game trails unless we need to divert against threats. There's a small village, so we'll skirt that."

She nodded, then held out her hand as if to motion him forward. "Lead on, old wise one," she jested.

Ken rolled his eyes at her. It brought a giggle she immediately stifled. They needed to focus on getting home.

Leading them back to the trail, Ken kept them faster than she'd expected him to carry with his injuries. As before, she constantly checked their six for trouble and wished they had a machete in case they had to go into the thick jungle to cut through the foliage and snakes.

Ken swept his gaze back and forth. Without any other support, this was the best they could do.

"Think the boys will make it tonight?" she whispered as she turned back.

"I don't know. It depends on whether they can keep the hostiles off our trail and avoid capture. They've taken out the guard towers, but as we've seen, they'll get replaced. We need to keep as many as possible inside the fence around Alejandro's home."

Frustrated, they left the agents to fend for themselves. She swallowed hard. She had to remember everyone could take care of themselves and more, but the need to protect rose in her. Right now, she needed to protect Ken.

Ken continued, "When we first left, four tangos cleared the field before Franks and Cowboy took out the guard towers. Those are the ones Doc led astray." He glanced at her and then looked forward, his eyes roaming the area and the ground below for threats.

"The team'll stay as long as they think a threat will come to us. Then they'll hoof it to Point Charlie or Bravo, depending on time."

"You've heard all that since we left? That sounds like a bit too much chatter." She couldn't imagine Ken allowing all that.

"No." He shook his head. "It's from our plan, what I heard, and what I know Franks will do."

In the future, at an op brief, she planned to remember everything, not only from the normal but from the victim's perspective. She'd never expected to be the one needing to be rescued.

They'd only stepped off their path when they heard rustling in the bushes ahead. Ready to protect themselves, they prepared for anything. Except the little boy dressed in next to nothing who'd darted away holding—none other than—a snake. Although she hated them, having a child bitten by a venomous one sent shivers crawling up her spine. When she was made to move out of hiding, Ken grabbed her arm, leaned close, and told her, "Safe snake."

The child scampered off, taking no notice of them or doing an excellent job of avoiding them, and she breathed a sigh of relief.

"We must be close to a village," Ken told her as they stepped back into the open.

They stopped briefly for what she suspected was Ken to

catch his breath and take more painkillers than had been in the first aid kit. Although mild, they would help with his pain without losing his edge. Doc would've ensured that to be the case.

On a break at about midday, they checked in with the team, stopped, and split a meal bar while rehydrating. A trek through the jungle taxed the body. If Bev really had to do this, why couldn't she have chosen the beach? Admittedly, running in the sand in her combat boots would tire her out quickly, but at least she could have swum afterward. The best part would have been no slithery things.

This not happening at all would be Sam's preference. What would've happened to Cody if they hadn't arrived? Thankfully, Alejandro had not abused him, but what had he been silently dealing with when his mother slipped off the deep end?

She'd fooled Sam. While she'd known her friend was losing it, she had no idea it'd gone this far. Even though it'd become obvious that Bev was a great actress. Sam missed the clues to this change.

Moving again, every so often, they halted and listened to ensure they hadn't been pursued, which made the day even longer.

Satisfied with their progress, Ken continued to lead her on a small trail and through the jungle, where paths appeared partially formed.

His limp became more pronounced. She didn't even ask. She put her arm under his to aid him. He didn't hesitate to put his arm around her shoulder and shift his weight awkwardly as she took the brunt of the weight off his bad leg. It made for tougher and slower going, but they'd make it together.

Keeping their rifles in their free hands, Sam praised that HIS made them all practice with their non-dominant hand. Always be ready for the unexpected.

She struggled under his weight but refused to admit it because he'd try to walk on his own again, and his crumpling to the ground was possible.

No matter how far away from the compound they traveled, their vigilance couldn't slip, but she couldn't turn and check their six. If Doc had eluded the men, he'd arrive soon to cover them. She'd rest much easier when that happened.

Until Doc or the boys arrived, she'd drop Ken in that small cave—also known as Point Charlie—and stand guard.

A sense of relief filled her when the roar of the Las Golondrinas waterfall reached them. Then, they'd need to travel to get him down the slope and not set off red flags. Trying to remember their terrain maps, she realized their path was about to get very steep.

"Approaching Point Charlie."

She almost missed Ken's low voice, immediately realizing he was updating the Franks and the team.

He stopped, and she immediately released him and turned, moving back-to-back with him, uncertain why he had halted.

"Copy." He touched the earpiece to turn off the mic.

Although she wished they'd had another comm system for her, at least Ken had one to keep in contact with the team. Along the way, he hadn't given her any more, other than the men had been engaged.

"Let's go," he ordered, walking without her support.

"What did they say?"

"We're to take shelter in the cave below the falls. When they can, the men will arrive and take a position to protect. We'll stay there for the night."

Unbidden, the idea of spending the night with Ken—not as a prisoner—sent a delicious shiver through her. The thought of him touching her—skin to skin—heated her face. Her breasts ached for his touch. Her body wanted him to be hers. That desire within her shocked her somewhat, but she'd always had a soft spot for Ken that she'd held in check during her marriage.

With Ken injured, it might be some time before their lust could be sated. Unless…her mind whirled with options as they passed bright, beautiful flowers along the trail.

Stepping from the path, her mouth dropped at the splendor of the Las Golondrinas waterfall. Above them, she spied towering mud and rock formations that looked like hidden elephants. A higher pool set under towering trees caught her eye. If only she'd been here to explore on her own. To enjoy the environment without worries of someone tracking her to kill or recapture her.

Scanning the area, a buffet of greens in the sudden vistas of broad valleys…the beauty of it lifted her soul.

Looking down the waterfall area, the cave remained out of sight, but the landscape before her wowed her even more. A vast blue-green pool that fed off the cascade lay below them. It would be an ideal place to swim and bathe, both with and without Ken. And a bath sounded heavenly.

They had two options to reach their destination: jump into the pool below or descend a twenty-five-foot steep bank of shrubs, plants, and loose dirt. The trail looked sketchy, but jumping would potentially ruin some of their equipment—like their weapons. Or, they could get injured, which Ken didn't need more of.

Without question, they took the sketchy trail.

"Be careful. It's a steep descent," he warned her.

Even though she'd known this, his repeating her thought had concern leaping inside her. "Can you do this?" He could barely walk on his own. She'd been half-carrying him.

"We'll go slow."

Slow. Great. Slow, and no one is protecting their backs. There was no one to pick him up if he fell.

Halfway down to their location, on a misstep, her heart nearly stopped at the thought of an uncontrolled fall. Dirt and small pebbles rolled around Ken's feet to the pool below. While she'd imagined them playing in the water, she didn't relish the two of them falling into it.

Ken stumbled as she had that thought, and his injured leg slipped out from under him. Horrified, she reached for him but only caught air as he fell the last few feet, making a large splash.

Losing her balance after grabbing for him to keep Ken upright, weightlessness wrapped itself around her as she plunged into the cool water with the weight of the backpack tugging her down, leaving her fighting to reach the surface.

Chapter Twenty-Five

Ken gasped for air in the cool water as he broke free of the surface, treading water with a rifle in one hand. He'd held it up in the fall but plunged too deep to keep it dry. He could strip it and dry the components as best he could without a kit. It may or may not be serviceable by the time they moved on to catch their ride.

In the meantime, they had Sam's piece because he'd also lost his SIG.

A noise caught his attention. He looked up, and horror gripped his gut, twisting it with no mercy as he watched Sam's flight through the air. Her head just missed a rock before she landed with a loud splash. He had to get to her. She'd hit the surface hard, too hard.

"Sam!" he yelled over the sounds of the falls. Without waiting for an answer, he swam to where she'd entered. Treading water for a moment and calling to her again, panic tried to seize him, but he fought it off.

With renewed vigor, he dove under the water. Even with the crystal clearness of the water, it took him a moment to locate her. A moment she may not have. She struggled with something, and when he got closer, he sighed with relief because she would survive this.

He didn't know she could move so swiftly and skillfully when he reached out to her. Her KA-BAR appeared at his neck, and if he'd moved before she recognized him, he might be floating down the river.

Before she removed the borrowed knife and sheathed it,

she struggled to tread underwater, with one hand holding the rifle and the other with her knife. He worked to free the backpack from watery tree roots. They needed the items in it, so he understood why she hadn't abandoned it.

Something twisted inside. She would've been trapped if she hadn't been able to slide from the straps. His hands shook at the depth of his feelings for her and the loss he would've suffered.

Not wanting the bottom of the pack to rip and their equipment to fall into the depths, he handed her his rifle and gave her a thumbs-up to return to the surface while he worked with it. Probably needing air in her lungs, she followed his order.

Cutting the strap was a last resort, as they'd still need to carry the pack. Nearing the end of his air supply, he worked swiftly to free the bag from the last branch. With the bag slung over one shoulder, he kicked hard to reach the surface, ignoring the pain of his damaged leg, before he had to take a breath. He'd prefer air to water.

Watching Sam struggle with both rifles, he stroked through the water toward her and led them toward the pounding falls. He arrived first, slipped into the narrow space behind the falls, then hauled himself up to sit on the small shelf.

Quickly, he dropped the pack and held a hand to Sam to collect a weapon. After she'd handed him one, he placed it on the shelf. Before he could take a second, she'd put it there and pulled herself into a sitting position.

Breathing hard, they looked around but remained in the spot, hiding from general view, resting. Glad they would stay put for the night and that Doc would be here to protect them. Maybe he could get enough rest for his body and his leg. This hadn't been nearly as bad as survival school or even when he'd been put through the wringer as a hostage in training scenarios. He hadn't been shot during those sessions, though, which made the difference.

They needed to move to secure the area, although with their rifles and her handgun wet, they only had knives to protect themselves. While they could do that, it had to be close combat, and he wasn't strong enough to defeat Alejandro's small army.

Gritting his teeth at the throbbing pain that settled once he rested his leg, Ken took too long to get to his feet. Sam narrowed her eyes, assessing him. He wanted to tell her not to worry. His injuries couldn't be that serious, or he wouldn't be able to stand. Although he'd never admit it, the movement took every bit of his resolve to bite through the pain radiating and burning through his leg.

"We made some noise when we plunged into the water, so be careful. You take that side." He nodded behind her to emphasize his direction. "I'll go this way."

"What about weapons?" she asked, concern hitching her voice.

"Go ahead and carry your rifle and Glock. It might work, but doubtful. Just the sight of you carrying might be enough."

Shrugging the backpack over both of his shoulders, they separated to recon the area. The pools on their level and above surrounded the jungle, making it hard to clear all the areas.

After clearing his zone as best as possible, he met Sam in front of the hidden cave.

"Clear," she told him.

He hated to give her this bit of bad news, but he wouldn't keep it to himself. "Our comms didn't like the swim. It's not completely gone, but it's garbled, and I couldn't tell if they heard me transmit." In his mind, something beat nothing at this point.

They'd received his last check-in for approaching the falls. They might assume his location in the cave could block his signal. Either way, the team would be here. He had no doubt.

One thing was for sure—he could count on the HIS agents.

Trying to instill some humor to lighten the atmosphere, he smiled and said, "Here we are, cradled in the jungle, standing beneath one of the most beautiful waterfalls I've seen. And the swimming hole—well, it was just too much to pass up."

Her smile brightened her face. "It is a paradise out here."

Drunk on the memory of their kisses and knowing no one could sneak up on them, he held out an empty hand. "What'd say we make this our first date?"

Her eyes widened, and she stood silent, her gaze moving between his face and hand. With the bruise on his eye still changing colors, he couldn't be much to look at.

A cold knot formed in his gut as a wave of apprehension coiled. Although he'd been joking, he held his breath at her response. Maybe the kisses they shared hadn't been as memorable to her. She'd given him the impression she wanted to move forward, but he could've read her wrong.

In a soft voice, she surprised him with, "Can we?"

Can we physically, or can we while on the run? Wanting to be truthful with her, he responded, "We still have to remain vigilant until the men arrive. After that, we need to rest."

Something changed inside her, and she flashed him a knowing grin. "So, just what kind of date are you taking me on? We've already gone on a nice hike and swim. A grand adventure. What more can there be?"

His eyes twinkled with mischief. "A gourmet dinner in a secluded spot."

She threw her head back and laughed. "Such a romantic."

The world of romancing a woman had eluded him. Most likely because the few women he'd been involved with hadn't been Sam. His heart had always been devoted to her.

Unable to find someone worthy of replacing the spot in his heart for her, he'd lived a primarily solitary life. It wouldn't have been fair to another woman not to have him fully hers.

After borrowing her Glock and removing a flashlight from the bag, he crept into the small cave, hoping no wild animal had made its home there.

With her wet weapon—which should generally be able to fire after that plunge, but he wouldn't hold his breath for it—in one hand and the flashlight in the other, Ken took a step into the cave where light from the lowering sun shot beams of light broken by shadows from the towering trees.

"I'll go," Sam offered.

He shook his head. Already, he hated leaving her to watch for a threat without a weapon. Any threat attempting to surprise them from outside wouldn't succeed. They'd have ample warning for him to return to her. But finding something deadly in the cave without carrying a weapon would be suicide.

The animal-free cave measured nearly the size of a good-sized living room. Plenty of space for their needs.

After clearing the area, he called Sam in to wait until the team arrived.

She stepped inside and toward the side wall where sunlight hadn't penetrated the area. Rubbing her hands up and down her arms, he wished they could start a fire. He reached into the pack and pulled out the small blanket that had been vacuum-sealed to save space. Although chilled by the temperature drop in their enclosure, he handed her the olive-green blanket.

"What about you?"

"I'll be fine until the men come. Then I'll swipe theirs." He could also grab a Mylar emergency blanket, but survive without it.

With a nod, she reached for the one in his hand and wrapped it around her shoulders like a shawl.

"How long do you think they'll be?"

Looking at the—thank God—waterproof watch on his wrist, like it held the answer, nothing but honesty could exist on an op. Touching his earpiece to activate the mic, he requested, "Status report." After nothing but an unreadable reply, he shook his head. "Don't know, but I hope soon. We need to get out of these wet clothes." He kept his eyes forward and maintained a nonchalant tone in his voice.

Even being cold, they removed their wet T-shirts, although she left her sports bra in place. Sam wrapped the blanket back around herself.

In only a few moments, his body temperature warmed. Not entirely because his pants still clung to him, but because it was better.

After that, without thought, she reached back and released her messy hair from its holder. Turning to watch her, he stepped closer as she ran her fingers through the wet strands now flowing over her shoulders, framing her exquisite face.

He needed to taste her mouth, to feel the softness of her breasts up against his chest, both with and without a clothing barrier between them.

Seeing her shiver, he closed the space between them. "Sam." He had no idea what he'd planned to say.

She turned to look at him, and he was floored by the passion, flaming desire, and maybe love that flared in her eyes.

He knew his focus should be on the cave entrance, but this woman enthralled him. They'd only just begun what could be—would be if he could convince her—between them.

"Do you remember our first kiss?" They'd never spoken of the moment since it occurred.

She nodded, and her eyes gleamed. "You were drunk."

That he'd been, but he'd not forgotten the feel of her soft lips on their unique taste, along with a hint of the strawberry margarita she'd been sipping. He hadn't forgotten the heat when he'd slid his hands over her lovely ass, pulling her tight against him, and how their bodies had molded together. He'd have taken her to his bed that night if he hadn't had morals.

It'd been a warm Thursday evening with the rain doing that annoying misting thing and the clouds covering the usually bright evening sky.

"You wore an incredible red dress because you and Beverly had been at some event before you two stopped in at the sports bar."

Surprise lit her features. While he couldn't remember what the women he dated before had worn, he couldn't forget the image of her. A small fire flamed in her eyes. A fire he planned to have blaze before the night ended. "What else do you remember?" Her tone moved to suggestive.

He took a step closer, then stopped when the tips of her breasts and hard nipples—from probably cold and desire— touched his chest. "Actually," he smiled slyly, "I remember when you entered, what you drank, and how long it took Adam to get you and Beverly to our table." He reached and lovingly touched her cheek, his thumb rubbing across her lips. "And, with your shiny hair reaching the middle of your back and your lips begging to be kissed with a clear gloss, you made a pretty picture."

Yep, he remembered every detail and hadn't let it go after turning her away. Sadly, but ironically, he'd worried about making Sam a widow when in fact, he'd survived, and the man she'd married had died while he'd survived.

Ken closed his eyes to fight back the pain of losing his best friend while he coveted the man's wife. Then kiss her again a year after Lance's death. She'd been right to push him away since she hadn't been ready.

"Ken?"

He opened his eyelids and saw tenderness behind the heat in hers. "I'm going to kiss you now." If she wanted him to stop, whether by words, expression, or movement, he would, although he'd prefer she didn't.

Sam tilted her head back to reach his mouth with her own. Even with only about a half-foot difference in height, kissing involved his leaning over and her rising on her tiptoes.

He gently nibbled on her lower lip until he sensed their combined passion mounting. Claiming her as his own, he kissed her with a possessiveness through which his love flowed.

As their lips moved over each other and their tongues fought for dominance, his anticipation ramped up to an almost intolerable level. He needed her body next to his, skin on skin.

Lifting his head, the memory of her face, as the evening shadows flitted across it, would dominate his recollections of her. She exuded a strength that had kept them from trouble, a tenderness that worried her about his injury, and the desire and love she offered him.

"Now ain't that nice," a man drawled.

Chapter Twenty-Six

Spinning around with a frantic heartbeat, Ken pointed the Glock at the cave entrance. He tried to push Sam behind him for protection like he would for a client. Instead, she'd tried the same thing with him. She also had her waterlogged weapon pointed directly at the man who'd entered their little sanctuary unannounced.

He'd shake his head at their loss if they didn't face a possible threat. Together, he foresaw them in for a wild ride in future assignments.

With a massive sigh of relief and a major ass kicking in his mind for allowing his defenses to be lowered, he ground out, "About damn time you arrived." Trying to remember, it hadn't been Frank's fault. He'd been surprised. It'd been his. Had it been anyone other than an agent, there'd be no telling what would've happened to the two of them. Then again, he doubted any of the men Alejandro had on his payroll could move as stealthily as his agents.

Franks leaned on the edge of the cave wall, which meant that he'd not only approached silently but also had time to watch the two of them.

Ken narrowed his eyes with a challenge to his second-in-command that he keep his mouth shut about anything he'd witnessed. The team would learn soon enough that he and Sam were together.

"Reagan wouldn't appreciate your profanity," Franks jested. "Soon, her swear jar will be full enough to pay for college through a doctoral degree."

Grimacing, Ken asked, "Do you really think she'll count damn as a curse word?" He shook his head, knowing they'd eliminated her fine while on operations. "Never mind. I'm glad you're here. What's our status?"

Franks quirked an eyebrow. "Go for a swim?"

"We decided to do a couple of high dives," he snarled back.

"Damn, Boss," said the man who'd just told him not to curse. "You took a lickin'."

"And kept on tickin'." Ken chuckled at their joke from some old commercial and regretted it. A sharp pain wrapped its tentacles around his chest. A chest already enflamed with the exertion of their travels. If he didn't breathe too deeply or laugh, only an ache resided in his bruised ribs.

Franks turned his eyes to Sam, and the softening in them made Ken want to reach out and choke the man, even though he knew it'd been out of the bond they'd formed and not anything sexual. He'd been jealous of how she'd quickly become friends with the other agents, but had no reason to, since they had agreed to remain professional at work.

"How you doing, Sugar?"

"Just wet. I can help with guard duty tonight."

Oh, hell no. She'd be in his arms tonight because he wouldn't let her out of sight until Beverly was captured or dead.

Franks shook his head. "Nah, you're a target. I'd rather protect the two of you for a change. Take the night to rest, eat, and recoup. With what Doc says about the boss's leg, we must start early to meet the bird on time."

Grumbling under his breath, Ken narrowed his eyes. "It's fine." He'd surprised himself with how far he'd traveled. While he'd been grateful for Sam's assistance, he'd still borne the brunt of his weight on his leg.

"Is Doc coming down to look at his injuries?" she asked, her voice lit with hope.

He'd like that too, but he also knew Doc wouldn't be pleased with the depth of them going untreated to this point, along with his running through the jungle.

"Yeah. I wanted to check in first." Turning back to Ken, he asked, "What do you need?"

"We need at least one—preferably two—weapons of any sort. We've got one blanket, but I'd like all of yours. We need to get out of these wet clothes and dry off. I'm sure Sam would like her own cover." While jealous because an agent saw Sam only in her sports bra, he had to remember she wore something similar when working out with the team.

Franks nodded, and a sly, knowing smile crept across his face before he pulled one of the handguns he had in a holster and handed it over. Ken wanted his holster and weapons back. He felt naked without them. "Doc'll bring the rest down with him. He's also got an extra bladder and some chow." He grinned.

With a quirk on his lips, Ken nodded in relief that his team had come together without him. He couldn't be prouder of them. "My comms are iffy."

"We figured that. We don't have an extra, but we're here with you now, so you'll be fine. Just be alert if you hear gunfire."

Like he needed to say that. "Where're you situated?"

"The top of the ridge is the only place someone can begin their descent or slip up the river by boat, so we've set up one top and one bottom while the third rests. We'll rotate every three hours once Doc is finished with you, and that'll put all of us awake before dawn."

With nothing to add since Franks had made the same

decision he would've, he thanked him and watched the agent retreat.

While they waited for Doc to arrive, he and Sam kept a reasonable distance between them, even though he wanted her back in his arms. Tonight would test him both physically and emotionally. They'd been right about him needing the rest, but Sam didn't tire him in the least.

With his agents protecting them, he relaxed somewhat, but not enough. He hadn't heard Doc approach.

The big man—easily the largest on the team in height, muscles, and broadness of chest—smiled when he entered, the cave roof only a few inches above his head.

"How's it going, Sugar? Boss?"

Of course, he'd ask the woman first. He loved women. All women. Too many women.

Sam smiled at him, and for a moment, Ken thought she would hug him. A spark of jealousy gripped him, and it took all his reasoning to release it and remember how she'd responded to him.

"I've got your stuff." Doc handed Ken a handgun—probably from Cowboy, since he also wore two weapons. The blankets he gave to Sam. "Would you lay these out so I can get a good look at his injuries? Make sure it's in the remaining light. You can move them later when it's time to sleep." He also held a full water bladder for her to take. "Electrolytes."

Ken grimaced, knowing the taste of them. He wanted to say he could manage independently, but bending over disagreed with him. In fact, getting up and down might be a challenge.

While his team had bonded and gotten to know each other as he had them, they'd absorbed everything about him. It tugged at his heart since he considered them family. "I can get back up." *Maybe.*

"Doesn't matter. I want you off the leg until tomorrow. You'll need to stay off it when we're back home. Pain level? Honest."

Ken scoffed. "Does it matter? I'll make it out of here. Now, are you planning to look at my wound?"

"Don't need to." He knelt by the pallet Sam had created. "You got shot. No matter if big or small, it still needs tending. Now, Sam, turn your back. I don't care whether you go to the side or back of the cave. Just don't block these last few rays."

"Why does she need to move?" Ken asked. He'd love to have her hold his hand through this, not because of fear but because it'd be soothing.

"Because you're going to strip for me."

"Where're my singles?" Sam piped in with a laugh.

"I'm worth more than one-dollar bills," he countered with his best seductive smile aimed at her.

"All right, you two lovebirds."

Ken stiffened. How had he known? If Franks had blabbed, he'd have him running drills sunup to sundown for weeks.

"Don't worry. Your secret is safe with me."

"But—" Sam sputtered.

With him? Not with the men or Franks? "How—" He stopped, realizing he'd given them away with only one word.

"Anyone with eyes could tell. Especially with how hard the two of you try to stay out of each other's way at HQ."

"No." Anger radiated from her.

"We'll discuss it later. Let's get Ken patched up so he can hold his *Barbie*. Or Sugar, in this case."

For men who'd never played with dolls other than

soldiers or GI Joe, they joked about him finding his Barbie every time Ken took a woman out. They'd even begun using the dollmaker's labels, like Cherry Pie Picnic Barbie Doll.

He'd heard that most of his life, so it slid down his back, but he thought it funny, so he'd played along, assuring them that his Barbie had gotten away, which had been confirmed.

Doc turned his gaze to Sam and raised an eyebrow. "Sam?"

She hurried to the edge of the cave opposite them, holding her wet rifle as if it comforted her. It probably did.

"Let me see the leg."

Sam turned to observe Doc take a look, only lightly touching once on the front and once on the back.

"Okay, your pants aren't stuck to the wound. Your fall into the water would have helped. It probably washed away some of the dried blood, but you've got some fresh, slowly oozing, and I'm worried about. Go ahead and undress. Let me know if you need help with the pants."

After some uncomfortable shifting and a groan or two bitten back, with Doc's help, he lay unclothed on top of a blanket with another covering only his privates. Resting his head on their pack, he could observe Doc examine him.

Like a licensed doctor, Doc poked and prodded enough to make it hurt worse. Ken wanted to order the man away, but thought better of it. He had to set an example for his team. If one of them needed care, he'd expect them to endure it.

"Well, as you know, the bullet went through. While unable to see inside your leg, I'm going on the fact that it's not bleeding profusely, and you can bear some weight, so you'll survive. Stitched, but your chest?" Doc heaved a frustrated—or maybe pissed off—breath. "Those motherfuckers."

"They actually put pressure on the gunshot wound to increase the pain, so I'd speak out."

"Speak out for what?"

As Doc pulled something else from his pack, he realized they didn't know. "They wanted me to give up our Old Man."

"Why would they want the Old Man?"

Ken caught his breath between his teeth. Doc was a bit late in telling him, "This might sting a little."

"They wanted Old Man and me." It felt odd calling Jesse such, but that's how the team—especially on an op—referred to their fearless leader.

"I can't stitch this without it being checked out, so I'm going to use some big-ass Steri-Strips for now."

Ignoring that assessment, he continued, "It's not only Alejandro. it's Beverly."

"We couldn't identify the car's driver who entered the compound." Doc's hands touched a few burns on his chest, and he held back a hiss of pain. "They're on the verge of being infected. Tomorrow won't improve since you'll be sweating right over them. But tonight, I'll put something on them to help in the short term."

When the man pulled another thing from his pack, Ken wondered how heavy that bag was. Doc carried a regular backpack, and with the larger size, he added medical supplies and not the measly first-aid kit one could buy at the store. It took a big man to carry a big pack like that.

As Doc applied goo to each of the ten cigarette burns, he moved on to all of Ken's issues. "Let's look at that mug." He prodded Ken's face.

Ken winced at the touch and how he must look to Sam.

"The eye didn't swell much, or it went down. I've got

something here for the lip, but it looks like you've been breaking the small scab."

Ken worried that he blushed at the fact that he had not cared about the discomfort when he kissed Sam. It'd been worth it.

"Otherwise," Doc said, "you'll have to wait out the bruising." Satisfied, he moved on. "How're the ribs after all that effort getting here?"

"They're survivable." Which was true. Even when he did something like laugh, a twinge went through his chest, but even that hadn't been too painful. "They feel fine while I'm lying here."

Doc winked. "How about we wrap them just in case you find yourself breathing heavily?"

Well hell. That hadn't been the least bit subtle. While he wanted to love Sam from head to toe, his limitations prevented him from doing so. Having his ribs wrapped for tomorrow's trek wouldn't be a bad idea. It might be wise since he did plan to kiss Sam—a lot.

"Go ahead," he said gruffly.

Light laughter filtered into the cave, and Doc's grin grew into the "I know a secret" type of smile that infuriated Ken.

At least Sam hadn't been offended or argued the point. Bonus there.

"Let's sit you up."

After wrapping his ribs and ensuring the bandages would hold, Doc taped the ends down and lightly smacked Ken's flank to get his attention.

"Now we need to get you on your stomach so I can check the entry point on the back of your leg."

He gingerly rolled over and exposed his ass in the air, bare to the world, and didn't allow for much confidence in his ability to protect. Doc pulled the blanket over his ass and administered the same treatment on the bullet wound on his thigh. Being prepared for the sting didn't make it feel any better.

Getting back to the op, Ken said, "She's off her rocker."

Knowing who he meant, Doc asked, "Do you think she'll keep tracking us?"

Turning his head to the side to rest on his arms, the image of Sam watching him filled his heart and soul. He knew he'd do everything possible to keep her safe, especially from the woman she called a friend.

She turned, their gazes locked, and the strength and resolve in her beautiful eyes bled into him. While she'd known the truth when they'd been Alejandro's guests, a rock-solid determination radiated from her.

"I do, and I don't think she'll stop at me and Old Man." Not after she'd provided Sam with a drugged drink. He hadn't even wanted to guess what had been mixed with their water. At least they'd caught it before finding out.

"Okay, you're done." Doc started putting items back in his pack. In a low voice, he ordered, "Don't overdo it." Then he stood and asked Sam about her health again before his next order. "I want you to rest. No." He held up his hand to forestall Ken's argument. "Both of you need to rest after your ordeal."

"It's not over yet," Ken argued, then thought about Doc hinting at him and Sam tangling limbs and telling him to rest —contradictory cuss.

"No, it's not. But now, you've got us watching your back." He turned, then slipped out of the cave, just in time because the shadows disappeared.

"Go ahead and set up some blankets deeper in the cave, far enough that the light shouldn't hit us in the morning."

She did, then watched him with concern. How

humiliating to his pride when he followed Doc's orders and rolled to the new space instead of attempting to stand and then squat again.

He cursed Beverly to hell. "Fucking bitch," he murmured. Because of that woman, the first time he had Sam naked, he could only lie there and watch while his body ached—not just from the beating or shot he'd taken.

"What was that?"

Bringing up her lunatic friend would only take away from their semi-relaxed moods. Instead of answering, he smiled. "Time for you to get undressed."

Chapter Twenty-Seven

By the time Doc departed, Sam's clothes had chafed her skin. She wanted nothing more than to remove them. With how they'd molded to her body, though, peeling them off wouldn't be easy.

"Come here," Ken requested from his position on the cave floor. She'd dropped the extra two blankets under and over him in a large pallet. She could've created two separate spaces since the other agents had provided four blankets, but she fully admitted she'd wanted to be close to Ken.

The smile on his face, even with his chin sporting a few days' growth, the purple beginnings of bruising, and a small split on his upper lip, gave the illusion he wasn't in any pain. She didn't know why he tried to fool her, but he'd failed. However, that smile did something funny inside her. Butterflies fluttered in her stomach, bouncing off walls to make themselves known.

While she'd seen him mostly naked when she'd turned around before Doc finished his work, seeing his bare chest now drew a different response from her. That concerned emotion had been replaced with a deep desire she no longer wanted to restrain.

Since she didn't move, he mostly repeated himself. "Come on, get out of those wet things. I'd help you, but I promised Doc I'd stay flat on my back for the night." He winked at her, and she wanted to shake her head at his playfulness amidst their situation.

She had things to accomplish first, and he knew it. She

considered dropping some water over his head to tempt her away from work. Technically, they both should be prepping for defense, but she'd give him a pass this one time. "You know I have to dry out our weapons."

"It was a test."

Hmm. "Is that so?" With a laugh, she collected the weapons that had taken a plunge and field-stripped them, drying the components and readying them for when they might need protection. Sitting on the floor, she caught Ken silently watching her. She wondered what he saw, or was he saving up his impressions to critique her work once complete?

Moonlight spilled over the treetops, distorting through the clear mist of the waterfall. Not much light filtered through the cave entrance, but what could be called romantic.

Satisfied with her work, she stood. She'd decided that while she needed to get out of her damp things, she wouldn't remove her underthings as the sports bra and boy shorts would provide a barrier to that unrestrained lust flaring in her core. "I wish we could build a fire, but I'm worried about our safety in getting noticed."

"Don't fret. The men have our backs. Believe me. I wouldn't lie here buck naked if not."

She almost choked at that thought. While she'd thought he'd wear his underwear, hearing he wasn't set her body on edge.

"What you do need to worry about are the *aluxes*."

Her eyebrows rose at his shift in the topic. What kind of story was he about to spew? "The what?"

"They're something like Maya leprechauns. They're well-known knee-high tricksters," he described with a fake Irish brogue—a terrible one.

She chuckled at both him and the story. "Is this a fireside tale you use on dates to woo the lasses?" She added her flair of Irish to the tail end of her question.

"Only those I trudge through a rainforest with." The sexy grin that could be patented spread over his face. "They're depicted on Yaxchilán engravings."

Enjoying his mischievous nature, she asked for more as she removed her boots and socks. "And what kind of mischief do they get into?"

"Word is that if you don't ignore their misleading noises, you'll get lost in the jungle."

She snorted. "Like that isn't already easy to do." Tackling her pants, she grunted when they stuck while attempting to pull them off. There was nothing like the struggle of pulling wet pants down your legs.

Ignoring her challenge, he continued, "There's also the spirit people who are known to transform into things like jaguars and crocodiles."

"That's okay. I'll pass on them as I've already been watching for jaguars." Finally, her pants were on the ground. The success of that task made her dizzy with joy.

Ken flipped back the blanket on the empty side of the pallet and patted the space next to him. "Come on, relax a bit. Wouldn't you tell your client to relax if the men had their backs? It's the same thing right now. We're in the client role, so we're safe and have to trust them while we recuperate enough to make the trek tomorrow and get out of this country."

She spread her pants out to dry, then slid under the blanket beside him, trying not to let their bare skin touch. Would she be able to control her desire? She had to because he needed to rest with his injuries. Disgruntled at their predicament, she told him, "I don't like playing that role."

"Neither do I, but Franks is running the show to get us to the rendezvous point on time since we escaped before the HIS rescue attempt. We must follow their directives as much as we may not wish it."

Jokingly, she said, "And here I thought *you* were my knight in shining armor. Well, Kevlar."

With many low-sounding pain groans, Ken rolled from his back to his good side. He propped his head on the hand of his bent arm, reached over with his free arm, and turned her toward him until the tips of her breasts lightly touched his chest.

She shifted to mirror his pose so they were on the same level. Although he said not to fret, she couldn't help it. "I still don't get—"

"Shh. Trust in them."

Had she been that obvious in what she'd planned to say? That's when she noticed something else. While he said to relax, his muscles were tense, ready to defend themselves if needed. She didn't feel so bad now. She could do the same, especially since she could reach her feet faster. However, she wouldn't doubt him in a crunch.

"I've wanted to have you naked beside me since the moment I met you." Slipping his hand up, he tucked a few damp strands behind her ear. "If I had pursued you, would you have chosen me over Lance?"

Wanting to jump up and tell him yes, she wondered if that were true. While Ken had always been serious and focused, he'd not been as lighthearted as she found him now. Maybe if they'd dated, she'd have realized that his mind— and probably his heart— wasn't ready for anything serious. Back then, his team came first. No woman would've replaced that.

With Lance, he'd made her and the team equal, which

she'd appreciated because she'd never wanted him not to have his mind focused when out with the other Rangers in life-and-death scenarios.

She hadn't been ready when he'd approached her as a widow after only one year. Timing for them had always sucked. This time, if they could get past this, she'd fight for them to finally have a chance.

Before she could respond, he said, "Don't answer that. It was wrong of me to ask."

"It's okay," she said as his hand moved to her jaw, sending delicious tingles from head to toe. "Honestly, I'm not sure." And while that first inclination had been to say yes, the actual answer settled in her with the truth ringing deep.

His hand settled on her jaw, and his eyes focused on her lips as his thumb slowly stroked them. "It doesn't matter. We have now."

Leaning toward her, he kissed her lips lightly, and her body warmed. Before she could kiss him back, he moved and placed light kisses over her face before trailing down her neck with a wet, hot contact that drove her to near madness with need.

"Sam," he whispered as his lips returned to hers, "I love you."

Not waiting for a response from her, his mouth covered hers with such a soul-searing kiss she wanted to weep her happiness.

His tongue caressed hers while he pulled her flush against him in a move that she suspected was painful for him. Not stopping, his hand roamed over her back. Whether he touched bare skin or over her underthings, her skin tingled with his every stroke.

Taking his time, his tongue coaxing hers, he made love

to her through their kiss. The want, the need of this man for her, had never been greater than at this moment. A moment when he'd been through hell, worried about keeping her safe, and now, if she read it right, he planned to please her.

Soon, the kiss made her entire body throb with a fiery need she hadn't expected from just their lips meshing hungrily.

He broke away and seemed to be catching his breath as she was. The lust, desire, and love pulsing in his eyes turned her to mush.

When she'd lain beside him, his semi-aroused state had been noticeable. While not the ideal time for this or Ken's physical state, she crafted a plan.

Since they'd been relieved of their duty, for the night at least, she didn't feel guilty about them taking this time to explore each other's bodies, no matter their future.

"I want to touch you. May I?"

"Ken"—seriousness drove her tone—"why ask, and why only ask sometimes?"

Searching her gaze, he offered, "I want to give you the choice. Now that I've got you, I don't want to do anything you're not ready for that might scare you off. Being around you, though, with this heat zipping between us, I forget myself, and I'm sorry to say that I just take."

How could she not love a considerate man, especially one who loved her in return? She'd be a fool to step back now. "Oh" was all she could say in response.

"After that, I want to make love to you."

Here? With the men outside? His injuries?

"If you're worried about the men, don't."

She truly wondered if he could read her mind. Either he had some extraordinary power, or, like he'd told her once, her thoughts were easily read.

"They already know we're together."

"What— How—" she sputtered.

"Trust me. They do."

She sighed and pushed for a serious face. "There's a lot of trusting you want me to do." She didn't know whether she jested or meant it.

He popped another quick kiss on her lips. "You're part of this family. We'd do anything for each other. You should've already realized that."

"I know, but them knowing about us? That freaks me out."

He chuckled and stopped quickly. "Based on what I've been told, you've been giving me hungry looks at HQ these last few months." He smiled slyly, and she wanted to give him a playful swat but was unsure of where he might be hurt. "So, are you going to let me love you tonight? I'll let you love me." His slow wink nearly did her in.

The man knew how to melt her panties without even touching her. His playful tone and actions always drew her attention, especially when he was directed at her alone.

She shook her head. "I don't think you're in any shape to love me. Besides, Doc said for you to lie on your back."

With a sly grin, he whispered, "I *can* lie on my back." He did, and she caught the grimace. "Besides, it's more painful to want you this badly and be unable to sate my desire. I would endure the world's worst pain to be inside you."

She must've looked skeptical because she was.

"Look, my ribs are wrapped, so as long as we don't press down on them, we're fine there. I know my mug isn't that great to look at, but you can still touch it. As you've noticed already, my split lip isn't stopping me. As for my leg, I can't be on top."

Her skeptical look must've deepened as he continued his justification.

"Okay, I'll hurt a little, but it'd be worth it. I want you, Sam, and I know you want me too. If it makes you feel better, we can wait until we're home and in bed for our first time. Or," he continued, "we can make a great memory right here." He moved his hand to her hips and waited. "Well?"

She couldn't even believe she was considering this. She only had her lust-addled brain to blame. "How about we start with the kissing and touching and see where we go from there?"

She'd thought his previous action and words had turned her into putty, but this smile—the one responding to her partial agreement—melted her into a puddle at his feet.

"Then, let's get to that kissing and touching thing."

Although not sure, she'd have sworn he chuckled under his breath. Wait until he realizes her plan.

Chapter Twenty-Eight

He'd had some bad ideas in his time, but Ken admitted this one ranked right up there with them. But no way in hell would he go back now. Had he not trusted the team to keep him safe, he wouldn't have considered being naked with Sam.

Truthfully, it hadn't been by his desire alone. Their wet clothing was the reason for their naked state—or close to it, but he'd take full advantage. He'd waited so many years to feel her beside him, underneath him, on top of him, and anywhere in between.

However, she'd been right. This might cost him, but he'd pay every penny. Asking her to wait now—when things were near perfect, except for a madwoman having them chased—would be worse than using a dull razor on his face while dry.

With a sudden need to confirm her readiness to take this plunge, he asked, "Are you sure? It hasn't been that long since—"

She cut him off. "I know. Since we've come back together as friends, some of the time, though, I think of you as not so much a friend but a lover."

Her words were tentative. Regardless, knowing she thought of him, his cock tented the blanket, and she'd yet to touch him. She seemed to be working hard on not doing so. What a contradiction she was. "So that means yes?"

Her low and melodious laughter reached him, down to his soul, and he knew she'd flipped all the way to their enjoying this short time together, protected by their brethren. He wanted to hear that happiness every day of his life.

"I'm worried about you." The touch of concern and desperation blended in her voice.

"Don't. Now, first things first, you need to dispense with that bra and panties."

She opened her mouth—surely to argue.

Before she could respond, he said, "They're wet, and we don't need a wet blanket or for you to catch a chill." He hoped she didn't think about their hair being damp, or his justification flew out the window.

After a moment where she appeared to be mulling over all the world's problems, she stood and went through a hilarious dance of removing them.

His breath quickened, watching her struggle with her black sports bra as she pulled it over her ample breasts. Her arms appeared stuck at one point, and based on her body tensing, she'd heard him laughing. Saying something probably blasphemous at him, she tugged and grunted until she removed it. Her narrowed glare at him had been just as comical.

Her sexy black underwear shorts slid off easier. With deep regret, he hated he hadn't been the one to remove them.

Once finished, she shivered, and he tossed back the blanket again. "Come on."

Without hesitation, she slid under the covers and turned close to him. As she slid to his side and snuggled in for warmth, he put his arm around her and pulled her close, urging her to rest on his shoulder.

"I don't want to hurt you," she whispered.

There'd be no way around that, but it wouldn't stop him. "I told you I'll be fine. Just watch the ribs and leg."

"Won't…if I'm astride, won't moving your hips hurt

your leg?"

Like hell, but right now, the thing that hurt stood like a flagpole in front of them. "That's why I won't be moving my hips."

She chewed on her lower lip, and his wood turned to granite.

They shouldn't even attempt to make love with his current condition and killers on their trail, but he wouldn't lose out on having her naked beside him. "How about we just play around a little? Like teenagers in the back seat of a car. You know, that kissing and touching thing." A chuckle escaped before he could stop it.

She laughed again. "It was more like pickups in the woods."

"You southern girls always have to be different."

Lifting herself, propped on her arm, she softly touched his face, whispering of an affection he didn't know existed. "I'm so sorry about your face. Well…everything."

"Shh, it's okay, honey. You didn't do this, and it'll all heal. Can you look at me like this and know this is the man you'll spend the rest of your life with?" It wasn't the right time to say that, but he had.

"I—"

Since he couldn't take back the words, he took the following words from her. With a hand on her face, he directed, "Kiss me."

Even realizing he didn't ask, he didn't stop. His lips glided over hers in a featherlight kiss until hers moved in a loving connection that fireworks shot through his body even before they opened their mouths and their tongues explored.

Her taste…soft lips…tongue…boldness drove his body to crave more of her. "God, I want you." A tremor slid through his body.

"No."

Every muscle stiffened. Had he heard her correctly? He leaned back and looked at her. "No?" Christ, he hoped she hadn't changed her mind about them.

Lifting herself on her arm in a sideways sitting position, twisted toward him, she pushed her damp hair over her shoulder and exposed what he hoped would be his playground.

She sighed, gliding her fingers around the wrap on his ribs. "I thought I'd stop it before you did or before you got too far to keep your right mind."

"Stop?" He gulped at the idea. Would he have? Truthfully, he'd set his mind to sex without thought or concern about anything else.

"Yes. You'd have remembered our situation or your injuries at some point."

"I don—"

Her finger slid over his lips to halt his speech. "I think you would've, and you'd have groaned about it. And," she pointed out, "probably left me with a fire that needed quenching."

Relying upon the team hadn't bothered him. The men wouldn't enter the cave without alerting him and Sam somehow, and with enough time to take a protective stance. His body would've been the problem. Even his turning to the side earlier had taken something out of him. Refusing to admit that but not wanting her to think he'd made it worse with her, he nodded. "You're probably right."

She narrowed her eyes, disbelief plastered across her face.

"Okay, it would've been tough to pull away from you, but maybe…no, probably…I think, more than likely, I would have. As for leaving you burning"—he winked, finding he'd done that playful action more often than ever —"I can take care of that right now."

"Actually, I was thinking about taking care of you."

The hand he'd been reaching up to touch her breast stopped, suspended in midair. Blood pumped faster to his groin, almost making him lightheaded with desire. "What're you saying?" His heart hammered. From his experience, clarity in situations such as this was necessary.

With blue eyes that brought pleading to a new level, she said softly, "You're hurt. Let me do this."

When he didn't speak, she continued, "Although not to diminish how you'd feel, if we have trouble, our response would be no different than if we slept."

Still, he didn't speak. He'd had oral before, but he and the woman participated fully. If he allowed her to give him pleasure without returning it, it felt selfish and a bit cheap. Granted, the thought of her mouth on him heightened his driving need for her. Could he settle for only that, though? He wanted to be inside her so badly it almost made him insane.

Not waiting for his response, she brushed her fingertips over the naked part of his chest, sending sparks flying to each nerve ending. When she leaned down and pressed a kiss to his neck, she asked, "Am I hurting you?"

Fire shot through him, and his arousal grew harder, shutting off the blood flow to other parts of his body. Including his brain. "What?" he asked breathily as she licked and tugged on his lower earlobe.

Whispering in his ear, she repeated, "Am I hurting you?"

Before he could answer, she skimmed her hand down his torso and below the blanket to grab his throbbing cock. He had waited a long time for her and wished he could do their first time justice, being inside her the entire night.

Slowly lifting her head, her breath quickened. "You have to tell me, or I can't do anything else."

In slow-motion, his mind muddled through what she'd asked. Her lovely breasts had that little glow from the moonlight glistening off them, and the fire in her blue eyes had his heart beating fast, just for her. Reaching a hand to her cheek, he wondered how he'd finally gotten lucky enough to have her by his side.

When the lust in her eyes morphed into what he thought was a concern, he remembered her question. No, she didn't hurt him. He was already hurt. "No," he assured her.

After a quick kiss on his hand, she used butterfly kisses across the bit of his chest, not wrapped or slathered with ointment, and descended to his swollen dick. At his indrawn breath, he thought she laughed. The touch of her hands…her breath…her lips…her mouth allowed a raging inferno in him to run wild and unmanaged.

The wet warmth of her tongue as she licked him from base to tip, as her hand glided up and down, sent an erotic shiver through his body. He dropped his head back and exhaled a lust-filled sigh. Selfishly—like he'd worried he'd be—he craved her mouth, taking him in deep. So deep.

He caught his breath when her mouth slid down, stopping at her fisted hand. Picking his head up—screw any pain from his chest—he reached down and lifted her hair to see her face and her loving him. He'd never last. He took a deep breath, fighting to keep from embarrassing himself and spilling at any second.

Trying to kill him, she added her tongue as she stroked up and down on him, her mouth keeping a tight hold. When she reached down and grabbed his balls, a primal groan tore from his chest as naked desire rushed through his veins.

"I'll never forget this sight. Your head between my

legs…your hair spread across my thighs…my balls nestled in your hand…my dick in your mouth."

She mumbled something against him, and the vibration while she sucked on his cock had him tossing his head back and gritting his teeth to forestall his release. At this point, and in other circumstances, he'd throw her over and pound into her wet heat without mercy.

Sucking deep breaths, he leaned back to watch her love his body.

The remaining blood settled in his groin, his balls drew tight, and that tingling at the base of his spine told him he was ready to explode. He clenched his hands into the blankets and closed his eyes to control the near ecstasy riding his body. He wanted it all. "Sam, my angel." He waited until she peeked up at him. "I'm gonna come real soon."

With a mischievous grin, she leaned back down. "Good."

They were going to enjoy their years together.

Ah, hell. She did some swirly thing with her tongue, and, with a guttural groan, that ecstasy he'd searched for but hadn't reached, grabbed hold of him and tossed his senses into a round of weightlessness as his orgasm ripped from him. It shook him to the core—a depth he'd never achieved with anyone else but expected with her.

Sam stayed with him and didn't move until he couldn't take it anymore. Smiling with sly satisfaction, he wanted to kiss her face. She kissed his neck, then snuggled beside him, appearing as sated as his body.

Once his limbs regained some semblance of control, the aches and pains he'd been oblivious to during the lovemaking returned. Worse, he'd tried raising his hips, and his thigh throbbed. All said, he still wouldn't have stopped.

Finally, together—heart rate, pulse, and breathing back to

normal—aches and pains in line, and the ability to speak returned. He prepared to say something to Sam but had no idea what. "Thank you" seemed awfully selfish. That damn word again. When he healed, he'd give her something to feel desirous about to ease his pain.

As he contemplated his options, knowing the first words after something so personal were critical, he peered down to see the expression on her face to gauge a possible reaction.

She slept. With his worrying about what to say, he hadn't noticed her breathing even out or her relaxing.

Smiling at his reprieve and her lovely form, he listened as Franks did another check. While their comm had been spotty, he knew the cadence and timing of what'd been said. All that mattered was that he knew they'd been safe while she'd done mind-blowing things to his body.

Knowing tomorrow would suck, he needed a genuine night's rest. Weapons at the ready, HIS having his six, and having Sam next to him, comforted him.

He sighed contentedly. With her head nestled on his shoulder, he kissed her on the forehead before he fell into his post-coital stupor and slept.

Chapter Twenty-Nine

Shafts of sunlight peeked into the little retreat he and Sam had created. They had to move before one of his men climbed down and surprised them.

If he hadn't trusted the men wholeheartedly, he'd never have let his guard down and had the erotic night with Sam, where she'd opened up to him. While he felt entirely selfish already, he'd never press her to move to the next step. Having her love his body like she had filled him with renewed hope, they could move forward, and soon.

Being warm, well-rested, and hungry, he took inventory of his body. His ribs were survivable.

Shaking some sense back into himself to finish his assessment and keep his mind off last night, he closed his eyes and focused. While sore and throbbing, his leg shouldn't prevent him from keeping up if they moved at a slower clip.

He glanced over at the beautiful woman curled into his side. Her relaxed features made her appear so peaceful that he hated to wake her with a reminder that her lunatic friend had been chasing them—and not to have afternoon tea.

He'd never cared for Beverly much when they'd all hung out together, especially him being the fifth wheel unless he got bored and found a date. But he'd dealt with the woman since she'd been important to Sam and Adam.

While Sam had been angry with her friend, he'd noticed her suppressed rage whenever she caught his injuries paining him. He wanted her to worry only about her safety and stay focused. He'd get through the hike. There was no alternative.

When they completed this op, he expected Sam to release her pent-up feelings about Beverly and the situation. He'd be there for her even if he had no idea what to do besides hold her. Making Beverly pay would be right on his list after Sam's emotional needs.

He'd worry about that later.

While he'd rested, he slept lightly and hadn't heard a peep outside. None of his men would've gone down without a fight, and if trouble had happened, one would've rushed to guard the cave entrance, alerting them.

Maybe they'd get lucky, and Beverly had abandoned her mad scheme. Ken couldn't fathom how Alejandro had bought into Beverly's plan, considering she wanted them dead because of her late husband. No piece of ass was worth someone else's life.

Ken woke Sam with a kiss, and her warm lips moved under his. When she opened her eyes, they widened with surprise, then a smile filled every feature, and she greedily accepted his mouth moving over her.

"Time to move," he whispered with their lips an inch apart. With a strong will, he pulled back and sat. The sudden jolt to his body almost had him dropping back to the ground in agony. He sat for a moment and breathed through the throbbing pain.

Beside him, Sam dressed but stopped when she saw him sitting. Like before, she came, crouched, and offered her shoulder for support. He wanted to decline because he needed her not to focus on his injuries. He quickly realized getting up would be his biggest challenge, and he couldn't fool her otherwise. Already, he'd shown too much weakness with her. He was supposed to be the protector…the hero. Yet she'd come to his aid the entire time.

This mission left them injured, betrayed, tortured, and starved, and she'd remained steady on their path to escape and elude. With all that and his reliance on her for support and cover, he liked being by her side, not just because he wanted to protect her. He had to figure out how to explain how much he wanted her to stay on the team because hiring her had been the right move.

"It's just stiff from sleep, but I admit putting on my pants will be tricky. Please help me get them on while I lie down. If you pull them up, I won't have to bend my knees to get in them and fall on my face."

She reached for his BDU pants and laughed. "That's a sight the team would love. Why don't I have my camera ready?"

"You'd best be careful there, you little minx."

The team had commented on how he smiled and laughed with them more often. They'd figured out that Sam had been the cause of the positive change.

After he suffered the humiliation of Sam dressing him with his growing erection—undressing would've been much more fun—they grabbed a crap-tasting bar Doc had left, drank some fluids, and quickly prepared to leave. As she watched with concerned eyes—what he'd hoped to avoid—he made a couple of rounds inside the cave to loosen his leg muscles.

Feeling good about his ability to travel independently, he clicked on his earpiece. "We're on our way out." He heard nothing but static, but he knew someone was responding. Going with his gut that all was well, he clicked off the mic. They snatched up the weapons she'd readied and showed themselves to the team.

Within minutes, the five of them—Sam, Franks, Cowboy, Doc, and himself—hiked up the uneven trail that hadn't been a piece of cake he'd hoped. Once he steadied in a regular, albeit slow, stride, with Franks in the lead and Cowboy in the rear, they continued to the extraction point.

On their journey, Franks updated him, but he didn't have much new intel. Cell signals were spotty inside the rainforest due to the thickness of the cover, and he didn't have the sat phone. Damn, Bev and her goons. He wanted his gear. Devon will be apoplectic about needing to replace it, along with everything else.

He stumbled over a tree root, and faster than he could imagine, Doc grabbed his arm to steady him. He nodded his thanks. There was a time when he would have been mortified to need the support and no doubt looking to see if anyone had seen his near miss. His ego was well past concern about such things. Survival was all that mattered.

The pulling of muscles when he'd tripped amped up the pain in his thigh. He bit through it until it settled again—something he could easily work through. They hadn't gone far, so he couldn't allow it to affect him this early in their trek.

He ignored the tug on his chest with his weapon in his hand. He searched the area—as they all did—but he'd been limited in turning. Doc whispered to him to keep forward so he could watch his step better and not injure himself further.

Ken nodded his understanding and trekked on.

But when he looked forward, his heart swelled with love and pride. While he'd still prefer she not put herself in danger, he knew this was what she was made for. His little warrioress sent a thrill of excitement through him when she slipped into that mode. Focused and fierce, she looked so damn hot in her BDU pants and a long-sleeve T-shirt.

Sweat trickled down his spine and his temples. Tossing a glance over his shoulder to confirm Doc remained behind him—as he'd done to Cowboy—didn't settle his nerves. His team had outstanding skills, but they'd passed too easily with them on an open—albeit narrow—path. Preferably, they'd continue unscathed, but unease clenched his gut.

Less than five minutes after those thoughts—as if he'd summoned trouble—noticeable movement in the jungle with trees and brush moving spurred them into action. Franks leaned back to Sam and said something Ken didn't hear. Sam dropped to the rear as Doc and Cowboy split off to intercept the potential threat.

Damn, his earpiece was dead. He wanted to yank it free and stomp on it, but left it in case the comm piece came to life. But, oh, how he hated not being the first in the know.

Franks picked up his pace, and Ken had no option but to follow him if he wanted to remain with the man. Sam had rescued him, helped him dress and stand, and now she had his back—again. Pride filled his chest. She was so fucking amazing.

"Dammit," Franks said. "Doesn't that bitch ever give up?" He halted them, looked down at his GPS unit, said something in the comm piece that Ken missed, and turned back to them.

"Wait right there," Franks ordered.

Before Ken could question it, Franks slipped off in the direction of the other two agents, blending into the jungle.

At least they didn't leave them unprotected. He and Sam did have their weapons. If they had to dash, he'd keep upright to prevent Sam from being held back.

Sam crouched, her chest heaving as she caught her breath. While both trained for endurance, a little rest wasn't unwelcome. A short one, though.

Waiting and not participating lanced his every nerve. He could hold his own with his weapons, but only if the fight remained stationary, which was unlikely.

With weapons at the ready, they surveyed their area and kept a watch in all directions for potential threats. Gunfire erupted in the direction the team had headed, and snapped their attention in that direction. As a rule, HIS avoided gunfire if at all possible.

Sam surged to her feet, and he pushed back to look around them to ensure their security bubble remained intact. A barely perceptible unnatural jungle noise behind him carried in the stilted breeze that slithered up his spine with a bead of threat. Although he tried to steady it, his pulse quickened, and adrenaline pushed him into his fight-or-flight mode. He made to spin around and protect them.

Before he could, behind them, arms reached out of the jungle, and out of the corner of his eye, horror bit down on him for Sam's safety. His heart pounded, and the reflex to fight raged in him. Those arms wrapped around each of them to prevent him and Sam from using their weapons. He couldn't hear but felt Sam's strangled cry as hands clamped over their mouths, and a roar came from him into his captor's hand. Within seconds, the jungle swallowed the two of them.

His stomach clenched and revolted as his heart churned within. Once again, Sam had been captured, and he'd been unable to prevent it.

Chapter Thirty

Frantically twisting and turning to free herself or grab a weapon, Sam's heartbeat went into overdrive, racing so fast she thought it would explode from her chest. While that racked her system, her mind remained cold, calm, and focused, yet slightly off-balance.

There'd been one man on each of them. She had no idea if more existed. Judging by where she hit his body, her threat stood at least six feet tall and had been strong enough to lift her from the ground. She didn't weigh overly much, but it still required a strong man to do so with one arm.

Since she couldn't wrestle herself free with her current tactics, she went on the attack—one of the only ways she could fight in her position. Her combat boots made an excellent sound when one connected with a knee.

"Oomph."

While it sounded more like surprise than pain, a short dose of satisfaction lifted her confidence. She'd go for the other knee before she got dirty. If she had to move to that tactic, it'd have to be with a fist instead of her knee since she faced away from him. Somehow predicting her movement toward his uninjured knee, her captor shifted out of her strike range.

"Easy, Sugar." The whispered name and command set her relief on a whirlwind. Bravo team had arrived. Then her ire rose. Why hadn't anyone told them? Ken's comm must be completely down. No wonder her team hadn't worried about leaving them where they had been. They would receive her boot up their asses for keeping them in the dark.

"Package is secure," Grits said low, presumably to all on their comms.

The thrill of anticipation crept up her spine. Even though he thought he could make it alone, they could get Ken to safety. She knew they needed help and not just because of his wounds. Alejandro had more men than they did—no sense playing the odds when you didn't have to do so.

She spun around and shot a look at Grits, ready to give him a piece of her mind for that stunt, for making her fear for her life, but he placed a finger over his lips. Hoping to hear over the loud pulsing beat of her heart in her ears, she closed her eyes, swallowed, and focused.

Hearing men hurriedly approaching from up the path they'd occupied, she silently thanked the agents for saving them from a firefight where Ken's mobility worried her.

The more they walked, the more pronounced his limp had become, and the slower he moved. The stubborn man wouldn't admit to his team he needed help any more than he already had. That male pride thing would be the downfall of men.

Glancing over, Ken stood firm, gazing at the tangos walking past them. Out of her peripheral, she caught Grits giving a hand signal, then Romeo and Celeb silently slipped out behind the men.

Whispering, she asked, "Aren't you going to send someone to help Franks, Doc, and Cowboy?"

Grits shook his head but never took his focus away from where his agents had left. "Listen."

Quiet reached her ears. The gunfight had ended. Her stomach lurched at what the result might've been.

"Franks called us off, or you know we'd have been there."

As if he could read her mind on their status, Grits quietly announced, "Friendlies incoming."

A collective sigh flowed through the group. Looking over her team, she zeroed in on her missing counterpart. "Where's Nemo?"

"He and Jesse are aboard transport to cover us in the open area."

It made sense to her, especially since they'd need two birds to extract them now that both teams had arrived. Nothing short of euphoria filled her. Then her mind slipped to what Grits had put her through. Before she could give him a piece of her mind, Grits again warned of friendlies before Romeo and Celeb returned, reporting the two tangos had been disarmed and were napping. She realized he'd been doing that for her and Ken, as the rest of the team had heard the others' inbound movement.

"Hey, Boss," Romeo's broad grin projected his pleasure at seeing them again or what he'd just accomplished.

"Aren't you tying them up or something?" Sam asked before Ken could respond to the welcome. They didn't need the men reentering the fight.

Grits shook his head. "No. We don't plan to stay or come back and clean this up. If we tie them, it'll be a death sentence for them. If we stay on schedule, they won't return to the compound with time to rearm before we're wheels up."

Not forgetting what Grits had done, she asked, "Why, pray tell, did you pull us off the track like that? Why couldn't you just step out?" Anger blended in her voice, but part of it derived from fear.

"FNG." Celeb shook his head and laughed.

"Celeb," Ken warned, and the one word inferred something she didn't grasp based on Celeb's solemn reaction.

They'd called her that since she'd been hired and in front of Ken. Although she'd prefer they didn't, she understood it as camaraderie. If Ken began treating her differently or challenged the men's actions, they would have big problems.

With Grits's nod, two agents took off at a good clip just before the remainder of Alpha team arrived. Seeing the entire team with the brush, trees, and hanging vines was difficult. Knowing they were there made the difference.

Grits glanced around the group. "Okay, Speedy and Casper are on point." He instructed each person on their position, so she and Ken—the targets—were covered on all sides. He'd left no room for threats to reach them without much trouble falling on their heads. "Are you ready to move?" He looked at Ken but didn't ask for what she knew would humiliate him in front of the team.

Little did he know, the men had focused on him. His limp and grimace of pain didn't go unnoticed by them either, no matter how hard he tried to pass himself off as unaffected.

Due to their number and to make less noise, they remained on the narrow trail where they could barely walk two abreast, especially with the broad shoulders of these men. With several agents in front and back, Grits strode on her left while Franks walked on Ken's right.

She wondered if Ken realized they moved at a more sedate pace than usual in what she suspected was meant to accommodate Ken. He hadn't told them to pick it up. Instead, he allowed Grits to decide and run things. It showed her how strong a man he was as a great leader, and how he followed his men without question.

The trail forked and opened up to the route they'd take. Based on how long they'd walked, they should be arriving soon. Maybe she just hoped they would because it meant they were that much closer to a ride home.

Having Grits next to her worked best since she didn't have a comm system. While she only heard one side of the conversation, she could put together most of it, and if she asked, he'd probably tell her. The team didn't keep secrets on an op. That could be deadly.

As they made their three-hour trek, Doc dropped back occasionally to check their six and return to take up his position at the rear. Based on Grits's one-word responses, the agents on point must not face any resistance. While she remained focused and ready, relief at almost being safe made her lightheaded. She refused to allow hope to bubble up in her mind until after they were airborne—way after.

They hadn't encountered any trouble and had almost reached the transport. Either Bev had given up, or they just hadn't been found. Both options worked for her.

Placing hers and Ken's extraction as a priority, she worried that Bev would escape them and not pay for her crimes. Although the crimes were committed in Mexico, she didn't know how they'd proceed. Bev could pay for sending her son to Mexico and for the kidnapping. Since she hadn't reported it to the police, their only recourse would be to ensure Cody didn't return to her clutches.

Based on all Sam had learned working with this group, Bev's actions wouldn't go unpunished. Somehow, they'd find a way, no matter how long it took them. She had no idea what the punishment should be for Bev's men shooting Ken, her holding them in captivity, torturing Ken, and attempting to drug them both. Then there was the shootout with their team.

Sam's heart ripped open at the thought that she'd brought this woman into their lives. She'd unwittingly led them all to where they could be killed. Refusing to allow grief to overcome her steadiness, she swallowed past the lump in her throat and shoved it down for consideration later.

Approaching the fork, she tensed since they would be more vulnerable. This far from the compound should have fewer threats. Granted, it took them longer to reach this point since they'd made the detour last night.

The thought of the previous evening had her nerves jittery with a need for Ken's touch to soothe them. A pulse flowed over her skin, leaving an erotic tingling that touched every bit of her.

"Take cover!" While low over the comms, Grits's urgent voice had everyone moving faster than a jungle cat after its prey but nearly noiselessly. Before he'd completed the order, he'd grabbed her arm and shoved her into the overgrowth, leaving his body as a target before he joined her under the shelter.

Glancing over her shoulder, she gasped, and her heart skipped a beat as Ken fell when he twisted. Instinctively, she moved to help, but Grits held her firm, preventing her from assisting. He pulled her next to him. "We won't leave him. You two are the targets. You stay with me. Period."

Half listening to her self-designated bodyguard, her stomach clenched, waiting for Franks to get Ken to safety. Franks reached down, and before he could get an arm under Ken, Doc raced out of concealment to help get Ken to his feet quickly. Her eyes nearly misted at the dedication of this team.

Although Ken could probably walk, getting up bothered him—they kept their arms around his back, not letting him go until they'd reached a safe spot and confirmed he could stand on his own.

Spread out for yards and yards. The team faced the trails

coming into and out of the intersection with weapons ready. An odd sort of adrenaline traveled up her spine, leaving her feeling like she weighed nothing while retaining control.

The next moment, fear gripped her, and if a hand hadn't slapped over her mouth, she'd have cried out, giving away their position. Her heart lodged in her throat as she worked to control herself. A big-assed snake dropped on her shoulder and left her quivering and all but ready to faint. Oh, how she wanted to shoot it.

Frozen to the spot, she nearly passed out from failure to breathe. Having ophidiophobia and trekking through the jungle didn't mix, but she'd had no choice. She'd thought Cody had been abducted, and then she had to get her and Ken to safety. Her fears be damned.

The snake quickly disappeared from her shoulder, yet her fright kept her immobile. Panic ran through her, and every cell in her body stood alert, expecting the snake to strike from whatever position it had taken.

"It's okay, Sugar," Ken whispered in her ear as a hand slid from her mouth. Relief, as she'd never known, flooded her, leaving her emotionally spent and living in an air of safety. The one man who knew and understood her fear had kept her from crying out while removing the object of her terror.

She spun around and wanted to fling herself into his arms and soak up his comfort and love, but she knew it was far from appropriate. That rescue meant more to her than getting shot at on an exit.

Smiling, he nodded back to the edge of the jungle. Turning, her eyes narrowed. Four men with rifles pointing forward raced toward them and abruptly halted, looking around as if lost. They must've realized the trail HIS would take to leave this Godforsaken jungle.

One of the men, a stout guy with thinning hair, appeared to be in charge of the foursome and said something that had them fanning out without entering the forest.

Like the agents on point, HIS didn't engage the tangos. Not out of cowardliness but because they didn't harm or kill unless necessary. Especially in foreign countries, worming their way out of trouble might not be easy. Their governmental contacts only went so high up the chain.

Focused on the four men, she hadn't noticed Franks slip up beside Ken behind her. If she hadn't seen Grits chatting with Ken, she probably wouldn't have. She gave herself an internal shake to wake up any of her senses dulled from the snake attack.

Once the tangos were a reasonable distance away, the teams slid back onto the path, took the left branch, and moved faster with heightened tension.

When they halted this time, they'd arrived at their last bit of cover.

Grits looked at his watch and cursed. An inappropriate giggle bubbled up at wanting to tell him he'd owe Reagan a couple of dollars, but now wasn't the time or place. She couldn't relax, even in thought. "Stand by," he said, presumably into his comms.

Franks and Ken pulled closer, and Ken directed, "Talk,"—always to the point when he led.

"We're five early." He grinned. "We got you here faster than we thought. Of course, you don't look injured to me at all."

Most of the blood had washed out of Ken's pants, but plenty remained.

Grits lifted his arm and pointed left to right. Half of the men spread out into the jungle. "Boss," he hesitated.

Ken nodded. "It's okay. Franks can get me there. I want

you on the bird with us."

"Planned on it." His grin widened.

The conversation confused her. As Ken and Franks moved in front of them, she was about to ask when the welcome sign of the helos' landing reached them. With two birds, the sound echoed around them. Not good if they were still being followed.

It sounded like they'd canceled the hot-loading. Grits must've been concerned whether Ken could launch himself into the bird fast enough. She'd had the same concern.

"On me. Alpha team, bird one. Bravo team, bird two. Keep your eyes open." Grits turned to her. "Your job is to get on that damn bird. No arguing. We'll protect you."

She moved the rifle in her arms. "I'm quite capable."

"What part of no arguing did you not understand?"

She quirked a brow, even knowing she needed to back down and let everyone do their job in this op. She hated that she couldn't be an active member even though she'd rested and replenished her energy.

"Look, Sugar. I didn't say you weren't capable. I need you to be away from any threat. That means you get your ass on that bird. No more discussion." He moved them back in front of Ken and Franks.

Not being able to be part of the protection was a hit to her ego. Yet, she was comforted that the team went to such great lengths to protect her and Ken.

Her heart pounded in her chest. Having Jesse and Nemo covering them bolstered her courage.

"Go, go, go." As they stepped out into the open, they ran toward their transport home.

With their sharpshooters in the birds and agents fanning out to protect her and Ken's trip, she had no idea to what extent Bev would go to recapture them or get to both Ken and Jesse simultaneously.

Her stomach tightened at the thought she'd almost been a part of this lunacy.

A shot rang out from the bird, and she reacted unconsciously, stopping and spinning with her weapon at the ready. Before she could search for targets, Grits wrenched her back around.

"What the hell did I say? Get your ass on that bird!" he shouted to be heard over the noise of the engines.

Three-quarters of the way to safety, she glanced over her shoulder and almost stumbled at the uncoordinated move. What she saw almost stopped her heart. Ken and Franks had gone down.

Not caring what Grits said, she stopped and ran toward them. Damn, if he didn't stop her by grabbing her arm again. She tried to wrench away, but he held firm. He leaned in close so she could hear. "We've got him." Doc rushed up from his position and helped the two men up. He'd nearly lifted them both himself. Ken had his arms around each of their shoulders, and they hustled forward.

Grits turned her, and they raced the remaining steps as their sharpshooters fired off more rounds.

Stepping on the rail and with her heart galloping away, she lifted herself to climb aboard. When Grits put a hand under her butt and pushed her in, she sprawled across the floor. Instead of feeling embarrassed about it, he yelled for her to move. "Now," he added in a firm yell.

With another adrenaline boost firing through her, she scrambled across the floor, carefully avoiding Jesse as he fired again. Once again, she turned and lowered her rifle to take up a support position, but Doc and Franks launched Ken onto the floor at her feet. Grits gave her a glance that bounced between her face and her weapon, so she set it aside and reached down to help Ken, but Doc leaped in—the big man was amazingly agile—and he quickly got Ken situated —no first-class airplane seats on this trip. Jesse might be kicking himself for running this op pro bono after adding two cargo helicopters to the final extraction.

Her eyes met Ken's, and he smiled at her. Her heart fluttered. All the walking and running had to have taken a toll on his leg. Not that they'd helped it the night before. While not a doctor by any means, she suspected the real doctor might have a problem with the wound not being stitched immediately. He'd likely give Ken that cane he hated back for a while.

The following men entered and took positions to protect the final agents entering. Those seated donned their headsets, and when Grits—the last to enter—made it aboard, he told the pilot to get them in the damn air or their bird would be decorated with bullet holes.

It wasn't until they'd flown well away from the area that the team relaxed and switched to a channel for just them so the pilots wouldn't have to deal with their chatter.

As the fear and excitement from the extraction left her, she trembled with relief and suppressed rage as they joked with Jesse about getting Reagan to change her rule. The fact that they weren't bound to follow orders from a child hadn't seemed to occur to them.

Looking at all the men, especially Ken, she'd never been more grateful for the team at her back. Her "friend" had been the one to terrorize them, whether through torturing Ken or men shooting at them as they'd helped her and Ken escape. And Bravo team must've done a quick turnaround to assist them. The past ten years, hell, even before that, almost seemed like a lie. HIS and the team who surrounded and supported her were real. Their connection was everything.

Relief swelled through her. She trusted Alpha team, but they'd been down to almost nothing agent-wise with her and Ken out of the mix.

"Old Man." She couldn't get used to some call signs, but she wouldn't be the one to disrupt what had already been established. "How's Cody?"

A smile stretched across his serious face. "He's good. Kate, Reagan, and Jason came home to be with him. Reagan follows him around and talks nonstop."

She didn't doubt it from the little she knew of his daughter. As for Cody, he could probably use someone the same age to be around. She could barely wait until she returned. Gaining legal guardianship might be challenging, but since Devon had already reached out to the proper authorities, she could only hope everything went rapidly. But Bev. Would she fight it? Sam had to find a way to have her sign over Cody's care permanently. She'd do whatever it took to find the woman and make it happen.

"I want to be included when you find a way to make Bev pay," Sam said.

The men glanced at each other with unease. "Sam," Grits said, his voice soft, "before Bravo team came for you, we stormed the compound looking for her and Alejandro. That's why we didn't join you right away."

Her breath caught. "Is she in the other bird?"

Her heart sank to her stomach at his hesitation like a leaded weight. His following words made her think of one person. Cody.

"We found Alejandro dead and her missing. We don't know what happened, but obviously, he'd been murdered."

Her stomach revolted, and she bit back the bile rising in her throat. What had happened to the woman she'd been closer to than her sister? Grief and anger washed through her in a painful gush. Sam could no longer treat Bev as a friend. She needed to pay for how she'd treated Cody and Ken.

Sam would be the person to make her pay.

With Alejandro dead— "But the men?" Why were people still chasing them?

Grits shrugged. "My best guess is they don't know yet."

Things had gone too far. Her entire focus had to be on Cody, since who knew what Bev would do now that she'd lost her chance to kill Ken and Jesse.

She didn't fight it when Ken put his arm around her shoulder and pulled her to him—with the whomp-whomp sound echoing off the helicopter, her ire ebbed, and a tear slipped down her cheek.

To protect Cody, Sam knew she wouldn't hesitate to kill his mother.

Chapter Thirty-One

Sam's task became apparent, with Cody safe and happy at Jesse's house within a virtual fortress and Ken off to the hospital under superb care. She raised her chin. "I want to go after her," she insisted to Jesse. "I know she was a part of this, even murdered Alejandro, but Cody won't be safe until we apprehend her." After Bev's actions, she couldn't bring herself to say friend, not even her former best friend.

"Sam, we don't even know for certain that she murdered him."

True, but something inside her cried to avenge all Bev had done to Ken and the emotional toll she'd laid on Cody. "I want her."

Jesse sighed. "You're smarter than that. Even if she did murder him, and we know she tortured Ken, it occurred in Mexico. Unlike going after Cody, where the parent hired us to extract him, going in to pull her back against her will is tricky. Especially with someone who's gone off the deep end like she has. We're not Mexico's favorite group right now."

She hated when he was right. While that made him a good boss, she still despised it. There had to be some way. They'd done shades of gray ops before. If Devon could locate Bev, Sam would go alone if necessary. She couldn't have Bev coming after Cody. Couldn't.

When she didn't speak, he continued in a more soothing voice. "Are you sure you're not misdirecting your anger? This isn't the first time you considered the need to avenge someone you love."

All the winds flew out of her sails in a silent whoosh. How could he be so calm about Bev wanting him dead, and Sam had almost contributed to it? Ken must've been awfully convincing when he and Jesse had spoken about her. The men had surprised her with their forgiveness and the confidence she wouldn't fall back into that trap that Bev had helped lay. As upstanding men, they assured her they trusted her to have their backs.

With a thought to Jesse's question, she took a deep breath and let it take away all her anger and assumptions about what had changed with Bev. Desperately, she hoped Cody could grow up not knowing the level of his mother's evilness and destruction. And she knew going after Bev wouldn't resolve everything, but it could make Cody an orphan.

The thought struck hard and almost knocked her down with its heavy burden. Whether an orphan or not, Cody would grow up with Sam. She'd have to talk with Kate and Rylee to see how they did it, to balance the demands of HIS and motherhood.

She'd see if they had a recommendation for a caregiver who could watch Cody while she worked.

"Sam?" Jesse's eyebrow rose as if realizing her mind had jumped the track.

She started. "You're right." Her words released a weight holding down her shoulders. "I'm so sorry, Jesse."

He waved it off as if nothing had happened. "You've already apologized, and I accepted. That's enough of that. Now that your head is back on straight, let's discuss this."

Keeping her emotions out of it, she nodded.

"The twins are watching Bev's house until they can be relieved by one of the teams. Do you think she'd go back there?"

Her first instinct had been no, but with Bev's mind, who knew what she'd do? With a sinking feeling, Sam realized she'd lost touch with Bev's thoughts and couldn't anticipate her actions. "I don't know. Maybe. She's not thinking straight, but she's also methodical. Wildly," she added. "She had all this time to try something, and I don't understand why now and how she thought her plan might work."

"I've been thinking about this," Jesse offered. "I think she'd hoped you would do the deed to keep her hands clean."

Bewildered, she started to respond and, out of long-standing habit, almost defended Bev. Then her mind began to whirl. "She got me riled up about it."

"Yep."

"She had convinced me the report was authentic."

"Yep."

"I considered doing something because of it."

"But you didn't do anything."

She didn't react because Jesse's tone told her he was helping her work through this. "And when I didn't react, she made other plans."

"Yep."

She'd toss something off his desk at him if he said that word again. "But why take Cody?"

"Because she knew you'd do anything for him. And if she took the fight to Mexico, she would probably get away with it because I guess Alejandro had the law in his pocket."

Closing her eyes and letting it wash over her, a renewed sense of purpose filled her, but one thing still had a hold. "I can't believe I allowed myself to be part of her trap. And to think I might've done something regrettable."

"Sam, first, I don't believe you'd ever have followed

through and allowed Ken or me to die. Second, why would you doubt Beverly, who was your friend? I imagine she was very persuasive, convincing you it was the only way."

She had been, but that didn't absolve Sam of not getting to the truth of such vital information before it all began.

Jesse shook his head as if realizing she didn't want to speak further. "I'm worried about Cody."

So was she.

"Since Beverly used the boy to execute her plans, there's no telling if she'll try again. She'll know he's been with you since we took him. She doesn't know where I live but knows where you do."

She opened her mouth to speak and closed it. Although she'd worried about Cody's safety, she hadn't thought through how she'd move forward.

"You're not alone, Sam. With us, you're never alone. You have some choices to make. AJ and Jake are watching your place in case she shows."

Had he brought most of his family back for her? A warm acceptance slid through her veins. "What about Trent's problem?"

Jesse picked up a pen and tapped it on his desk, focusing on it until he spoke. "They caught the men in the act, and Devon tracked them back to who'd been giving Trent trouble. With this situation, they cut their vacation short to be here for the team,"—the corners of his lips twitched into a smile—"and you."

Flabbergasted—an emotion she rarely felt—and unsure what to say except "Thanks" again, she smiled. "You said I had choices." While she had an idea, she'd never pass up something from his brilliant mind and experience.

"No matter your choice, you'll have a HIS guard."

She nodded in relief that she wouldn't be Cody's only

protection.

"There's an extra couple of rooms at my house, and you two are welcome there. As we've said, unless she recently found out, she doesn't know I live here and couldn't pass the security Devon's had built around the place."

She nodded and waited. He tapped his pen more, quicker this time.

"You could go back to your place with an agent."

There seemed to be another option, though she couldn't think of what it might entail.

"Although my least favorite, you could check into a hotel. Mind you, the last two options can be with or without Cody. He's welcome here as long as needed to keep him safe."

While room service and daily bed-making appealed to her, she couldn't do it in this situation. There were too many people to consider. It was too difficult to control. Going back to her place would be comfortable. She knew all the nooks and crannies of her home and neighborhood.

While she wanted to stand and fight Bev, she chose the one who kept her and Cody safe. "We'll stay with you."

The movement of the pen stopped, and he tossed it down. A broad grin spread over his lips. "The right choice."

With a suppressed laugh, she wanted to ask him why he'd even given her a choice. Then she remembered he wanted her to see that she controlled her life…her decisions…her actions.

Now,"—his firm tone made her gulp at what might come next with this change—"are you ready to see Cody?"

Pleasure flowed through her, bringing a smile to her face. "Yes," she said emphatically. "I am. How is he?"

Jesse stood, and she followed suit. "He's fine. The only thing he says about his mom is that he doesn't want to return to her. We didn't prod him, figuring that'd be best for you to do since you know them both."

Damn Bev. "I'll see what I can do. If all else fails, I'll get him into counseling or anything that might work."

He nodded his approval, and that somehow made her feel comforted in her choice. Jesse's daughter, while an infant, had lost her mother. As a father, he understood a parent willing to go to any length for their child.

And Cody was now her child. No matter that she didn't give birth to him.

Following Jesse out of the room and the building to enter the back of the family's home, her palms turned clammy, and she discovered nervousness had taken hold of her. To finally see him again.

When Cody saw her, he rushed to her, and they held each other so tight she didn't understand how they took breaths. Joy and the most beautiful thing she'd ever felt rained over her. If this was what motherhood involved, she understood why delivering a bowling ball from a tiny hole made it worth it.

"Aunt Sam, am I going home with you?"

Tears misted her eyes at the hope in his voice. "What do you think about staying here with me another day or two? Then you can come home with me?"

He could've knocked himself out with how swiftly he bobbed his head. "Yes."

"Well, okay." She grunted hard and then laughed when Cody hugged her tightly. Tears sprang to her eyes, and she closed them quickly and planted a kiss on the top of his head. "I love you, kiddo."

She opened her eyes and watched as he raised his head to look at her, happiness lighting his face. "Love you, too." He gave her one more squeeze before turning away.

She would use the time to learn all the basic parenting stuff to get her through at least the next week or so. She hoped that together, they'd be able to fumble their way forward. Being the cool aunt had been fun, but she knew she'd have to find equilibrium. Smiling, she thought she might keep one or two of the tricks she'd used for special occasions.

Jesse approached her as Cody scampered off, yelling to Reagan that he was staying longer. The grim look on his face had her insides churning.

"Ken," she whispered. It had not been easy to choose which important task to tackle first when they arrived back in Baltimore. With the two men in her life safe, she'd decided to go after Bev because the woman threatened them.

Although she'd wanted to rush to the emergency room to see Ken, Jesse had reminded her that she'd drag two agents with her. Instead, she'd decided to wait and see him when they finished his treatment. That's been a hard pill to swallow—waiting—and maybe she'd been wrong, but by morning, she'd be by his side, no matter what.

When Jesse didn't respond, she wondered whether he'd heard her. His reluctance to tell her anything made her body twitch with worry. "What? Tell me. Is it Ken?" Her pulse raced, and an invisible hand clenched her heart, waiting.

He nodded. "Yes, it's about Ken." He paused, and she thought she might have to wring his neck to get the words out. "They're keeping him overnight."

The floor fell out from under her. If she didn't already want to kill Bev, she would now. "I need to see him," she said weakly. Screw pulling two agents to go with her. They'd understand.

"I figured you would. While I get everything ready, why don't you take a shower? You and Kate are similar sizes, although she informed me you were, uh—" He waved his hands near his chest, and even though everything around her was in turmoil, she wanted to laugh at his discomfort. Who knew big, bad Jesse—their Old Man—could blush and stumble for words?

"Anyhow," he said, trying to salvage things, "we'll have some of your things brought over here later."

Eager to get to Ken but knowing she needed the shower since she still carried the stench of their jungle trek, she nodded, then followed him to a bedroom with a private bath.

As hot water sluiced down her skin, memories of their encounter in the cave brought a smile to her lips. Tingles spread over her skin, filling her core with desire and need. There would be a time soon when they could be together. She was determined to make it so. A passion-laden, languishing sigh escaped her.

After drying off, she pulled her damp hair back into a ponytail and donned the donated clothes. The pants were a size too big but came with a belt, and the blouse was too small. Worried the buttons might fly, she sought out Jesse for a T-shirt.

She wore Jesse's overlarge T-shirt and set off with Franks and Stone, who'd returned from cleaning up at HQ.

As she climbed into the back of the SUV, she realized she hadn't asked Jesse how severe Ken's condition was and hadn't brought any identification or a phone.

The man addled her brain. With a smile, she admitted that she wouldn't change it for the world.

Chapter Thirty-Two

Ken sat in the hospital bed, wondering how he'd let the doctor convince him to stay overnight with a damn IV attached. His leg wounds and burns showed minor signs of infection, which didn't surprise him with the sweat, blood, humidity, and temperatures he'd endured.

The doctor had called him "Lucky," considering his leg wound left him with minimal damage. The doctor cleaned the wound using a pair of tweezers to grab the fabric. It'd been torture. They had to staple the entry and exit wounds since the injury had been open so long that sutures wouldn't work. Thankfully, they'd made it happen with some grumbling about how he'd made their job more difficult by waiting.

Once again, he'd walk out of the hospital with a cane as the muscle damage didn't appear too extensive. He'd gladly take that if it meant Cody and Sam were safe.

Besides, he had to convince Sam to marry him. If his wounds worsened, he'd have a hard time of it. With Sam came Cody. Being a father to the boy didn't faze him. While he'd never considered a family, Cody was Adam's son. He'd respected Adam and would be honored to do right by his boy.

Whether Sam would allow it turned over in his mind. Being independent, she may want to go it alone first. He wouldn't give up. He wouldn't let her go a second time.

After another lousy hand of poker with Doc, he tossed down his losing hand and looked at the clock on the wall.

Sam should arrive soon. Not fast enough.

Doc's deep chuckle bounced around the room. "Time won't move faster because you keep checking it."

Ken wiped a hand over his face and sighed. Doc was right. His friend kept him company, and he wouldn't discount the time with him. "Deal. My luck is about to change," he joked.

Picking up his newly dealt cards, he silently cursed. Another shitty hand. That reminded him. "Did you hear if Jesse talked to Reagan about her swear jar?"

"Oh yeah." Doc laughed hard, and Ken impatiently waited for more. "Now, I heard this secondhand, and I came straight here. Anyhow," Doc continued, "Reagan had been in HQ with Devon. She jumped up when the teams strode in and asked how much money they owed her."

Ken closed his eyes and laughed. He hoped Cody wasn't as precocious as Reagan. "What happened?"

"Jesse took her into his office." He shrugged. "No one knows what was said, but Reagan came and asked for a meeting. Of course, the teams complied. She informed them that it wasn't okay to cuss while they were on ops, but they didn't have to pay her. Cowboy said she tacked onto that unless they wanted to pay her."

Ken chuckled. "Leave it to her to find a way around what her daddy undoubtedly told her."

"Do you think you'll be a parent soon?" Doc asked as though an afterthought while he drew more cards.

Yes, he would. "If she'll have me."

"Oh, I think she will."

His stomach was unsettled with nerves. "They're taking a long time. They left—"

Laughing, Doc cut him off. "I know how long ago they left. Did they put a worry drug in that bag? They probably just got caught in traffic."

Before he could respond, the door swung open with a force that almost sent it crashing against the wall. Only the mechanism on top of the door stopped it.

Sam, wearing an overly large T-shirt and jeans, came to a screeching halt and stared at him, her eyes never straying to Doc. Her wide-eyed gaze gradually warmed, and electricity zinged between them.

While he'd been physically injured, he'd worried more about her and the emotional turmoil this incident had caused. Maybe asking her to marry him so soon hadn't been wise, but with her, he didn't always think right. His mouth tended to run away with itself.

Dropping the cards still in his hand while Doc moved, Ken presented her with one of the widest grins he could muster. He'd only been given a common painkiller, so the smile truly came from within.

Moving farther into the room, she halted at his side, leaned down, and kissed him as if no one else was in the room. Maybe Doc had already left. He didn't care.

Her lips brushed his in a soft, lingering kiss, enough to tingle through his body. Much more of this, he'd yank her onto the bed with him and show her how much he loved her.

"Now, that's the best greeting I've received since I was held here against my will." While not entirely true—the last part—it sounded good.

"I can't imagine how the team or the hospital staff would greet you, but I hope this was the best." Her eyes were alight with mischief.

With their gazes locked, love and desire flowed perfectly between the calm of a lake and the raging waves of an ocean. He'd given up so many years with her, but finally, he had her.

Reaching out, she took his hand and threaded her fingers through his before she sat in the chair beside his bed. "I would've been here sooner, but—"

"It's okay. You're here now. How are you? And how's Cody?"

Her gaze remained riveted on their joined hands, and something gripped his insides. What did she fear?

"We're fine. We're going to stay at Jesse's for now."

"That's a good idea."

The sadness on her face when she finally looked up at him caught his breath. "I'm sorry, Ken. I—"

Hoping to reassure her, he squeezed her hand and smiled. "Sam, don't. There's nothing to be sorry about. Not for Beverly's actions or yours."

"But—"

He cut her off and steeled his voice to stop this craziness. "What's done is done. Some things don't need revisiting."

When she dropped her head, he changed the topic. "Since you wore your nightgown to visit, does that mean you're crawling into bed with me?"

She looked down at the black HIS T-shirt he knew couldn't be hers. "It's not a nightshirt. It's Jesse's T-shirt. Kate's shirts didn't quite fit."

Redness crept up her cheeks, and he found it adorable. Trying not to chuckle at what she'd said because anyone with eyes—especially a red-blooded male—knew the difference in the women. "I see." He bit his tongue not to say something that might land him in the doghouse, especially since his mind had wandered to holding them in his hands and having them against his chest.

Squirming because his thoughts were derailing, he cleared his throat, smiled, and went all in. "Why don't you climb into bed with me and let me see why the other shirts wouldn't fit?"

She laughed, and he couldn't decide if he preferred the sound or the expression on her face at the action.

Her eyes twinkled in merriment, but a deep longing sat on the edges. "While getting caught with my pants down by the team doesn't appeal to me, getting caught by a hospital worker seems ten times worse."

"Well, come lie in my arms. I need to feel you and know that after everything, you're safe."

After a glance up and down the blanket covering his body, she bit her lip. "I don't want to hurt you."

"You won't. I'm not that bad. Now come here."

Relief that she'd stood to join him whipped through him. He hadn't realized how important that step was to ease his fears.

A knock sounded on the door, and she stopped her progress. Alarm flashed across her eyes before she spun around, her hand slapping her thigh where she kept her holster. Only now, she didn't have one.

He had little concern because his weapons rested under his pillow. When the doctor had taken him back for care, Doc had sought approval through the security department. Although unorthodox, at one time, Jesse had permission for HIS because of prior security details. So there'd been no problem with him retaining his weapon.

Besides, his men already watched the door, so it shouldn't be anyone not approved. Still, with one hand gripping the stock, he said, "Come in." He could whip it around and fire in no time if it was trouble.

The door opened for Franks and Stone. Both wore frowns. Before he could greet them, Franks glowered at Sam. "You were supposed to wait."

His eyes widened as he knew Franks's pain. "I take it

your clearance ran into a snag, and Sam didn't wait?"

Turning to Ken, Stone said, "New guard. We almost threatened to call his boss to get our standing approval."

Sam reached down and slid her hand into his. While she probably didn't realize it, her small action made him feel ten feet tall.

"Thanks for seeing Sam here," he told the men. "I know you'd have liked to go home after this."

Stone shook his head. "No. We want to be here so that crazy woman doesn't catch up to Sugar." Realizing the possible impact of his words, he turned to Sam and sheepishly said, "No offense."

She laughed, and the music of it touched him deep down. "It's okay. Bev is crazy."

"We're here until you're ready to leave, Sugar."

"Thanks, Franks. I want to stay all night if we twist an arm and get approval. Is that a problem?"

His slow smile appeared. "No problem. We'll take care of the approval and take over for Romeo and Celeb. We'll just be outside."

"But—"

Ken cut her off. "Thanks."

Once the men exited, she turned to him. "Why did you stop me from offering the couch or the chair? I can't sit on both at the same time."

"Because we need privacy."

"Ken, I told you we couldn't here."

He grinned as mischief grabbed hold of him. "I'm not talking about that. I'm talking about you coming over here and lifting your shirt so I can see the evidence of why you couldn't wear something from the other women."

Chapter Thirty-Three

After a night of dozing in one of the most uncomfortable hospital beds he'd encountered, Ken woke early enough to watch Sam sleeping in the chair beside his bed. Again, she had that peaceful glow about her.

The Sam he knew…the Sam he loved…the Sam who loved him. He'd endure almost anything for her happiness.

When she'd invited Franks and Stone to take turns on the couch, he'd hoped their arguments would win. Sam had been more persuasive, and Franks slept on it now, his feet hanging over the edge.

As if an alarm clock had buzzed, Sam and Franks awoke simultaneously. She smiled at Ken with a warmth and love that reached deep and fed his soul. He may have loved her before, but the woman she'd become completed him.

He closed his eyes and groaned. Had he really just used a corny movie line to describe the two of them? If the team found out, he'd lose his man card.

Franks sat with his legs over the edge of the couch, running his hand through his blond hair. It did nothing for his rumpled appearance.

Sam shifted in her chair when he stood and stretched, dropping her feet to the floor. "Is it true you're going to helicopter school?" she asked Franks. Until now, Ken had been the only one who knew for sure, as he'd given Franks time off for training. The team had its rumors, making it near impossible to keep something from them…the men and women who made up a family.

Franks shrugged as if it meant nothing. "I have been for a while. Our schedules don't always make it easy to attend regularly."

Stone entered the room, pushing a phone into his pocket. His gaze instantly zipped across the small space, and Ken would bet his agent hadn't missed anything. "The doc is doing rounds early and will be here in a few minutes. Will you be ready?"

With a nod, Ken turned to Sam. "Why don't you take Franks to get some breakfast, then bring something up for us?"

Sam opened her mouth, probably to argue, but Franks stopped her. "I sure could use something to eat. Dinner last night left a lot to be desired."

Once Franks led Sam out of the room with a backward look and nod, Ken turned to Stone, knowing Franks would keep her away for a while. "Tell me."

"Nothing. From what Cowboy says, Devon's about to pull his hair out since he can't locate her." He shifted, looking uncomfortable, and a cold hand gripped Ken's insides. "Well, I know now isn't the best time, but remember when Devon talked about having someone on each team that could help with the load at HQ?"

Relief whooshed through him. He'd already had an inkling that Stone would be the person on his team who'd be interested. With mostly military special operators, Ken knew those veterans wouldn't ride a desk, but Stone had been FBI and, from what Ken had learned, pretty damn good with computers and research. "Uh-huh." He paused and assessed his agent. "And you want to work at HQ. Be our Devon?"

"I do."

"As long as you realize it's when we're up, you're boots on the ground with us unless Devon and I decide you'd benefit us better behind the wheel. Or, until we expand the team."

"I know it might get busy, but I want to help more. I'm no Devon, but I had a lot of practice at some of that computer magic he's capable of doing."

"When we get back—"

A doctor, who seemed too cheerful early in the morning, interrupted them. With great patience, Ken allowed the man to examine every wound, then poke and prod him until he wanted to lash out.

With a prescription for pain medicine and some ointment for his burns, Ken waited for the nurse to speak with him and all the stuff that went with checkout. Sam and Franks arrived as his release papers were finally placed in his hand.

Never happier to leave, he hustled them out. He wanted her to be secure once again.

When they drove through Jesse's gate, Sam directed them to take her to the house first so she could check on Cody. Even though they'd discussed the security measures on Jesse's land, she still worried about his safety.

Kate met them at the door, and Franks and Stone turned down the path to HQ. He stopped at the mess as she, Kate, and Ken walked by the family room.

"They created blanket tents last night," Kate informed them. "I just haven't gotten to it. They were up most of the night trying to keep everything from falling. Once they conked out, Jesse shored it up so it didn't drop during the night."

"Where's Cody?"

Kate's pleasing smile eased his tension. "He's with Reagan, riding Winglet."

Sam frowned. "What's a Winglet?" Kate had to be messing with their heads. Then again, if Reagan was involved, there was no telling.

"He's a horse," Kate said, like he should know that. "Haven't you heard her mention him? She talks nonstop about it."

"I didn't realize it'd be here. I thought she rode at a training place."

"She did, but she drove me nuts wanting to go all the time. It was easier to buy the horse and hire a groom. The barn's been unused for so long, so we didn't have to build anything."

While not well-versed in the cost of keeping a horse, he knew it would be an expense someone like him couldn't afford. But with how down-to-earth Kate acted, he often forgot she was a multi-millionaire. She didn't usually spoil Reagan to this extent, so the little girl must've been a significant pest. "So why the name Winglet? It's not a usual one."

"Reagan just comes up with these things. I never question her creativity or the originality unless I've prepared for a long, and I mean *long,* justification."

"I want to see Cody," Sam said with determination.

He did, too, and even though security was tight, he always wanted someone with the boy.

"Sure. Go out the back and take a golf cart down the winding path to the left. It's back a little to keep the smell away."

Sam took a step in that direction.

"Oh, I know how hard it is to sleep in the hospital with either the uncomfortable chair or a nurse checking in every couple of hours. After you've seen Cody, go up and rest. He'll be busy for a long time. When he's back, I'll watch him until you wake."

"Wait," Ken asked Kate, but also directed the word to

Sam, "who's with them?"

"Brett, the trainer, and Rylee."

"Is she—"

Before Ken finished, Kate anticipated his question and nodded. "She is."

A small weight lifted from his chest when he realized someone was close to Cody and armed.

"One more thing, in case I miss you when you return inside, Sam. While you were gone, Emily went to your place and picked up some clothes, and I grabbed a few things from your locker. It's all in the chair in the guest room."

With that parting speech, she walked away without a backward glance. She hadn't asked if they'd need two rooms. The family respected their privacy.

He had to figure out why Sam hadn't argued to go to HQ after seeing Cody. Sam had a relentless drive to go after Beverly from what he'd learned from Franks.

He'd have to watch her and hope he did what was right by her and Cody.

Jesse met them on the path and inquired about his health. Realizing something was up, he exited the cart and told Sam to proceed. Despite the curiosity in her eyes, it was clear she was torn between staying and going to Cody.

Going to Cody won out as it should. He'd rather be there, too, but he needed to hear what Jesse had to say. "I'm going to the house."

Before she drove down the path, he circled the vehicle and gave her a quick kiss. "I'll meet you in a few minutes."

She hesitated. "Promise to tell me everything?"

"Yes." And he would, even if he knew it might hurt her. He hated to give her bad news. Professionally, she needed to know it to do her job.

As she drove away, he watched her back in that oversized T-shirt. She hadn't even wanted to stop and change out of it.

Without taking their eyes from her, Ken asked, "Whatcha got?"

"She's back."

Jesse hadn't needed to identify the "she" because it'd only be the bitch on the run.

"Devon doesn't know how she got back without triggering anything. A neighbor told AJ he'd seen her lurking in the neighborhood."

Anger pumped fast in his veins with a cold lick of fear that she'd get to Sam somehow. "Do they have her?"

Jesse shook his head. "No. We sent Casper, Speedy, and Nemo to the area to help AJ and Jake cover it more thoroughly."

He digested that for a moment with confusion. "Why Bravo team and not mine?"

"I almost sent yours."

"So why didn't you?" Ken asked, his brows raised.

With tight lips, Jesse offered, "Because I thought your team would want to be here when we brought her in."

He nodded his gratitude. "Okay. Think we're going to have any problems bringing her here?"

Jesse shook his head. "Shouldn't, but we can't hold her. Once she realizes that and pushes to leave, we'll keep an eye on her, along with Sam and Cody."

"They can't live here forever." They'd live with him as soon as he could get her to agree. A sigh escaped him.

"What's wrong?" Jesse asked.

He shook his head. "I just hate Sam dealing with a woman—her friend—who betrayed her."

"You can't protect her from all the hurts in the world."

"I know. She's quite capable of taking care of herself. Hell, she basically rescued me. I just wish I could hand her a perfect world."

Jesse chuckled and slapped him on the back. "Spoken like a true man in love."

He couldn't disagree with that statement.

"On a brief sidetrack, our attorney is almost done with the paperwork on Cody. It was a good call on your part to jump on it early."

A lump formed in his throat at the generosity of the Hamilton family. "Thanks."

"Anything for you, Ken. We've been together for a long time. You're my family too."

Good God. His eyes misted, and he corralled his emotions.

"Are you going to marry her?"

Without hesitation, he answered, "Yes."

Jesse reached forward and slapped him on the shoulder blade. "Let us know when the big day is."

"Well," he hedged, "she hasn't actually said yes."

Ken didn't find it funny like his boss. Jesse threw his head back and roared with laughter.

To change the subject, Ken asked, "Kate mentioned us resting. What's all that about?"

"Sam needs to rest and step back until we bring Beverly in. The intensity of her desire to find the woman doesn't mix with what we need to do. We've learned about how that passion can screw up an op."

He figured it was something like that. "Why not just sideline her and let me get back to it? This was my assignment, to begin with."

"Because," Jesse said, "I think you're the only person who will make her step back."

He'd never neglected his duties or allowed something or someone to take precedence. The only time he'd missed an op was when his father died.

Already feeling like his family was in danger, he disregarded his aches and moved forward with what he had to do. He had to keep Sam and Cody safe until Beverly was in their hands.

"How do you expect me to do that? She'll go rogue as soon as I tell her she's out. Anything to protect Cody."

A corner of Jesse's lips twitched. "I'm sure you'll think of something."

He flipped Jesse the bird and strode off.

At the corral, Cody sat astride a beautiful brown horse with a white stripe down its head.

Pride infused him at the sight of the kid on the horse and Sam smiling while resting her foot against the bottom rail of the wood fence. He had a feeling they'd visit quite often.

Coming up beside Sam, he leaned on the top rail while his fingers itched to touch her…feel her silky skin…pull her close to his body…. His blood heated at each thought.

Boy, he had it bad. He clasped his hands tightly to keep them where they were.

"I want him with us," she said.

Her use of "us" sent his heart into an unnatural beat. He knew she meant now, but…. "You want to tear him away from this to make you feel better? I'd like him with us, too, but he won't be happy. He's safe with Rylee and Brett."

She let out a weary sigh. "I know. I just…."

Screw not touching her. He turned to her and pulled her into his embrace. "You're just acting like a mom who cares."

Into his shoulder, she said, "I just worry about him. He's been through so much."

He kissed the top of her silky strands. "I agree, but being with Reagan has been good for him. It's like a big sleepover to him. Don't take that away right now."

"Okay," she reluctantly agreed.

Stepping out of their embrace, he said, "Come on, let's go lie down. You look worn out."

She tossed him a flippant grin. "Gee, that's nice to say."

He shrugged. "Had to be said." Grabbing her hand, he led her to a golf cart, up the path, inside the house, and to a guest room, holding his breath from time to time when she lagged.

Leaning back, she eyed him with small slits in her gaze. "How'd you know I'd be in this room?"

With a sly grin and wink, he responded, "Trade secret."

Entering the room, he closed the door and walked her back to it with slow, easy steps as if it were a dance they'd perfected. Being this close to her, his breathing grew heavy and his heart light. The woman tied him up in knots he'd purposefully never undo.

The love and desire that gleamed in her eyes and on her face nearly sent him over the edge. Bringing his hands up to rest against the door on either side of her head, he noticed a slight tremor. When she licked her lips, the tight grip on his patience snapped.

"I've waited long enough for this."

Chapter Thirty-Four

Sparks of pleasure shot between them, igniting the fire he'd built within her. His lips descended to meet hers, taking his time, letting his tongue explore the inside of her mouth before languidly tangling with hers. He acted like they had all the time in the world, but she knew they'd get called back to HQ at some point.

Pushing that thought aside, she took advantage of the time they had. The events in the cave were foreplay, and Ken, despite his injuries, came at her with the force of a hurricane.

When his lips moved hungrily against hers, shooting a bolt of lust to her core, her hands fluttered over his chest, then he stiffened. Remembering his burns, she pulled back, unsure.

With a "Fuck it," he pulled her snugly against his heated body. A small smile came to her lips at his low growl.

With the hardness of his arousal against her, she wanted to throw herself, spread-eagled, on the bed and tell him to love every inch of her. Yet she wanted him to sprawl out like that so she could feast. Their future would not get tiring.

As his lips moved to her neck, she tilted her head and all but mewled as she rubbed herself against him like a cat. When he spread red-hot kisses over her neck to her ear and back, she almost missed when his hands slid down, reaching the hem of her shirt and tugging it up.

Against the need in her body, she straightened and moved her hands to his, stopping the movement. "Didn't you say the doctor frowned at you when he found out about your idea of 'activities'?"

That infuriatingly sexy grin spread across his face. "Yep."

She arched her eyebrow. "Didn't he say you shouldn't do anything until healed?"

"Yep."

If possible, that grin grew. "So, what are you doing?"

"This." With her hands over his, he lifted the huge T-shirt she wore.

"But—but, your leg."

"Screw my leg. Now," he said with a raspy voice, "get that damn contraption off."

It took her a moment to understand he meant her sports bra. She'd hated wearing the dirty thing, but going braless to the hospital hadn't been an option. Of course, seeing her struggle with it in the cave probably gave the impression that it was impossibly difficult to remove. But it'd been wet then. It was thankfully easy when dry.

With what she hoped turned out to be a saucy grin, she stripped the undergarment off and whirled it around her finger like a stripper, then slung it across the room.

His eyes darkened, desire resting within.

When he stepped back and surveyed her naked torso, self-consciousness burst forth, and she almost covered herself. Almost. Having that first real night with someone one loved shouldn't make one nervous, but there it was. She shoved that thought aside, opened herself to him, and smiled.

She searched his eyes for any clue to his thoughts. Then she saw it. He devoured her with a nearly bursting hunger.

When his eyes left her breasts and returned to her face, he opened his mouth to speak, but nothing came out. He tried again. "You're perfection."

"I'm not even fully undressed yet."

Slowly, a grin slipped across his face. One that turned her insides and had her craving his touch…kisses…and loving. "We can correct that right now."

Stepping toward her, their eyes remained locked in a smoldering embrace that could've set the room ablaze. He reached for the top of the jeans she'd borrowed. She didn't protest as he unbuttoned, unzipped, then slid them down before she stepped out of them.

"Damn." Licking his lips, he looked at her non-underwear state, then at her. "If I'd known you'd been commando underneath, I'd have removed those pants long before now."

Smiling, she reached for his shirt, but he stopped her.

"I'll do it."

Seeing the few spots on his chest where he'd been burned almost put a damper on things. Would every time she saw them remind her of how she'd nearly allowed her ex-friend to talk her into killing the man she loved and her boss? She'd have to remember the positives—she and Ken came together, they had a significant connection in the cave, the team came out to support them, and Cody was going to be safe with her.

He must've realized she began to cool because he tilted her chin up so she could look him in the eyes. "Don't. They don't hurt, and we're safe." His lips gently touched hers, moving slowly over her mouth while a hand sneaked in and played with one of her breasts.

Bad times forgotten, she leaned into his touch with a moan of pleasure. Once she responded and everything flared up again for them, he shifted his kisses to her breasts, moving from one to the other, leaving them heavy and eager for his lips and tongue. When his mouth grasped a nipple and sucked and tugged, she cried out at the jolt that shot to her core.

Needing to touch him but not wishing to break away from the pleasure, she reached toward him, rubbing his erection through the jeans. It wasn't enough, so she reached for the button.

On a growl, he said, "Bed."

She didn't argue but worried when she saw him unable to bend as he removed his jeans and underwear. He'd adjusted by pushing both down as far as he could while standing, then sat on the edge of the bed and pushed them down, toeing them off at the bottom.

His magnificent cock stood at attention, and she wanted it inside her more than she wanted her next breath. They belonged together, and they belonged in a loving embrace and act.

Her mind whirled at how difficult it'd been for him to remove his jeans. The doctor said he shouldn't do this. She was selfish and didn't want to stop, but maybe she should. Well, she'd tried that already, and he'd argued. Hurting the man she loved didn't sit well with her.

"Ken—"

"Quit, Sam. I'll be fine if I'm not on top. The muscles in my leg aren't ready for that. Lie here beside me, and let's do that—kissing and touching thing." He settled on his good side and patted the space beside her. This looked awfully familiar.

Smiling, she crawled over beside him. Propped up on elbows, they faced each other with little space between them.

She tried to move closer, but he halted her. "I need space to touch you."

Need radiated through her, pulsing at her core. She didn't

want to wait.

Each kiss reached deeper and deeper into her heart that he'd set free. Free from the hate…free from the darkness… free from her refusal to live life as she should…free to love again.

While his mouth slipped down her neck on a path to her breasts, her hand slid down his body past a well-defined chest and a taut stomach. He stiffened, and a moan slipped from him when she gripped his cock. Although she'd already seen and touched him, it felt new—a new step in their relationship.

As if to keep up with her exploration, his free hand burned its way down her body, then moved between her thighs.

"Sweetheart, you're wet for me."

He didn't have to tell her that. She knew. "I want you inside me." While she'd love more foreplay, she didn't wish to wait any longer. She pulsed with her need for him.

He grinned and rolled onto his back. "You don't have to tell me that twice."

A giggle bubbled out and didn't fit in their setting. It went to show how easily they meshed.

Straddling Ken, she avoided looking at the burns but noticed something she'd somehow been missing. A round scar as big as a nickel stood out near his left arm socket. Tentatively, she reached out and touched it. She didn't need to ask.

"The bullet hit around the edge of my vest. Bled like crazy. That one evened up Jesse and me saving each other's lives, dragging one back wounded from a battlefield of sorts. Then, he got hurt again."

Tears misted her eyes at all this man had endured in his life.

"Enough of that. If you don't slide yourself down, I'll pick you up and do it." He closed his eyes and tensed. "Shit. Condom."

"Oh." In her mind, she screamed, *Nooooooo!*

"There's one in my wallet. Back pants pocket."

"I'll get it." She climbed from the bed, nearly ripping his wallet from his pants pocket, to return to bed.

Without a word, she opened the package and rolled the condom down his length. Straddling him again, she positioned herself on him and smiled.

He repeated, "If you don't slide yourself down, I'll pick you up and do it."

Without arguing, she grabbed him, and when she slipped his cock inside her, her world changed. Once she was fully seated, no one else in her life would do.

With his hands on her ass, he moved her to a tempo that flamed the burning inside to a raging wildfire. She wondered if she could die from this much bliss.

"Sam, you feel so good. So tight. So perfect."

She leaned down to kiss him, but he shifted her up slightly to place his mouth on her breast.

As she rode him, each movement built upon that fire, and only he could extinguish it and send her floating into that pleasantly sated place.

"We were made to be together," he said before clamping onto a nipple again.

"We were." Sitting back up, she adjusted her hips and moved in a rhythm that, if the tension in his jaw indicated anything, led him closer to the edge as it did her.

Moving faster as her core throbbed in the desperate need for release, he growled, "You're killing me."

With a grin, she kept going, feeling euphoria spiraling through her. When her eyes squeezed shut, and her head dropped back in surrender, she contracted around him, knowing it brought him closer to his release.

As if in tune with what she needed, he raised his hips to push deeper into her and groaned. Her breath caught, and her eyes shot open to look at him with concern. The movement had to have sent a shock wave through his injury.

"Don't you dare stop," he ordered.

Unable to stifle a moan, she obeyed his order and rode him, taking every bit of pleasure he gave. She launched headfirst into a contentment that swallowed her whole.

Barely conscious, she heard a rumbling growl, and her name as release overtook him.

She dropped onto him, sliding a bit with their sweat. Both were breathing heavily. She felt his leg twitch underneath her. Lifting to look at him, the pain in his face couldn't be denied.

"It's okay," he assured her. "Letting it rest will do the trick."

"Will you be able to walk?" She couldn't handle it if she'd made him bedridden.

He reached for her cheek with a shaky hand, and she leaned into his palm. "Yes, I will. Don't worry. Come on, curl up here. We should get a few hours of sleep while it's offered."

"Maybe we should've waited until you were fully healed."

"No way would I have changed this moment. I'd endure any pain, as nothing in this life beats the feeling of being inside you—body and soul. That damn poet or whoever coined the phrase had been right. Love does conquer all."

Although she'd never expected something so poetic from him, as his bookshelf held only thrillers, she had to agree with the statement. The two of them had come a long way and overcome many obstacles to come together. The strength of their love was their foundation.

Slipping off him, she stood to get something for them to clean up. Once clean, she curled up beside him as he'd asked. She'd have done it anyway.

With his eyes closed, Ken slipped his hand through strands of her hair, and she welcomed the tender touch.

"I love you." She hadn't meant to rush it out but held her breath, waiting to see what he said in response. Sure, he'd told her he loved her, but how would he receive this?

Thinking he hadn't heard her since his hand hadn't stopped or even faltered, she prepared to repeat it, but her nerves were shaky.

Tucking a strand behind her ear, he lifted on his elbow, then looking into her eyes, he asked, "Sam, sweetheart, the question still stands. Will you marry me?"

Sam stiffened at the knock on the door, and he growled at the intrusion.

Kate's statement had her blood running cold. "They've got Beverly."

Chapter Thirty-Five

Sam jumped up from bed, and adrenaline raced through her body. "What? Who? Where?"

"They picked her up, trying to break into your home. Ken, Jesse's asking for you."

Her breath caught at the implication. Thank God she hadn't taken Cody to her house. But what did Bev want now? Too many possibilities existed that she'd prefer not to entertain.

Surprisingly, Ken had dressed before she'd even laid out a top. He kissed her on the nose. "I'll see you over there."

She gaped at his leaving her, but understood he had his role to play. She raced to get herself ready, wanting to figure out how to stop her friend's madness and refusing to allow the team to exclude her.

Pulling out the clothes that Kate had brought for her, she frowned. What did one wear to confront someone who'd played such an essential role in their life, only to find out they'd been manipulated and set up?

Sam dropped to the edge of the bed. Several emotions jumbled within her until she couldn't figure out how she felt. The two that stood out the most were gratitude for HIS and all they'd done and uncertainty at what was to come. Make that three—her love for Cody and Ken.

Could the three of them make a loving family? While Ken had asked her to marry him before, they hadn't talked about his feelings for the boy and becoming a father. Not everyone could step into that role effectively.

Shrugging, she shelved it and focused since she couldn't figure it all out at the moment. She then accessorized after slipping into a pair of jeans and a T-shirt that actually fit.

She looked at her appearance in a full-length mirror and then pulled her hair back into a sloppy bun with the elastic band she'd used earlier. Even though Em had picked up makeup for her, she rarely wore it since it rubbed off on her rifle butt, and it also had a slight fragrance that a breeze could capture, alerting anyone to her presence. She bypassed it for this meeting.

Satisfied she'd prepared for the coming battle, she exited the room to stop short when she saw Kate waiting.

"I thought you might want to know that Ken leads the interrogation."

She wanted to lead this with all her being. Bev couldn't get away with what she'd done. But that wasn't her role in this Op. Sighing, she'd trust the agents to get them through this. Her team had never led her astray, even when she'd almost gone that way. If they said let Ken lead, then Ken needed to lead.

"Before you argue, think about it. She despises Ken and will get blistering mad and probably share everything to spite him since she thinks we have no authority."

Bewildered, Sam asked, "I didn't think we had authority. When did it change?"

Kate laughed. "We don't have it, but we won't let her realize she's right and can leave whenever she wishes. Besides, we have the authorities on the way."

Her mind whipped back to what was most important. "Where's Cody?" Her breathing rushed in and out, frantic as her eyes roamed the area.

"Calm down." Kate's soothing voice and soft touch on her arm slightly relaxed her.

She trusted and believed in this woman. She'd never allow something to happen to the children.

"He and Reagan have challenged each other to some hot game they've displayed on the big screen. Rylee is still with them, and AJ and Jake are also hanging out."

Relief spread through her body, allowing her to end this madness that could haunt Cody for years. "I have to see him before I go."

Kate raised an eyebrow. "Are you sure you're ready for him to see you like that?"

When she'd accessorized, she'd strapped on a replacement weapon—thank you, Kate—on her thigh. She hadn't thought much about it as it'd become a part of her. Cody might not understand, and she wouldn't do that to him. "Just watch him for me, please."

A soft smile graced Kate's lips. "There's no need to ask. Now, I do believe they're waiting for you to begin."

Her eyes widened. Waiting for her? The camaraderie of the team had her eyes misting with love.

Kate nodded. "Yes, Ken went over to get spun up. He says to trust him."

How many more times would Kate say to trust Ken? From what she'd learned—albeit by the gossipy men on the team—Kate hadn't trusted Jesse one iota when they'd met, and he'd tried to protect her. "Wait, what does spun up mean?"

Kate shook her head, but a grin remained on her face. "Oh, the military guys tend to use it. It's when you're reading into an op late or new intel has arrived. He'll quickly devour everything new collected about Bev and the situation."

"Okay." She'd try to be the excellent agent who knew her place. And that place wasn't stepping over her boss's toes, no matter how nice they were rubbing up and down her bare calves.

"Are you ready?" Kate asked.

Ready as she'd ever be. No case had ever been this personal. She hoped no more would be. She nodded and walked through the large kitchen to the back exit and down the HQ path. After typing in her code, she took a deep breath and opened the door.

Breathing slowly in and out while walking down the hall to keep her ire down, she ducked into the war room and stopped. All eyes turned to her, support and caring evident in every pair. She looked at her team and almost wept at their solidarity.

This made her plan to leave them so gut-wrenching.

Chapter Thirty-Six

Maybe others didn't notice, but being attuned to Sam's nuances and looks, her eyes' fast display of emotions surprised him. She'd walked in with apprehension and maybe a bit of fear. Then he'd caught a glimpse of gratitude and love, which he attributed to her notice of the team's support.

That final emotion in her eyes when she stopped short of the agents had to be sadness. He couldn't comprehend it at this distance and couldn't question it or support her until later. That knot of worry about how she'd handle this interview sat as a lead weight in his gut.

Her happiness was his, and when she hurt, he did too. She'd suffered enough that he had to end this for her, however he could. He loved her too much to allow this emotional torture to continue.

Today, he'd finally slain the demon that had been breathing its lethal fire at her for years. He'd almost wanted her to stay away, but knew she needed to be there and see this through, no matter how painful. If Beverly slung her vile words at Sam, his restraint might not be tight enough to keep him in check.

He stepped toward her. "Are you ready?"

With a slow nod, her weak voice called to his heart. "Yes." As if realizing how she'd sounded, in a firmer voice, she repeated, "Yes."

Ken led Alpha team agents into one side of the conference room. They'd discussed building an interrogation room but hadn't had much need for one. They'd only brought a few people to HQ and preferred not to bring anyone into their domain. However, maybe they should consider the idea.

Beverly sat on one side of the long, thick walnut table with Grits and Romeo standing guard behind her, flanking her seat. The conference phone and other toys Devon supplied for the room had been removed. No sense in giving her any opportunity.

Across from Beverly, he offered Sam a chair beside him before he sat. This had been his first look at the woman since she'd been brought to HQ. He'd been surprised Jesse had allowed that, but he'd heard she'd been blindfolded from Sam's home to this room and had bitched about it so much they'd threatened to gag her. He wouldn't have put it past them.

He couldn't tell if her wrinkled, blue, silky top and wild hair had more to do with her mental or on-the-run state. Either way, she looked like a woman who'd taken a dive over the edge.

In a planned role, Jesse walked over to him, dropped a blue folder on the table in front of him, and then took a stance to Ken's left. Instead of sitting, Jesse stood with his arms crossed over his chest, which was how he imagined all the men behind him standing. Pride swelled in him at this team.

"Hello, Beverly," he said evenly.

She hissed at them. At least, he couldn't describe it as anything else. She turned to focus her attention on Sam. "You backstabbing bitch. We had such a great plan, and you backed out."

When Sam tensed, Ken lowered his hand below the table and squeezed her leg.

"Name-calling won't get us anywhere. There is one vital thing we are going to accomplish today."

In a quick, jerky motion, Beverly crossed her arms over her chest. "I'm not doing anything with you, husband killer."

Ken flinched at the name, not because he felt he'd earned it, but because he wished Adam had never lost his life. Maybe then Beverly wouldn't have done this.

With no need to drive his mind down that road, he continued on course. He tapped the folder in front of him. "When you first called Sam about Cody being missing, you started a chain of events that were not all within your control."

Her eyes bored into him with hate and contempt, but he didn't care. One thing would get done without her admitting to anything. Some things were more important than others.

"See, when we figured out you'd somehow played us at Cody's expense, we started our own chain of events—fully outside your control. Before we even rescued Cody,"—he refused to call him her son—"we had our attorneys start some paperwork." He didn't mention Devon had spoken with FBI Deputy Director Arthur Hall when they'd realized things were going tits up.

That got her attention. Her eyes widened, and she sat up straight. Maybe realizing her slip, she narrowed her eyes and acted as if she didn't care.

"You *will* sign this document to give Sam custody of Cody." Granted, he had no clue what level of guardianship, adoption, or whatever the HIS attorney had included. The man had just promised that Sam would go home with the boy.

Beverly jammed her thumb in her chest so hard Ken expected she'd bruise herself. Good thing there were witnesses here, so he didn't get blamed. "My son is mine.

No one else gets him." She looked at Sam with venom in her eyes. "No one."

Ken chuckled, and with the intensity of Sam's stiffening, he knew he'd thrown her. She didn't know his game.

"Oh, I think you'll sign. Not only is it in Cody's best interest, but you've also become a very wanted woman."

Fear washed across her face. "What do you mean? I didn't do anything in the US."

"You mean besides allowing your son to be kidnapped and transported out of the country?"

With a smug attitude, Beverly leaned back and crossed her arms again. "I didn't break any laws there." At the number of snorts behind him, her startled look said she must've rethought that.

A weapons buyer who'd been busted in Georgia had admitted Beverly had been at a purchase with Alejandro. Apparently, it hadn't been the first time, but they wouldn't bring it up for Sam's sake. They'd leave the arrest and investigation to the alphabets.

He went for another tactic. "How'd you get back from Mexico so fast?" And, he wanted to add, without triggering an alarm.

"Alejandro had plenty of resources for me to use. The right amount of money greases many palms."

"I didn't realize you had a lot of money."

"Alejandro always said what's his is mine."

"And now it's all yours?" he hedged. Although he didn't need it, he wanted her to confess to Alejandro's murder. They were handing her over to the FBI either way, but it'd be satisfying to accomplish it. But Cody came first.

"Of course," she said flippantly.

"How did Alejandro die?" He held his breath, hoping she'd turned smug enough.

"I shot him. Just like I should've shot you instead of toying with you until that asshole"—she pointed at Jesse—"arrived."

Devon, who'd situated himself by the door, slipped out quietly at her confession.

Leaving that line of questioning there and not hinting that she'd hung herself, he tapped the folder again. "You've just admitted to killing Alejandro and using his resources to return here."

"That's a crime in Mexico. You have no authority."

He didn't, and it showed she'd been sane enough to plan this to escape punishment. "You're right. I don't."

That surprised her and took the wind out of her sails.

"See, what I meant by you confessing to killing and using his resources is that those people whose money he took to buy guns or who he owes for the guns will be very interested in how to access what they consider theirs. Now, I imagine if they knew where to find you...." He let it hang with whatever assumption she chose to make. They would not be so low as to let her loose with those dogs or lie to have her sign the documents. She didn't know that, though.

He slid the papers across the table, and Grits held out a pen. They watched her like a hawk, knowing a pen could be a mighty weapon.

As if she'd discovered something funny, she smiled that odd smile that curled his blood. With a shrug, she signed everywhere before Grits snatched the pen from her and picked up the papers.

She wore that smug smile again. "It doesn't matter what you think. It needs to be notarized, and without that or either of our attorneys present, those papers are worthless."

Now Ken's smile grew smug. This wasn't their first rodeo dealing with crazies. A man in a crisp, gray suit stepped from the back of the room. "Beverly, meet our attorney, Sebastian Davenport, and the man who will notarize what you just signed and verify your verbal approval." Sebastian slipped around the table, collected the folder from Grits, and departed.

Anger slanted across her face so deeply her features began to morph into something sinister. They already knew that to be here, but her look seemed to change. "You tricked me."

"How's that?" Ken asked.

"You said you'd turn me over to those who want Alejandro's money if I didn't sign."

"Actually," he said with too much joy, "I never said that. I only said what if they knew where you were."

Her eyes narrowed, and crimson crept up her neck. Whether in anger or embarrassment, he didn't care. Before she schooled her features, her face fell. He freely admitted this was the first time he'd enjoyed seeing someone else's pain. It could be wrong of him. Too much about her brought out his "not giving a shit" flag.

With that paperwork, Sam would be free. Cody would be hers. She had no idea what else they'd planned, and he hoped she could accept it as needed for all involved.

Devon returned with a harried man in an ill-fitting tan suit. FBI Special Agent Finley Anderson. The agent had never impressed him, but he still was FBI. It'd taken him so long to arrive that they hadn't waited and had started without him. Fin—as he hated to be called, so, of course, they called him that—could have the tape of the session, along with the honor of taking her into custody.

The FBI wanted info on Alejandro, the same as the Mexican government. They could play their little wars without HIS being in the middle.

After this transfer, HIS would wash its hands of the situation. But they'd always keep Beverly in their sights. The woman had hurt one of their own and her child for vengeance.

Beverly turned her glare on Sam and pointed a finger. "This is all your fault. I'll find a way to make you pay for helping him escape and taking my son away from me." Her evil stare flitted to him, then back to Sam. "Maybe I'll finish what I started with your lover. You never should've crossed that line to be with someone like him. One of the men responsible for your husband's death. You sicken me."

He opened his mouth to speak, but figured Sam needed to respond even though every cell in his body wanted to reach out and protect her. To show his support, he lightly squeezed her thigh and waited.

"I feel sorry for you, Bev," Sam said softly. "You wasted so long in misdirected hate and almost had me fooled, almost convinced me to do something I could never take back. Jesse and Ken didn't kill our husbands, and I think you know that. The terrorists who shot up the convoy are responsible. And if I hadn't had this great group and the love of a wonderful man—" She turned to him, and he wanted to kiss her and thank her for the show of love. "—I wouldn't have realized what I'd been missing…would still be missing. I only hope you'll realize it before too long." She paused, and the sudden change and steel in her voice ricocheted up his spine. "Touch Cody, and I'll kill you."

Beverly's eyes did that narrowing thing again that had annoyed him—time to transfer her to the FBI.

"Beverly, I want to introduce you to FBI Special Agent Finley Anderson. He's here to—"

He didn't get a chance to finish. She screeched to Agent Anderson, "Did you hear her threaten me? I want her arrested for threatening me, and they stole my son."

Ken rolled his eyes at the woman's stupidity.

"I just arrived. I didn't hear a thing."

She pointed to the door. "You got here a few minutes ago."

He'd heard of people being crazy-stupid, but he'd thought it meant something else. He began to think most of Beverly was playacting.

Fin shrugged. "Sue me."

Ken almost burst out laughing at the agent's response. He imagined the FBI wouldn't have approved, but it seemed a perfect retort to Beverly.

Her mouth opened and closed in a fishy motion.

For some reason, Ken raised his eyebrow at her while she did that, and it didn't please her.

When Agent Anderson moved to Beverly, Ken's men retreated. They were done. They'd accomplished what had been necessary.

It finally struck Beverly what was occurring. "You can't arrest me. I've done nothing wrong. You can't let them take me. Sam, make them stop."

Hoping Sam would remain stoically silent, Ken shrugged nonchalantly. "As far as I'm concerned, they can dump you in the Bay." Driving his gaze into her to confirm the depth of his following words, he said, "Stay away from Sam and Cody. It's not a request."

"Let's go," Fin said to her, with a hand urging her to stand.

Ken turned to Sam—with nothing in the room keeping his energy and love from her—and with all tenderness asked, "You ready?"

His heart nearly broke at the pain in her mist-filled eyes. While the interview had been short, as they didn't want to dive into Alejandro's mess or the full extent of Beverly's craziness, they achieved their goal of ensuring Cody was safe and lived with Sam.

Sam took a deep breath and appeared to hold it. When he thought he might have to help her push out the air in her lungs before she passed out, she released it slowly and nodded. "Yes. I want to see Cody."

"So do I. You two will be safe from now on, Sam. We'll always know where she is, and with all that she's been involved in, I doubt we'll see her on US soil again outside a cell."

"Why would she be in a cell in the States?"

Hell. He walked a tightrope here, wanting to keep Sam in the loop and protect her feelings, knowing her friend had dropped that low. "Just trust me."

With a shout of "Gun," the room erupted in activity and shouts. A shot was fired, and Ken found himself on the floor with air whipped from his lungs and Sam on top of him.

The sounds of a struggle with Grits loudly asking who he assumed was Fin, "What the hell were you thinking, jackass, not having your weapon secured?"

Franks knelt beside him, calling to Sam. The fact that she hadn't moved sent a ball of dread to his heart. Had she been shot?

Thinking briefly about what had happened in those split seconds, he hadn't been focused across the table because Fin should've had Beverly in custody. Sam had turned away from him toward Beverly. His pulse raced as he remembered Sam's eyes widening as she'd stepped between him and Beverly's line of sight.

A low guttural growl of grief rose from deep within his chest. "Sam?" He couldn't see her face since her back was pressed against him. He wanted to roll her off him and see if she'd been hit, but knew he could do more damage if she'd been injured.

When she still didn't move or respond, his gut churned at the thought of losing her after finally reconnecting. They'd been so close to Beverly that Sam would've taken the bullet in her chest or somewhere on her torso.

He had to stay positive because he didn't want to live without her. Frantically, he reached around her to see if he could feel where she'd been shot. Large hands shoved his away.

Relief gushed from him harder than he'd expected possible, realizing Sam had worn her Kevlar vest. That must've been the "stuff" Kate had retrieved from her locker. He tensed again, but not as tightly as before. At that close range, some severe damage could still occur.

"Boss?" Franks asked.

"I'm fine. Sam?"

"Doc's looking her over. He wants you to stop trying to touch her."

A "screw you" came to mind, but he held it back since their instruction enabled them to help her.

"Is she—" He couldn't go on because he knew you should never ask a question you couldn't handle the answer to.

"She's just unconscious. The vest stopped it, but she'll have a big-ass bruise. Be patient while he checks for other damage."

Thank you, God, for allowing the woman I love to live.

"Okay, Doc said we could lift her off you."

"Please do." He had to see her, make sure she was okay.

After they lifted Sam off him onto the floor beside where they'd landed, he leaned over her when he heard that infernal woman's hurtful words.

He swiveled toward Agent Anderson, ignoring Beverly's words. "Get her the hell out of here, and don't forget to add attempted murder to her list of charges."

Not waiting to see how they got the crazy woman out and to the agent's car, he knelt beside Sam and held her hand tightly in his. Stroking her pale face with his other hand, the softness and thoughts of when he'd held it between his hands and kissed her deeply called to him. Something reassuring him.

Yet, he didn't know if he could handle this—her constantly being in danger. If it weren't HIS, she'd no doubt return to SWAT or something equally dangerous. It'd be ten times worse because he couldn't keep an eye on her.

With a painful-sounding wheeze, Sam opened her eyes. "Burns," she whispered, agony sounding strongly in her voice.

Doc had already cut her blouse and unstrapped the sides of her vest, ready to lift it to see the damage. It became apparent she wore another T-shirt beneath it, and Doc would have to cut it also. Even though he expected her to have on her sports bra, she might not, and the men shouldn't see a lacy concoction on her. He didn't want Doc to see her that undressed either, but desperate times….

Turning around, he found Franks and told him to clear the room. Franks nodded as if understanding and ensured the team exited.

"Give me a minute, Sugar, and we'll get everything off," Doc said soothingly.

Her wide eyes searched the room and landed on him. While he hated to see her in trouble, knowing she wanted him at that moment had him standing ten feet tall.

Casper slipped in, handed Doc a med kit, and offered help, but left at Doc's refusal. Ken thanked the man for not adding another body seeing her down to her sports bra.

Sam closed her eyes as if biting off the pain. He took her hand, clasped it, and lifted it to his mouth, kissing the back of hers.

When Doc gave her a shot, she stiffened but relaxed a moment later. The Sam he knew in Georgia had an immense hatred for needles. The burning pain had to override it.

"How's that?" Doc asked as he opened the vest.

She grimaced, and he almost asked Doc to stop, but the man needed to triage her.

"I've got to cut the shirt to see." Doc waited for her to nod before he continued. When he opened the shirt, Ken had to hold back his raging anger at Beverly. Instead, he focused that energy—positively—on Sam.

The shot had landed on the left side, lower rib. A large blotch of deep red marked the spot of impact. He wanted to lean down, kiss the spot, and would if it'd remove the pain.

Based on the location of where the wound was—since he hadn't worn a vest—it would've hit him in the gut.

"Were you hurt?" she asked him while Doc prodded at her chest.

This woman, who'd considered wanting him dead, had not only helped him escape death, but she'd stepped in front of a bullet for him.

"No, sweetheart, you were a fool for stepping before that bullet. But I love you for it."

"You weren't wearing a vest."

With how form-fitting hers had been designed, he hadn't realized she'd worn hers. So used to seeing her in it with the clothes she wore, it hadn't caught his attention. He kissed her on the forehead with a newfound tenderness. He'd never known a woman could save him emotionally and physically. Realizing there'd been no doubt, the woman who could achieve all that would be Samantha Milton. Soon to be Samantha Patrick.

Her stepping in front of a bullet for him sealed the deal. In his mind, the action was as close enough to a yes for him as it got.

As her voice weakened, she said, "Thank you. Thank you for having her sign the papers for Cody."

"I didn't do it just for you, sweetheart. I did it for Cody and us."

A wide smile grew on her face, but her eyes became glassy, and her pupils changed. He snapped his head up to Doc. "What the hell did you give her?"

"Calm down. It's only a mild painkiller. We're reworking our approval to stock something heavier." He looked down at Sam. "Sugar, I don't believe you've broken your ribs, but you could have fractures that I can't see. Do you want to go to the hospital and get them X-rayed?"

She shook her head. "No. It doesn't hurt when I breathe. It burns and throbs where it impacted."

"What do you think, Doc?" Ken asked. "Should she go?"

"I'll always advise going, no matter the injury, as I'm not a full-fledged doctor, nor do I have all the tools and equipment needed."

Ken almost growled. "Fuck. That didn't answer my question."

"I'd recommend she go because I imagine there's a fracture or two—probably small. But they won't be able to do anything but wrap them tightly."

"I'm fine. I don't need to go to the hospital." Then, she promptly passed out.

"Shit, Doc, what the hell's wrong with her?"

As he checked her pulse, Doc said, "Don't worry, that's probably the painkiller."

Frantic, with his blood pulsing through his veins, he decided. "I'm taking her to the hospital."

"She's going to be pissed at you," Doc warned.

"I don't give a damn. I just want to make sure she's okay."

"All right. Let me wrap these ribs first, or transporting her will be more painful than it needs to be."

Impatient, Ken urged him on. "Hurry the hell up."

The medic chuckled as Doc wrapped her ribs with Ken holding her up.

"What the hell is so funny?"

"You owe Reagan a lot of money."

Chapter Thirty-Seven

When Sam woke in the emergency room, her first thought was panic for not understanding why she'd ended up in the hospital's care. Her eyes landed on Ken, and she relaxed. Then she took in a deep breath and groaned through the pain. Ken squeezed her hand, and she settled back, waiting for the doctor.

She had a couple of hairline fractures. The doctor had expected worse, but Devon had the best vests money could buy. The only good thing about the experience was that she had another mild painkiller. Unlike the men who tried to be all badass, she'd take hers when needed and when able.

After a quick release, she wished she had taken one, but she wouldn't while driving. She and Cody had left Kate's house and were finally going to hers. With all that happened, she forgot to ask about getting Cody's stuff from his old home.

Before she'd left Jesse's home, Ken stopped her. He had some paperwork and stuff to do to square away all they'd done in Mexico and at home, so he'd told her, "I'll meet you at your place this evening."

She'd nodded, glad he'd be there. She had much to discuss with him about her future and theirs. "I'll stop at the store and pick up something to cook. Any preferences?" With a coy smile, she asked, "Do you still like steak and potatoes with no veggies best?"

He grinned. "Sure. But I eat my vegetables now."

"Any in particular?"

Glancing at Cody, he responded with, "Whatever Cody eats."

A warm smile spread across her face as he'd already begun to include Cody.

Jesse walked up to them and handed a small duffel to Cody. "Here, buddy." He looked at Sam. "We picked up a few things at the store. Madison and Emily flew to Georgia and packed up his room. The boxes should be here tomorrow. We'll bring them to you."

A love that only a family carried washed through her for what they'd done for a child they hadn't known. Gratitude swamped her, and she knew those two words weren't enough, but it was all she had. "Thank you."

Cody looked up at Jesse with admiration in his eyes. The easy smile Jesse gave the boy warmed her heart for Cody's happiness.

Jesse nodded at the boy. "I want to have a quick chat with you. Let's walk this way."

Cody didn't ask her. He followed mindlessly. A frown dimmed her smile. *What were they talking about?* Cody nodded a lot but didn't say much.

She whispered to Ken, "What's going on?"

He grinned. "Jesse's just talking with him."

Shocked at that response, she sputtered before she got out, "He's too young for the talk."

Grabbing her arm to stop her from interrupting, he said quietly, "Not *that* talk. Trust him."

"Why is Jesse doing it and not you?"

A sigh escaped him. "He doesn't really know me yet. Jesse brought him home and has made a positive impression on him. It's best this way."

Completely confused, when the two returned to her, she raised her brows at Jesse, but he remained tight-lipped. The quirk at the corner of his lips narrowed her eyes at him. What was the man up to?

She'd figured out she had a lot to learn about kids. Cody had gone to the back seat when they arrived at her car. "I know the age in Maryland is under eight years old, but it's safer for me back here in the middle seat, but only if it has a shoulder strap." He slid into the seat and had her wondering just how he'd learned all that, and then Reagan came to mind—the little fountain of knowledge.

On the drive to her apartment, the light began to dim as they navigated rush hour traffic more easily. It had been one of the longest days of her life, but Ken and Cody were now safe from Beverly.

"I've never been to Baltimore before," Cody said.

"I can show you all over if you want."

"Reagan says I need to see the aquarium."

She wondered how many of his statements would begin with "Reagan says." "You do. I'll take you as soon as we can go."

"Can Reagan and Jason go too?"

"I'll see what we can do."

After another uncomfortable silence, anxiety ruled her, so she asked, "What did Jesse tell you?"

"Oh, Mr. Jesse reminded me I'm the man of the house and am supposed to look out for you. I'm not sure how I'll do that."

She held back her chuckle but couldn't stop the smile that crept across her lips. "Did he now?"

"Yep. And he said that even if you get married, I'm supposed to look out for you, but I can let your husband be the man of the house." He quieted for a moment. "I like that idea because that's a lot of pressure being the man of the house. I mean, I don't even have a job to pay the bills." He sighed, and based on the noise, he kicked at the back of the passenger seat. She let it slide since this seemed so important to him. "If you don't get married, I guess we'll have to cut back until I can get a job. Mom always spent a lot of money on clothes, so you might wanna not do that."

It got harder not to laugh. Jesse had tried to pump up the boy's importance, but Cody had taken it all wrong. "I'll tell you what. Since I already have a job, how about I pay the bills, and you can just watch out for me?" She hadn't wanted to add the last because she feared to what lengths he'd take it, but she figured since Mr. Jesse—who had made hero status in Cody's eyes—said it, Cody would do it.

"That might work. We don't have to make a decision right now."

So grown-up already. While Cody was the same age as Reagan, Kate had warned her that kids were more grown-up than they appeared.

Seeing the business she needed to visit, she navigated traffic to the parking lot. Turning in her seat, she looked back at the excited Cody. "We won't be long here, and then we'll get you settled into your new room."

Objective completed, she drove the few miles to her modest two-bedroom starter home. After parking, Cody stood in the driveway and looked around in circles.

"Do you like the area?"

He nodded. "Just checking for bad guys."

Her heart nearly stopped. She didn't want him constantly worrying about Bev and any goons she'd had around. "Do you expect any?"

Shrugging, he joined her at the open trunk. "No, but if I'm going to look out for you, I need to know my surroundings."

Well, well. Jesse had gone a little deeper than she'd have

wanted. "Did Mr. Jesse tell you that?"

"No. Reagan did."

Shaking her head, she held back a laugh. This had been serious business to him. "Well, I promise I've checked out this neighborhood and feel good about it."

"All right. You told Mr. Ken you'd be stopping by the grocery store, and you didn't."

She inserted the key in the door and told him, "I already have what he'll eat."

"What about me?"

"Do you like pizza?"

His eyes lit up. "What kid doesn't?"

She pushed the door open, turned off the alarm, and closed it behind them. "We can order you some if you don't like what I'm cooking."

"Maybe if I'm the man of the house, I should eat what you and Mr. Ken eat."

Sam smiled brightly. "Can I tell you a secret?"

Cody went from serious to excited and bounced on her brown suede sofa when he sat. While she knew he'd like the secret, he probably wouldn't keep it. Hopefully, she was able to get to Ken first. "There's going to be a new man of the house soon. Would you like that?" Having Cody accept him sat paramount in her heart. The kid had been through a lot, and she wanted him to have a stable home where he could love and respect his parents.

Cute, little, brown eyes widened. "Is it Mr. Ken?"

Holding her breath at his following response, she could only nod.

"I can accept that."

Relief washed through her at the boy's acceptance of Ken. She tossed the dress, still wrapped in the dress bag from the department store, over an armchair.

He pointed at the dress. "Are you getting married tonight?"

Laughing, she shook her head. "No. I haven't agreed to marry him yet."

"But he asked, right?"

"He did. I'm going to tell him yes tonight."

"When I get pizza?"

The short attention span of a kid made it challenging to carry on a conversation. "Yes. How about I show you your room? It'll need decorating. We can do it together."

The shocked look on his face when he stood nearly knocked her over. "You mean I get to choose?"

Damn Bev. She should've taken Cody sooner. "Yes. You think of what you want, and we'll go to the store or shop online to fix it up."

"Woohoo!" He took off down the hallway, Sam following at a more sedate pace.

He peeked into her room and wrinkled up his nose. "That's too girly. I hope it's your room and not mine."

It appeared her life would be holding back a lot of laughs. "It is. Yours is over there." She nodded to the only other bedroom.

"My other bedroom was yellow."

Her breath caught. That'd been the first time he'd mentioned anything about his life before now. She knew she had to be prepared for it, but it still burned. "Do you want it yellow?" She hoped not. Before Bev learned the sex of her baby, the two of them had painted that room yellow, and she'd planned to repaint it with Adam when he returned.

Sorrow gripped her again at the loss they'd both suffered. At what Cody'd suffered without a father figure. Well, he'd sure have one now.

"No, I'd like blue. Can I have blue?"

"You sure may. There are a lot of shades of blue to choose from."

"I just want blue." He turned back to survey the room with its double bed and dresser.

Maybe she'd change it out for a single bed for more room. She'd find a kid's desk for him and a computer. Having a TV in the room wasn't happening.

Bouncing his butt on the bed, he gave her his approval. "I like the room."

She wouldn't have known what to do or say if he'd said he didn't like it. "Okay, I'm going to shower and prepare for dinner."

"Are you going to wear that dress Miss Megan got for you?"

Megan—AJ's wife—had arrived at Kate's to help. The women got their heads together, listened to Sam, and told her not to worry. Besides what she'd found as sexy lavender underthings, they'd bought her the red dress she'd promised Ken she'd wear when they returned. Not usually a dress person, they had to purchase heels too. Even though everything was her size, she hoped it all fit since sometimes sizes were off.

It hadn't been the same dress she'd worn when they met, but styles had changed.

After a quick shower, she looked around for Cody and found him at the table. He drew a pencil on a pad that she expected Jesse to have purchased for him.

"What're you drawing?"

"Winglet."

Curious about his artistic talent and memory level, she asked, "May I see?"

He shrugged and handed her the pad.

"Wow!" His work was magnificent, and his memory

was outstanding. While she didn't remember the horse exactly, this drawing brought it back to her mind. Looking at his work, no one would believe it of a child.

Handing back the artwork with pride, she smiled with warmth and love. "You have an amazing talent."

He shrugged again, but she noticed the slight lift in his shoulders at the compliment. Not responding, he accepted the book and went back to his work.

With her shower and the food prep completed—not at the same time—she ventured back to her bedroom and donned the dress. It fit snuggly with the bindings around her ribs, but it wasn't a vulgar snug. Used to wearing long pants and Capri pants, the dress stopping midway between her thigh and knee made her want to pull it down to keep from showing so much skin.

She couldn't understand the top half. The dress went over the shoulder, but on the arms, there were holes and more sleeves, so her shoulders showed. The rest of the dress was simple and plain. She could deal with it.

Remembering it was for Ken and not her, she slipped into the heels and returned to the front of the house, where she heard Ken speaking with Cody. Something inside her twisted that while it had been Ken who had answered the door, Cody shouldn't be opening it. She didn't want to explain all the evils in the world.

"Are you getting settled in?" he asked Cody.

She shouldn't eavesdrop, but she wanted Cody to have that alone time with Ken, plus she was curious.

"Yes. Sam says I can paint my room blue. Will you help?"

Happiness infused her body. Her heart filled with love for these two men.

"I sure will."

"Good, because since you're going to be the man of the house, you should do that kind of stuff."

Her hand flew to her mouth. There were apparently no more secrets with Cody in her life. It'd only been a few hours for him to hold it.

"I will be the man of this house, but I'm thinking that maybe instead of painting this room, we buy a bigger house, and you can paint a room there blue."

While surprised at Ken's confidence, she really shouldn't be. He'd pushed forward since they thought they might die. It made her wonder if they moved too fast. Then she remembered their growing friendship and connection since she'd started working for HIS.

"That'd be good because I didn't tell Aunt Sam 'coz I didn't want to hurt her feelings, but that's a small room, and the bed is a little hard."

A touch of hurt tried to worm its way inside since being unable to provide Cody something that he liked ate at her. She shouldn't design things just to please him, but starting a new life, she wanted him to find it safe and loving.

Ken chuckled. "Don't worry. You can go with your Aunt Sam and me to find our new home."

"Can I order pizza now?"

With that question, Sam entered the room as if she hadn't heard a thing, but Ken's cocked eyebrow told her he suspected she'd been there. Once he took in her dress, looking her over with hungry eyes ready to wolf her down, he smiled and closed the distance between.

Her pulse quickened, and her heart beat overtime at his nearness. No man had ever had blood rushing through her veins with desire and love like this man.

In a low, husky voice and with that infuriatingly sexy grin, he leaned close to her ear and growled, "I can't wait to peel that dress off you and make love to you all night long."

Feeling the heat rising up her neck and the whispering touch of the air when he spoke, she nearly melted at his feet. She just stood there, incapable of anything other than breathing, and that was a feat in itself as it had deepened in an erratic pattern.

They both boasted minor injuries, but she knew they'd make it work. Lord, help her when they are at full strength.

He chuckled and stood straight again. "I like the dress."

It took another moment before her senses returned, and she almost snapped at him for making her feel like mush in front of Cody. This could be a problem when they are married.

She cleared her throat and looked at Cody. "Cody, do you want me to order you some pizza now?"

"If you give me the number, I can do it."

Sadness filled her insides. He shouldn't know how to do that at this age. Maybe know how but never have to. She wanted to ask how often he'd done that and find out why when Ken's light touch stopped her from responding.

"How about we do it together?" he asked. "I'd like to learn what type of pizza you like."

"Pepperoni."

She should've expected that. "I'll leave you two to get to know each other better, and I'll start up the grill."

Ken looked about to argue, but Sam nodded toward Cody.

Once the grill had warmed, Ken walked out on the patio with a plate holding the steaks. Without a word, he placed them on the grill and closed it. Setting down the plate, he turned to her. "How'd you manage to get that dress? I know you didn't have one in your closet."

With indignation, she huffed. "How do you know I

didn't?"

He chuckled. "Come on, Sam. You never liked wearing heels. They typically go with dresses, so I can surmise you don't have very few dresses in your wardrobe."

The man knew her too well. Avoiding crossing her arms and pouting like a child, she remained truthful. "All right, Megan got it for me." Not wanting to indulge his curiosity, she changed the subject. "Anything happen after I left?"

"Not really. We debriefed—you'll do yours tomorrow—did some paperwork." His features softened. "Sam, about today—"

"There's nothing to talk about."

The pain in his eyes drove into her.

"This whole op almost killed me, and not physically. I couldn't stand the potential of you being hurt and then getting shot—" He gulped.

She'd planned to wait, but now was the right time. "Ken, I'm leaving HIS."

The shock on his face quickly morphed into concern. "I won't lie and say I would prefer you weren't there, but only because I don't want you to get hurt. I also don't want you to go to another dangerous job."

"I've still got most of Lance's life insurance policy, and Sebastian said something about getting money to help raise Cody through Bev's finances so I can take some time to transition."

His light touch on her shoulder drew her closer. Since Cody had ruined her answer, she'd plugged ahead.

"Why are you quitting, and what will you do?"

"I honestly don't think Cody should have two parents who work in a dangerous job. He's been through so much already." She shook her head, not quite ready to forgive herself for not seeing just how much he'd suffered at the hands of Bev. "As for what I'll do, I went to the gun range on the drive home today, and I'll begin teaching various courses. Some they have, and some I'll design."

Before she spoke, he appeared to be holding his breath. Huskily, he asked, "Do you mean it? Cody's two parents?"

"Yes. But I don't think we should get married right away. Cody needs to know you and feel comfortable before we can become a family."

He swooped down for a kiss but first whispered, "I'll wait as long as I need to. I love you, Sam."

"I love you, too."

His lips had barely touched hers when Cody slid the patio doors open. "Pizza guy's here." Then he spun around and ran to the front door.

Ken growled. "I'll be right back. Turn the steaks for me."

She did as instructed, noticing they were on their way to being overdone.

Warmth slid through her; she'd been blessed with the love of two fine men. If anyone had told her before now that Cupid's arrow could hit the bull's eye twice, she'd have scoffed at them.

When Ken returned to the patio, he automatically checked the steaks and grimaced. "Don't get me wrong, I'm going to love having the kid around, but there will be times when I want you alone."

"I want that too, but I'm not sure how we can manage that. I have no family here, and while Kate offered, that's a long drive to their home."

A mischievous grin formed on his face. "Danny offered to babysit."

He continued to shock her. "Franks?"

Shrugging, he turned back to the grill. "He watches the Hamilton kids a lot."

"Doesn't he have a girlfriend or someone he's seeing?"

Ken took the steaks from the grill. One side wouldn't be done much, but the other side compensated for it. Instead of medium-rare, they had a suitable medium. "Don't know. Didn't ask. It's not my business."

"I like Danny, so I'm making it mine. I plan to make it my mission to find a woman for him," she affirmed.

"No offense, sweetheart, your history with the ability to choose a woman is suspect."

She smacked him on the arm, and he acted like she'd wounded him.

Trying to soothe things over, he said, "But you don't know many women in Baltimore."

She smiled brightly, full of confidence, before she winked at him. "Never underestimate a woman's determination."

About the Author

Sheila Kell writes about romantic men who leave women's hearts pounding with a happily ever after built on memorable, adrenaline-pumping stories. She is a four-time winner of the Readers' Favorite Book Award for romantic suspense and contemporary romance.

As a Southern girl who has left behind her days with the United States Air Force and as a University Vice President, she can usually be found in central Florida with her family and cats. When she isn't writing, you can find Sheila with her nose in a good book, trying to leash train her cats, or wishing she had a genie to do her bidding.

Ways to connect

https://www.sheilakellbooks.com

https://www.facebook.com/sheilakellbooks

https://www.goodreads.com/sheilakellbooks

https://www.bookbub.com/authors/sheila-kell

Sheila loves to hear directly from readers. Feel free to email her at sheila@sheilakell.com.

Don't miss out on new releases, exclusive excerpts, and giveaways! Join her newsletter: https://www.SheilaKell.com/subscribe

Join her Facebook Reader Group:

https://www.facebook.com/groups/sheilakellbooks